ON
CLOUD
NINE

ON CLOUD NINE

a novel

KELS & DENISE STONE

BETWEEN THE SHEETS
PUBLISHING

Published by Between the Sheets Publishing

kelsdenisestone.com

Paperback ISBN: 978-1-964675-02-2

ebook ISBN: 979-8-9864169-3-9

On Cloud Nine

Editing & Proofreading:

Caroline Acebo at Brass House LLC

Caroline Knecht

Isabella Bauer

Cover Design: Chloe Friedlein

Author's Note

This book deals with mature themes such as childhood trauma, anxiety, and male infertility. We hope that we've taken great care in addressing these topics.

To all the mirrorballs—when you're shining for everyone else, remember to shine for you too.

Chapter 1
Molly

"ARE you seriously making out with someone at our wedding shower?" I gawk, watching my soon-to-be husband devour a woman like she has the last blackberry pavlova stuck down her throat.

"Oh. Hey, Molly," Lance says, taking a step back and buttoning up his shirt with the laziness of a stagnant breeze on a hot summer day.

Nobody can see my *perfect* fiancé in the closet with another woman—especially today.

Lance Bradbury has always been good at putting on *the act*. Why couldn't he wait to swap spit with one of the staff until after the festivities?

"Please wrap this up," I plead. My stomach wrings into knots.

"Calm down, this is part of the arrangement, remember?" He shrugs and swipes at the lipstick on his chin. The caterer hesitantly looks between us.

"Not here, and not today." Panic slews in my veins. "What if people saw?"

"Who'd be poking their nose into one of my closets?" He

notices my fretful expression. "Fine, just give me a minute." My fiancé turns to his necking partner and whispers incoherently.

He's the worst.

In the year I've been engaged to Lance, we've never been fond of each other.

Well, maybe that's not *entirely* true.

He's keen on what my family can offer him. We're wealthy. We have a name that is engraved into museum halls and hospital wings. In our world, the difference between old money and a hot-off-the-press multimillionaire is stark. Lance can't buy class, but, through our marriage, he can secure a legacy for his own family.

Bradbury-Greene. In three short months.

I roll my eyes at his hushed whispers and turn back to check the damage.

The throng of New York high society litters the Bradburys' Tribeca residence. Down the hall, the first floor holds two hundred people—half of whom I cannot recall the name of. They're dressed in monotone suits amid white orchid center-pieces, seemingly unaware of my fiancé's indiscretions. Midday light floods through the large windows, making the high ceilings seem enormous, yet I'm suffocating.

Then I see the sharks of the Upper East Side. Portia Royce, Emma Elingdale, and Miranda Laurel beeline toward me. Their Jimmy Choos and Manolos clack along the hardwood.

A banshee wails in the distance. At least, I think it does.

Relax, Molly. You've been trained to handle this.

Straight spine. Glimmering smile. Polite laughter—not too loud, not too high-pitched, just right.

My lips pull upward. I gently glide the closet door shut, but Lance wedges in an oxford, trying to exit.

"There you are, doll." Portia swings one of her almond-shaped nails in the air. Heads swivel toward us at her screeching tone. I must get these three out of this hallway and away from the closet.

"Portia! So lovely to see you here." My voice quavers. "Have you had a chance to check out the ice sculptures in the backyard?"

Lance makes a terrible wall with his body to conceal his mistress. My ten-carat engagement ring feels more like a restraint than a symbol of commitment.

"The only ice I do is cryotherapy. Besides, this little situation seems far more chilling." Portia is only a few inches away, peering her razor gaze over Lance's shoulder. "Are you and Lance having a little *coup d'état?*"

Certainly she doesn't know what that phrase means. Although this is beginning to feel like a seizure of power.

"No," I respond and nudge my elbow into Lance, trying to get him out of the way. We need to shut the door.

Portia's eyes widen with intrigue. *Oh no, she saw.*

"O-M-G—Lance, were you in there with someone else?" Her neck cranes around us.

"He wasn't!" I play up my best laugh and edge closer to my fiancé.

Emma pulls out her phone. My heart drills against my chest.

"He totally was." Portia pushes past Lance and flings open the closet, revealing the woman reapplying her lipstick. "Is that the caterer?"

"It is, isn't it?" Emma says. "I recognize her from my mother's bruncheon last Tuesday."

My world spins as dozens of eyes peer at us. I'm exposed and vulnerable. Whispers flood the lower floor, trailing into the hallway.

Is that Molly Greene?
Guess he couldn't wait until after the wedding.
Ugh, I already bought them a gift.

I need to go somewhere else, vanish, except there's nowhere to run. Nothing else for me to do.

My body reacts. Flushing, sweating, and trembling.

Miss Molly Greene, soon-to-be wife of Lance Bradbury. That's who I need to be right now, but the mask keeps slipping.

I can't do this. I can't handle this.

Tears pinch my eyes. My jaw aches from my forced smile.

Then I see him.

Matthew Hudson.

My coworker. My friend. My crush.

And he's heading straight for me. I knew I shouldn't have invited my colleagues from the Oceanic Research Organization.

His cool blue gaze slices through the crowd. His usually messy jet-black hair is slicked back.

My pulse lets up before a camera flash burns my retinas.

"This is so juicy." Portia taps on her phone, likely breaking the news to everyone who's anyone.

My guests begin to filter into the hallway. Lance refuses to chime in and help repair this chaos. Instead, he kicks his foot back and forth like a bashful schoolboy.

Does he find this amusing?

That's the thing with families like the Bradburys—they don't understand the kind of scar a mishap like this one can leave on a legacy.

It's essential that I gain control of the situation.

"Thank you all for coming." I engage my most commanding tone. "But there's been a bit of a misunderstanding here…"

My ears ring with the gossip that's floating around the gathering crowd.

"That's right," a familiar voice chimes in. Someone is pushing past the stuffy suit jackets. It's him again. Matthew.

What in the world is he doing?

Gasps come from the socialite wives. Frowns from the business partners. *Splendid.*

In a matter of minutes, I've become the main attraction of the month. The only topic that will be discussed at the next dozen social engagements.

Matthew rushes toward me. For the past three years, he's been my secret office crush, and now he's looking at me with an intention I've never seen before.

Instead of his usual work uniform of trousers and a button-down shirt, a tailored suit hugs his muscular build. He looks good—a weak-in-the-knees kind of handsome.

I ping-pong my panicked gaze between him and the crowd of watchful eyes, trying to comprehend what's happening. More phones shoot up, recording the scene.

Are the rest of my coworkers watching this train wreck among the crowd? What about my actual friends? I knew I should've kept my guest list to family only and saved myself from this embarrassment.

"We didn't want it to come to this," Matthew declares as he reaches me. "But it's time you all knew that Molly and I are in love."

My soul leaves my body, and it's as if I'm watching every-thing from above.

"*We are?*" I gulp, but the quick turn of his brows makes me rephrase my words into a statement. "We are."

There's no way he's reciprocated the feelings I've had for him. Feelings that go beyond our very professional, very platonic friendship.

Gasps fire at us like a round of bullets.

"Impossible," Lance snaps. The hallway feels like it's shrink-ing. "Who even are you?"

"Matthew Hudson," he says confidently.

"Hudson? Of the *Hudson* River?"

"Uh, n-no," Matthew stammers, palming his neck. "Just Hudson. I suppose Hudson of Massachusetts."

"Never heard of them before," Miranda whispers over her

shoulder.

One moment, I'm squished into a doorway, smelling Lance's Fahrenheit cologne. The next, my coworker's hand is on my lower back, a place it's been only once before, a very long time ago. Those dreamy blue eyes sear me.

Matthew Hudson cannot be in love with me. *No way.*

"Kiss me?" he asks.

"What?" I whisper.

"Trust me."

"Am I dreaming?" I must be. Because this whole *knight in shining armor confessing his love* thing only happens when I'm safely tucked into my bed, reading one of my romantasy books.

Matthew's head shakes. I am definitely not dreaming.

There's no time to respond. No time to process.

I connect my lips with his, and I'm officially kissing the charming, gorgeous, and quiet Matthew Hudson. I've imagined this for years, but my daydreams do our kiss no justice. I lean into it, memorizing the mint on his breath.

After what feels like an eternity and is somehow all too soon, he pulls away. I stand beneath his watchful eyes, winded and confused.

I try for a calming breath. My lungs fill with vetiver and musk. His scent. Earthy and sensuous.

"Okay, who is this Clark Kent knockoff?" Portia squeals with delight. "And what on earth is he doing kissing our Molly?"

"That'd be nice to know," Lance agrees.

Around us, bafflement grumbles from the guests. Matthew tucks me under his muscular arm, and my panic ceases.

"This is, um, Matthew." I yank myself out of my daze. "My coworker…he's a really successful ecopreneur." Could this be my escape from marrying Lance? Exchanging one relationship for another? Would my parents even allow it? I have to try. "And…he's right. We're in love!"

"For this level of drama, I would've worn a better dress," Emma babbles to her friends.

Ignoring her, I search the crowd of overly curious faces for my mother's copper hair or my father's wiry eyeglasses. Not here yet. *Ugh.* They're going to lose their minds when they find out about this.

But I still have time for some damage control.

Sure, I've probably sabotaged the Bradbury investment in my family's business. That doesn't mean I'm going to cause more harm to the Greene name by wasting another second under these watchful eyes.

"Well, thank you all for coming today. I assure you, there's nothing to see here," I enunciate in my best public relations voice. "Please enjoy the hors d'oeuvres and the violinist."

The caterer slides out of the closet and rushes down the other side of the hall, away from the guests.

It's Lance's turn to goggle at me. "Molly, we're not done."

"If the lady wants to be, I think we're quite finished." Matthew steps forward, towering over Lance. His jaw tenses beneath his five-o'clock shadow.

I force a nervous giggle. "Yep. All done."

Focus, Molly. Focus on fixing this. Not on how taut the lines of Matthew's face look.

The crowd hesitates and then disperses, sweeping Lance away with them.

I rush down the hall, pull open the third door on the right, and step into the Bradbury family library.

When the door latches shut, a shiver zooms up my spine. I spin, finding myself in Matthew's arms.

"What have you done?" I take a few steps back. I can't linger too long in his embrace.

"What have I done?" Matthew's voice is filled with dread. Or is it concern? Regret? He swipes at the creases in his forehead.

"You kissed me?" I ask because I still can't believe it.

"I did." Matthew steps closer, and I distance myself, my hamstrings colliding with a desk. I'm pinned. "I'm sorry, I—" He hesitates. "That was so inappropriate. But I saw your face, and everyone was whispering about you. I mean, the asshole was hooking up with someone else. I couldn't let you deal with that alone. I just—I acted."

"Did…did you want to kiss me?" I slap my hand over my mouth. Is that seriously the best question I have? Not: *Why'd you cause a scene?* Not: *Did you mean what you said about being in love with me?*

"Um, are you alright?" He deflects, and it's enough of an answer for me. This is all just one heroic rescue.

Am I alright? No. I'm not remotely alright. Absolutely not. I must've been the worst kisser ever. Dismay joins the nerves humming beneath my skin.

"Of course. I'm fine. Everything is fine." My voice cracks, but I hide it with one of my best smiles. "Oh my goodness. Wait. Did anyone from ORO see?"

"No. Just me. Everyone else was in the gardens," he says. One less thing I'll need to run damage control on.

"Please don't tell them."

"I won't."

"Okay." Tears brim my eyes. I can't cry in front of him.

"Here, take this." He hands me the beige handkerchief from his breast pocket.

"Oh, I don't want to stain it. My mascara would never come out."

"It's meant to be used. I don't mind." I'll buy him a new one and drop it off at his desk on Monday. I grab the soft fabric from his fingers and blot it under my eyes. "Also, you can't be fine, Molly. You just caught your fiancé cheating on you."

I stare up his six-foot-one frame. There's a small bend in his nose I've never noticed. Rugged and unexpectedly out of place. I have the sudden urge to ask him how it got that way, but when I open my mouth, nothing comes out.

No diversion. No answer to his worried expression.

It's always been different with Matthew, my real personality slipping into our conversations at work. I've had to keep my guard up around him. Something about the way he looks at me makes me want to pour my whole soul out to him.

It's terrifying.

I only like revealing parts of myself that will make people happy. Currently, that seems impossible.

"He…um, it's just, I—I don't actually want to marry Lance. We have an arrangement." The faint whisper doesn't even sound like my voice. Regret envelops me. I haven't told anyone that my marriage to Lance is a sham.

"I wouldn't want to marry him either after what he did out there." Matthew's brows furrow. My eyes are on his lips.

Oh my goodness. *Pull yourself together, Molly.* You're soon-to-be Mrs. Bradbury-Greene. Not some girl with a monster-sized crush who's incapable of articulating one rational thought.

"It's not like that. I mean, I know about the caterer, the waitresses, the old flames," I explain. Matthew stares at me, stark, cold judgment burning in his eyes. "But we've worked something out."

How could he understand what it's like to be in my Hangisi jewel buckle pumps?

It's silly. I have everything I want, but the pressure of the Greene legacy constantly rests on my shoulders. If only I had a sibling my parents could pawn off for their business proceedings —though I'd never wish this kind of life on someone else.

"Molly," Matthew says in a low voice that makes my bones tremble. He touches my arm, lighting up my skin like a city regaining power. "Please help me understand what's going on here."

"Our families set up our marriage." My mind races, and the

words come pouring out. "I have to tie the knot before my twenty-seventh birthday. It's a Greene family tradition and the only way I can access my trust."

And I need that money. Without it, I may never have autonomy. It's my only opportunity to have something for myself. Open my own business and follow my own dreams. A piece of me my parents can't control.

A fifty-million-dollar reward for a loveless marriage doesn't seem *that* bad.

When I look up at Matthew again, his face is entirely unreadable. Great. He probably just thinks I'm a spoiled rich girl. Maybe I am.

"I see," he begins. "Wouldn't your parents want you to be happy? To not marry someone you don't want to? Surely there are alternatives."

Does that truly happen? Are there parents out there who prioritize the joy of their children above their own needs? I doubt it.

It's the burden of being a Greene—in a world filled with riches, we're not meant to feel the luxury of genuine happiness.

"No alternatives. At least, not any my parents would approve of."

Matthew's eyes narrow. "Why do they have to *approve* of your husband?"

I need to rejoin the party. Chaos must be ensuing out there, but I can't move.

"A clause requires it," I reply.

"Uh, okay. That's a bit strange." Yup, that does it. Matthew won't look at me the same ever again. At least I'll be quitting ORO after my wedding and can hide from this mortification forever.

"I know it probably seems that way, but my great-grandparents, Oliver and Clara, got married at twenty-seven and opened the first On Cloud Nine resort together. It's tradition to follow in their footsteps. As a wedding gift, all the Greenes receive a trust."

The tradition is dated, and quite unreasonable, but their intentions were good.

Fall in love. Begin a life of commitment.

The hopeless romantic in me has always thought it was sweet.

"Okay, I hear you. Except why Lance? Doesn't the fact that he just publicly humiliated you cancel out the whole approval clause?"

"I wish. The Bradburys are helping us fund a large resort expansion on the Gold Coast in Australia. Besides, I'm really just trying to get my fifty million dollars."

He pauses, scanning my face. I look away, nervously rubbing his handkerchief between my fingers. "What's more important to you?"

"Huh?"

"Your family's business or your trust?"

No one has ever asked me that before. Choosing has never been an option. "The trust." I admit the unspeakable out loud. "Look, it's pointless. My time has run out. My birthday is in five months, and I have to be married before then."

Otherwise, the trust gets invested in the family business, and I'll be without my money and without a husband.

"If you just care about the trust, then why don't you marry me?"

Shock slaps me harder than the TMJ massage I got last week. "I can't let you—"

"Does this tradition prevent you from getting a divorce?" he interrupts.

"Possibly."

"If it doesn't, then marry me."

A weight sinks into my gut, causing my muscles to weaken.

It's as if the ground beneath me has given way and I'm free-falling into an abyss of uncertainty.

"What?" My voice comes out harsher than intended. Everyone has unspoken motives, but I can't figure out Matthew's.

"I want to help you. It's simple. Look, we'll pretend to be in love, get engaged, you'll get your trust, and you won't need to marry Lance."

His boldness is overwhelming. My knees buckle.

This is my way out.

Sure, my marriage will still be a business deal, but one that would actually benefit me. One that I agreed to.

"What's in it for you?" I blurt out.

His indecipherable expression remains steady. "Fifty million dollars is a lot of money. I've been contemplating a new project," he says, looking down at me. "What if we split your trust?"

That leaves me with twenty-five million dollars. Is that enough? It has to be. The door handle rattles behind Matthew.

"That could work, but do you even understand what you're offering? A lot of expectations come with marrying into my family and—"

"Marriage isn't that important to me." There's a coldness in his tone, and he gives me no time to ask why. The door handle clatters again. "We'll tell your parents we've been in love since we first met at work. I can win them over."

"I—" The room spins around me. I can't catch my breath. He's looking at me with those discerning blue eyes, and I can hardly stand it. It's like he's daring me to take a chance, to take control of my life.

Will my parents see right through me? But the alternative is worse.

"Okay, let's do it." I agree right as the wooden doors swing open.

Vivian Greene is monumental. She's dressed in a Chanel

pantsuit that matches the tweed fabric of my dress, and her heirloom pearls dangle off her neck. "There you are," my mother's voice bites out.

With a deep breath, I give my new fiancé a nod, sealing the deal.

Chapter 2
Matthew

WHY DID I decide to play the hero?

I know why. It's her. Heart of gold, sweet as sugar, lovely Molly Greene.

She's hardly a damsel in distress. Around the office, she's graceful and composed. Today, I don't even recognize her.

Molly's long, spiraling red curls are suffocating in a bun. Her face is bare, swiped clean of the familiar colorful makeup that usually blankets her radiant amber eyes.

Christ, half of our office is here. What if everyone saw me confess my fake love for Molly?

Nothing good comes from mixing work and feelings. I learned that the hard way.

But I couldn't stand idly by as my friend was being humiliated in front of dozens of people. The moment I saw panic flood into her face, all my rational thoughts ran off course. I had to fix it.

"Mom," Molly implores. "Please, let me explain."

Vivian Greene looks tyrannical. She gives her daughter a sour look, clearly conveying that Molly will be the one to pay for my uncharacteristic act of chivalry.

Why isn't she out there grilling Lance for embarrassing her daughter?

"You have five minutes, Molly—*five*—to break it off with Mr. Hudson of Massachusetts and get back out there to reconcile with Lance. We need to clean up this nightmare you've created."

"No." Molly's lip trembles. The same plump lip that was just pressed against mine.

"What do you mean *no*?" Vivian snaps.

"We're in love," I chime in. *Why am I unable to keep my mouth shut?* The only people I'm this protective of are my family, yet today's events have brought out a side of me I've never known.

"That may or may not be true, but my daughter is engaged to Lance Bradbury." Vivian shoots Molly a seething glare. "And she should be out there, acting like his fiancée."

"No, Mom, please listen." Molly looks smaller than she usually does. Younger, even. I suppose we are ten years apart, yet I've rarely felt that difference until now.

"This deal with the Bradburys is important to your father, to our business," Vivian bites out.

"I understand that, but my trust allows a love match." Molly tries to steady the tremble in her voice.

How many clauses are in this trust?

"We already discussed this. Now come." Vivian turns toward the door. Molly remains stuck to her spot on the library floor.

"Don't you care that Lance was caught with the caterer? At our wedding shower?"

Molly hasn't mentioned her fiancé much. There was always something that felt off about their relationship. Lance never came as a plus-one to the office events she organized. I assumed he was a busy guy, and he is…just not with work.

Vivian's exterior seems to fracture, as if she's finally hearing her daughter. "You know we've—" She shoots me a look and lowers her voice before turning back to Molly. "Your family is counting on you."

"I love Matthew." Molly utters the words out loud. I force myself to ignore the brief spark they ignite in my chest.

"If I may interject here." I clear my throat. "When I saw your daughter today, it made me realize I've been head over heels for her since we first met. I had to act."

Vivian addresses Molly. "What is this need to *act*? Have you been sneaking off to meet with this man?"

"N-no, of course not," she stammers.

"We've been respectful of the arranged engagement, but I know we're both certain about our feelings. It was only a matter of time before we felt ready to tell you," I lie.

"This is not the time nor the place for this. Molly, you need to get yourself together and fix things with Lance." Vivian spears her pointer finger into the air. "Remember where your loyalties lie. You have five minutes, and I expect to see you out there."

Molly fidgets with the ring on her finger, an extensive stone on a plain silver band, and watches her mother leave.

Maybe I haven't quite pieced together how opposite our lives are.

Hell, her fiancé's family owns a townhouse in Tribeca with a library of antiquarian books and a shelf filled with pristine first-edition classics.

Molly's eyes are glassy as she gives me a skeptical look. My heart aches. I hate seeing her like this. "Is twenty-five million dollars enough for you to marry me?"

"As I said, it's not a big deal to me." Love has been off the table for so many years, I can barely recall how it feels. But this is Molly. My friend. It won't get messy. "We can figure it out."

Sure, I'm an entrepreneur with a cozy five-bedroom home in the suburbs of Greenwich. I paid off my mortgage. I invest in start-ups. All in all, I've done well for myself.

But the money she's offering is life-changing. There's no

point in denying I've had *the itch* again. A lingering desire that I didn't expect to feel after starting my first company, Plastech. The plans for my next venture are already drafted, and this could be my chance to start EcoDrones off on the right foot.

"Are you sure about that? You just met my mother."

Sure, Vivian was frightening, but she's nothing I can't handle.

I nod. "We tie the knot. You receive your trust, wire half to me, and we get divorced."

Our arrangement will only take a few months. A year, tops. A low-stakes marriage with no chance of us falling for each other.

Maybe in another life, our office jokes would lead to something more. But I haven't let my thoughts go there since our first year of working together.

She was only twenty-three then—far too young—and I had sworn off dating.

The latter is still true. Only difference now is that Molly needs my help, and I have a way to fund my project.

"Okay," she says. "I'll try to convince my parents we're a love match. It may work."

"Sounds logical to me."

She inhales, looking flustered. "Let's talk tomorrow. I really have to try to fix whatever is going on out there." Molly reaches for the door.

"Tomorrow," I confirm.

How hard can it be to fake a marriage to a woman like her anyway?

Chapter 3
Molly

MY FINGER HANGS at the doorbell outside the white French doors of the Greene Estate. I hesitate, briefly considering fleeing the nineteen-acre Scarsdale property instead of facing either of my parents, but I press the button.

Last night I was in a possessed fit, tossing and turning in bed while contemplating Matthew's marriage proposition and the agreement we made in the library.

Could it work?

Unlike my marriage to Matthew, my union with Lance would be trickier to unravel. Ending the engagement now is a better PR strategy than a messy separation.

The worst-case scenario would be getting stuck with that sleazeball until the day I wither away—*'til death, or possibly tragic golfing accident, do us part.*

If Matthew can endure a few months of being married to me before we file for a separation, I may be able to keep my trust and end up a divorcée. We'll call it a *conscious uncoupling event* like I read about on Goop.

This meeting must go perfectly.

The door locks click open.

A housekeeper stands in the doorway. An unfamiliar stout woman with graying hair, in a simple black uniform, whom I haven't seen before.

My mother is peculiar about almost everything, which makes it hard to retain staff. Hiring employees for the Estate is a full-time job.

"Hi, it's nice to meet you. I'm Molly." I give the woman a quick wave.

She returns a smile and gestures for me to come in. "Welcome, Miss Greene. Your mother is waiting for you on the back patio."

I read the name tag on her uniform. "Thank you, Caty."

As I step into the foyer, a chill runs down my spine. My eyes take in the familiar surroundings—the spotless, winding staircases, the glittering crystal chandelier suspended from the center of the ceiling, and the gilded mirrors that reflect the vast space.

The house is painfully silent, as always, save for my clattering J'Adior slingback heels. Passing through the first kitchen, which is perpetually filled with year-round peonies, I enter the southern kitchenette that leads to the backyard. The doors are already open, linen curtains picking up the fall breeze.

In the distance is a signature On Cloud Nine pool in pristine condition, lined with blue and white tiles. My dad let me pick them out in a small shop in Porto. It's always been special to me that he used those exact tiles at the resort he opened in Portugal.

I rarely make decisions about our family's hospitality dynasty, but sometimes, when Dad is around, I get to suggest a color for curtains or an activity for the daily agenda.

My mother always insisted on keeping me away from the resorts. Despite the fact that I grew up around the business, she thinks I'd become too overwhelmed or a workaholic like my father.

According to her, I'm better positioned as a well-behaved socialite, working a *simple* job.

Resentment prickles in my chest. My role at the Oceanic Research Organization has never been easy, but my parents only see what they want to see.

I spot my mother beneath her umbrella, afternoon tea set up at the four-seat table she's occupying.

She's wearing an impeccable black dress, heirloom pearls hanging in their place around her neck. Her beige Chanel ballet flats match the embroidered cashmere cardigan on her shoulders as she scans the pages of a large binder behind her oval Bottega sunglasses.

Probably a schedule for one of the many autumn socials she's planning.

My father sits beside her in a pair of wiry glasses and a collared shirt, typing away on his phone.

They seem oblivious to each other's presence. There are no secret glances across the table, no tender touches exchanged as they work together.

The way it's always been between them.

Hollow and bland. Automated. As if they've been programmed into stiff movement.

Well, almost always.

I cling to the years when we were a happy family—at least, what our types of families may define as happy. Things shifted once my dad took over the On Cloud Nine resort with my Uncle Davis.

My life would mirror theirs if I married Lance. Saying yes to the Bradburys—even for an opportunity to expand our resorts to Australia—means choosing a life where I become an empty husk of myself.

Lance and I would buy the biggest mansion Westchester has to offer so we'd never run into each other. At parties, we'd pretend we were in love, and then every night he'd have a mistress around to keep his bed warm. Yes, my parents and Lance would be happy, but I don't want to spend my life on country club autopilot, pretending to be a cookie-cutter wife.

My parents don't notice I'm here. I clear my throat, not wanting to interrupt either of their focuses.

"Hello." I smile.

"You're late," my mother says without taking her eyes off the materials in front of her.

I look down at my JLC Reverso Duetto watch. One minute past three o'clock and already starting off on the wrong foot.

"I couldn't help but admire your Itoh peonies," I lie. She doesn't seem flattered by the phony compliment. I approach my parents, taking a seat on the cushioned chair opposite them.

Dad looks up from his phone and gives me a curt nod.

We sit in silence. I wish they could act even remotely content to see their only daughter. Just once. If I didn't speak, I'm sure they would spend hours not acknowledging me.

It's lonely, like it's always been.

A blaring reminder as to why I can't live this way anymore. A pretty bird in a gilded cage. Primed and groomed for the highest bidder.

I fumble with the fabric of my white Altuzarra trousers, the ones my mom sent to the townhouse last month. Nausea hits my gut. I love my mother, but navigating her is like walking through an open minefield.

There's no more delaying my inevitable plea. Things need to change. I understand that now.

"Mother, Father." My voice shakes.

"Speak up, Molly. We don't have all day," she says.

"As we discussed yesterday, I'm not marrying Lance," I blurt out.

Did I just say that again?

Panicking, I shove a small cucumber sandwich in my mouth before I say anything else I regret.

The food turns viscous, getting caught in the back of my

throat because I've forgotten how to swallow. I try to suppress the impending coughs, tears brimming my eyes.

I want to shrink into a ball, but I violently hack instead.

This is what happens, isn't it?

You speak your truth once, and then suddenly it's death by cucumber sandwich.

"Are you alright, doll?" my father asks, but doesn't look up to check if I've asphyxiated. I'm not as important as whatever is on his phone.

"Of course she's fine, Ray." My mother flashes me a look I wish resembled concern rather than annoyance. "You must be more careful. Remember, small bites."

Vivian Greene is the epitome of kindness and cruelty all at once.

I compose myself and fight against the adrenaline coursing through my veins.

"Did you hear what I said?" I attempt.

My mother removes her sunglasses. "We've spoken about this, Molly." Her amber eyes burn through me. "All the arrangements have been made for your wedding. You should be grateful the Bradburys overlooked yesterday's *situation* with such grace."

"Did they overlook their son's activities with the staff?" I say. Vivian frowns.

"We have to be strategic," she reaffirms.

Yeah. I've been figuring out how to strategize being around her my entire life.

It took two years of constant pleading for my mother to let me move into our empty Upper East Side townhouse. After that, I wasn't around to play puppet at her random gatherings, and it was worth every attempt at compromise to no longer be a part of her matchmaking schemes.

Back then, I was thankful the Greene trust stated I had to be twenty-seven to get married, but that time has flown by.

Despite all my efforts to become the daughter they've always wanted—working a job that looks great on paper, getting a degree from Cornell, the family alma mater, wearing the clothes she curates for me, smiling at soirées, and asking *how high?* when they say jump—it hasn't been enough to escape being a pawn in their business proceedings.

"As much as I want to help with the expansion and get us the capital we need, I can't." I muster up the confidence to say it. "It so, unfortunately, happens that I'm in love with somebody else."

I hand over the information to her like an opponent in a tennis match, patiently anticipating the next move.

"Not with the man from yesterday," she states, not as a question, but as fact.

"Matthew Hudson is a successful entrepreneur." I present my case. "He graduated summa cum laude from MIT, developed a technology that's cleaning plastic out of the ocean, and makes generous philanthropic donations. He's kind and a gentleman. I'm certain he could be an appropriate match for me." I announce the achievements exactly how I practiced them this morning.

Matthew's accolades list is long. He always lends a helping hand at the office. There's the month he organized career days for undergrads from all the city schools to get introduced to sustainability. He also has an adorable sense of humor. His prime accomplishments should be enough to convince them he's suitable for me.

"Molly, Lance is a phenomenal match for our family," my mother asserts as she crosses her ankles, sending her knees to one side of her chair. "Besides, we already drafted the business plans for the Gold Coast expansion. Right, Ray?"

My father doesn't respond.

This is how my parents can ignore all of Lance's glaring red flags. The Bradburys are real estate developers who have been itching to climb their way up the social ladder. My family wants to expand our resorts to Australia, but they need capital. We may be billionaires, but most of our funds are tied up in investments and properties.

It's simple. The Bradburys want status, and my family needs money. Our union would be mutually beneficial for everyone except me.

I'm just the icing on the cake—holding everyone together.

"Would it not be possible to expand without there being a marriage involved?" I suggest despite already knowing the answer.

"How many times have we had to tell you?" My mother flashes a frustrated look at my father, who still doesn't notice. It's always a curious dynamic, how little power she has in the resorts, but how much of her reign she exercises in keeping the family name strong. Dad is the only one here who decides what happens at On Cloud Nine. "Finding a new investor of this size would be impossible. The Bradburys are our best chance."

"Lance doesn't care about me, Mom. Don't you want me to be happy?"

"We can't always be happy." My mother's nose crinkles as if she's bitten into a lemon. "What is this truly about?" She targets me. "You've been engaged for a year. Every attempt to push back this wedding has been exhausted, and you'll finally be married in three months. Our decision is final."

My heart sinks so far in my chest that it feels as if it's collapsed out of my body.

"But Matthew is—"

"A stranger." My mother shuts down my attempts. "Have you thought about what people would think if you abandon your engagement to Lance? Or how your betrothed will react?"

What would happen if the public knew that Lance has been with more people than I could count on my fingers and toes? Probably nothing.

Things like that don't matter around here, especially if you're a man. *Ha.* I bet Lance went home with the caterer after yesterday's debacle.

Men receive high fives when they get mistresses. Women get labeled as easy and exiled at all social gatherings.

Do I want to feel that level of humiliation for the rest of my life? A Greene daughter—not allowed to join the business, not able to choose her own husband, not capable of having her own ventures and ambitions.

"I could just lie low until things blow over. There's something new every week." I have one last move to make. As desperate as it may be, I need to try.

"Our family name will not be that *something new* next week. It was enough to have a stranger kiss you when the board was present."

I inhale, readying my final argument. "Oliver and Clara married for love." All the photos of my great-grandparents in my father's office prove that. "Lance and I are not a love match." I keep the statement neutral, not wanting to give her more reasons to dispel my terrible attempts to convince her.

My father looks up from his phone. The mention of his lineage piques his interest more than the family in front of him.

Great-Grandpa Oliver was his biggest mentor.

"You said Matthew was an entrepreneur?" My father adjusts the glasses sliding off his nose.

"That's right. Started off his career in venture capital before deciding to build a company that focuses on protecting the environment," I recite as though this were my own job interview.

My father appears curious. "How old is he?"

"Thirty-six," I say.

"That's only a few more years than us, Vivian." Dad leans toward her, not quite touching, but an inch closer. "Is this love you have genuine? Are you certain this man isn't using you?" my father pushes.

I try not to be hurt by his questioning. Of course he's

doubting my judgment. Quite hypocritical, especially after they've sold me off to a man who definitely doesn't have the *right* reasons in mind.

But I have to be convincing now. He's my only hope.

"Yes, I'm certain. I love him, Dad," I lie. "I truly love Matthew Hudson."

He sighs and faces my mother. "I think we should allow her to complete the On Cloud Nine marriage course with this man. I believe there's one in Sedona next week."

Did he just agree to let me try?

"What?" I struggle to comprehend his response.

I didn't have to take the course with Lance. My mother vetoed it since he was already an approved choice.

"You cannot be serious." Her voice turns gravelly. My father's gaze remains stolid. "What about the business plans?"

"I can manage the Bradbury agreement for the time being."

Wrinkles—the ones she spends thousands a year to cover up —crease my mother's forehead. "Think of what's riding on the Gold Coast," she blares. "More than our name is at stake."

"The trust allows it." Dad gives me a small nod. I'm as giddy as a rocket ship, ready to launch out of my seat and run over to him with the biggest embrace. "He sounds like an appropriate enough fellow."

I'll be the one person in my family who hasn't gone through with an arranged marriage, but at least I won't be the only Greene not married by twenty-seven.

If I don't fulfill *that* part of the tradition, I'll never hear the end of it. And, worst of all, I wouldn't receive my trust, and my chance at independence would be cut short.

The money would just be funneled back into the resorts.

"Ray." Defeat is apparent on my mother's face.

"Let her do this, Vivian. We took the course when we were engaged." He clears his throat. "Don't you remember? I believe we had quite a splendid time in those yoga bonding sessions at Lake Champlain."

"That was ages ago." My mother ruffles the hem of her black dress. She seems bothered by him bringing up the memory. *Or is she flattered?*

"How nice it would be if time could stand still," my father sighs. "I say that she can marry Matthew if they approve her course. If not, Molly will continue with her marriage to Lance." He turns to me. "Do you agree to those terms?"

I nod vigorously, unable to contain my excitement.

"This is a mistake," my mother huffs. "There is no way you're doing this." She gathers her belongings and leaves.

"Thank you," I whisper to my dad, who's already returned to his phone.

The suffocating anxiety drains from my veins.

My mother thinks I'm bluffing, and I can't wait to show her what I'm made of.

I can put on a convincing act. Never been an issue before. I played the perfect fiancée to Lance for a year. I can do it again. This time beside a man who's selfless and kind.

Worry returns to my chest.

Matthew.

What if he's decided to call the whole thing off?

THE DOOR SWINGS open on the second knock. I blink, trying to register my shirtless coworker standing before me in a pair of gray sweatpants. A warmth melts through my body, starting at the pit of my stomach and blooming into my cheeks. I try to look anywhere but at his, um, bulge.

But I fail, oh so terribly.

My mouth waters. Yes, actually waters.

Has Matthew Hudson always had that *thing* beneath his usual pair of navy-blue trousers or khakis?

I force my eyes back up to his, but not before they glide over his very toned torso. His shoulders are burly. A chest that looks firm to the touch. Across the olive-toned skin is a smattering of hair. So manly.

My pupils probably resemble saucers. I've never seen a man like him up close. He's *grown.*

On Matthew's handsome face, a round pair of glasses sits on the bridge of his slightly crooked nose.

I gulp.

Who is this man, and what has he done with the one I've come to know at the office?

"Hey, Mol," Matthew sputters. "Ah, sorry about this." He gesticulates at his hunky bare torso. The way I see it, there's no need to apologize. I could practically lick the skin on his chest right now. "My nephew just spilled his entire soda on me. Please, come in."

I've forgotten how to speak.

Sure, I've daydreamed about Matthew at the office on numerous occasions. I mean, how could I not? He's literally a save-the-world hottie—a little shy with a healthy dose of nerdy.

My breath quickens. Oh my. What is happening?

Unlike now, I've always had the self-control to brush those fantasies away.

"Nephew?" I manage. "This must be a bad time."

"No, come inside," Matthew repeats, motioning into his home. From the doorway, I spot a grand staircase with intricate woodwork and arches that lead to a beautiful kitchen. There's a fireplace in the living room with a mantel covered in family photographs. Two couches sit opposite each other. Beyond the cozy space lies a sprawling backyard garden. "Aaron's staying the night. My sister and the rest of her family all got food poisoning, so I offered to take him off their hands."

A fluffy brown cat peeks its head between Matthew's ankles, looking up at me with large russet eyes. He leans down and picks up the little animal, hugging the kitty to his bare chest.

Goodness.

He's a cat daddy too. How could I forget?

"Are you planning on standing there all day?" He shoots me a playful smile.

My heart flips in my chest. Hands clench and relax.

What have I gotten myself into?

Chapter 4
Matthew

I'VE SCARED the woman I'm supposed to marry. I nervously tug at the collar of my clean T-shirt, as if the half-naked appearance that I greeted her with will become any less traumatizing.

Spoiler alert: it doesn't.

Molly sits in front of me in my living room, crossing and uncrossing her legs for the ninth time. Sunlight pours through the sliding doors that lead to the backyard, casting shadows on her pale complexion. She takes a sip of water, then sets her glass down. There's a small drop clinging to her plush bottom lip. She licks it away, and her eyes meet mine.

"First off, I appreciate you giving me a way out of this marriage with Lance. I realize that I'm asking a lot of you," Molly says, stroking her fingers over her throat. "If you change your mind, you can back out at any point."

"Thank you, but I'm a man of my word, and the proposal still stands." I shift beneath Bear's weight on my lap and give his ear a scratch.

I researched as much as I could about Molly's family. They're a tight-knit group in the hospitality industry, widely known for their On Cloud Nine Resort Group, which was founded by Oliver and Clara Greene when the newlyweds purchased their first hotel. The same type of affluent individuals I've worked with for years.

I can manage this.

Plus, with the promise of twenty-five million dollars, I'd be a fool to turn down the opportunity.

Molly watches me, mulling over my words as if they're a puzzle she's struggling to solve.

Her eyes wander over the photos of my family on the mantel. "I'll share the arrangement details, and then you can decide."

She sounds like a well-rehearsed executive. The formality is chilling, but that's what this is—a business arrangement.

"Fair enough. Go on."

Molly leans forward. "As I already mentioned, the trust requires that I follow tradition and get married by twenty-seven. The Greenes are allowed a love match, which is what we'll pretend to be for my parents' approval. But what I didn't mention is that we have to complete a marriage preparation course."

Huh. That's weirder than I expected, but rich people do odd things all the time. "Like counseling?" I tilt my head to one side. Bear kicks his feet in his sleep.

"Yes and no." Molly pulls her hair out of its clip, sending her red corkscrew curls across her shoulders. She almost looks out of place here. White trousers. Fancy heels. This is a household of hiking boots and old books, but seeing her among my things is bringing up that feeling again. The same one I felt when we briefly kissed and my diaphragm froze. "Oliver and Clara wanted future Greene generations to experience the same bond they had when they opened the first On Cloud Nine. So, they created a marriage course. It's offered at every location around the world."

"Okay." I blink. She's never this rigid when we chat at the

office. "What does it entail? As long as it's not a blood sacrifice, I think we'll be okay."

She doesn't laugh. Instead, her eyes crinkle with concern. "No, nothing like that. It's a series of workshops and tests to ensure we're compatible before you become an official member of the Greene family."

"I'm quite good at taking tests." I wink. This time she blushes, her hard exterior beginning to fade. "When can we get started?"

"Right." She hesitates, chewing the inside of her cheek. "The only thing is, um, well... The course is two weeks long, and it's in Sedona."

Fourteen days. In Arizona.

I rearrange myself on my couch, waking Bear. He stares at me with a disgruntled look and climbs off my lap. *Grumpy boy.*

"That's a long time."

Work has been slow, but can I take two weeks off? My team counts on me. The next few weekends, I'm signed up to help clean up the Appalachian Trail. Thursdays, I mentor students in the Enviroworks club I started at MIT. Plus, I told my sister that I'd help take Aaron to his hockey practices.

Molly interrupts my thoughts. "I'm sorry; I know you have a whole life."

"Hmm. I suppose I can move some things around, and I have a ton of vacation time."

Postponing my volunteer work should be fine, and my mentoring is done over the phone. Aaron might feel disappointed, but I'll only miss the beginning of the season.

"Really?"

"Yeah. It's worth it to get EcoDrones off the ground sooner."

"Right, of course, your project." Molly's eyes widen. "Does anyone at the office know? Are you working on it with Ollie and Robert?"

"That's the plan. They've expressed interest. But the technology is costly." My friends and I poured our souls into Plas-tech. The start-up bled money faster than a gambler at a casino until we merged with ORO. We've been hesitant to take the leap again.

"Makes sense. If you don't mind me asking, what is EcoDrones?"

"It's going to help with reforestation efforts after wildfires. Pretty much a fleet of drones that plant new trees." I planned on spending the next few years saving and engaging new investors while researching, but twenty-five million dollars is the jump start I need. I won't have to beg for capital like I did with Plastech.

I can suck up missing a couple of my obligations. Especially when this technology could create a real impact after the horrid wildfires we've experienced over the past ten years.

"First you're getting rid of eighty thousand tons of plastic in the ocean, and now you want to focus on forest restoration? Is there anything you can't do?" She lights up, and I'm glad to see a glimpse of my Molly back. Well, not my Molly. But my friend.

"It's no big deal." I shrug, attempting to shake off feeling like some kind of vigilante when she puts it that way. "Anyway, what happens in this marriage course?"

"Right, it's easy. We'll do some activities, like couples yoga or an intention-setting class. An instructor will pass us. And that's it. You don't even have to spend your free time with me if you don't want to." Molly chuckles nervously, eyeing her empty glass.

I reach for the water carafe on the coffee table and pour her more. "Is that what you'd like?"

"No, I—I love talking to you." Her cheeks coat with an adorable pink. "I mean, I enjoy it. You're—you've always been great to talk to."

Warmth returns to my veins as she bashfully grins at me.

"Well then, it's settled. We've hung out plenty of times at the office. We'll just do it in Arizona now." It can't be that much different. I've never been let down by my gut feeling. "So, how quickly do you think we'll be able to get a divorce?"

The sooner the better. That way, Molly can pursue a genuine relationship with a man who can love her and start a family with her.

"Um, so it may take a few months for us to get married, but then once we do, the trust will come through. I'll wire your half, and then we'll begin the paperwork. We'll have a prenup. You can use one of our lawyers or retain your own counsel." Her formal tone returns and clips through the room. "The process should be pretty quick."

"Makes sense to me." It's better this way. I stopped planning for a traditional storybook relationship years ago. The plans I made with my ex came into my life as swiftly as she left. "I can manage two weeks in Sedona, a prenup, a wedding, and then a quick divorce." I tip my head toward her.

"Is next week too soon to leave?"

"I'll have to make some calls, but I should be able to arrange everything by then." She brushes her hair over her shoulder and nods. "Let's discuss the actual faking of our relationship. What will that entail? I want us to be in sync," I say.

For this to work, clarity is crucial. Except sometimes even that's not a solid guarantee. My abdomen tightens.

When I was with Laura, we talked about our future often. I was sure we were on the same page. Both powerful executives with a white picket fence, nice cars, and unlimited vacations. We planned on being perpetual DINKs. I assumed she'd be happy. Until she left.

That won't happen here. Absolutely fucking not. Molly and I will lay everything important out on the table.

Her voice strains. "Well, my family cares about their image…a lot. So, we'd have to be convincing."

I watch her carefully, trying to understand why her family wouldn't let her choose the person she was going to marry. But I'm sure it'll be fine.

Focus on the things we can control.

"When we get to On Cloud Nine, are we going to share a room? Sleep together?" I attempt a distraction.

A blush creeps across her face again. "Oh gosh, no. I'll be sure to book separate rooms."

Her reaction unsettles me. My shoulders feel heavy. I'm not sure why. Of course she'd want her own space.

Eyes on the prize, man.

Twenty-five million dollars. Helping your friend.

Not feeling bummed about a girl not wanting to share a room with you.

"Great. If that's what you're comfortable with." I nod, swiping my palms on my sweats. "What about PDA?"

Her eyes go wide. "Hmm?"

"Should I put my arm around you when we're in public?" I clarify. "Can you tell me what you and Lance did?"

Molly cringes. "Um…we never discussed what I'd prefer. Lance assumed he could touch me, hold me, even kiss me."

"What?" A pit grows in my stomach.

"No, it's fine." She tries to laugh it off, but there's nothing funny about what she casually shared with me. "It was just some touching here and there. Kissing in front of other people. Nothing…like that."

I wouldn't put it past him.

There's a stretch of silence because my reaction is probably crossing some kind of line. Really, Molly doesn't owe me another explanation. But my body remains tense. "I hate that he ever put his hands on you."

"It's in the past." Molly bangs her knees together. I can tell she's uncomfortable as she throws on her brave face.

"I'm never going to put you in a position where you have to

do anything you don't want to." No is a full fucking sentence, there's no other way around that. My pulse refuses to settle, and I stretch out my fingers, willing it to calm down.

"Thank you." She averts my gaze. "And the same goes for you. I don't want to touch you if you don't want me to. Even if it's pretend."

"Works for me. But, if you wanted me to…well, I wouldn't mind touching you," I admit. "So we're a convincing couple, of course." Oh, hell. I'm making this awkward. "As long as I have your permission. You can take the lead here."

"Um, how…" She hesitates, mustering up a question. "How would you like to touch me, Matthew?"

Her body pressed into me. Her mouth on mine. My mind is flooded, overflowing with the smallest details from our brief kiss. Did she taste like…cider? Is that even possible?

I shake away the memory.

"Maybe we could hold hands?"

Molly nods. "I'd like that."

"Hugs are quite nice."

"Very." She swallows heavily. "I think those t-two are good," Molly stammers. "We definitely don't need to kiss again or anything. My parents never kiss, so I doubt they consider it an important part of a relationship."

It's been a long time since I kissed someone, apart from the uncharacteristic display yesterday, and never someone like Molly.

"What do you think about kissing?" I ask before I can stop myself.

"I enjoy kissing," she admits rather candidly. "Sometimes, I just want to drown in someone's taste for hours."

The blood traveling to my dick has clearly not received the memo that we're hashing out the details of our fake—*very fake*—relationship.

"Sounds nice." I clear my throat, adjusting myself in my sweats. "Once this is over, I hope you get to do that with a person you want to kiss."

She deserves it. Someone who likes her without pretending or arrangements. Just because she's her.

"Maybe." Molly glances away, peering at the garden outside.

"Okay, so, starting at On Cloud Nine, I can hold your hand and give you a hug," I confirm. "Until you'd like me to stop."

"Yes." She nods.

"She's pretty." A whisper comes from the corner. Aaron hides at the foot of the staircase, his duckie footie pajamas peeking out from behind the wall.

How could I forget my nephew was here?

"Aaron, get over here, buddy," I call out to him, and he timidly waddles over to us. I lift him up onto the couch. He hides behind my arm. "He's not normally shy," I tell Molly, whose nervous demeanor has dimmed. Instead, she's grinning, waving over at my nephew.

"Hi there." Her voice rises, friendly and sweet. "I'm Molly." Aaron abandons the refuge behind my T-shirt and tries to hide his toothless smile as he waves back at her. "I like your pajamas a lot," she says. "I think I have the same pair at home."

My imagination enforces no self-control as an image of Molly in duckie pajamas—entirely the opposite kind of footie pajamas my nephew is wearing—flashes into my mind. No, these are incredibly inappropriate pajamas. The kind that would make even a grown man like me blush and giggle like a schoolboy. It'll take more than my crossword puzzles to swipe that image from my mind.

My nephew cackles and sprints out of the living room, zooming around the kitchen island.

"He's a sweet kid." I get off the couch, keeping my attention between Molly and Aaron. "But he has the energy of a firecracker."

Molly follows me into the kitchen as I try to wrestle my nephew into my arms. It's no use. He darts around, dodging our legs.

"Kids are so cute." She grins and takes a seat on the barstool at the island. "I've always wanted to be a fun aunt, but, you know. The whole no-sibling thing."

My heart tramples over itself. Molly clearly said she wants to be an aunt, not a mom. The weight of insecurity from my past resurfaces. I can't fixate on what she said. She's only twenty-six. Kids are probably the furthest thing from her mind right now. But in a few years, that'll change.

I swallow, pushing the thoughts away.

"It's the best. You can spoil them rotten and then send them home when you want to sleep in." I pull out sliced fruit from the fridge and set Aaron up with a tablet on the kitchen island.

The entire time, Bear and Molly observe each other with equal intensity. Man, it's adorable.

I interrupt their telepathic exchange. "How are you feeling?"

Molly's neck jerks back as though I've hit her with a frying pan. "Me?"

"Yeah. All of this must be really difficult for you."

"I'm not sure I have the words to explain what this means to me." She evades my question. "It feels like you're my only shot of securing my trust without Lance being in my life."

"Hey, Mol, look at me." I walk around to her seat, positioning myself beside her. She peeks up at me from beneath darkened lashes, her eyes hiding so much she's refusing to say. "We're in this together. You're *my* best shot at funding my project. The forests won't be planted without you."

"Forest!" Aaron yells from behind her, making her laugh.

"What should we tell everyone at ORO?" Molly is still

looking up at me. "I was already thinking about leaving after I got my trust." Her gears are spinning again.

"I think I'll also be leaving ORO, after we get divorced." I keep my voice low, motioning between us. "So we should just tell people that we've been an item for a while. It'll be more convincing."

"Okay," she agrees. I drop my palm on the island beside her. "Well, then, what do you want me to call you? I mean, in the relationship sense."

Right. "Um, what would you prefer?"

She considers me for a moment. "I guess until my parents approve our marriage, I—I'd be your girlfriend."

My girlfriend.

"Sounds right to me." I attempt a reassuring smile, but the nerves kindling in my chest are impossible to ignore. "Boyfriend and girlfriend."

"I've never had a boyfriend before. Not even a fake boyfriend."

"What do you mean? Ever?" My fingers curl for no reason.

She must have had some kind of relationship in the past. *Is Molly a virgin?*

Where on earth has my head gone? *Stop it, man.* It's not my business what her love life looks like, even if I'm a bit curious.

"Uh." She slants her body away from me. I take a step back, sensing her discomfort from our close proximity. "With Lance… we were at a dinner when the terms were arranged. I was single when I sat down at the table, and by the time they brought out the crème brûlée, I was a fiancée. And before that…well, the dating options are slim when you're in my position. The decent guys are taken or decrepit." Molly laughs casually.

Doesn't seem like she's been given a choice on anything in her life.

How have I never noticed before?

"Well, you'll also be my first fake girlfriend."

"What about a real girlfriend?" Her voice is small. "I mean, you don't have to tell me, sorry."

"No, it's fine for you to ask. We'll definitely have to get to know each other much more if we're going to make a convincing couple. I doubt knowing what color mug you use at the office for each corresponding workday would be enough to spell out that we're in love."

The smile on her face vanishes. "What?"

Molly has a tendency to walk around the office, saying hello, and she's always carrying a different colored mug. I'm certain everyone's noticed. It's her thing.

I pull at my collar again. "Your mugs," I clarify. "On Monday it's purple, and on Tuesday I think it's green—"

"You know about that?" She pulls her knees together, almost knocking them into me.

"Yeah, it's no big deal. The little things make a person interesting, right?"

"*Right…*" Molly doesn't seem convinced. "I guess it would be smart to exchange personal profiles, just in case we're probed."

"Good thinking." I nod. "We can compile fact sheets about ourselves and quiz each other until I'm fluent in Molly Greene and you're fluent in me."

It'll cover all the important things—I'll just be sure to leave out the granular details about my relationship and medical history. My infertility and what happened with my ex have no place here.

This is pretend. Why burden Molly?

"Great." She seems to shrink a bit, but I can't tell why.

Aaron's tablet clatters behind her as he nibbles at his fruit.

"Anyway, to answer your previous question, I haven't had a partner in years. It just hasn't been in the cards. No one really fits into the life I've built, and, well, I guess I've been too busy to look." I pocket my hands into my sweats. "Hopefully that doesn't dissuade you too much."

"No." She shakes her head back and forth. "We can figure out how to fake being in a relationship together."

"We can do this." I give her a nod. "It's like a new work project."

"Only pretend." Molly smiles.

Chapter 5
Molly

"Y‌OU'RE GETTING DIVORCED."

"No," I sigh, yanking a silk blouse out of my suitcase and tossing it at Lily.

"She's getting married," Avery clarifies. She grabs the top and neatly folds it onto the pile of clothes on my bed.

"Only if my parents approve," I remind my best friends. "He's just my boyfriend for now."

The thought of Matthew Hudson being my boyfriend has been one I can't stop mulling over.

My brain—or body—can't comprehend the fact that this is all a ruse. The past couple of days, the anxiety of us spending two weeks together in such close quarters has caused me to lose sleep.

It must be a side effect of my melatonin and stress cocktail.

That's it. It has to be. Or my little white pill needs a dose adjustment.

My friends and I have spent the last hour going through my closet. Lily, my old roommate, lives across the street. Avery is a quick park walk away. They insisted on helping me pack even when I assured them it was unnecessary. But they wouldn't take no for an answer and showed up with an extra cheesy pizza.

My favorite kind. They know me so well.

"I still don't understand how we missed all of the drama at your wedding shower," Lily says. "Or how you managed to stand with Lance at the end to thank everyone for coming."

"It was fine. I didn't want to draw any more attention." I barely remember the rest of that day, thankfully.

Lily strolls over to my dresser and pulls out pieces of lingerie I have no business taking with me to Arizona. "I wish you'd told us your parents set you up with that bread slice of a man. How's he handling the split? Did he just shrug his shoulders and swap spit with someone new?"

"He's…" I try to find a word to explain Lance's reaction to the news that I was ending our engagement. But nothing suitable comes to mind. Nothing to help define exactly what led him to send me thirty texts over the past week. "Hurt. I think his ego is bruised. But he never really liked me." My thumb instinctively rubs the inside of my now empty ring finger.

His messages replay in my head.

LANCE

We need to talk

Stop ignoring me Molly!!! Since when do you not answer?

We're getting married in less than three months

Your driving me up the wall

If I had Lily's confidence, I would have responded to the last one with: It's you're*.

I won't give in to his empty threats. I'm tired of worrying about what Lance wants. Honestly, he's probably used our shattered engagement to gain sympathy from other women. Though I don't understand how anyone can be attracted to someone who prioritizes hair pomade and status over forming a real connection.

"I hate him even more. How could anyone not like you?" Lily rolls her eyes.

"You're sweet." I smile.

He's not the only one confused by my behavior. My mom can't wrap her head around the fact that I'm standing my ground. She keeps calling and asking me if I've come to my senses or if I've scheduled the last fitting for my wedding dress, a starch white custom Vera Wang that's hard to look at. If they approve my wedding with Matthew, I'll pick my own dress.

Just have to make it through the next two weeks. That's all.

"Seriously, Molly, all you had to tell me was, *I gotta marry this douchehat for money*." Lily walks back to the bed, a pile of colorful fabrics falling from her arms and onto the sheets. She brushes back the long braid of black hair from her shoulder and raises one of her plucked brows at me. "I would've said, *Thank fuck, that makes so much sense*, and then helped you get out of it." She laughs so easily.

Lily Rodin has no issues speaking her mind, and I wish I could crack the code to her confidence.

"I guess I was embarrassed," I admit. I wrap one of my fingers in a loose curl on my chest, twirling the strand until it turns frizzy. Or maybe I was guilty, a little ashamed. I was ready to give up a piece of myself to keep my parents happy, to continue a legacy that's been around for generations.

The pressure of my world requires me to be pliant, and I finally said no.

Does this make me selfish? Would that even be a bad thing?

"There's nothing to be embarrassed about." Lily gives me a reassuring smile. "Besides, I think the situation worked out for the best. You get to be married to a sexy, nerdy hottie with gorgeous blue eyes."

My body flushes with warmth at her words. Matthew *is* sexy. I wonder what he's doing. Sitting on one of his couches, maybe reading a book, his cat curled up in his lap?

"Lily's right." Avery grins, tucking her blonde bob behind her ears. "I know you've always had your eye on Matthew, but when he's around you, it's like he's hypnotized."

"He is not," I insist. Heat floods my face.

Avery looks at me as if she doesn't believe me. She's spent the most time around us. Maybe she's been more perceptive than I have. Matthew and I obviously talk at the office—less so since I've been engaged to Lance, but we're friendly.

"The relationship is fake," I remind her as much as myself.

"Yeah, yeah." Lily waves off my deflection, her long nails batting at the air. "I pretended once, and you know how that ended."

I do. Both of my friends have found their soulmates in two brothers. Lily fell in love with Nico Navarro, a man who practically rolls out the red carpet for her every time they step into a room.

Avery is no different. She fell in love with my boss, Luca Navarro, who treats my friend with an enviable tenderness.

I ache for a pure love like either of theirs. Lily with her fiery passion and Avery with safety and security.

But could I have what they have?

What kind of love is even meant for me?

I doubt any man who falls for me would be happy with my true self. He'd only like the shapeshifted version I'd present to him.

"Everything works out how it's supposed to," Avery sings. She picks up a rose-colored La Perla embroidered bodysuit and waves it between us. "Now, if you bring this with you, I'm sure you'll have a much more enjoyable trip."

"Or this," Lily chimes in, holding up a floral-print slip that's more lace than actual fabric.

I grab both of the undergarments from them and walk back to my dresser. "I can't bring these with me. Who would I wear them for?"

"Matthew," my friends say in unison.

"Absolutely not." I return to the bed with a set of appropriate pajamas. Though the idea of Matthew's hands running over the fabric of my lingerie sends a tingle of electricity up my spine. "There's no need for us to make things more complicated."

"*Need* and *want* are very different." Lily stuffs a few more lacy sets into my suitcase, replacing the pajamas I packed. I'll fix that later. "What do you actually want?"

"My trust," I reply because it's the only thing I'm sure of.

"Fair enough," Lily concedes.

Between breaking off my engagement and managing the ramifications from the drama at my wedding shower, time flew by. I leave New York City in sixteen hours. I'm not remotely prepared, despite the two packed suitcases already waiting for me in the foyer downstairs.

"I'm certain your parents will love Matthew," Avery declares confidently. "He's simply a great guy. There's no better way to put it."

It's true. Matthew was Avery's boss before their start-up merged with the Oceanic Research Organization. She knows him better than I do. When I told her I needed to take time off to fulfill the terms of my trust's marriage course, she approved. If anything, Ave was a tad disappointed that my sudden relationship with Matthew wasn't real.

"You know what they say." Lily's green eyes flare with mischief. "It's always the quiet ones."

"Huh? What about the quiet ones?"

"Cut it out, Lil." Avery shoots her a knowing stare, one I desperately want to be a part of.

Sometimes, when I'm around them, I feel so out of my league. Unlike the girls I grew up with, Ave and Lily are cool.

They are funny and loyal. They're self-made and always say what's on their minds.

Complete opposites of the person I am.

Although we're close, I'm secretly afraid that I'm taking up space in their life with my problems.

"I'm just saying, the gentlemanly, brooding type usually has a lot more *fun* than it seems." Lily emphasizes the word *fun* the same way she does when she references a particularly erotic scene in one of her books. Being best friends with a romance author has opened my eyes to things I hadn't quite known I wanted to try.

Role-play, sex outdoors, and even spanking. My cheeks heat.

I shouldn't think of Matthew and those fantasies at the same time.

My eyes widen. "No way. There won't be any kind of *fun*. Matthew's just being nice. Besides, he has twenty-five million dollars at stake in this deal."

Lily stuffs another highly inappropriate bra into my suitcase. "Nico was quite *nice* to me this morning."

Avery scrunches her nose, not wanting to hear about the things her brother-in-law has done to her best friend. "You better be careful, or one of those *nice* mornings are going to turn into a twenty-two-pound baby." Ave is a new mom to a beautiful girl, Kaia.

Now it's Lily's turn to flash an exaggerated frown. "Fuck off."

They both explode in laughter. I can't help but join in.

My heart beams at the little sanctuary our friendship has created for me. I'll never be able to repay them.

Their giggles turn into stories about all the different ways a twenty-two-pound baby can come about.

I haven't had a *nice* morning in a long, long time.

Maybe the resort will change that.

I smother the thought. Matthew and I are a business arrangement. There's nothing *nice* about that.

I'M NOT ashamed to admit that I've cyberstalked Matthew on more than one occasion. When we first started working together, I may have let my crush on him dictate many of those late-night internet searches. However, I wasn't remotely prepared to review fifteen pages of facts about my new fake boyfriend.

I'd be lying if I said I hadn't memorized every word he sent me.

He got Bear five years ago when his brother, Myles, discovered that his new baby, Willow, was allergic to cats.

The organizations he volunteers for and donates to took up a whole page. *Terribly attractive.*

He hates the word *bulbous* because he had an English teacher who used it one too many times.

His first car was a Chevrolet Cavalier, which Matthew bought with the money he made tutoring during high school.

He's been in one long-term relationship before, quite a while ago. The entire flight, I haven't mustered up the courage to ask him about it. Maybe that's only a question for *real* girlfriend territory.

"Favorite ice cream is strawberry with a scoop of chocolate?" He shoots off another personal tidbit from my fact sheet.

"That's correct." I nod, unable to resist sinking deeper into the soft leather seat on my parents' private jet. Matthew looks too chiseled and firm in this lighting.

Business only, Molly.

He's made it clear that he wants a divorce as soon as possible.

Sure, we're becoming fluent in each other, and this game of back-and-forth quizzing is making me melt where I sit. And, yes, there's the fact that when I look at him, I replay our rushed kiss at my wedding shower over and over.

The kiss felt like passion, fire, something I thought…I don't know what I thought.

Everything that unfolded was merely a gentlemanly rescue, not a genuine interest in me.

"Explains why we only have two flavors for office birthday parties." He cocks his head at me.

"Hey!" I feign offense. "If I'm planning the party, then I might as well get something I like."

Matthew chuckles. The deep sound rekindles the butterflies in my chest. "Seems only fair."

"What about you? You didn't put any ice cream in your profile."

"I suppose I didn't," he says. "I love a good creemee."

Huh? If I were drinking water right now, I would've performed a spit take all over him. "A what?"

"It's a Vermont thing," he explains casually. Clearly not picking up on the pure provocation of the word. "Avery would know what it is."

That doesn't sound like something either of my coworkers should be discussing. Is it a new sex move?

Goodness. My pulse quickens. I'm severely out of the loop.

I lean in close, lowering my voice so the cabin crew can't hear us. "Is that how Kaia was born?"

"*What?*" Matthew's eyebrows knit together in confusion.

"Like, is it some kind of slang for, you know…um, *you know*." He doesn't seem to register my meaning. "For…*doing it?*"

He erupts in a fit of laughter that reverberates around the jet.

"It's just soft serve ice cream. Where's your mind, Molly?" He swipes at his jet-black hair, his biceps rippling in his shirt. "Tsk, tsk. That's positively filthy."

"*Oh*." My cheeks probably match my fuchsia Ulla Johnson manet blouse. "You have to admit, it does sound a little dirty."

"Well, now that you mention it." He shakes his head, grinning from ear to ear. "I'll never be able to order one again without laughing."

My lips part, my legs going with them. *Gosh.* How do I play this coolly? "Maybe when we get back home I can order one for you. You know, so you don't laugh."

I positively sound like a robot right now.

"I'd love for you to order my creemee for me, Mol." He keeps a straight face for a millisecond before bursting into laughter again. The anxiety and stress of our arrangement thaws slightly.

But then reality sets in.

Will we be friends after the divorce? With neither of us staying at ORO, will we keep in touch? Are these my final weeks with Matthew?

It's like each time I enjoy myself, I ruin the moment by worrying about the future—a future I so desperately need for myself.

Game face, girl. Put on your game face.

"We have our ice cream orders down." He scrolls on his phone. "Huh, but you didn't list a favorite color?"

Matthew's eyes connect with mine. Would it be totally weird if I told him that I liked the specific shade of blue of his eyes, with flecks of another color I can't make out from this far?

I settle with, "I like all of them."

"Every color?" Matthew's grip on his phone grows firmer, bringing out the veins in his hands.

"If I could live inside a rainbow, I would." I try to suppress my swelling smile. "What about you?"

His gaze glides over my curls, lips, and nose before meeting my eyes. "I'd have to go with red."

A surge of excitement dances across my skin. Does he appreciate my hair as much as I appreciate his eyes?

This exchange of information feels like flirting. I don't want it to end.

I have an overwhelming urge to close the gap between us. I stretch out one leg slightly closer to his. The distance diminishes, and my palms become sweaty.

The crook at the top of his nose comes to my attention again. "So, in your fact sheet, you mentioned that you've broken your nose. Is there a story?"

"Oh, well." He rubs the back of his neck, fingers tangling in the hair there. An almost bashful look in his eyes. "I'll tell you, but please know, it was a different time in my life."

"What happened?" I perk up, ready to memorize a part of him he's never shared with me.

"I was nineteen. My sister called me crying from prom. Turns out her date was hooking up with someone else under the bleachers. So, I drove over there, and I, um…" He glances at me nervously. "I put the guy in his place, to say it politely. He got in one good punch, but he never spoke to my sister again."

"Wow," I say, sinking further into my seat. Seems like saving me from Lance wasn't the first time Matthew has stepped in to play hero.

Oh crap, does he see me as his sister or something? How does Matthew even look at a woman he desires?

"I don't want you to think I'm a violent man." He straightens quickly. "Hell, I never even killed a spider after that, but seeing how upset my sister was… It just hit a nerve."

"You don't have to explain yourself. I think it's admirable that you would stand up for her like that." Even a little attractive. Okay. Extremely freaking attractive.

Obviously, I've read too many romantasy books with the *who did this to you* trope, and it's altered my brain chemistry. But that fact doesn't stop my eyes from lingering on the smattering of hair peeking out of the top button of his shirt.

The attendant curtain flies open, and Elizabeth walks over to us. "How are you both? Can I get you another drink?"

"Oh, wait, I got this." I interrupt Matthew before he has a chance to answer. "He'll have a whiskey sour."

He nods. "And my girlfriend will have a seltzer with a wedge of lemon, please."

My heart betrays me, rushing and hammering in my chest. Matthew Hudson just casually called me his girlfriend.

He's probably just getting comfortable with the term.

"Are you sure you don't want another champagne?" Elizabeth asks me, a cordial smile on her face.

The world beats to the rhythm of my pulse. *My girlfriend.* My chin trembles. "Oh, uh, sure," I say, even though I haven't finished my first flute.

"Perfect, I'll get those drinks for you right away." Elizabeth disappears to the back of the plane.

"You rarely drink." Matthew leans forward and settles his forearms on his thighs. "I mean, I've never really noticed you doing so over the past couple of years."

The confirmation that he's been watching me almost forces my hands over my face. First the colors of my mugs. Now this? *No.* Surely I put that in my fact sheet. I can't remember now.

"Yeah, I like the occasional glass of wine or champagne, but not much lately." I shrug, feeling insecure about my decision. I don't want champagne, so why'd I say yes? Drinking on my Lexapro always makes me feel woozy. "There's probably an open bottle back there, and, um, I would hate to be wasteful."

"Okay," he says. He doesn't push the subject further, but something's off.

Matthew remains mysterious. I don't know how to act or what personality to wear for him. It's agonizing to be around someone who notices things about me.

Don't forget that he's always paid amazing attention to detail. No other reason.

"Let's get back to, um, the questions." I wring my hands together. "Okay, here's an easy one. When is my birthday? Yours is on the first of January." A fact I already knew from memorizing most people's birthdays at ORO.

"February twenty-fifth."

"Correct." I pause. "You have five siblings? Myles, Mitchell, Maya, Mac, and…oh, don't tell me." My eyes close, and I tug my lip between my teeth. I know this.

"Madison," he affirms.

"Ugh, of course." My shoulders relax. "Your parents have an affinity for the letter M."

"We used to get teased about it at school, since we're all pretty close in age, but our mother's name is Mary. I guess my dad wanted each of his kids to be named in her honor."

Matthew seems to light up at the mention of his family, unlike the dread I feel when my own is mentioned. The way his cheek rises more to the left when he smiles is achingly attractive.

I swallow. "That's sweet. I'd love to meet them." The sentiment slips out, but I mean it. It'd be nice to be around a happy family for once.

"Maybe you can." He rubs the stubble on his jaw.

"What do you mean?"

"Every year during the holidays, my family holds what we call the Hudson Olympics. My parents come up with various games, and my siblings and I compete in them," he says proudly. "Now that everyone's grown up and married off, except for me and Madison, the tournament has become a couples game. If you come, we can team up."

My head almost shakes in disbelief. "You want to introduce me to your family on Christmas?"

"I mean, if we're not divorced by then, and if you don't have plans," he offers.

"No," I say, clapping my hands together. "Apart from the annual Winter Ball that my mother throws, my parents attend business soirées during the holidays." Last Christmas, I was alone in the city. "So my calendar is *wide* open. I'd love to go."

"It's settled." His hand meets his knee, his thick fingers flexing again. "There's no rule about two friends competing."

The word stings, but that is what we are. *Friends.* "What kind of games do you guys play?" I attempt to hide the disappointment in my voice.

"We don't know what to expect until we arrive. Last year, we built gingerbread houses from scratch. There's always skiing or snowshoeing. My parents love to keep us on our toes." The holidays aren't for a few months, but he's already excited.

"As long as it's not cooking, I think I could help you win," I jest. The closest I've gotten to my kitchen is to chat with Chef Hugo about his family in Italy. "Do you know your way around the kitchen?"

"I'd like to think so." He winks. "My dad taught me to cook."

Seriously? A bit of drool gathers at my lip. "How are you still single?" I laugh, sending one of my hands out into the air in front of me.

Then I realize I crossed a line.

Oh no.

Matthew looks stiff, pulling away into his seat again. The pilot comes over the intercom. "Please fasten your seatbelts. We'll be landing in ten minutes."

Here we go.

Chapter 6
Matthew

I NEVER HAD A BUCKET LIST, but I might need to start one after the past twenty-four hours.

Fly on a private jet. *Check.*

Flirt with my fake girlfriend even though we're meant to be strictly business. *Check.*

Take a marriage preparatory course at a five-star luxury resort. *Almost check.*

Lie to my family about all of the above. *Sadly, check.*

I hate not sharing my life with them. But if this playing pretend doesn't work out, I'd rather not spend the holidays hearing about it. I brush the thought from my mind.

Even in October, the weather in Arizona is harsh. Around us, the great canyons are monumental. Cacti in terracotta vases surround the On Cloud Nine property in the distance.

A town car speeds toward us, stirring up plumes of reddish dust.

"That's going to be Lolita Deveaux, the person who's in charge of approving our course," Molly says, looking ahead. Her springy curls wind around her face, the sun bouncing off the tip of her button nose. "She's a licensed couples therapist and a leading expert in the intimacy and relationship space. Oprah named her one of the top one hundred visionaries of our generation. You wouldn't believe the schmoozing it took to have her work for us."

"That's super impressive." Hopefully, the quizzing session we just had will be enough to convince an actual expert we're in love. Nerves prickle in my chest. *Alright. Guess it's time to get the show started.* "You ready?" I ask.

She nods. "Yes. We can do this. I'm prepped and quizzed."

"I'm going to put my arm around you; is that alright?"

Molly turns to me, and I wish I could see her gaze behind her sunglasses. "Uh, yes. Good thinking."

I gently drape my arm over her shoulders and draw her close.

The scent of red ruby apples, bright and fresh, engulfs my senses. The smell reminds me of the autumns I spent trampling through an orchard as a child. It makes me think of home.

This is going to be a long trip.

Maybe I can use these feelings to my advantage. It's normal to be attracted to someone like her. It'll make this act we're putting on all the more convincing.

The car pulls up before us. A tall woman with short gray hair and deep tawny skin exits the vehicle.

Molly gives me one final nod before her expression is engulfed in a radiant smile that mimics the one she wore during her wedding shower. Mollybot 2.0. *New personality secured.*

"Lolita!" she calls out.

"It is a pleasure to see you, dear." Lolita embraces Molly's hands and looks over at me. "You must be the wonderful Mr. Hudson who's captured our sweet Molly's heart."

"It's a pleasure to meet you." I flash her my best grin, ignoring the simmer of electricity coursing through my veins as Molly's shoulders rise and fall beneath my arm.

"Welcome to On Cloud Nine," Ms. Deveaux continues.

"We're elated to help you and Miss Greene cultivate your budding love through tranquility and rejuvenation. If I understand correctly, you have requested two rooms for your stay?" She eyes me with a nonjudgmental smile.

"Yes," Molly confirms. "We're waiting for our wedding night."

"Ah, how special. However, I spoke with Mrs. Greene, and it seemed most appropriate to place our beautiful Molly and her lover in the Unity Suite."

Molly's body stiffens in my embrace. *Great.*

We agreed we weren't sleeping together, but this is a luxury resort. The rooms must be huge. We'll figure out a way to make sure she's comfortable. There won't be observers making sure we consummate our union like in medieval times. Right?

"Shouldn't we keep the room for a couple who's actually on their honeymoon?" Molly's voice pitches upward, the way it does when she's uneasy.

"Bonding young love involves cohabitating," Lolita declares. "I guarantee the journey you'll be taking with me over the next two weeks will strengthen your relationship."

A knot tightens beneath my rib cage. All this talk of love is making me tense.

"Is there a Unity Suite with two beds?" Molly rubs her hands together. "I kick around in my sleep."

"No. Unfortunately, the only available room has one bed."

"Well, we both like sleeping. It'll be great to do it together for two weeks," I blurt out. *Wow. Smooth, man. Real smooth.* The corner of Molly's mouth quirks up. "Besides, maybe you can finally let me know if I talk in my sleep."

"I'm sure you have many interesting things to say, like the various synonyms for the word *bulbous*." Molly breaks into bashful giggles. I knew sharing my ick would come back to bite me in the ass.

But if her laughter follows the word, then I think I can bear hearing it a few times.

Her laughing fit turns into a snort. She claps her hand over her face. "Oh my god. I'm so sorry; I snort sometimes when—"

"Why are you apologizing? I've heard your laugh before." I drop my arm from her shoulders and look at her. "It's adorable."

Her eyes twinkle so brightly I can see them through her sunglasses. A rushing sound fills my ears. Is that my heartbeat? No. Must be the heat.

Lolita interrupts our moment "Ah! You two are truly in love. Inside jokes are so important in relationships. Let's get you over to dinner, and the staff will take care of your things."

Triumph floods my veins. We're putting on a good show.

We climb into the back of the town car and make the brief trip through the five-hundred-acre property. For the next hour, Lolita and Molly give me an extended tour, sharing details about the healing powers of canyons, the exclusive workshops, and the different workout facilities.

We receive a calendar of activities—all optional except for the scheduled inclusive mealtimes. I scan the list. Yearning Yoga, Seductive Stargazing, Passionate Pottery, and Couples Groundwork.

Interesting. Honestly, I won't complain if Molly has to put on one of the workout sets she occasionally wears to the office.

I roll my shoulders.

Molly walks ahead of me, a small bead of sweat rolling down her neck. One of her tightly spun curls clings to her skin. The lone strand drags down her nape. She looks back at me, peering over her sunglasses and giving me a smile. My mouth goes as dry as the desert we're standing in.

She's really easy on the eyes.

"HELLO, MOLLY AND MATTHEW," a hostess coos, welcoming us into the resort's main restaurant. "Your table is this way."

Apparently, we arrived just in time for the seven-o'clock dinner. Lolita didn't give us an opportunity to go to our room and change. My shirt is clinging to my body from the walk around the grounds. Molly, however, still looks polished. The pink fabric of her blouse hugs her curves, and she put a small ribbon into her hair, pulling her long curls away from her face.

Damn. My fingers tingle.

Through the windows are stunning views of the dusky desert mountains. The restaurant's open kitchen has chefs at work. We're weaving through guests enjoying their meals when Molly stops walking. Her body turns to stone.

I spot a woman with familiar copper hair. She's sitting with her back to us, at a table I assume is ours. "Is that your mom?"

"What is she doing here?" Molly faces me as she whispers. "I—I swear I had no idea she was going to be here."

"Don't worry," I assure her. "We can do this."

Vivian must just be checking to make sure we arrived safely. I'm certain most parents call, but when you have several jets, why not see for yourself…right?

Molly brushes her hands over her clothes. Worry creases her face as we approach the table.

"Ah, there you are." Vivian looks down at her watch. "Five minutes past seven."

I guess the schedules here are strict.

"M-mother." Molly stumbles through the word, disbelief still heavy in her voice. "What are you doing here?"

I pull out a chair on the opposite side of the table, extending my hand to help Molly into her seat. Vivian's hawkish gaze sears into me like I'm performing in a one-man show called *Awkward Interactions with Potential In-Laws.*

"Hello, Mrs. Greene. I didn't realize you were joining us." I try to hack at the thick tension.

"Please, call me Vivian. Mrs. Greene was Ray's mother." She reaches forward and adjusts her glass on the table. "Doll, what are you wearing?"

Molly's rehearsed smile falters. "I just threw this on," she explains. "We haven't had a chance to change."

"Well, not to worry. I made sure to bring a perfectly curated wardrobe with me. Something with a bit more *class*," Vivian adds.

What's wrong with Molly's clothes?

"Thank you," Molly utters through tight lips. "Will you be here long? I didn't realize you planned to attend the course with us."

"I was shocked when I heard from Paul that you booked the jet, so I had to see your arrival for myself. I didn't think you'd go through with this—or that you wouldn't consult your own mother before telling Lance that the engagement was off."

"I told you last weekend."

"Yes, but we thought whatever's gotten into you would have blown over by now." Vivian tilts her nose up.

I'm so out of my comfort zone and unsure how to handle this stare-off between them.

"We're thrilled to be here," I say. "Your jet is very nice."

I never imagined those words would come out of my mouth. Is that even a compliment?

"Thank you." She faces her daughter. "Did you appreciate the move to the Unity Suite? It'll be more appropriate for your experience here. I'm almost certain you two haven't spent nearly enough time together at your little assistant job. You can consider it my gift to you." Vivian's Cheshire cat smile could cut glass.

"My job is important." Molly seems irritated. We've only been here for five minutes, and her mom has already belittled her twice.

"Of course, doll. We all know how vital assisting others can be."

My nostrils flare at the blatant disrespect. "Without Molly, our offices wouldn't run. She's the glue holding all of ORO together."

Molly's mouth gapes.

Vivian appears annoyed by my remark.

"Let's dive into your plans here." Ignoring me, she pulls a journal and a fountain pen from her bag. "Like my mother-in-law did for me, I took over the privilege of handcrafting your stay." Vivian gives us a piece of neatly pressed stationery. "I'll be leaving later tonight, but I wanted to ensure that Lolita will monitor you and give me daily reports. So will the state-of-the-art cameras. All of this is to guarantee that you're succeeding in your course."

Cameras? That's overkill.

Molly wears a broken expression. Sure, I've picked up on our ten-year age difference a few times, but the gap is obvious when she's bickering with her mom. Although, I suppose Molly's occasional spells of worry and anxiety at the office make a lot more sense now. This level of scrutiny is bound to make anyone feel uncomfortable in their own skin.

We scan the meticulous agenda. The days are jam-packed with activities from eight in the morning until late into the evening.

Feeling uneasy, I tug at the collar of my shirt.

How many yoga classes will it take to prove our love?

"This must've taken you the entire flight to plan," Molly says, looking resigned to the extensive list before us.

"It was worth it." Vivian smiles, watching us expectantly.

Moving us into one room, forcing us to spend all day together…is Vivian trying to overwhelm us?

Does she already know this is fake?

We have to prove her otherwise.

Hell, it's twenty-five million dollars for the both of us. Molly's independence. EcoDrones.

Our fire seasons are getting longer, and the destruction is going to permanently ruin our ecosystem.

I need to stick this out. It's only two weeks.

I can do this. *I can do this.*

"Thank you." I give Vivian a polite nod. "Your effort to enrich my love for your daughter is so kind."

Mrs. Greene seems taken aback by my compliance, and I'll count this as a small win for the evening. "My pleasure. I'm sure it's a privilege for someone like *you* to visit one of our family jewels."

It's impossible to miss the way she emphasizes the word *you*, as if I'm less than. Molly stiffens again at her mother's poorly delivered jab.

I, however, am not remotely offended. Intimidation is the lowest form of social warfare. Little does Vivian know, affording one of the eight-thousand-dollar-a-night rooms here would barely put a dent in my account balance. But frivolity isn't my thing. I'm a simple man.

"Your generosity knows no bounds, especially when I get to have the family *jewel* by my side at all times." I hug her daughter close.

My patience, nonetheless, has an expiration date. I may need to teach Vivian Greene a lesson or two about boundaries.

Chapter 7
Molly

OF COURSE MY mother shows up to check on me.

How did I not anticipate her scheme?

My chest sags with guilt. Matthew is surely violated. How could he not be? Our easy-peasy marriage course now consists of countless activities, all under the surveillance of Lolita, my mother's new spy.

He's sacrificing his time and energy to raise money for his reforestation project, while my mother's orchestrating one of her silly games. He stood up to her. No one, apart from Dad, has the nerve to talk back to Vivian Greene.

But there was Matthew—confident, composed, and smart.

"I can't believe her," I say as the door to the Unity Suite latches shut. "I completely understand if you want to leave now."

"I'm not going to leave." Matthew flicks on the light switch, illuminating the room, which is decorated in earth tones and elevated southwestern decor.

Everyone has a breaking point. *Don't they?*

My eyes brim with tears. I can't believe I'm crying in front of Matthew—again. He grabs a tissue and hands it to me.

"Thank you." I sniffle, blotting my eyes.

"Anytime."

My face turns hot as a wave of embarrassment washes over me. I pinch my eyes closed and then open them. "I promise I don't normally cry this much," I attempt to assure him.

"You don't need to hide your emotions around me." He boyishly pockets his hands, making his trousers hug his thigh muscles.

I gulp. The longer I stare at him, the calmer I get. *Is that so wrong?*

"Thank you. I know my mother isn't pleasant, but my parents are always there for me, even if their methods are unusual." Regardless, Matthew doesn't deserve her wrath.

If she knew how he'd spend his portion of the trust payout, would she still act this way?

Probably. She would be annoyed it wasn't being used to expand the Greene legacy.

My heart pirouettes at his lack of response. Is he irritated? Upset? What on earth is he thinking?

He should storm off or yell. Instead, his eyes fill with compassion and understanding. Does he pity me?

Matthew places his hand on my forearm, and goosebumps fizz along my skin. "I'd do anything for my family. I won't leave you here, Molly." The words barely register. "The forests need replanting, remember?"

Right. The forests, our arrangement. That's all this is.

He breaks the connection.

Then I'm fully aware of where I am. The panic from dinner made me forget all about our sleeping situation.

I'm alone in a hotel room with a man.

"So, about this bed in here," Matthew says, walking into the bedroom.

Oh boy. Untamed heat floats around my body.

Is it desire? Seriously, *now?*

I toss my tissue and walk toward the room.

The room with just one bed.

One freaking bed.

What if he wakes up in the morning and sees me? The real me. My two different selves, Socialite Molly and Work Molly, sword fighting until they expose Just Molly.

Abashed, I hover in the doorframe of the bedroom.

They spared no expense for the Unity Suite. The bed is enormous, made up with ivory linen sheets. One wall is floor-to-ceiling windows, with views of a private outdoor patio and the expanse of canyons beyond.

On the opposite side of the bedroom is a walk-in closet beside a master bath, which includes a large soaking tub and shower. Arranged on the counter are signature On Cloud Nine towels and plush bathrobes.

"I can take the couch, and you can have the bedroom," I offer. "I'll schedule a massage in the morning, to help work out all my kinks."

His eyebrow quirks up. "Do you have a lot of those?"

"Couches?" I squint.

"Kinks."

"Uh, I meant because my neck gets tense. All that time working at a computer." I attempt a laugh. "You know, it's the leading cause of stiffness."

"Stiffness. Right." There's a tick of a smile on his lips as he turns away from me. "This is a huge bed." He bends, gliding one of his fingers over the sheets. The fabric ripples beneath his touch. His biceps bulge in his button-down.

Matthew's eyes bore into mine, illuminating me like a spotlight. Even now, when I'm half holding it together, I don't want to shy away from him.

Ugh, I'm screwed.

I don't know how to handle being in such close quarters with a crush.

The room bubbles with silence. "Yeah, the sheets are organic."

"Lovely. We wouldn't want our sheets to have pesticides," he teases, trying so hard to make me comfortable. I do feel safe. I *am* safe. I'm just overwhelmed out of my mind right now. No big deal. "How tall are you? Five foot three?"

"Five foot three and a half," I clarify, straightening my back.

"Forgive me for missing the important distinction." He tsks. "Now, we're going to be here for two weeks. You've mentioned you'd like to take the couch, but I'm worried about your kinks." He stifles a gruff laugh. "I don't think sleeping in the living room would be quite as comfortable as this bed."

"No, probably not."

"If I can make a suggestion." He cocks his head at me, and I nod for him to go on. "I think we'd be able to share this vast bed without disturbing each other. Of course, only if you wanted to."

He's so charming.

I glance down. Yep, still here. I haven't melted into a puddle. Still solid, human Molly. *For now*.

"Y-you'd want to sleep together?" Lance would've taken the bed without a second thought.

No. I don't want to think about my ex.

There's no competition between him and Matthew.

"We're both adults," he reminds me. "I don't move around a lot in my sleep, and you're quite petite. I'm sure we can fit in a gigantic bed without causing too much of a ruckus."

Sleep together.

Sleep in the same bed. In one bed. With Matthew Hudson.

Someone pinch me. Anyone, seriously.

I've never shared a bed with another person, let alone with a man who looks like *him*. A squeal brims my throat. I shove it back down as best as I can.

"Right, of course we can sleep in the same bed together." I nervously brush a stray curl out of my eyes. He's probably just thinking about this logically. "It'll be more convincing for the housekeeping staff."

"Sounds good. For now, I'll take the side closest to the door."

The most gentlemanly thing to do. Must he be so thoughtful?

Maybe in another life, where I'm a normal girl with a normal family, I could spend hours kissing a boy like Matthew Hudson. Touching his shaggy jet-black hair and gazing into his blue eyes while lying in the same bed. But that's not happening tonight.

"Sure, if that's what you're comfortable with."

"When I was younger, my parents would have all the kids share rooms during family vacations. Obviously, as the eldest, I had to take the bed closest to the door. You know, in case we were attacked by monsters or zombies." He chuckles. "I guess I haven't quite shaken the habit."

"It's nice to know that I can count on you to protect us from the boogeyman." I smile.

I'm sure if I could see myself from the outside, I'd catch myself standing here, cherry red, hair a mess, mascara splotchy, and grinning like an absolute fool.

But he's so nonchalant. I shouldn't be nervous.

For the next hour, we get ready for bed. I took the first shower, and Matthew's in there now. I dig through the neutral wardrobe my mother had the resort staff unpack for me. I hate it.

On the other side of the closet, steam pours out from beneath the bathroom door. My crush is naked. Only a few feet away. Suds likely cover his toned body as he lathers up his...*oh my goodness*. My core pulses. I gulp, slowing down my breath.

Pajamas. Focus on finding something to wear. I open the top dresser drawer. Inside are sexy robes, lace bralettes, and corsets.

Ugh, I'm gonna kill Lily for messing with my suitcase.

Why do I own all of this? There's never been someone I've wanted to show my collection to. But lingerie gives me confidence—a sprinkle of self-esteem. A way to express myself, especially when I'm muted in plain clothes.

I open the next drawer. An avalanche of thongs bursts out.

"Oh no!" I yip, attempting to shut the drawer.

The bathroom door swings open, and steam follows Matthew out. "Everything okay out here?"

"Yeah." I shove the fabric back into the dresser. When I turn to face him, Matthew Hudson is shirtless again.

Not only is he shirtless, but his hair is damp. Droplets of water cascade over his shoulders and bare chest. A towel hangs loosely off his waist. One sudden movement, and it could fall to his feet.

Gravity yanks my bottom lip down. We're both half naked, standing a few feet from each other. Only a robe and towel between us.

This is a dangerous situation.

He smirks, inquisitively tilting his head to the side.

"Are you hiding something over there?" *He knows about the thongs.* Matthew must be a mind reader.

"I didn't pack anything to sleep in." I shrug casually.

"No pajamas?"

His eyes drop to the floor. Then I see it, a pair of panties—which is a generous term since it's just a strip of lace.

"Uh, none." My cheeks burn as I cover the thong with my foot.

"Do you normally sleep naked?" Matthew chuckles, readjusting the towel on his waist.

"I—uh, naked?"

"Well, if you didn't pack any pajamas, one may presume you don't sleep with any." A hint of mischief ripples off his face.

My damp palms swipe across my robe. "No, um, I must've just forgotten to pack them."

"Here." He retrieves a stack of clothes from his side of the closet and hands it to me. "You can sleep in these."

The T-shirt and cotton basketball shorts are soft and worn in. "Are you sure?"

"Absolutely." He disappears into the bathroom. "I have another pair."

I press the fabric to my cheek. How many nights has he slept in these?

He strolls out a minute later. "Bathroom's all yours."

I yank the shirt away from my face. Great. He almost caught me acting like a creep. I grab a pair of panties and rush into the bathroom, where I slip on Matthew's oversized shirt, tug on the most appropriate underwear I could find, and eye the basketball shorts. They'll be too big. The shirt already hits below my knees. This should be fine.

I tuck my hair into a bun and return to the bedroom. Matthew is in bed, wearing the same pajamas as me.

"We match," I chuckle.

But instead of the jovial mirth usually dancing in his eyes, there's a darkness.

It unsettles me.

Nervously, my gaze slips over his tan skin against the stark white sheets. Beneath his shirt, the outline of his pecs is obvious. Matthew oozes manliness and coziness. As if tempting me to snuggle up beneath his burly arms and drown under the weight of them.

A breath catches in my throat. *What am I even thinking?*

"Do you think we should send out a Christmas card? Matching pj's and all," he jokes, snapping me out of my depraved daze.

"Maybe we can get a set for Bear." I smile and wade over to my side of the bed, where I quickly climb beneath the covers and lie parallel to Matthew.

He is so far away. It's like there's an island between us. An island of neutrality.

Perfect.

"The pillowcases are nice." He rearranges the stack of pillows beneath his head.

"They're silk. I sampled hundreds of them before finding these."

"It's like sleeping on a cloud." Matthew runs his hand over the fabric. "That was incredibly cheesy. Of course that's what it's supposed to feel like."

I stifle a giggle. "Silk is better for your skin and hair. It's especially good if you have curls like I do."

"I guess I'll have to get some for my bedroom at home."

My pulse picks up again. Did he mean for himself or for me? Why am I moments away from kicking my feet and squealing at the idea of Matthew Hudson buying silk pillowcases for me?

We haven't even discussed living together. It's a tad soon. He must want to care for his really nice skin.

He reaches for the light switch above the bed. "Well, we should get some rest."

I nod and tuck my knees close, keeping my eyes on him.

The room is enveloped in darkness, with only a faint glimmer of starlight seeping through the blinds. His breathing is barely audible.

My hand scoots closer toward him, and, as if he's mirroring me, Matthew's fingers do the same.

They remain in the neutral zone, right beside each other.

Light pinches my lids, and I stretch my legs out wide. I can't remember the last time I slept so well.

Then stone-cold reality hits me. I slept with a man. As silently as possible—and, of course, for fake boyfriend research purposes—I roll over to face Matthew's side.

It's empty.

My heart crinkles like a piece of used wrapping paper.

Where is he? I lift the covers. He's not here. I sit up, resting against the headboard.

Did he move to the couch in the middle of the night?

Oh no. Maybe I snore. "Matthew?" I call out.

Silence.

Through the cracked bedroom door, I can barely see into the living room.

What did I expect, that we'd wake up together? He'd roll over and give me a sleepy smile?

That's silly. Fake relationships don't have cuddly mornings in bed. Disappointment washes through me.

I need a distraction.

After taking my Lexapro, I grab my phone and pull up my reading app.

There's no better way to escape reality than with a book. Especially when the book includes dragons. *Wings and fangs, here I come.*

Over the next hour, I rotate between scanning the same page over and over and inching my way toward Matthew's side of the bed. The faint whiff of his smell refuses to stop beckoning me over, and I'm too weak to resist.

Without a smidge of rationality, I toss my phone and sniff his pillow.

Wow. My mouth waters. It's heavenly. Vetiver. Earthy, woody, and smoky. Heat builds in my core.

Was I always this depraved?

The front door swings open.

Oh god. He's going to see me smelling his pillowcase like some kind of deranged stalker. I straighten up and launch myself far away from his side of the bed.

From the tiny crack in the bedroom door, I watch Matthew come into the suite, his skin damp with sweat. A white towel hangs over his neck. Somehow, he looks bigger. Is that possible?

My mouth hangs open. He's…*gorgeous.*

How hard is he going on the weight machine if he looks like that?

Matthew glances toward the bedroom, and I sink down into the covers. There's no way he saw me.

I peek my eyes open. A wide grin meets me through the doorway.

"Good morning." He lifts his hand, the one I almost touched last night, in a small wave. "How'd you sleep?"

"Good morning," I call back, but he's already out of view. "Slept great. What about you?"

"Best sleep I've gotten all year. Must've been those organic sheets," Matthew says from the living room. The faucet in the kitchenette turns on. "I was reviewing our schedule, and it looks like breakfast is in thirty."

"Okay, great. I'm just getting up." I hike up onto my knees and stretch over the edge of his side of the mattress. One brief glimpse of him in all his sweaty glory, and it'll put all of my tainted thoughts to rest.

"Do you know what this Lover's Labyrinth activity on your mother's agenda is going to entail?"

"No clu—" Suddenly, my palms slip off the sheets, and I tumble onto the shag rug with a large *plop*. I'm face down, but my legs remain on the bed.

Oh my god.

"Um, Molly?"

I open my eyes. Matthew stands by the door, observing my klutziness.

"Yeah?" My voice cracks. A breeze tickles my thighs. No, no, no. I should've worn those damn shorts. My lace-covered behind is out in the wind for all to see.

Just close your eyes and pretend to be invisible.

"Is this a morning stretch I don't know about?" He appears above me. I crane my neck sideways. His six-foot-one frame seems exceptionally tall from this angle. "Or do you need help?"

He outstretches his palm. Veins cord his forearm. Then my gaze falls a few inches to the left.

I gulp. Great. My fake boyfriend's bulge stares back at me. A bulge that looks particularly…um, enticing under his workout shorts.

It's rather well-endowed. At least from way down here.

"Uh." I look away, reach for his palm, and scramble to pick myself up off the floor. "Thank you."

"You alright?"

"Just peachy."

Something in his gaze lights up.

Why did I say that? Ugh. He probably didn't even put it together. I mean, Matthew's older than me. I highly doubt he's making the connection between the peach emoji and my exposed butt.

"Very peachy indeed," he laughs. Nope, he definitely got it. "See you in a sec." He enters the bathroom and shuts the door.

I collapse onto the bed.

I'm in need of a very cold bath.

Chapter 8
Matthew

A WEEK AGO, everything was normal.

Now, I'm halfway across the country, waking up next to my achingly beautiful, off-limits coworker.

I glance over at Molly as we walk through the property. Should we be holding hands constantly now that we're around people?

The sun beats down violently, but Molly sports an all-black outfit. *Is this her way of mourning her engagement to Lance?*

Instead of looking at her face, which is the only appropriate place to look, my gaze slips to the outline of her full breasts beneath her sheer shirt. They're cupped in a bra that matches the lacy underwear she wore this morning. A damp sheen coats her chest, the skin hiding beneath the dark fabric.

How the hell did she manage to fall out of bed?

Another item to add to the bucket list. Seeing the peachiest ass. *Check.*

My icy shower this morning did nothing to wash away the image of her wearing my goddamn T-shirt and those fucking panties.

Christ.

I need another workout session to calm myself down. My dick hasn't gotten the memo that we're just sleeping next to Molly, not sleeping *with* Molly. These thoughts are why I didn't linger after I woke up.

No one has ever smelled quite like her. Those damn red ruby apples.

Who am I? Snow White? This is ridiculous.

"It's a hot one today." Molly attempts a laugh.

"Are you sure you don't want to go back up to our room and change?" I ask as we continue our stroll. It's barely noon and already eighty degrees.

"I'm comfortable." Beads of sweat coat her brow. "My mom may be checking the cameras, and I'd rather wear something she flew out for me."

Molly obviously loves and respects her parents, but to what extent? Family isn't supposed to micromanage you. No matter how much money sits in their bank account.

"Why does she care so much about what you wear?"

She looks over at me, resignation on her face. "Bright colors give her headaches."

How selfish. Has Vivian ever heard of ibuprofen?

"Well, I think you always look nice." I smile at her.

"Oh, thanks. You always look good too. I mean, not in bright colors—though if you wanted to wear more color, I'm sure a saturated forest green or a deep indigo would do your blue eyes wonders." She stumbles through her words.

Has she given this a thought before?

"Forest green or deep indigo," I echo. "I'll keep that in mind."

We turn behind a building and are greeted with wild, viridescent hedges standing ten feet tall. I cringe. How are they providing enough water for these in the middle of a desert?

"Good morning, Molly and Matthew." Lolita waits for us at

the arched entryway to the maze. "Welcome to the first day of the rest of your lives."

Intense.

"Hi, Lolita." Molly skips ahead of me. "When did we start adding mazes to our resorts?"

"It's new," she explains, while pulling a metal contraption out of a tote bag that hangs off her shoulder. "You'll be trialing the journey."

"I don't want to overstep, but lush foliage in Sedona? That seems like an improper usage of the natural resources here." Molly's using her presentation voice.

Has she sounded this attractive at the office all these years?

I mean, we both work at a conservation organization. It's not a coincidence we'd think the same environmentalist thoughts.

"We're using reclaimed water to maintain the hedges," Lolita explains.

"Hmm." Her shoulders tense. "I'll just bring it up to my father. Don't let my rambling keep you from what you were saying. Sorry."

"This Lover's Labyrinth will be like nothing you've ever experienced before." Ms. Deveaux holds up a padlock with two separate cables coming out of it. "If you will, please extend your wrists out like this."

We mimic her outstretched hands, and she laces my left wrist and Molly's right one together with the cable, securing the lock between us. We're handcuffed together.

Bondage with a fake girlfriend. Another item to check off the bucket list.

"Is this necessary?" Molly asks, staring at our wrists.

"The exercise will challenge you to overcome difficult situations together." Lolita recites her wisdom. "A couple who can navigate life's complexities by standing beside one another and not running away can survive any bump in the road ahead."

Our arms drop to our sides. But because of our height difference, Molly's hand lifts, bouncing near my hip. She goes rigid when her fingers brush against mine.

"Are you comfortable?"

She nods before turning to our instructor. "Do we get a map? The maze looks huge."

"Love cannot be understood with a map. This will be your opportunity to organize your own wonder." Ms. Deveaux must only speak in riddles.

We approach the archway, and with one final look at each other, we step into the maze.

Three dead ends later, sweat drips off my forehead, burning one of my eyes. I hope the other compulsory activities aren't this draining.

"In your fact sheet you said you like to read, but what genre?" I ask, trying to focus on anything except the heat.

"Oh, it's called romantasy." Molly peers up at me through her thick lashes. Her hand is still brushing up against mine.

"Is that the title of a book?"

She stifles a laugh and gives me a waggish look. "No, it's a combination of romance and fantasy."

I should've put that together. "Is that what you're always reading during your lunch breaks?" On more than one occasion, I've startled her while she's blushing behind the pages of some tome-sized hardback.

Molly bites her lip. A thrill gallops through me.

"Sometimes, if I'm at a really good part, it's hard to wait until I get home to find out what happens."

"I get it. Especially with fantasy. Hours slip by, and the next thing I know it's two in the morning," I chuckle. "I'll have to add something with a little more romance to my own collection."

"You should. It makes the stories more fun. The drama, the tension, the pining." Her voice rises with glee. "I didn't know you read fantasy books. I've always taken you for more of a biography kind of guy."

"I've been enjoying all the assumptions you've had about me." I give her a playful nudge. "But I like to mix it up. Fantasy, biographies, research papers."

"What's your favorite mythical creature?" she asks, watching me scrupulously.

"High elves," I reply with a sly grin. "Their entire purpose is to gain knowledge. I bet they have access to the best libraries."

"Interesting choice." Her voice is low and seductive. Or maybe I'm imagining that it is. A gorgeous woman is speaking to me about elves—teen me is aching for a high five right now.

My heart thunders. "Perhaps we could find a book to enjoy together?"

Suddenly, Molly misses a step, falling against my side. I catch her and pull her close. Amber eyes find me, her gaze melting over my face like honey.

Time slows.

A memory resurfaces from when I first started at ORO. We were at an old bar on the Upper East Side. Molly seemed more carefree back then. She was taking salsa classes, and one drink too many turned into us dancing for hours. My hands ran over her hips as the lights strobed above us.

The night never went anywhere. Laura ruined that for me—after her, I swore I'd never mix business with pleasure again.

The next day at work, Molly never mentioned it, so we just moved on. Shortly after, she started to bring up Lance in conversations, and she was never quite as freehearted as that night. Even after three years, I haven't forgotten the way her waist feels beneath my palms.

"Y-ye-huh, a book, together?"

I'm thirsty for a tall drink of water…or for Molly. Another kiss? Just one more, to savor her. Then I'll put all these thoughts to rest once and for all.

My dick twitches against the fabric of my trousers. *No.* I clear my throat and steady us upright.

"Yes," I confirm. "A book, together."

"Sorry for losing my footing. These Loewe espadrilles are a nightmare." I have no idea what that means, but nothing about her body next to mine felt like a bad dream. She speeds ahead, pulling me along by our wrists. "To answer your question, I, uh, I'd love to read a book together."

"Great, we'll have to find something," I say. "What about you? What's your favorite mythical creature?"

"I like griffins." Molly flashes me a smile with her pink lips. "I'd love to ride one."

"That makes sense; they embody strength. I'm sure any griffin would be honored to have you as a rider." I halt. I did not seriously say that. *A GRIFFIN WOULD BE HONORED TO HAVE YOU AS A RIDER.* I'm losing my mind.

"I think they'd feel the same way about you," she laughs.

There's no point in denying it anymore: we're flirting again. We should probably stop before it goes too far.

What did we even talk about at the office?

"I definitely thought we'd be able to figure out this maze pretty quickly." Although I gave up trying ten minutes ago.

"Nothing at On Cloud Nine is easy," Molly sighs, using her free hand to swipe at the strands of hair sticking to her face. "Well, actually, the typical stays are. We've earned Condé Nast's Most Relaxing Destination award for eleven years in a row."

"You never really talked about the resorts at work. I don't think I truly grasped that your life was like this."

"I try to keep both of my worlds separate." Our fingers brush again. The friendly distance between us shrinks the more we roam around this hedge maze from hell.

Last week, Molly was a hardworking executive assistant at one of the world's most prestigious ocean conservation firms. Now, she's that, and also a woman who dresses in all black in the scorching Arizona heat just in case her mother is spying on us.

I'm struggling to mesh her contrasting personalities.

"Do you ever feel like you're split in half?" I prod.

"All the time," she whispers. "But I'm honestly fine. I'm good at being flexible."

"Flexible or sacrificing?"

Molly shrugs and then fans herself with her free hand. "They really need to put hydration stations in this maze. It's too hot to be without water for this long."

Guess her shapeshifting is an off-limits topic. But I want to know more about this other side of her.

I attempt a different direction. "I'm surprised you don't work for the family business. You have a lot of ideas for the resort."

"It was never an option. My mother didn't want me to follow in my father's footsteps. Besides, I have two cousins, Dave and Larson, who will be taking over the resorts—if my dad ever decides to retire. Though I doubt that'll happen."

"How does that make you feel?"

"Sure, it would've been nice for my parents to see me as a suitable contender for being a part of the company. But," she replies plainly, "adding water stations and pillowcases are small, insignificant changes. Nothing life-changing."

"Everything complex is made up of simple things."

Her gaze drops to the dusty ground. "I suppose you're right."

"Your current job isn't any easier, and you still seem to manage to do everything your family requires of you."

Molly stays late when meetings run over, and she's always the first to fill in when folks call in sick. A true jack-of-all-trades.

"I don't think my mother sees it that way, because I'm just an assistant and got the job through my father."

She can't believe that nonsense.

"A title doesn't make the job any easier. Also, I remember your first boss, Johanna. She was a pill."

"Yeah." Molly frowns. "Vivian only hears what she wants to

hear. But it's fine. I genuinely like my job. Taking care of others comes easily to me," she says softly. "My dad may have helped me get the interview five years ago, but I picked the company. Johanna was a real inspiration. She left her family fortune and started ORO from the ground up."

"Is that something you wish you could do?"

"I'm not sure." She shrugs. "What about you? How'd you get involved in conservation?"

"I've always felt a connection to the greater good," I explain, swiping at the back of my neck. "I invested in sustainable companies at my VC firm. It became clear that the oceans were transforming into a giant trash can. That's how Plastech was born." Well, that, and things with Laura falling apart. "I recruited Ollie and Robert for the mechanical aspects, while I secured the capital for the project."

"I guess if you're an entrepreneur, you just know?" Molly appears genuinely curious. A glimmer sparks in her eyes.

"I always started businesses as a kid. Lemonade stands, trading baseball cards, and pawning off my brothers' things. But don't tell them that."

She giggles, swaying in and out of my proximity.

"Maybe I can introduce you to some people when we get back to New York?"

Huh. I guess I hadn't considered how door-opening being around someone like her could be for my business.

"I'd love that. Thank you." I flash her a smile. "What about you? What are you planning to do with the money from your trust?"

"Can I be honest with you?" she asks, looking around at the hedges, seemingly suspicious of being caught.

"Of course."

"Well..." She hesitates. "I don't want to be perceived as just another rich girl who doesn't make a difference. I want to own a business and make an impact on someone's life. I want to re-create the way people feel when they come to On Cloud Nine. But on a smaller, more personal scale. Maybe my own inn?"

Molly has a hidden passion for entrepreneurship. That's news to me. News that makes her even more alluring.

Perhaps I can mentor her. I advise other people all the time. Starting your own business is hard. Terrifying, even.

"That's really cool, and just so you know, the offer to help goes both ways. If you ever want to brainstorm, I'm your guy."

"Thank you." She averts her gaze to the hedges. "I don't know if I could even handle breaking into hospitality on my own."

"I'm certain you could do it," I say.

She stretches her plump lips into a wide smile. Our gazes lock. The tension between us is palpable.

Her pinky glides up the side of my hand. Shivers hurl down my spine. What else could those fingers do to me? Or what could I do with them?

I know I shouldn't, but I have the urge to kiss Molly Greene.

A demanding urge.

Her laughter. Her smile. The way her touch has been indenting my skin the entire time we've been trapped in this maze.

Molly swipes at her hair, but a loose strand remains glued to her round cheek. Instinctively, I reach to brush it away.

A mistake. A huge mistake.

Molly takes a startled step back. *What have I done?* In a blink, a hedge swallows her whole. Our binds tug me along, and I topple forward, bracing myself above her.

"*Ahh!*" she screams.

As I regain my balance, the branches dig into my palm. I wrap my free arm around Molly's waist and pull us away from the hedges. She's light in my embrace, delicate almost. Once we're on our feet, she remains pressed up against the vegetation.

The lacy fabric of her bra is only two measly pieces of

clothes away from my bare chest. Despite the fact that I'm super dehydrated, my mouth waters.

"I'm such a klutz," she laughs, collapsing her forehead onto my chest. "*Ouch*."

"What's wrong? Did you get cut?" I fiercely scan her body.

"My hair." She reaches her bound arm behind her, dragging my hand along with it. "It's stuck."

"Hey, I got it; let me help."

Carefully, I unwind her strands from the tangled mess of ficus leaves. She tenses up beneath me. I can't ignore her warm breath against my chest. Leaves rustle around us in the stiff breeze. I linger on the soft texture of her curls between the pads of my fingers.

When the last strand is plucked loose, I hesitate, not wanting our closeness to end.

"T-thank you." Her smile is golden, her lips plush. Molly leans into me, fitting all too perfectly. I'm consumed by her damn smell again.

I get light-headed as it fills my mind, my lungs, my body. Blood rushes into my cock, which is throbbing in my trousers.

Can she tell I'm fucking hard against the slope of her stomach? She must be able to.

My palm desperately grips the curve of her jaw, my eyes hungrily fixating on her lips.

Our breaths come in short gasps. Each one of mine is a small release of the tightness building inside me.

This feels too real.

I need to close the distance. The desire is becoming visceral.

Just one more kiss. Just to get it out of my system.

"Matthew." Her mouth drops open. I swallow, trying to steady my pulse. Has she changed her mind about our kissing agreement? I definitely have. "You—"

"There you are!" A voice scratches my eardrums. "I've been

looking for you. You were meant to be exiting the maze over an hour ago."

Lolita marches toward us down the hedge path. My jaw clenches. I get the feeling that Molly and I won't have a lot of alone time under all of these watchful eyes.

Molly unwraps herself from me, getting back to my side. "We got a little distracted."

"Of course you lovebirds did." She winks. "The exit is right at the next bend."

Right. That's all this was, I attempt to convince myself. *A distraction.*

I force a smile. I've never had to be this *on* for so long. Hopefully, my solitude in the mornings will be enough for me to recharge after these supervised days.

Chapter 9
Molly

"RELATIONSHIPS ARE MESSY, which is why you and your soulmate will need to commit to molding your love into something that can strengthen your imperfections," Lolita announces from the helm of the pottery studio. In front of her, various finished ceramics sit on a wooden table. "But love can also be fragile." She picks up a bowl and smashes it on the tile floor.

I shriek. Matthew grabs my hand over the pottery wheel, trying to calm me down.

"Sorry," I gasp, catching my breath.

"Don't be. That was horrifying," he says.

The rest of the couples in the class remain unfazed by Lolita's antics.

Some sit beside each other so rigidly, you'd think they were also pretending to be in a relationship. Though, on our left, a couple in matching paisley shirts and white aprons are giggling and playing footsie.

There's a camera in the ceiling at the far corner of the room. We've been diligent about our act since we arrived, and I'm certain we're putting on the performance of a lifetime.

But are Matthew and I being affectionate enough now?

He's still holding my hand. This is the longest we've touched since our almost kiss in the Lover's Labyrinth two days ago. At least, that's what I think would've happened if our relationship coach hadn't interrupted us.

But we'd already agreed we wouldn't kiss, and Matthew has been respecting the rules valiantly. He hasn't made any obvious moves on me at our other mandatory activities. It was merely heat exhaustion and the fact we were cuffed together.

After helping free my hair from the hedges, he probably held me that extra second because we were just putting on a show. Like we are now.

"Remember, do not fear the mess; embrace it." Lolita's voice pulls me back to reality. Around us, couples pick up mounds of clay.

"I guess we should get started." Matthew scoots his chair slightly toward mine. His perpetual five-o'clock shadow hugs the strong outline of his jaw oh so nicely. "Have you done this before?"

"When I was younger." I grab a slab of clay. "Have you?"

"Never. I'll need you to teach me." He playfully quirks his brow at me. "Sadly, that means I can't re-create that one scene from *Ghost* like the couple over there." Matthew nods toward one of our senior classmates, who's massaging his wife's arms as he sits behind her. The look on her face is a tad amorous for this early in the morning.

"You've seen *Ghost*?"

"My sister, Maya, forced me through every single romance classic when we were in high school." Matthew connects his forearms to the tops of his thighs, leaning toward me. "Apparently, they were meant to help me with girls."

"I doubt you ever needed help in that department." I shut my eyes. *Why do I manage to say the most inappropriate things when I'm around him?* My crush is getting out of hand. "Um, honestly, I always pictured you as more of a documentary type of guy."

"Do you picture me often?"

My eyes fly to his. Butterflies, or woodpeckers, come alive in my stomach. "I…"

Matthew's stoic expression cracks, and he grins at me as if he knows what he's doing. "I love documentaries," he chuckles. The sound is lush as it pours over me. "I'm surprised you've watched *Ghost*. I thought that was a little before your time."

"*My time?*" It's my turn to raise a brow at him. "You're only ten years older than me, not thirty. Besides, *Ghost* is a classic."

"I was born a few years before that movie was released. Does that mean I should consider myself a classic?"

"You've both aged well." I share my most ill-suited thoughts out loud again. "You're not old; that's not what I was saying. It's that, you know…I just meant that you look good."

"You look good too," he says. I'm about as mushy as the clay in my hands. Definitely growing too attached to his flattery.

"Y'all are cute as a button." Someone to our left gives my shoulder a tap. "Aren't they cute, Jerry?"

"Reminds me of when we first were married. Are y'all here on your honeymoon?" Jerry smiles. The paisley shirt couple look at us expectantly.

"No, we're on vacation," Matthew clarifies.

"Young love." The woman sighs dreamily. "Makes me miss the days when we looked at each other like that."

Like what? I want to ask them. They must be talking about all my gawking and stuttering. Guess my crush is coming in handy after all.

"How long have you been together?" I love hearing about people's meet-cutes.

"Thirty years," Jerry broadcasts.

"That's commitment. My parents have been together just shy of forty," Matthew says, beaming at any mention of his family.

"It goes by so fast. Shucks, we saved for six years to come to this resort for the fancy honeymoon we never got."

Six years. My heart sinks. That's a long time to wait. I've had access to over a hundred resorts my entire life, and I never quite put together that others may have found the experience to be once in a lifetime.

"Oh stop, Jerry," his wife teases.

"You're worth every penny, honey." He kisses her. "We met at her boyfriend's baseball game. He had the worst throwing arm, but I'm thankful for it, because it led Gigi to chat my ear off the whole game."

"Well, you sure were the better catch."

We all laugh.

They're too sweet. I should speak to Lolita about comping their stay, or extending it. They should spend more time here if they can.

"How'd you two meet?" Gigi pries. *Oh no*. We haven't rehearsed this story before.

"Wo—" I start.

Matthew interrupts me, taking the lead. "It was my first day at the office where Molly worked. My company was contracted to collaborate with her company." He uses his confident CEO voice, and it sets me on edge. "I remember it like it was yesterday. The nerves of walking into a new place. But then I saw Molly. Her wide smile hit me like a shot of caffeine, and she wore this bright green dress, which somehow made her curls look like a firestorm. I barely got any work done that week." He gives me a slow and sexy smile.

The room feels stuffy. He must've thought about this.

I barely remember that day. I was too frazzled making sure Plastech's offices were set up properly.

"Adorable. You are very pretty, dear," Gigi hums, but my mind stays lost in his story.

"My wonderful potters, I'll be back shortly," Lolita announces, causing me to snap together. "You have thirty minutes to explore your projects before I return."

Jerry slaps his palm on his lap. "Oh, we better get back to it."

"Nice chatting with you." Matthew nods and returns to the clay in front of us. He casually dropped a memory that's causing me to have heart palpitations, and now he's sitting here entirely unbothered.

"Convincing story," I croak.

"Because it's true," he says plainly.

"You, um, have an exceptional memory. But are you sure it wasn't a blue dress? I could've sworn—"

"It was definitely green." His tone is uncompromising. The backs of my arms pebble. Okay. It was green. *Definitely green.*

"Um, where were we?" I need a distraction from the jumble of emotions bouncing around in my chest.

"I'll follow your lead."

"Right. First, we're going to pick up the clay." I lift the clump from the wheel. Matthew cups the backs of my hands with his. The touch is electric. I'm still not used to feeling his skin on mine. "And slam it on the wheel to make sure it sticks."

We drop the clay. A loud smack rings in my ears.

"Good job." Matthew grins. The praise flares heat into the tips of my ears. "What's next?"

I hit the foot pedal beneath the table. "We bring our wheel to life and use some of the water"—I nod to the pail beside our pottery wheel—"to begin sculpting."

"Got it." He dips his hand in the water, moistening each of his long, calloused fingers.

The whole intelligent artisan look has officially made it onto my list of hottest things I've ever seen. It's as if he's a craftsman in one of my romantasy stories, working natural material into a rare gem to save the day.

Is he the type of man who fixes things around the house? All on his own? What else could those veiny hands fix?

My thighs clench together in my seat.

I've never once been turned on in public, and now it's happening daily. A side effect of my anxiety meds is that it takes a little while to get the spark going. But Matthew's been lighting up that need inside me nonstop.

"What would you like to make?" he prompts, snapping me out of my thoughts.

Most of the other couples are making bowls like the one Lolita shattered. Gigi and Jerry are inhaling and moaning as their clay morphs into something phallic.

I only hope that I can have that kind of passion with someone one day. Unabashed desire and love for each other.

"Vases are nice. Maybe we can make something to hold the dahlias you grow at home," I suggest.

"Noticed my dahlias?" A boyish grin dimples one of his cheeks. His hooded eyes crease, and the stubble on his chin gathers.

Matthew's rough knuckles are caked in clay. I want to trace the lines in his fingers.

To pretend better, of course.

Instead, I dampen my own hands and step on the pedal again.

"They're my favorite."

"A vase sounds good. There's a camera on the other side of this room; I'm going to move closer, okay?" I nod. Matthew scoots his chair to my right until he's inches from me. He follows my lead as the soft clay glides smoothly around my fingers. "How's that?" he whispers from beside me.

"So, um..." My throat constricts. I need to focus on the

instructions. "Very good. We just have to press our fingers into the center to shape our vase."

The smell of vetiver and the graze of his knee cause a taut feeling to deepen in my stomach. He nods and presses into the center, while I hold the exterior of the clay. The moment his pointer and middle finger apply the slightest pressure, my core floods.

If there wasn't a kiln on site, I'm certain I'd be able to use the heat between my legs to harden our vase.

His precise movements hypnotize me. Delicate but deliberate strokes. Clay catches in the hair along his arm. My insides are vibrating.

How would it feel for those same strong fingers to glide—

"This is fun." Matthew interrupts my thoughts.

"Mhm."

"Why don't you give this part a try?" He takes one of my hands and guides my fingers into the hollow center of our vase.

Up and down. In and out.

Plutonium must be coating my cheeks because the radioactive heat coming off my face is deadly.

"You're a natural," I croak.

Really?

A natural?

What am I trying to imply? That he's running rampant, fingering clay vases left and right?

I'm a drooling mess.

"Are you kidding me? You're absolutely incredible at this." Matthew squeezes my hand. A current of static jolts up my arm, and I yank back, folding a portion of the vase. It's not ruined, but one side is oddly shaped.

Oh no.

"I'm so sorry." I rush for the water, drenching my hands and attempting to fix the damage.

Matthew drops his forearm onto my thigh, shattering my frantic concentration.

"You don't have to keep doing that." His large palm covers my hand. The gesture is calming. All the radioactive sensations are quickly subdued. "You don't have to keep apologizing for simply being. It's just a vase, darling. We can make another one."

The statement takes me aback. So does the fact that he just called me darling. *Did anyone else hear that?*

The creases around Matthew's eyes appear. It's as if he's realizing that he said it too. He's too ridiculously handsome to go around giving people nicknames. I want to rub my hand over his smooth stubble. To thank him for his patience.

I open my mouth to speak, but in the corner of my eye, a spark catches my attention. Reluctantly, I turn away from Matthew's blue gaze—and then my heart collapses into my stomach.

Near the southern windows, a bunch of newspapers are smoking beside an electric outlet.

"Fire!" I yell, shooting out of my seat. The sculpting and whispering freeze over as my classmates turn toward me.

Okay. Relax, Molly. Remember your training.

"Everyone, please remain calm. I'm a fire warden." I hold my hands up and begin motioning to the patio door. "Slowly make your way toward the sliding door on the opposite side of the room."

People scurry, some running toward the exit, some collapsing the chairs in their way.

Didn't I say slowly?

The glass door to the patio slides open as the small fire grows, sending up wisps of smoke.

Think, Molly, think. You always ace this training. I'm not worthy of my bright red warden hat if I can't get this under control.

"We've got to go." Matthew grabs my hand, waiting for me to follow him.

The extinguisher hangs beside the front door, and I drop Matthew's hand, sprinting toward it. "I can fix this."

"Molly, what are you doing?" Matthew runs after me, but I'm on a mission.

I pull the fire alarm, sending the blaring of sirens and red lights through the studio. Sweat pours down my face. My mouth is dry. That fire needs to be stopped.

"Matthew, stay back," I call out, unlatching the fire extinguisher from the wall.

Oh goodness. I hope I can remember how to use this thing. *Okay, pull the pin.* My breath clamors. My hands are unsteady. *Molly, you've been the fire warden at ORO for five years. You know what to do.*

I inhale a small breath, suppress a cough, and release the pin. I aim and squeeze the handle.

In a blink, I'm launched back by the pressure of the white foam exploding out of the can. The hose snakes around, and I gain control of it as best as I can, then point it toward the fire.

"You got this!" Matthew yells.

"She's saving us! Our bowls aren't going to be ruined," someone whoops from outside.

The hose slips away from me again, flailing around.

"It won't turn off." I fumble with the trigger, but it's stuck.

"Let me help." Matthew's fingers slide over mine, his torso pressing into my back.

We're suddenly so close. So, so close.

Fire. Smoke. His chest against my head. The extinguisher drops to the ground.

He spins me around; relief skips across his face.

My heart pounds with the fury of a jackhammer.

I know the fire was small, but I'm certain the flames would have engulfed us before I even got to kiss him again.

I mean, talk about bad timing.

"Kiss! Kiss! Kiss!" A chant comes from outside, or from my mind. I can't tell.

Matthew grips the curve of my jaw with intention. His eyes hungrily stick to my lips. Without thinking, I shoot up on my toes and crash my mouth onto his.

Wow. The taste of smoke intermingled with musk. He's rugged, with a chin covered in stubble that tickles my skin. When he parts his mouth against mine, inviting me in, I struggle to resist the urge to intertwine our tongues.

Even though it feels so right, it's also so wrong. Isn't it?

I pull back, catching Matthew's gaze, which is enveloped in darkness.

Did he want to keep going as much as I did?

"I—I, uh, I'm so—"

"No, it was just the moment." Matthew steps back, adding distance between us and brushing his fingers through his hair. "We got ahead of ourselves," he chuckles.

"Right." I nod. Of course he didn't want to kiss me. "All that adrenaline. The chanting. Don't even worry about it!"

A peck, only the briefest brush of lips. We've gone three years without kissing, and now it's happened twice in less than a month.

Light floods into the room, and some students rush from the patio and out the front door.

When the stampede stops, Matthew's arms are still draped over me.

"What's going on here? Is everyone alright?" Lolita appears beside us.

"There was a small fire," I manage around my dry throat.

A round of applause comes from the room.

"She saved the day!" a woman cheers.

I begin laughing. Cackling. Louder and louder. My side prickles with a stitch, stabbing below my rib, and I keel over. I can barely get myself to stop when I hear the rest of the class join me.

Nothing like a little disaster to shock me back into reality.

But my thoughts linger. I want to kiss Matthew Hudson again. And I don't want it to be pretend.

Chapter 10
Molly

"I'm so glad Lolita was able to get the outlet at the pottery studio fixed," I call out, making quick work of bobby-pinning a loose curl to the base of my low bun.

"Yeah, I still can't believe that happened."

After class today, I spoke to Lolita about extending resort vouchers to all of our classmates and making sure everyone is accommodated. Even though the fire was two days ago, the memory is fresh. I'm glad I was there to help everyone. My fire warden training finally paid off. Nobody got hurt, and the building was saved. *Because of me.*

"I checked my mother's agenda for today; it looks like we'll be making baskets." I enter the bedroom. "Do you think we'll learn different weaving techniques?"

"Actually, I was thinking we could do something else," Matthew says.

The cool hue of the morning sun sprinkles over Matthew's body sprawled out on the bed. He's handsome, as always. If he didn't sprint out of bed right when he woke up, would he look like that?

"What did you have in mind?" I whisper, taking a seat on the edge of the bed. A pit forms in my stomach.

He props himself up on the pillow. "Well, I booked us a pool-side couples massage."

"Oh. Um, I—I think we should stick to the agenda." My throat dries. What if Lolita tells my mother we're skipping activities? Vivian made it very clear we're being watched.

"Honestly, I'm getting a bit tired of being *on*. Maybe some time away from all the pretending can help us both decompress?"

A shroud of disappointment covers me. *Right.* How didn't I anticipate this? Pretending to like me must be taxing.

"Okay." My face falls into a frown. "But, uh, I'm worried if you don't come with me, then my mother will find out and hold our absence against us." The words are uncomfortable. They make me sound like a child. Is that how Matthew sees me?

I wince, wishing I could vanish.

"Let's try to be realistic. Basket weaving will not prove the love we have for each other." *Our fake love?* "Lolita can't be upset if we rearrange our schedule to be, well, together." There's no emotion in his voice.

Our relationship guide isn't who I'm worried about. He doesn't know my mother.

But I can't force Matthew to go. He clearly doesn't want to.

"You're right," I lie.

He sits up beside me. "I'm happy to be here, but when I'm back home, I have a day to relax. We've been operating at over a hundred percent for Lolita and the eyes in the sky. Why don't we take it easy today?"

All I hear is that I'm exhausting.

This must be a pity invite. Matthew's just being nice because that's who he is. A nice guy.

There's no point in denying that I've taken up too much space in his life.

"If this is all too much, we can call the whole thing off." I swallow. Guilt swoops in as soon as I say it.

"It hurts my feelings when you bring that up." Matthew looks at me, but I avert my gaze.

Great. Of course this is happening. I share the smallest part of my feelings, and I'm doing it all wrong. He's just confirmed I'm hurting him.

"I'm not going to call off our arrangement, and I haven't given you a reason not to trust me," he says.

Arrangement. Right. The twenty-five million dollars he needs.

Because what person would actively choose to deal with all of this? With my family? With two weeks of putting on appearances and taking part in silly activities?

Who would choose me?

"I'm sorry." I reluctantly pull away from him and head into the closet.

"Molly." He follows me, not letting me hide. Must he do that? My teeth clasp around my bottom lip, and I hold back a heavy sigh. If he'd just let this go, then I could flip a switch and become the person who could make him happy. Not exhausted. "I'm doing my best, but I need a little time to recharge. To just *be*. I'd like to do that with you. There are very few places where we don't have to put on an act."

"You don't have to explain yourself. I get it." I slip on my Saint Laurent loafers.

He shakes his head, palming the back of his neck. It'd be nice to spend the day with him, but I can't.

There's no reason he should give up his time to rest because of me. I'll cover for him if Lolita asks. That's fine. *I'm fine.* The thudding in my ears continues as I stride toward the door.

"You're leaving? Let's talk through this."

"I really have to go." I fumble with the doorknob.

"Molly, are you not going to finish the conversation?"

"Sorry."

The crease in my forehead deepens as I dash out of our suite.

WHACK.

A stick pops free from my poorly assembled picnic basket and slaps me in the cheek. The stinging pain barely registers. My mind's been so preoccupied with what happened.

Guilt claws at me for storming out on Matthew. I panicked. Full-blown, mountain-sized panicked.

Ugh. What was I supposed to do? Manipulate him into coming? Like my mother does to me all the time?

My frown deepens. He's probably drafting up a contract termination as we speak. Okay. Maybe that's excessive. We never signed a contract. But still.

I know he's not committed to me. Matthew is solely devoted to his reforestation project.

He'll divorce me as soon as he can. And what does it matter? That's what we agreed to.

I just figured that after our kiss in the pottery studio, things would change. But for the last couple of days, he's made no advances and showed no interest.

Who am I kidding?

Matthew doesn't want me. Not the real me. I'll never be good enough. I'll never please everyone. Especially not by being myself. I have to keep *that* girl locked in a vault.

Instead, I must turn into the woman who can convince my parents to let me marry Matthew so I can secure my trust.

Nothing else is important.

Lolita notices me glancing around, my abandoned basket on the blanket in front of me. She smiles and gives me a soft wave.

Is that sympathy? Pity?

"Where's your other half, dear?" Lolita stands over me and swipes at the curly pixie cut across her forehead. Kindness, not scrutiny, fills her brown eyes. It calms the worry strumming through my chest.

"Oh, um, he wanted to take some time off today," I explain.

"Ah, yes, that makes sense. Mrs. Greene's agenda is rather detailed." She gives me a soft grin, and it feels like we're on the same side for once. Are we? "But why aren't you with him?"

The question stings.

"Well, we had this activity planned today," I say.

"Oh, dear, it's fine for both of you to do something else. I understand that your mother has given you a lot to accomplish, but between you and me, I believe it's important to take some time and discover your own interests here."

Seriously? I could be getting a massage with Matthew. No cameras. No mandatory activities. Not miserably panicking about my mother's impossible demands.

My breathing halts. Did my mother jam-pack our days because she knew it would cause friction between us? Was that her plan all along?

Irritation snakes through me.

Of course my mother's goal was to get me to fight with Matthew. I played right into her hands. I can't keep running anytime life gets hard. I need to find Matthew and apologize, or I may as well give up and marry Lance.

Not an option.

But how do I even begin to address this with Matthew? Are we already doomed?

A question perches on my lips. "Lolita, is it normal to have disagreements?"

She kneels down and places a hand on my shoulder. "Of course, Molly. Falling in love is easy. But we're all individuals with different interests, schedules, and backgrounds. Discovering your partner is the most beautiful part of staying in love.

Disagreements are inevitable, but it's how we handle them that strengthens our bond. Communicating vulnerably isn't instinctive. We must learn that, together." She gives my shoulder a soft squeeze.

"Thank you, that helps a lot," I say. I handled Matthew's and my argument the way I've handled every sparring match with my mother: I panicked. I ran.

Embarrassment flushes my cheeks.

Matthew's demeanor during the argument was calm and logical. He's the only person who's seen this vulnerable side of me. The side that doesn't know how to make someone happy.

It's frightening.

As if Lolita can read my mind, she says, "I see you two together. Your energies, they complement each other. Where you sparkle, he is fire on the hearth. Give yourself grace. Love comes with growing pains." She nods and walks away.

I need to find Matthew and apologize. I owe it to myself, and to him, to fix this.

I can't afford to push him away.

Chapter 11
Matthew

I CAN'T BELIEVE she ran off.

Our arrangement won't work if we can't talk things out. If we aren't on the same team.

The afternoon sun peeks over a stucco wall as I wait for the masseuse to arrive for the couples massage I booked. No point in letting the session go to waste.

I wish Molly were here, putting sunscreen on and talking about her books, or whatever she feels like talking about. Hell, we could have been lying out here uninterrupted. I figured she'd enjoy a massage, given the kinks she brought up when we first arrived.

Would this misunderstanding between us have occurred if I'd told her I needed a break sooner?

Maybe Molly doesn't want to hang out with me when we aren't pretending to date.

That damn kiss in the pottery studio has been messing with my head.

Christ. I palm the frustrated crease in my forehead. Women haven't been on my mind for years, and now Molly's living rent-free in my thoughts.

I stretch out in the cotton folding chair.

The only places in the resort that aren't being monitored are our suite, the private pools, and the trails around the resort. I find myself second-guessing everything—are we touching enough, am I asking the right questions—when I'm aware I'm being watched.

I did the right thing by staying back, but I should've shown Molly some more kindness and patience.

This is her normal. She must constantly battle this kind of scrutiny from her family. A pressure point waiting to snap.

I only have to deal with this lifestyle for a short while.

I don't want to be another person who adds to her anxiety.

Out of the corner of my eye, something red catches my attention. *Her.* Curls bounce around Molly's shoulders; her eyes are hidden behind her sunglasses. She walks down the stone path that leads to the pool.

She came.

"Hey," I say, pulling the chair beside me closer, offering her a seat.

"Um—can we talk?"

"Absolutely."

She sits, nervously weaving her fingers together. "Okay, I'm actually not sure how to start this, so forgive me if I'm awkward."

"You're safe with me, Molly." I hesitate, but then I reach over and cover her hands with my own. "I want to talk this out."

She takes off her sunglasses, staring at my hands on hers. "I —I don't know how to act when I've upset someone, or, frankly, when I'm feeling, uh, upset myself." She frowns, slumping into the folding seat. "Sorry, I haven't vocalized this to someone who isn't my therapist."

"It's okay, take your time." I squeeze her hands.

"Whenever there's an ounce of conflict, it's like my body shuts down. Just stops operating. I hate it. I know it's irrational to run away from arguments and immature..." With another hefty inhale, a tear drops out of the corner of her eye. She doesn't bother swiping it away. My heart aches. "It's embarrassing that whenever someone upsets me, I simply want to disappear," she heaves. "As if I could close my eyes, and *poof!* no more arguments. But when that doesn't work, well, my next best approach has been running from people before they can abandon me."

Another tear.

"Hey, hey." I tug at her fingers, pulling her a smidge closer, and freeze. I want to wrap my arm around her shoulders, crush her into my chest, let her tears drench my shirt. *Does she want that?* I hold her hands tighter, causing her knuckles to redden. "I'm listening; I hear you."

Molly focuses on me. The tremble of her chin subsides. "I'm sorry I never really checked in with you. I know all of this pretending to be in love is a lot, and I expected you to submit to my mother and her agenda, like I always have. Everything feels like a crisis situation, and I'm just trying to keep it together."

"Molly." My voice uncharacteristically cracks at her tears. I clear my throat. "We're a team, and I'm not abandoning you. You don't have to handle everything on your own. I'm all in here. I'm all in with you. Even after the divorce, if you need me, I'll be there."

The same way I have been for all the years we've been friends.

The only thing I should focus on is learning how to manage these extremely complicated situations. Not on my suddenly awakened desires and muddled emotions from earlier. We're from two different worlds and ages apart. Surely we were going to have a learning curve.

"I know, Matthew. I'm trying to accept that. It's silly, but I have a hard time believing anyone is telling the truth or that they don't have a hidden agenda. I trust you—or at least, I want to trust you." Her amber eyes flash at me, looking panicked.

"Trust is built over time," I assure her. "It's like when I first started working at ORO. It took a while for my team and Luca to get along, but we banded together. What I'm trying to say is that I'm patient, and I'll be here."

"I appreciate that. I feel disappointed in myself, because I'm an adult. I should know how to disagree, how to say what's on my mind and in my heart and be able to hear someone else do the same," she says. "But people have always treated me like a child, and, well, that's why my trust is so important."

How could Molly be expected to act like an adult when her family treats her like she's not capable of standing on her own two feet?

"I get that. And I'm sorry I didn't mention I was getting a little burned-out. I'm an introvert, so, as much as I can throw myself into work and volunteering, I usually need time to rest. Honestly, I didn't know how to tell you that among all this surveillance and pretending." At the word *pretending*, she stills. I hate the lines I'm drawing, but they're necessary.

Molly confirmed that her trust is the most important thing here.

She wriggles out of my grasp. I'm guilty of missing the warmth of her touch. "I didn't consider how exhausting this is. I can be *on* all the time. It's the only way I know how to act, and, well, I'm aware that I'm a somewhat draining presence."

"No," I interject hastily. "What I'm trying to say is, I'm sorry if I came off harsh. I wish I'd given us the opportunity to come up with a compromise together rather than just booking the massage. I was tired of your mother's packed agenda, of needing to put on a show every day, but you do not drain me."

Quite the opposite. I get a burst of energy around her. The *real* her.

"Okay." Molly wipes away the stray tears beneath her eyes. "You're not upset that we fought?"

"No, not even a little." I straighten my spine and lean back into my chair. "Fighting with the people you care about isn't a bad thing, as long as you're both kind and honest with each other. It helps people grow closer."

"Nobody really gets me like you do."

I hope that one day she gets to fall in love for real, and that whoever has the privilege of being with her sees her like I do. After our divorce, that's what Molly deserves. A partner who could create a family with her where no one's expecting her to put on an act.

We sit in silence for a few moments. It's not awkward, just stiff.

The afternoon light ripples along the water in the pool. Stucco walls reflect the heat beaming down onto us.

Our first disagreement.

What would a normal couple do in a situation like this?

A high five for airing out their grievances and then makeup sex?

Well, we definitely can't do that.

Her petite nose scrunches the way it always does when she's a little unsure. It's adorable.

"What do you say we keep our massage plans and try to move past this together?"

She nods. "I'd like that. Thank you for planning something and wanting to include me."

"Of course. We gotta take care of all those kinks, right?"

Molly allows herself a throaty laugh.

"You know, I was wondering...well, maybe we can..." She hesitates, looking around. "Do you want to come with me to the On Cloud Nine library this week? It's one of my favorite parts of our resorts, and Lolita said she'd give us some flexibility with the schedule. It'll be super low-key. No need for cameras or performing." Molly races through the words so fast, I barely catch them.

"We can read one of your—what was the genre called again?"

"Romantasy?" She giggles lightly, recrossing her legs and leaning forward. Life rushes back into her. *Much better.*

"That's the one." I edge closer to her, causing our knees to touch.

Molly watches me. "I'd really enjoy doing that with you."

"Me too."

"Okay." She gives me one of her big smiles, all teeth and gums.

"Okay," I echo.

<hr>

OBSESSIVE LUST. Nine letters, across.

Limerence.

I type the word into my phone. Are my daily crosswords being curated just for me, targeting my unspoken thoughts?

Molly stirs beside me. The trickle of sunlight decorating her complexion bounces over to her hair, which is sprawled out across the ivory pillowcase. Her breaths are soft, barely causing her chest to rise and fall.

This is why, for the past six days, I've run out of our suite before she wakes up. So I wouldn't gape at her like some kind of neanderthal.

How could anyone resist admiring her?

She lets out an audible moan, stretching out her legs beneath the piles of blankets on top of us. Her mouth widens like a lion's.

Fucking adorable.

I stir around between the sheets, adjusting my shorts. My cock obviously hasn't received the memo that we're platonic.

Focus on the thing in front of you and not on Molly's full ass shifting its way to your side.

Puzzle. Crossword. Focus.

Unbending. Five letters, down. That's easy.

Rigid.

Like the throbbing erection scraping against my boxers. Hell, I'm thirty-six, not sixteen. But I can barely control myself waking up beside her.

Dammit.

She moves again. This time, her soft curves press up against my hip bone. The letters in front of me blur. My breathing halts.

I can picture her in my bed at home, waking up beneath the weight of my blankets. Maybe Bear would curl up at our feet as Molly nestles into my arms, her breath warming the skin of my chest.

She flips over, snapping me out of the daydream. One of her arms wraps around my torso while her leg straddles my own. It climbs up my knee, to my mid-thigh, until suddenly…

"Oh." Her voice hums in my ear. "Matthew?" Molly shuffles away, and I miss the brief cuddle immediately. "Uh, sorry—um, what are you doing here?"

"Good morning." I flash her a casual smile that I hope doesn't translate as, *Hi, I've been creepily watching you sleep.*

Molly sits up and leans against the headboard, coming eye level with me. I push my glasses up my nose.

The freckles above her top lip are brighter than I've ever seen them. I want to trace my mouth over each one, connect them like a constellation. My T-shirt swallows her whole. *To be that shirt.*

Christ. I'm jealous of my own clothes.

"What?" Molly says shyly. Her eyes are still heavy with sleep.

"Hmm?" I break my concentration on her.

"Is something wrong? You're looking at me all funny."

"No, not at all. You're just adorable first thing in the morning." The words are yanked out of me before I can zip my lips shut.

What has gotten into me today?

Molly's palms stick to her face, and she peeks over her fingers. My cock twitches in my boxers. *Seriously?*

"You're, um—" Her flustered voice cuts short as her gaze slides onto the erection I'm likely doing a terrible job of hiding. "Cute too."

The corners of my lips tug up. My blood heats a degree. "Thanks."

I don't think I'm ever going to get tired of her compliments.

"If you want to stay in bed and rest, then I can go on a walk and give you time alone." She pulls the blankets off of herself, ready to leave.

"No need," I say in a hurry. "I actually got you something. Stay here."

While Molly was in the shower yesterday, I made a quick call to the front desk to request a small delivery that should change up this morning's routine.

I retrieve my surprise from the front door. A plain coffee for me. A bright orange smoothie for Molly. The newspaper rests on the tray as well, the daily crossword waiting for me.

An app is fun, but there's something about the ink bleeding onto your fingers and the smell of pressed paper. A phone is no substitute.

I walk back into the bedroom and freeze in the doorframe.

Woah.

Molly sits on her knees atop the mattress, her pink lips smiling right at me. The faint morning glow shines around her.

She's striking.

Beaming and unruly.

The self-control I had a few minutes ago vanishes as my imagination paints a vivid picture of how she'd look above me, of how my hands could trace the curves of her body so lazily, memorizing every inch of her skin.

"Orange-You-Tasty?" she chimes.

Yes, beautiful, I'm sure you're delicious.

Snap out of it. It's just the name of her smoothie.

I steady my grip and present her with the tray. "That's right. I thought you'd want to read your book in bed this morning, and I could do my crossword?"

"You do crossword puzzles?" Her eyes widen with surprise, her bottom lip sneaking between her teeth.

"Yeah, after I'm done working out, which is usually what I'm doing most mornings," I explain, taking a seat back on the bed. "I didn't want to wake you with all my scribbling and muttering."

"Oh, I wouldn't mind scribbling or, um, muttering." Molly's cheeks rise, and I kick myself for spending the last few days alone in the lobby. "So it's totally fine for you to hang here sometimes if you'd like. Obviously, only if it's good with you."

"I'll make it a habit to be here more often."

Her shoulders shimmy the way they do when she's excited, as if her body is a sparkler on New Year's.

An hour later, we're sitting in the Adirondack chairs on the patio outside of our suite, glasses empty. I'm two clues away from finishing my puzzle, and Molly is sucked into her book.

It's nice being around her.

She's different today. After our vulnerable talk yesterday, it feels like we can just *be* without the veil of our fake relationship suffocating us. Just two coworkers, hanging out in their matching pajamas at a five-star resort.

Ha, normalcy!

She sits with her knees tucked up to her chest, my T-shirt stretching over her legs. Her face is bursting with emotions, frowning or stifling a laugh.

Suddenly, she gasps. Her gaze shoots up from her phone and finds me watching her. "Oh, sorry."

"Did you get to a good part?" I set down my paper.

"I just finished the book, and they left it on a cliff-hanger. The main character, Ripley, well, she's learned she has new powers and—" Her face contorts, the explanation cut short. "Wait, you probably don't want to hear about any of this."

I tilt my head to one side, beckoning her. "On the contrary; I want to hear everything."

"Really?"

"Yeah. Why don't you tell me about what happens to Ripley and how she got these new powers?"

Molly smiles brightly. She begins, and her whole mood lights up. When she's like this, her true self, I could listen to her talk for hours.

Chapter 12
Molly

THE RESORT LIBRARY is a sight to behold. Two stories, stained glass windows, and a winding iron staircase that leads to a treasure trove of books. All surrounded by the beauty of Arizona's desert. There aren't any guests here as we meander through the shelves, tilting our heads to read the spines.

We spent the morning together, and now we're skipping away from the agenda…almost like a date.

No. I shake my head. This can't be a date. We just agreed to read a book together. That's all.

It's natural for couples to spend time alone. *Right?* That's basically what Lolita said.

"There's nothing like the smell of old books," Matthew says, picking up a dusty, leather-bound cover. The book creaks as he opens it and inhales, closing his eyes behind his glasses. "So, so good."

My heart races. A warmth spreads through my core. This reaction to something so innocuous is exaggerated, but I can't help it.

Matthew Hudson is dreamy. Books or no books.

The collar of his button-down shirt peeks open, revealing

olive-toned skin and a bit of chest hair, which looks unruly. Manly. Oh so manly.

Please make this day a wet dream I never wake up from.

I need help. Serious, intensive help to get me to snap out of every dirty thought I've had about my fake boyfriend.

He's awakened a part of me I didn't even know existed. Since we arrived, it won't leave me alone. I grow wet, my nipples hardening against the fabric of my shirt.

Oh my goodness. I'll need an extra-long bath before getting into bed tonight.

"When I was younger," I start, attempting to muster up a distraction, "I spent a summer at an On Cloud Nine resort in Italy. There was a perfume-making class, and I remember wanting to replicate the smell of old books. So, I found a ripe, smelly tome of some kind and ripped a page out of it to boil for my signature scent."

"*No.*" Matthew gasps playfully and reshelves his book. "How old were you?"

"Hmm, maybe around nine."

"Was the sacrifice worth it?" He tilts his head. His glasses catch a hazy light from one of the stained glass windows, brightening up the blue of his eyes.

What was it Lily said? It's always the quiet ones.

I'm very interested in learning the true meaning of that phrase.

"It was the most wonderful perfume." We loop around one of the shelves, passing a section on Arizona horticulture.

"You are such a delinquent," he teases.

I'm starting to love sharing with him. Pieces of myself I never told anyone about.

We climb the staircase to the top floor. The cool metal railing glides under our hands.

"When my dad was in meetings with contractors and property investors, I used to spend hours reading in the little nooks up here. Sometimes, I even fell asleep in the tan chair beneath the window." I nod to the corner of the space.

"I don't blame you," he says. "I love a good library."

I'm glad it hasn't been awkward since our fight yesterday. I actually feel closer to him.

Lolita's advice echoes in my mind. *Communicating vulnerably isn't instinctive. We must learn that, together.*

I like learning with Matthew.

"Me too." I lead us toward the fantasy section. "I'd always stuff a suitcase with books when we'd make our summer resort trips. The books would get read quickly, and my dad got tired of sending the hotel staff out to get me new ones from the local bookstore. So, we added libraries to the resorts." I smile at the happy memories, the ones I try to cling to.

"I can only imagine all five-foot-three of you hoisting a suitcase up these stairs," he laughs.

"I don't think I was even five feet tall, but I was determined."

"Not much has changed." He winks.

Why was that so hot?

"Did you spend a lot of time reading as a kid?" I pluck a random book off the shelf.

"Yes." He stills beside me, craning his neck to read the spines. "A family of eight under one roof turns into chaos rather swiftly. Reading was how I escaped the noise." He tells me about some books he's loved. I hang on to his every word, entranced.

"Ah, I'm sure you caused a ton of trouble sitting beneath the covers of your race car bed, reading *The House of Mirth*," I giggle.

"*A ton*," Matthew says sarcastically and runs his hand through his hair. "Also, no race car bed. But I did like to collect model car replicas."

"Will you show me your collection during Christmas?"

He studies me for a moment. Was talking about the holidays too presumptuous? He invited me to his family's annual party when we first arrived, but maybe he didn't mean it. Or perhaps he was being polite.

"I can, though I'm pretty sure my sisters painted all my cars pink."

"Your sisters have good taste." I put my book back and stroll forward. "It's funny how different our experiences are. I escaped loneliness through books, while you sought quiet."

"You're not alone now."

Now. Because we have an expiration date. I doubt either of us wants to talk about what happens *after* all of this. For the first time in my life, I want to live in the present. With Matthew.

"So." I keep wandering through the shelves. "What should we read?"

"Maybe one of your favorites?" His striking eyes concentrate on me, as if I'm more fascinating than the stories hiding on the shelves.

Matthew's behavior makes me feel significant. It's like every time he looks at me, nothing else matters but me. Maybe I'm imagining it. But I'd like to live in the fantasy a while longer.

"I'm not sure I could pick just one." I sigh, running my fingers over random spines. "Should we go to war, or on a quest?"

"Let's go to war," he says decisively. "Perhaps there's something with elves?"

"I know just the thing." Two rows over, I squat down, looking for a copy of one of my favorites. "Hmm, it's not here." I stand up and scan the shelves. The dark spine with purple lettering sits right in the corner at the top of the bookcase. I tiptoe for it.

"Let me." He leans over me. Vetiver and musk hit my senses. "This one?" he asks. I gulp and nod. He retrieves the copy of *The Stone Court.*

"Thank you," I croak, taking the book from him and tilting my head up to meet his gaze.

"What's it about?"

Matthew hasn't taken a step back, and I don't want him to.

I just need to keep being this version of myself. Confident, unafraid. Anything to keep his gaze locked onto mine. My heart thuds.

"A corrupted kingdom and Serienna, their griffin-riding savior. She's also an elf," I explain as succinctly as possible. "But we could pick something else…"

"No. I want to read something you love." He takes the book and flips through a few random pages.

I want to kiss him so badly it hurts. To taste him. My midsection feels like tightened ribbons.

"Oh, this is interesting." His voice is low, if not a little sardonic. "'Serienna rocked her hips against the length of his velvet-wrapped steel as Damien—'"

"Oh my god." I go for the book; my cheeks burn.

"Hey, I'm reading here." Matthew uses his height to his advantage, pulling the pages up high. "'Damien's breath grew more ragged, but not once, no matter how overwhelming the pleasure of feeling her on top of him was, did he let go of his hold on the…'" He pauses, and shivers zoom down my spine. His erotic recitation sounds like one of my favorite audiobook narrators. "On the griffin? *No way.*"

Of course he opened right up to one of the sex scenes.

Universe, you're a cruel beast.

"Let's just pick another one," I stammer.

"Are they, um?" His eyes flash with a hint of wickedness. "Having this *adventure* while in the air?"

I can't help but giggle, and I give up my attempts to get the book back. "It's fantasy."

"And what about you, Molly?"

"Me?"

Matthew shrinks some of the distance between us. The book

pages press into his abdomen, and the cover onto my chest. His breath caresses the hot skin of my cheek.

Can he hear the way my pulse is pounding?

"What would you like to do on the back of a griffin?" His voice is low and seductive.

I bite my lip, trying to suppress a moan. An actual moan. Because I'm losing my mind.

Get a grip, Molly. The warning is pointless, because I only want to hold on to Matthew's strong arms or broad shoulders.

I need a response. Preferably one that isn't, *I'd like to have you take me on the back of a griffin.* Or in this library. Or in the bed we've shared for the past six nights. "Fly," I manage through a rasp.

"And what makes you feel like you're flying in real life?" He looks down at me, targeting me with his gaze.

My heart is about to plummet out of my chest.

You, I want to respond. I want to admit it earnestly. *Can I?*

No.

"I'm not sure," I whisper.

"Be brave." He bends forward. "Tell me. Could I do something to make you feel like you're flying?"

The surrounding books seem to fade away, like ghosts disappearing into the night.

I've never made the first move. Should I right now?

Can I be bold and go after what I want?

I hesitate, as if I'm trapped in some kind of slow-motion spell. Then I spread my palm across his pec.

My body hums with need. And, boy oh boy, am I ready to fall apart.

Matthew reaches one of his hands to bracket my jaw. I'm small and vulnerable. Yet somehow so undeniably safe.

I want to go for it. I want to be the girl who unabashedly takes what she desires. A mask I've never tried on before. Hopefully, it's a perfect fit.

My toes rise until, somehow, all too slow and all too fast, we kiss.

His lips are soft, and it's as if I'm tasting an explosion of colors for the first time. His hand moves from my jaw to the back of my neck, leaving a wake of heat.

"Mmm," he moans against my mouth. Is that because of me?

I'm alive. I'm flying. The air glides over my skin as his tongue parts my lips. The book between us crashes to the ground.

It doesn't matter. Nothing matters as much as this.

Matthew's arm wraps around my waist, dragging my body so close to his. Tasting him is now a craving I know I'll never be able to shake. Every fiber of my being is effervescent.

Is it possible to feel like the sun?

The skin between my thighs grows slick. My hands vine their way around his neck, pulling him closer. Our mouths hungrily explore each other. Our breathing syncs, a muddle of silent groans.

"You." Matthew's breath brushes against my lips. "Are." My back hits the shelves. "So fucking precious."

A lustful possession purrs through me. *Is he heaven?* He must be.

I hike up onto the shelves behind me, settling myself on something firm.

Kissing my fake boyfriend in the fantasy section of my parents' resort library is the wrong thing to do, but I can't stop.

Matthew slips a hand beneath my thigh, steadying me against the shelf. The other hand dances at the crevices of my neck, his fingers pressing into me as if my skin were an ancient text and he was trying to inspect every inch.

"Matthew." I shiver.

He pulls away, his irises dimmed with darkness. "Tell me

what you need, baby." His voice is heavy, dragging through me. Something pushes up against my stomach.

My eyes shoot open. No way. I press closer.

Matthew's getting hard.

Wow. *Am I doing that?* I am. He wants me as much as I want him.

"I need—" I begin, but my request is cut short.

"Excuse me." A gentleman on the other side of the aisle clears his throat. "Are you planning to check out any books?"

Oh god.

"Um." I slide down the front of Matthew's body, adjusting my hair and my matching Balenciaga set, which has crumpled together.

I bend down, picking up the book we dropped while Matthew grabs the second copy of *The Stone Court* from the top shelf.

"We'll be taking these two." Matthew grins.

"Wonderful." The elderly man takes the copies and disappears behind the shelves.

Matthew holds my hand and follows the librarian. My heart pitter-patters in my chest, and the flames inside me slow into a simmer.

I just kissed Matthew Hudson. In a library. A perfect moment that's only found in books. No, it was better than perfect. That kiss surpassed fiction.

TOWERING rock formations and cacti surround our trail. I kick a small pebble off the stone pathway and steal a glance at Matthew. He looks well rested. A perpetual, soft grin has been kissing his face since we woke up.

Kissing.

I, on the other hand, couldn't sleep. My mind refused to hit stop, or even pause, on the kiss we shared in the library.

How Matthew lifted me up against the bookcase, settling his gigantic frame between my legs. How his tongue trailed along mine as if he were savoring some kind of ripe fruit. How his fingers fisted the curls at the base of my neck. How he moaned into my lips.

I've had a few kisses before. But I've never been *properly* kissed. An air-stealing, world-spinning, dizzying type of kiss, one that made me want to rip all my clothes off.

Until yesterday.

Neither of us has mentioned the ki—*incident* since we left the library.

As soon as we got back to our room, I ran into the shower and then promptly tucked myself into bed, where I pretended to be asleep. If it wasn't for the copies of *The Stone Court* on our dresser and the lipstick stain on his shirt collar, I would have been sure I made the whole thing up.

Does he regret it? Or maybe he didn't enjoy kissing me?

Isn't the third time supposed to be a charm?

Sure, the kiss at my bridal shower and at pottery were around other people, a way for us to put on a show, but we were alone this time.

Maybe he knew the librarian would find us and report back to Lolita. Matthew's smart like that. Strategic. Intelligent.

I mean, what did I expect to happen? He'd pick me up in the library, carry me over the threshold of our suite, and ravish me right there on our bed?

Yes.

That is exactly what I expected.

My heart shrinks in my chest.

Unfortunately, I can't morph into one of the cacti on our trail and chameleon out of this situation. Add shapeshifting to the list of reasons why living in a fantasy world would be so much better.

We round another bend. I'm pretty sure we have an hour more of this scheduled, torturous trail walk before we get breakfast. I can't stand the quiet anymore. I have to know what he's thinking.

"So." I attempt to sound casual. Is that really the best I can do?

Let's kiss again.

Let's skip breakfast.

"Hmm?" Matthew glances over at me, unfazed.

"Aren't these sunrises some of the best you've ever seen?" I conjure up a question, averting my scattered gaze to the sky.

I have no game. Zero. Literally, *ZILCH*!

Sure, Arizona has beautiful sunrises. When the sun comes up, the desert turns into a canvas of orange, pink, and blue. The colors bleed together like a spill of watercolors.

But *sunrises*?! I'm thinking about jumping his bones again, and this is all I can come up with?

"They're beautiful." He halts in place.

"Yeah." I tug on my linen Simkhai Valeria midi dress. The white fabric is sheer against my skin.

Matthew's brows perk up with curiosity. "Anything on your mind?"

I must be so obvious with my inability to keep cool about the whole kiss thing. Must I have such an unforgiving lying face?

"Um—yeah. I just—" I shift in my spot. "The griffins got me all worked up last night," I blurt out.

Nice. Lovely. Splendid.

Am I kidding?

Of all the things I could have said. Anything and everything at all.

If our charade wasn't my only ticket to freedom, I'd throw

myself into a cluster of desert flowers and spend the rest of the trip hiding in the canyons.

"The griffins?" His eyes narrow, a charming smile creasing his face.

"You read my favorite book out loud," I offer as the worst explanation known to humankind. "In one of my favorite places, nonetheless, and we just got carried away. Right? I mean, things like that happen. Libraries are very erotic places."

Yes, excellent. I'll get that printed on a T-shirt when I'm back in New York City.

"You're talking about our kiss?" He leans closer. The shadow his frame casts over me teleports me into yesterday. I take a step back, and my ankle brushes against something sharp.

"Ye-*ow*!" I jolt and look down. A harmless cactus sticks into my skin. One second, the short prickles shock me, and the next, I'm wrapped safely in Matthew's arms.

His face is blank except for the glimmer of amusement in his eyes.

"Sorry," I say into the space between us. *Ugh.* I'm trying to stop saying sorry. It's frustrating that I can't turn off the autopilot response.

"Don't be. I'm glad I'm around to keep catching you."

I blush. "I'm a bit klutzy."

"Are you sure you aren't doing it on purpose?" He smirks.

"Uh—" The words catch in my throat. Is my crush subconsciously sabotaging me? Oh no. "On purpose?"

Matthew lets go of my waist, and I almost chase after his touch. "Well, there was the maze," he begins.

"Ah!" I shriek with laughter. "Funny."

He doesn't seem amused. "You were saying?"

"We probably shouldn't do that thing we did again," I whisper reluctantly.

"Kiss?"

"Yes."

Matthew zeroes in on me. "You don't want to kiss again?"

No.

"Yes."

His eyes pierce me, a crease in his forehead deepening for a moment before it softens. Then he nods.

"Okay," Matthew says, not offering another response before walking ahead of me again.

My heart drops, sucker punching me in the gut. This man is impossible to read.

"Hey, wait up." I lengthen my strides to keep up with him, my shoes kicking up red dust. "Don't get me wrong; it was very, um, good—very good, actually—but it's probably not smart of us to do it again. Right?"

He turns toward me but keeps his feverish pace on the trail. "*Good* would be the last word I'd use to describe what we did in the library."

I'm jogging after him now. "W-what word would you use then?"

"Astonishing."

My stomach sours. This isn't going how I wanted it to at all. What am I meant to say?

I want to kiss you, Matthew Hudson? I want to complicate your life even further? I don't want to pretend with you?

Those options are entirely off the table. I've already dragged him through my messy life. Besides, relationships—real, healthy ones—don't start off with lies and pretending.

The crushing weight of guilt nestles in my chest. I'm selfish for wanting more, for hoping he'd protest, take me by the shoulders and lock his lips on mine again.

He specifically said that he doesn't want a relationship. I mean, he's repeatedly brought up getting divorced because the only reason he's doing this is to fund his new project.

Astonishing could mean the kiss was surprising. A reason to be taken aback.

That *must* be what he means.

Not earth-shattering or incredible. The kiss was just a jumble of forced proximity and pent-up emotion.

We can't take our eyes off the prize here—we must remain convincing. I fiddle with the fabric of my dress. I can't make this conversation any more awkward than it already is. I need to change the subject.

I glance around, noticing the horse stables in the distance. "I wonder if my old horses, Honey and Maple, are still here."

Matthew traces my gaze, his muscular legs working tirelessly through the slope of the canyon. "You ride?"

"I used to, a long time ago." I heave a tired breath. Is he trying to run away from me? "I did dressage competitions for a year."

He scrunches his forehead, thinking. "Is that something to do with training?"

"Yeah, how'd you know?"

"Just a guess." Matthew shoves his hands into the pockets of his trousers, causing his biceps to flex. I gulp. "*Dresser* can mean *to train* in French."

"You speak French?"

At this question, he slows. "*Un peu. J'ai pris quatre ans de français à l'université.*"

"Oh…" I'm speechless. He's a gorgeous, grown man who does crosswords, reads books, and speaks a lick of French. *A lick.* My body trembles. He's out of my league. I clear my throat. "Yes, dressage is pretty much a choreographed dance between you and your horse. Though I haven't competed in over ten years."

"Do you not like riding anymore?"

"No, I do," I clarify. "My horse, Sunburst Symphony, is back in New York. She's a little too ornery in her old age. What about you? Do you know how to ride?"

"The summer between high school and college, I worked at a

camp. I got stationed out at the horse stables and learned everything I could, but I haven't been on horseback in years."

Why couldn't he have said no? Now the image of him riding a horse will be seared into my brain all afternoon. Jet-black hair flowing in the wind. A shirt with the top buttons undone as he gyrates his hips back and f—

"Molly?" Matthew waves his hand in front of my face.

"Huh?" *Focus on the real him, not the romantasy version your brain is insisting on concocting.*

"I asked why we haven't done any of the equestrian activities at the resort."

"What do you mean?" I'm unsteady.

"I've scanned the very detailed schedule, but not one activity in our last week here includes horses. Maybe we can try to swap something out of the lineup to go ride Honey and Maple?"

He's right. My mother knows how much I like riding, and she chose not to include it in our itinerary. I had one close call as a teenager, and after that she's always voiced her disinterest in me picking it up again.

The memory sours my mood. *Screw it.* There's no point in letting her worries and fears control every single one of my actions. Isn't the whole point of pretending to be in this relationship to move on from that?

"You're right. Let's go see them right now." I divert us from the path of our scheduled hike.

It's time to break free from the should-do's and start letting myself off my own leash.

MOLLY

I kissed Matthew.

I SEND the message to the group chat and immediately want to take it back, but I need to talk to someone. The first two kisses with Matthew I could write off as being pretend, but something about this one was different.

AVERY

This seems like phone call worthy news!

LILY

Ummm, excuse me? Details. NOW.

AVERY

When?

MOLLY

On Saturday.

LILY

You've held on to this information for two days????!?!?!?!?!?!?!

AVERY

How was it?

MOLLY

Pleasant.

LILY

That's the kind of word you use to describe a hug with your grandparents

I need more

MOLLY

It happened in the library.

LILY

What section?

MOLLY

Romantasy, between the letters S and T.

LILY

Those are the BEST letters to kiss between.

AVERY

Did it get frisky?

MOLLY

At one point, both of my feet stopped touching the ground.

LILY

Shut up.

Was there tongue?

MOLLY

And petting. Very heavy petting.

AVERY

Ooo la la, Molly, you're audacious

So have the kisses that followed been just as magical?

MOLLY

We haven't actually kissed again.

LILY

Did you not like it? :(

MOLLY

I liked it very much.

AVERY

Does Matthew have a cold?

MOLLY

No?

AVERY

Are you sick?

MOLLY

No, I'm feeling fine.

LILY

If you liked the kiss and you haven't contracted some kinda medical condition that's preventing you from locking lips with a gorgeous man…

WHY HAVEN'T YOU KISSED AGAIN?

MOLLY

We don't want to add physical stuff to the relationship.

It'll just make the divorce messy.

AVERY

Sometimes a good kiss is worth making things messy ;)

MOLLY

I honestly don't think Matthew even likes me like that. He's doing me a favor.

LILY

Kissing as a favor?

MOLLY

My parents may not even approve of our marriage.

AVERY

How could they not like Matthew? He's the definition of unproblematic

I can send a letter of recommendation on his behalf!

Do you think it would help?

LILY

Dear Mrs. Greene, Matthew is a fine, responsible man who would make your daughter come in every library around the world. XO, Avery Soko

I can't help but laugh.

AVERY

It could help

MOLLY

I appreciate it, Ave. But I doubt my mom would be that easily convinced.

Look, I don't know. My feelings are all over the place.

AVERY

Have you ever considered this may be real? That you've developed actual feelings?

LILY

Or that you're just very horny sharing a bed with a hot man??????

Are my feelings valid, or have Matthew and I been forced together? Is my crush inflating my emotions? Ugh. Not this again. I can't possibly get myself to believe there's more between us.

I've never been in love, so how would I know what it feels like?

MOLLY

I can't spring any of that on him. What if he feels obligated to pretend to like me?

LILY

Obligated? He would be so lucky to have a chance with you

MOLLY

He hasn't given me a reason to believe that he's thought of me like that.

AVERY

Have you asked him? Or told him you're starting to feel something for him?

MOLLY

I haven't.

AVERY

But he kissed you back

MOLLY

Yes.

LILY

And is he a man with eyes and a brain? Is he spending all of his time with a beautiful, smart, kind woman who, let's be honest, we all know he has a little thing for?

MOLLY

I guess?

I know my friends are right, but Matthew said a relationship doesn't fit into his life. Whatever is happening between us is simply a testament to how good we are at pretending.

Chapter 13
Matthew

WE STUMBLE in late to our scheduled activity. Lolita flashes us a glance.

"Sorry." Molly covers the smile cresting her lips. We lost track of time during our makeshift book club this morning. She spent the entire time blushing over the heated plot of *The Stone Court*. Who knew that someone so innocent could be reading such filthy books? I've been missing out on an entire genre.

I shrug. "We got lost."

"Not a worry, the resort is *very* difficult to navigate at times." Ms. Deveaux winks, a hint of sarcasm in her voice. "Get settled in."

The walls of the yoga studio are painted black, cloaking us in darkness apart from the faint glow of candles at the center of space. We quickly take a place on our mats.

"Welcome to Yearning Yoga, where you'll be connecting to your lover through breath and touch," Lolita says. "First, adjust your mat so it's parallel to your partner's. Then sit back-to-back, legs crossed in front of you."

Molly may not want to kiss again, but touching isn't off-limits. I should've checked the class description and worn thicker shorts.

We give each other tight-lipped smiles before turning around and pressing our spines together. Her soft hair tickles the skin of my bicep. My heartbeat turns unsteady.

"You alright back there?" I ask.

"Yep."

"On your next deep breath, reach your right hand backward to rest on the left knee of your partner for a seated twist," Lolita explains.

"This is a bit silly, isn't it?" Molly says playfully.

"Only a little."

Her hand drops onto my knee, and I mimic the movement, stretching my spine. Her hand glides farther up my thigh as she twists deeper into the stretch, letting out a soft moan. My dick throbs.

We're thirty seconds into this lesson, and all I can think about is kissing her again. Maybe I took it too far by laying it on her at the library. Seriously, what was I doing asking her how I can help her feel like she's flying? But I wanted to feel her lips on mine.

Kissing again will complicate things. Sure, we can't have a future together, but I can't help it. I haven't felt this invigorated in ages.

But I won't give in to my desires. The people in Molly's life rarely listen to her wants, and I won't disregard her words. We only have five more days here. I can do this.

Damn, though. I could've stayed in that library for hours.

We move through a variety of couples positions. Forward bends, assisted downward dog, twin tree poses. I didn't expect much from this Yearning Yoga class. Especially not the sound of Molly's angelic, breathy noises as she contorts her body into the poses.

I've been dropped into a torture chamber.

They should consider renaming this class to Hour-Long Lesson in Self-Control.

"Our next stretch requires balance and trust." Ms. Deveaux's voice wades through the room. "Sit flat opposite each other, and touch the soles of your feet with your partner's."

Molly faces me, a sheen of sweat coating her brow. I shift in my seat, attempting for the hundredth time to hide my unfaltering erection. Thank fuck it's dark in here.

"Now, as you lift your legs toward the ceiling, grab your partner's hands and straighten your spine. Your bodies should make a beautiful letter V in this boat pose."

Molly gives me a quizzical expression. "We can skip this one." She clears her throat, sensing my discomfort.

"No," I say quickly. "Let's give it a go."

We do our best couples boat pose, and my core burns. I squeeze her fingers. My knees remain bent because of our height difference, but Molly's firm legs are straight. Her eyes are closed in concentration. She lets out another groan, sinking deeper into the stretch.

"Remember, class, moaning is a primal response. It helps loosen your inhibitions and heighten the experience of being present."

My primal urges are screaming at me to abandon the overtly erotic pose and climb onto Molly's mat. Drive my tongue deep into every delicious inch of her mouth, reenacting what happened in the library two days ago.

"Inhale deeply and sigh out your breath," Lolita interrupts. I do as she says, because if I don't breathe, I may pass out.

This yoga class is absolutely no help in keeping my mind off of exploring the physical parts of our relationship.

Would Molly's eyelids flutter? Would she make the same low moans? Can her legs stretch this far back when I'm buried inside—

No.

It's haunting me.

She's haunting me.

I readjust again, trying to dull the ache in my balls.

This class is just the cherry on top of my creemee. Okay, maybe that word does sound a little dirty.

"Now that you've connected with your bodies, slowly come to a comfortable position on the mat." Ms. Deveaux rises and starts to light a few more candles, awakening our dark abyss. "Take your time. When you come to your seat, scan your body and see how you feel."

Hard, very hard.

I rise, snatching the blanket beside my mat and strategically positioning it over the protruding hard-on in my shorts. I face Molly. She gives me a sleepy smile.

"Are you okay?" she asks. "You look a little flustered. That was a hard stretch."

I give her a reassuring nod. "Hard indeed."

Christ.

Lolita grabs a tray and walks around the class. "Our practice helps unlock your inner desires. The next portion of our exercise will require you to write down something that's keeping you from having the most rewarding intimate experiences of your life."

"What?" Molly croaks, catching the attention of the class. She nervously tosses her own palm over her mouth, looking mortified.

"We all have blocks that prevent us from being our true selves, in the bedroom and out in the world. Sensuality is fluid, and it's a part of our identities." Lolita hands each of us a slip of paper and a pencil. "Until you address this hurdle with yourself, you'll never be able to clearly communicate what you need to your partner."

Molly blinks at her paper.

What's she going to write?

What makes her feel good? What other books have her blushing?

Get it together, man. I need to write something down.

Alright. What's keeping me from having rewarding intimacy? Incredible sex? Sensual hurdles?

The questions drip over me like a leaking tap, awakening the difficulty this particular topic always brings.

Let's see. I haven't had sex in years. Truthfully, I'm not sure I can even recall the last time I craved intimacy. After the incident in Boston, I did my fair share of dating in New York. I tried, I did, but I'd always end things before they got too serious.

My current situation isn't any better. Fake marrying a woman so we can split her multimillion-dollar trust doesn't exactly scream intimacy, lust, or sexual discovery.

I was never one for casual flings, so I'm drawing a blank. How is someone supposed to have good sex without a connection? Without trust?

I stare at the blank strip of paper. I'm as empty as it looks.

You're not good enough.

Oh hell. I shake the thought out of my head. Years of therapy, healing, and repairing, and somehow, the crushing feeling of my infertility is confronting me again.

What has been keeping me from having a relationship?

I just stopped trying.

I gave up on love, let it gather dust behind a shut door in my mind.

I jot an answer down and fold the note in half. Regret shadows me. Lolita did say we get to keep these confessions to ourselves, right?

Molly drops her pencil on the mat, crumbling the small sheet of paper in her fist.

"Does everyone have something written down?" Ms. Deveaux asks. Everyone nods in response. "Perfect. Now, face your partners and share your confessions."

For fuck's sake. Molly presses her fist to her chest.

"We don't have to do this," I whisper. Even with the intrigue of finding out her answer eating away at me, I'd rather not share my note either.

"I see a lot of you are hesitating." Lolita waves her hand. "In order to truly transform your relationship, you and your partner must learn to be unapologetically vulnerable. Why stop yourselves from having the best sex of your life simply because of your egos and fears?"

Our instructor could moonlight as a lawyer with arguments like those.

The room erupts in a wave of whispers. Couples take turns sharing their deepest secrets.

But Molly and I aren't a real couple. We could just make something up.

I go to tell her exactly that as she unravels her paper and leans over to me. "Uh." Her eyes narrow, as if she's reconsidering her decision. "I don't orgasm during sex."

"What?" My eyebrows knot together. Jesus, I hate myself for my lack of decorum. But she's twenty-six years old and never had an orgasm during sex? What about with herself?

Inexplicable uneasiness folds over my body.

"I know, it's so embarrassing. I don't even know why I said anything. I think I'm just doing something wro—"

"I'm sorry, I'm going to interrupt you." My fingers grip the blanket on top of my lap. "There's absolutely no possibility, in any scenario, that you're doing something wrong."

"You're sweet for saying that."

"I'm not trying to appease you. Is it something you struggle to experience…" I pause for a moment. Diving into my fake girlfriend's sex life may be crossing all sorts of lines, but I need to know. "When you're alone?"

She shakes her head. "No, um, no issues with that. It just takes me a long time to get, uh…" She scoots closer to me and lowers her voice. "*There* with someone and, well, oftentimes, the wait for me to do *that* kind of ruins the experience."

My frustration morphs into red-hot anger. On what green earth does making a woman come ruin the experience? I hate that someone hasn't taken the time to give her absolutely everything she deserves.

I inhale a sharp breath, a heaviness settling in my chest. "You're not ruining anyone's experience." My voice is flat. "It's the people you've been with," I say through a clenched jaw. "Any man who doesn't focus on *your* pleasure before his own isn't worth a second of your time."

"It sounds selfish when you put it that way," Molly whispers, her fingers fuss with her note.

"Sex *is* selfish, Molly. It's selfish to want to take every inch of your partner for yourself, to crave, want, and ache for someone. Any prick who was lucky enough to be with a woman like you and didn't spend every single minute of it taking you all for myself..." Her eyes widen. *Did I just say that?* "For *themselves*. Himself. Uh—" I clear my throat. "What I'm trying to say is...he isn't worth a damn."

The plush curve of her bottom lip drops open, glistening in the soft light of the room. She straightens her spine. "How can you be so sure?"

"Because if I were in their shoes, I'd work tirelessly to show you colors you'd only see while you're with me."

Dormant feelings push past the dust and blockage. Virility returns to my veins.

Dammit. I want her.

That kiss in the library.

This woman.

I'm not sure how much longer I can keep pretending this suffocating attraction means nothing.

"Oh—that's—wow, um." As much as she tries to hide her

reaction to my words, the rise of her smile is obvious. I've gone too far. "Enough about me; what's on your note?"

My note.

I almost forgot.

The sheet is crumpled in my fist, and I unravel it, reading my own handwriting.

I can't have children.

"Uh—" I scramble for something to say. I'm not ready to share this part of myself yet. "I can never give someone what they truly want."

"What does that mean?" She angles her neck toward me, clearly wanting an explanation. "Does it have anything to do with your previous relationship?"

Crap. "That was a really long time ago. I only meant to say that I can't give a partner my everything."

"I don't know much, but from what you've just described, I mean, I think you could definitely give me an orgasm." Her hand runs up her neck. "A hypothetical orgasm, is what I meant to say. And not even me—ha!" Molly forces a laugh, adorably flustered. "Just a someone. Anyone!"

I want to do that for her. But the reality of my own note reminds me why I can't give in to my feelings. Being rejected by Molly would be devastating.

"I just don't need something serious with someone." My tone is more final than I intend. Molly flinches, the sparkle in her eyes dimming. "Look, these exercises were a bit intense. I'm going to head to the room for a reset."

"Oh, okay," she says, and I don't give her any more explanation as I bolt from the studio.

A nerve hardens in my jaw.

It's better this way.

THE ABSTRACT PAINTING hanging on the wall of our suite's living room reverberates as I slam the front door.

I needed to get out of there, throw away the note that she definitely can't read. There's no good reason to inform her of my inadequacy, but I hate that she was so honest with me and I ran.

Isn't that exactly what I told her not to do during our fight?

"Dammit." I drag my palm over the damp strands of hair stuck to my forehead. I walk over to our small kitchenette and fill up a glass of water.

Yoga is hard enough without having to hide a hard-on the entirety of the class, touching Molly's warm skin, and having to share deep, intimate secrets.

What the hell is up with this resort? It's as if half the activities are supposed to make you extremely turned on.

What am I even thinking? We're in a marriage preparation course. Of course that's what they're supposed to do.

I was certain I'd be able to handle it.

As I chug down my glass of water, the image of Molly's perky ass and spandex-wrapped curves sears itself into the backs of my eyelids.

I can't keep thinking about Molly like this. We agreed that the physical exploration—Christ, I sound like Lolita now—wasn't going any further than that one kiss in the library.

Absolutely not.

I find my way into the bathroom, turning the shower to a blistering cold, and strip off my clothes. My cock springs out of my shorts, achingly hard. *Ignore it.*

Then I see my demise.

Hanging from the hook on the back of the door is one of Molly's bras.

A lace one. The fabric is cream with a pattern of pink flowers.

She's everywhere. In this room, in my head, in the boiling blood in my veins.

I reach for the undergarment and realize my mistake. The lace is soft and delicate, like her. I trace my fingers along the seams.

She'd look so beautiful taking this off for me. Could I take my time with her and give her the orgasm she deserves?

I jolt.

No thinking about Molly naked. This thing must be my kryptonite. *I need to get rid of it.* I'll just put it back for her, get it out of our shared bathroom, and get on with my shower.

I fling open the door and stare at our bed. Her side by mine. Most nights, Molly shuffles closer and closer to me beneath the covers. I have to mummify myself with our sheets to resist scooping her into my arms and not letting her go.

My cock aches. A shot of pain wraps around the base of my spine.

No. I'm stronger than this.

Dammit. It's literally just a bra! I'm a grown man getting hard over fabric.

I loop into the walk-in closet, leave it on top of Molly's dresser, and return to the icy shower. The cold droplets pellet my skin. I lather my palms with soap and drag the foam over my body.

The scent of red ruby apples consumes me.

I force my face into the water again, attempting to wash away her smell, but the sweetness grows potent.

My eyes shoot open. Perfect, I've lathered myself with Molly's body wash. My palm meets the tiled wall. I need to resist. I focus on my pounding pulse.

Thrum.

Molly's laughter.

Thrum.

Molly's flushed cheeks.

Thrum.

 Molly's bra.

A creak sounds outside. I still. Is Molly back? But her typical, singing *hello* doesn't come from behind the door.

Fuck. My free hand reaches for my cock, and I hate myself for the dragging grip over my length, but I give in. My eyes are sewn shut, my heart galloping as I keep a feverish pace.

I shouldn't be touching myself while thinking about my fake girlfriend, my coworker, my friend. But the argument is flimsy when my mind conjures an image of Molly's eyes rolling into the back of her head as she moans beneath me.

My palms possessively trace down her rosy skin. I anchor myself over her. She smiles, her gaze locked on mine. My lips smother her in kisses, my tongue devouring her neck and full breasts. The reddish tint of her nipples as they harden between my teeth.

She's wet for me and makes a groan as my fingers circle her swollen clit. Her body arches into mine as I play with her pussy. I'd commit hours to her, try numerous toys if that's what it took to get her there.

"Matthew." My name drags off her lips. I pick up the pace, stroking my cock vigorously.

"You're exquisite, darling; every inch of you is exquisite."

"Matthew," she says again through a lazy smile, and my balls cinch together with a heavy weight.

"Just like that, Molly." I push my fingers into her, and her breath catches when I angle myself deeper. "You just let me make you feel so good."

I need her.

I need to feel her, fill her, taste the way my cum drips out of her beautiful pussy.

The confession is enough to send me over the edge.

"Matthew?" Molly's real voice, not the one my mind conjured, comes from behind the bathroom door.

"Uh—" I catch my breath. The release from my orgasm is still pounding through me. "Yeah? Are you okay?"

"I'm good, just checking to make sure it was you in here. I heard someone talking."

"It's me. Just reciting something for a presentation," I call out. My forehead connects with the tile. *A presentation?* "I'll be out in a second."

"Take your time."

The cold water fails to calm the heat flaring in my veins. I open my eyes again, struggling to jolt myself out of my salacious daydream.

I'm a wreck.

Chapter 14
Matthew

"WE'RE HERE," Molly announces as we approach an outdoor kitchen set against a beautiful canyon backdrop. Lolita's wearing an apron as she stands among the various burners and open flames on the stone countertops.

"My favorite lovebirds," she chimes. "Welcome to today's Inferno Infatuation activity. Hope you brought your appetite."

"What is all this?" I ask as we walk toward our own private station.

"Your fact sheet said you enjoyed cooking." Molly gives me the softest nudge of her shoulder.

"I do." I can't help the smile breaching my lips. "But didn't we have an aerial meditation class today?"

"We did." She shrugs, the slightest hint of fire in her eyes. The strap of her frilly blouse falls, and she swipes it over her shoulder, revealing *the* bra. That damn piece of clothing that caused me to lose it yesterday. "I figured you'd like this a little more. At the very least, you can laugh at how terrible I am in the kitchen."

Before I have a chance to respond, Ms. Deveaux cuts through our conversation. "We all know the saying, *Trust your gut*. But today's activity will involve trusting your lover. You'll use all of the tools and farm-fresh ingredients available to you to nourish your partner by making their favorite meal." Molly gives me a very tense smile. Lolita continues, "There won't be any conversing with each other before you begin."

Thankfully, Molly wrote that she loves extra cheesy pizza in her fact sheet.

Twenty minutes later, I'm kneading dough onto the wooden board in front of me.

At On Cloud Nine, they spare no expense. We're making each other dinner from a fully stocked and refrigerated pantry under the late afternoon sun. The environmentalist in me has been struggling with the level of excess, but we won't be here for much longer.

"Ugh." Molly groans beside me, tossing another egg into the sink. She's definitely not preparing my favorite childhood meal —my dad's scallion cheddar biscuits.

"Are you still not going to share what you're making?" I eye Molly, who's made a great effort to hide her mystery dish.

"Do I need to call Lolita over here and have her walk through the instructions again?" Her authoritative tone makes me chuckle.

"No, ma'am," I say playfully and get back to my dough. Molly tosses one more smashed egg into the sink. Her back is tense. She must be getting irked. "Trust me, when I was first learning to cook, I served plenty of shelly eggs and burnt toast. But nobody masters something on the first try. Or, in my case, the second. Or third."

Molly peers over her shoulder at me, wiping the frustration from her brow. "You have a tendency to make a lot of good points."

The compliment floods my chest with warmth.

"How are we doing over here?" Lolita floats over to us, observing our stations.

"We're trying," Molly laughs. A swift crack, and a small cheer comes from her side. I glance over to find a clean, no-shell egg drop into her mixing bowl.

"And succeeding." I smile.

"It seems like the both of you can handle it from here," Lolita says, making her way to another couple.

Molly does a little celebration dance. It's ridiculously cute.

"Good job, darling."

Her eyes flash to mine. "You've called me that before."

Caught red-handed. I clear my throat, picking up a ball of mozzarella cheese and bringing it to my grater. "Trying to stay convincing, remember?"

Molly gives me a sideways glance and returns to whipping her eggs with a fork. "Right. Well, would you like a nickname?"

I don't hate the idea of her having something to call me. Something only for Molly to say. "Do you have one in mind?"

She thinks for a moment, pondering the question with care. "Ollie always calls you Mattie."

"And he's lucky he's twice my size, or I would've put an end to it long ago." I shake my head, pressing harder on the grater.

"Alright, no Mattie. Maybe I'll stick with Matthew. My Matthew."

I halt. Did she just say that?

My Matthew.

Before I can prod her about it, Molly pours her egg mixture into a pan. The sizzling washes away the bit of tension between us.

"Mr. Hudson?" Lolita's voice sounds beside me, and I force my attention away from Molly's extra-focused stare over the burner. "Please save some cheese for the rest of us."

I look down into my bowl, which is overflowing with a mound of mozzarella.

"There's no such thing as too much," Molly jokes, and I collect all of the shredded pieces.

As the sun disappears behind the canyon, painting the sky in bursts of orange and red, our classmates begin enjoying their meals. I take my pizza out of the brick oven and stroll toward Molly. She set us up at a picnic table away from the rest of the class. In front of her sits a plate covered with a napkin.

"You can't possibly eat what I made when you've conjured up this." She admires my piping-hot pizza. "Seriously. Are you hiding some kind of magical talent?"

"Maybe I wasn't being totally honest," I tease. "My dad taught me the basics, but all those videos of Gordon Ramsay in my search history are why I'm this good."

"Gordon is a little scary. He catered an event for us last year," she says nonchalantly and grabs a slice.

"What?" Sometimes I forget how wealthy Molly's family really is and how different our experiences have been. The casualness of some of the things she says makes me feel really out of touch.

Would being in a real relationship with her always entail that level of adventure and excitement?

"Oh, it was nothing. When I was a kid, we hired all kinds of chefs to cater the elaborate, themed barbecues my dad used to throw."

My brows shoot up. "Themed?"

"Yes. My favorite one was for the Renaissance. I was probably seven years old and got to eat a giant turkey leg with my hands while wearing a pink ball gown." She takes a bite of her pizza, her eyes rolling back as she chews. "This is so good."

Has she always eaten pizza this erotically?

"Thank you," I say, my gaze not able to leave her face. "You really had the world at your fingertips."

Molly stills, setting down her slice. "Yeah. It comes with its perks, but I assume most children can touch the furniture in their homes and run along the corridors. Not at the Greene Estate. All playing was done in the playroom, and all running was done outdoors on a small track beside the tennis courts. I always wonder if it would have felt as lonely as it did if I'd had siblings."

I can't even imagine what that must have been like for her.

"Trust me, when you meet my brothers and sisters, you might take that back," I chuckle.

Molly plasters on one of her fake smiles.

"I'm sure that's what all siblings say, but I imagine it's nice to have someone fighting by your side. Or, at the very least, just on your team." She shrugs and takes another bite.

"That's true. Maya has always been one of my best friends." My stomach growls, and Molly regards the plate she made for me. "I'm quite excited to find out what surprise you cooked up for me," I say, lifting the napkin off of my plate. A bagel sits in the middle, though it looks like it has seen better days. I lift the top of the bagel to reveal eggs that somehow look both over and undercooked. But the bacon looks crispy, and the cheese is more than half melted. I smile. "A bacon, egg, and cheese?"

"I know I didn't make the meal you put in your fact sheet, but you always bring one of these in on Fridays. Do you hate it?" Sweet of her to notice something so minute about me. Molly reaches for my plate, a blush reddening her cheeks. "Ugh, you know what, why don't we split this pizza? Honestly, I think it's best, if you want to avoid food poisoning."

"Hey." I drag my plate back. "My *girlfriend* made me this."

"She must not like you very much," she giggles.

"I think she likes me just fine." I take a bite of the sandwich, trying to chew through the burnt taste and runny yolks. This is horrible. *Just keep chewing and smiling, man.*

Her shoulders shimmy with joy as she watches me eat her creation.

"Molly," a voice calls out beside us, and we turn to face Gigi and Jerry, the couple we met during our pottery class. "Sweetest dear, we cannot thank you enough for your kindness."

The blush on Molly's face turns wine red. "Oh," she laughs. "Um, it's no big deal. *Really*."

"No big deal?" Gigi sets both of her hands on her hips and turns to me. "Not only did we get our nightly rate cut in half after that small fire in the pottery studio, your lovely lady here gave us a free week to any On Cloud Nine resort in the world."

"Airfare included." Jerry pulls at his suspenders, beaming.

Christ. I've never doubted Molly's kind heart, but this gesture was more than a set of good manners.

"It was nothing." Molly waves, an attempt to dismiss them.

"She's a keeper." Gigi winks at me. "We'll let you get back to your lovely dinner. We just couldn't resist coming by and letting you know how much we appreciate you."

They scatter off, leaving us in an empty silence. The last remnants of the orange sky cascade across her face.

"That was really nice of you," I say.

"They saved up for six years to be here," Molly replies. "Everyone should have the opportunity to experience luxuries like this."

"You know, you'd be terrific in hospitality." I tilt my head toward her. "Have you thought more about the inn you mentioned when we first got here?"

"Oh." Her eyes dart around, landing on Lolita, who is laughing with other guests several feet away from us. Molly leans across the table. "Honestly, I have."

"Tell me about it."

"I don't actually like how inaccessible our resorts are. It hadn't quite hit me until I spoke to Gigi, but it's not right," Molly explains. A sense of urgency coats her face. "Everyone should have the opportunity to enjoy the luxuries of On Cloud Nine. Maybe my inn could have similar offerings, but at an affordable price with a focus on sustainability. Is that too much?"

Wow. I want to kiss her again. I shake the thought from my head. *Let's keep this professional. She's talking about her future.*

Molly's parents were trying to auction their daughter off to the highest bidder so they can make more money, and she's worried about people having access to the grandeur her family's business provides.

How is she cut from the same cloth?

"That's a wonderful idea. An affordable inn with the offerings of a five-star resort. There's certainly a market for it in this economy. Where would you want to open up something like that?"

"I'm not sure." Molly slumps back into her seat. "I think it has to be in New York…I want to stay close to my friends and family."

Hmm. "Have you thought about mentioning it to your parents?"

At the suggestion, she visibly freezes over. I shouldn't have asked. I already know they kept her away from their hospitality conglomerate, but would it be so bad for her to turn to them for advice?

"I—I don't want to," Molly whispers. "I know it might seem silly when I have access to every resource imaginable, but I think I need to do this on my own, even if I don't quite know how to purchase a property."

That's admirable. I promised I'd be here to help her as long as we're together, and there's no reason that can't start now. "Have you heard of Zillow?"

"No, what's that?" She takes another bite of pizza, the cheese stretching off of her slice.

"It's a real estate website where you can look for homes and land. Kind of like…" I search my head for something she'd be able to relate to. "Like Sotheby's."

"Oh." Molly perks up. "Okay, that's cool. Maybe I can try to find my inn there?"

"Excellent idea. I can help you put together a business plan and break down your first few years of operating expenses."

A smile pulls across her pretty face. "I'd like that a lot. Can we put something together when we're back in the city? I'll scope out a few places and start making a serious game plan."

Her determination is so attractive. But come on, how could I not feel that for her when she's got that focused wrinkle in her nose and a glimmer in her amber eyes?

I force a calming breath. "Sounds like a plan. Have you picked out a name already?"

Molly turns as red as the tomato sauce on her slice. "Um, yeah. I was thinking…The Griffin." She looks up at me. "Is that cheesy?"

I can't help but smile, and Molly mirrors me. "Not even a little bit."

"Lovebirds, I don't want to interrupt your beautiful moment of connection, but the rest of the class has left." Lolita taps on our picnic table. I look up and notice the sky bleeding into darkness, stars appearing through the deep blue. The plates in front of us are empty, and the rest of the tables are desolate.

"Wow, time really flew," Molly laughs, shooting out of her seat nervously. "We'll get out of here."

My heart sinks into my chest. I glance around, not wanting our evening to end. At the edge of the outdoor kitchen, there are a few lit bonfires with Adirondack chairs. "Actually, Lolita, we're going to finish off our evening over there."

Ms. Deveaux claps her hands together, smiling. "Wonderful idea, Matthew. The stars are in their element tonight, and you might as well enjoy them before our Cozy Crescent session begins at midnight. I'll leave you to it." She gives us a wink before departing.

"I hope you don't mind," I say.

Molly tucks her hair behind her ears. "No, uh, I'd really like to stargaze with you."

Wonderful.

"Take a seat. I'm gonna grab something really quick."

Her round eyes spark beneath the starry sky. "Are you planning a surprise, Hudson?"

"Just something small." I toss my hands into my pockets, stretching out my arms. "The least I can do after that wonderful bacon, egg, and cheese."

"Well, now I know you're lying," she laughs and makes her way over to the Adirondack chairs.

I gather marshmallows, graham crackers, and a bar of chocolate from the pantry, along with some skewers before sitting next to her.

"How do you feel about s'mores?" I stab a marshmallow and hand it over to Molly.

"Best. Treat. Ever." She smiles over the fire, twirling her skewer.

In the haze of the flame, her face is all rubies and gold. She glows as the fire crackles in front of us. She's beautiful. Always has been. But she's also brave, vulnerable, and strong. I don't think I've ever met a person who's intrigued me more than her.

I've read hundreds of books, studied for thousands of hours, graduated at the top of my class at MIT, but for some reason, I'm struggling to define the feelings I have for her.

I only know that when I look at her, it's like my cup is full. Colors feel brighter, the air tastes sweeter.

"Matthew?" Her voice is low.

"Yes?"

"I'm going to need the rest of the ingredients." She looks down at the chocolate and graham crackers in my hands.

"Right," I laugh, handing them over.

She assembles her own treat.

The sleeve of her goddamn frilly blouse falls again, trailing down her arm. A blue thing that has been bothering me since I saw her put it on this morning. I can see the outline of that damn bra.

The top cups her breasts and cinches at her waist. Between her cleavage is a little white bow. I want to undo it, undo her.

My cock pulses against my jeans.

I'm almost mad at her for wearing it, as irrational as that sounds in my own head. It's making me want to lose control. But would that be so bad?

If we lost control for a little while?

"I'm so excited for this." She shows off her s'more. "Actually, do you want a taste?"

Yes. I'd really enjoy one of you.

"Uh." I pause, glancing down at my chocolate-stained and crumb-covered fingers. "I'll make my own in a sec."

"No, no." Molly hovers her s'more at my mouth. "Just take a bite of mine, seriously." She brings the sweet, sticky treat to my lips. Her amber gaze is locked on mine as I take a bite. My blood warms in my veins. "How's that?" She watches me with anticipation.

I finish chewing. "Great, thank you."

Why do I sound like I'm signing off on an email?

"Yum," she groans, taking her own bite. *Fuck.* Chocolate smudges along her mouth.

What would it taste like on her tongue? On her neck? I need to find out. Without an ounce of control, my hand reaches for her. I trace the pad of my thumb along her full bottom lip.

Christ.

Molly flutters her eyelashes up at me, looking all too bashful for the exceptionally tense exchange. I start to pull away, but she reaches for my wrist and glances down at my thumb.

"Uh, s-sorry," I stutter.

In a blink, Molly's tongue travels over the chocolate stuck to my skin. My heart stops.

Holy hell. I may die.

She drops my hand and looks back toward the fire.

"Maybe, after we get divorced, you can come to The Griffin for stargazing and s'mores," she says casually.

Her words are like a nail in my chest, the opposite of her rekindling touch. A reminder that this moment, with this beautiful girl, has an expiration date.

There's no other option.

OLLIE

is bear allergic to fried oreos?

MATTHEW

Please don't feed my cat fried oreos.

OLLIE

c'mon, seriously? not even a bite?

MATTHEW

Zero bites.

OLLIE

fine, m8. how's arizona?

MATTHEW

Having more fun than expected.

OLLIE

as happy as i am for you

work has been boring without you

MATTHEW

Don't worry I'll be back soon and we can get started on EcoDrones.

OLLIE

please don't tell me we gotta go back to a coworking space

they have the worst chairs

> my back can't handle it

MATTHEW

> I'll find one with very nice chairs.

OLLIE

> i don't believe ya

IT'LL BE nice to work on a project without having to rent the cheapest space available on the island of Manhattan. Depending on how quickly I can use the funds from the trust to develop EcoDrones, we may be able to look into getting a permanent home for our business.

OLLIE

> how's the whole fake dating thing going?

> fallen in love yet?

I stare at the message.

I suppose I love all my friends. And Molly and I have known each other for three years. So, by that logic, of course I love Molly.

But the feeling I get when I look at her doesn't quite match the feelings I have toward my other friends. It's different. Probably because I'm attracted to her. Any human being with a heartbeat would be.

Molly could ruin a man with just her smile.

I can't deny the dormant emotions that she's been awakening in me. But the ache of my past clings to every crevice of my body. That yoga class and the confession I wrote down about my infertility are stark reminders as to why I can't kiss Molly again.

Sharing my inadequacy with her isn't an option. What if she thinks something is wrong with me? What if she regrets kissing me?

Selfishly, I don't want to do anything that would change the way she looks at me.

Maybe some deep part of me is afraid that I'm simply not worthy of her.

I glance over at the seat beside me. Molly's engrossed in a book. The feelings of not being good enough swallow me whole, but I force them away. Exposing this part of my life won't do us any good, no matter what emotions are brewing inside of me.

MATTHEW

We're having a nice time.

I gotta go. Chat soon?

I'll tell him about the kiss when I get back. Knowing Ollie, he'd probably fly all the way over here just to chat through the details. It's been a long time since either of us kissed a girl who meant something to us.

OLLIE

THAT'S ALL YOU'RE LEAVING ME WITH
MATTIE?

MATTHEW

Don't feed my cat oreos.

OLLIE

you bastard.

I pocket my phone, stretching my legs out in front of me. The clear blue sky hangs above us as we sit on the patio of our suite. Insects hum around the arid canyons.

"Can we talk about something?" Molly says from the Adirondack chair beside me, fidgeting with the pages of her book.

"Of course." My half empty coffee sits on the table beside today's untouched crossword puzzle.

"Well, my parents arrive in a few days to let us know their decision."

The last week and a half has flown by. We're almost at the finish line.

I pivot toward her to give her my full attention. "Are you nervous?"

"Yes."

Should I be? "Have you heard from them since your mom left?"

"The occasional text, but nothing about us," she explains.

I don't know her parents well enough to understand if that's cause for concern. We've been doing great in the course, even if we're stepping off of the agenda occasionally. Lolita certainly hasn't indicated that's an issue.

"Can you ask them how they're feeling? It may ease your worry a bit," I suggest. "Or we can ask Lolita for an honest update? Given the way she's acted the past couple of days, I doubt she's spying on us."

Molly's lips roll against each other. There's a nervous crease in her brows.

I try to calm my own unsettled pulse. Her parents will definitely approve of our marriage.

"You're right," she answers, pulling me back to the present. "Maybe I'll give my mom a call tomorrow. They're just unpredictable sometimes."

I wish I could do something to assure her, but my only confidence rests in the fact that we're abiding by the terms of our arrangement.

It's best to begin thinking about our future.

"Maybe we should talk about what would happen after they give us their approval," I say. "I should've asked this before we left for Arizona, but would we have a wedding?" My question sparks more uneasiness.

"My mother would probably say it's bad optics to have a

wedding so soon after calling off the marriage of the century with Lance, so we may just elope."

The thought saddens me. "If you could have a wedding, what would it be like?"

Her eyes widen with surprise, the way they do any time I ask her about her own preferences.

"I know it's a bit silly, but I've always wanted to wear a colorful dress." She smiles beneath the smattering of sun on the patio. "No white or beige, but something bright and beautiful. All my real friends would be there, and just my mom and dad, without any of their business connections. No fancy frills, no pressure to perform, no expectations. Just me and my husband." She looks over at me.

Just me and her.

No. *Stop it, man.*

I try to shake the vivid picture of her fantasies from my own head. "Sounds really nice."

"I'd want flowers of every color, and—" She blushes.

"What?" I readjust in my chair, picking up my coffee and taking another sip.

"It's silly, but maybe a horse to ride off on with my new husband, just like in the books."

I tilt my head toward her. "Nothing that you want for your special day is silly."

She goes on telling me about her perfect wedding, as if she's held it in her whole life and she's finally been given permission to let her thoughts run free.

Some long-forgotten part of me seeps into her daydream.

A cake topped with pounds of raspberries? *Yes.*

Snow falling? *Absolutely.*

Sharing vows in private? *Anything you'd like, baby.*

The requests are so small, and yet I want to give her all of them.

Maybe while we still have a few days here, I can give her

even a fraction of what she wants. With the stables on the property, there's no reason she can't live out her riding dreams.

"What about you? I know you were in a long-term relationship; did you ever think about what you wanted your real wedding to look like back then?"

The word *real* catapults me out of my daydream. Molly wasn't talking about marrying me. *No.* Her real husband will get to give her everything she wants. At least, I hope he does.

"We never got to that part." I set down my mug, feeling uneasy. There's no point in dodging the questions anymore. I need to nip this in the bud. "It was a long time ago. Laura and I met at work, and our lives just meshed. It was easy. Comfortable. But we both realized we wanted different things in the end."

"What kind of things?" Molly asks, tucking her knees into her chest.

Despite the years of therapy, I still struggle to make peace with how quickly things fell apart. Laura and I had our goals aligned, I'm certain of that, but my infertility diagnosis put the reality of our future into perspective for her.

I glance at Molly. Another temporary future looking back at me. One that won't come with so much hurt. At least, I hope.

"I wanted to launch Plastech and focus on my career." I keep my answer short before deflecting the conversation away from my past. "I know you said it may be a few months before we get married. Would we have to move in together?"

"Lance didn't have to live with me, before or after our engagement, so I doubt it. And after we're married, we could probably live apart." She hikes her knees up to her chest. "Maybe we just host an event or two at my place, to make it seem like you live there before we get divorced?"

"Alright." Our future, or lack thereof, sits heavy on my chest. That means only four more days of waking up with Molly.

It's not enough.

Maybe we can pretend that it is.

Pretend that we're not broken.

Pretend there aren't a million reasons why we shouldn't make this complicated.

Pretend the future doesn't exist.

I know it's wrong, but I want more time with Molly.

Chapter 15
Molly

I SHOVE away the uneasiness in my body and throw on a dazzling smile before answering my mother's call. My familiar Socialite Molly mask feels poorly fitted today.

"Hey, Mom. How are you?" The last time we FaceTimed must have been when she pocket-dialed me from Bergdorf's four months ago.

Vivian barely looks at her phone. Her amber eyes are focused on something in the distance.

"Molly, your father and I will be arriving in Sedona in three days," she reminds me, tugging at one of her pearl earrings. A lump forms at the base of my throat.

"Wonderful. You'll have the opportunity to see what a good match Matthew and I are while you're here." I pace around the suite. Thankfully, Matthew's doing his morning workout at the gym and doesn't have to witness this terse exchange.

As much as I like to daydream about our happily ever after, I know I can't possibly tie him down to my family.

My mother finally peers down at her screen, a stern expression coating her face. "I assure you, we've been getting all the reports, doll."

"Great." I nod. A stretch of silence sits between us, and my brain uses it as an excuse to turn the anxiety in my belly into panic. I have not missed this feeling. At all. "Well, thank you for letting me know."

"Are you in a rush?" Her voice is all thorns.

"No." I flop down onto the leather couch. "Of course not."

"Have you made good use of my agenda?"

My heart thuds in my chest.

The trust. *Thud.* Going back to being Miss Molly "Doll" Greene. *Thud.*

"Yes. Lolita even encouraged us to spend time doing activities we both enjoy," I say. "Three years of knowing each other have given us a lot of shared hobbies. The way you have polo with Dad."

"Hmm." My mother raises her brow at me, watching me closely over the video call. "We'll see about that."

Her statement is a gavel dropped between us. She hangs up. Panic continues to flood my chest.

This is how things have always worked: my mother makes decisions, and I abide by her requests.

But something's been shifting the past couple of weeks, something that even my thunder of nerves can't wash away. A change is coming from deep within me. Once I get my trust, I won't be able to run away from it any longer.

"So, I wanted to make a suggestion." Matthew leans against the doorway, rubbing his damp hair with a towel.

He's in a Henley shirt with two buttons undone, tufts of hair peeking out. I've been staring at his chest for the last two weeks and still have an urge to run my fingers through the tangled manliness awaiting me.

Something about his undone, casual sex appeal has me spinning out of control.

Why does he have the audacity to look quite so adorable, cozy, and sexy all at once?

How is it fair?

Wait, can a person even look cozy? I have no idea. But Matthew does. Cozy to the touch.

"Molly?" He snaps me out of my very obvious gawking. "You still there?"

I glance up at him. "Um, yeah. What's up?"

An expression that clearly says *I know you're ogling me* lights up his face. "I wanted to propose something."

My heart beats louder in my chest. "Isn't that how we ended up here in the first place?" I tease.

"Touché." He continues to swipe at his strands, his muscular biceps tensing in all the right ways. "But something a little different this time. I was thinking—"

"I love it when you do that," I blurt out, lifting up onto my toes as if I'm about to float away. *Wait.* "Did I just say that out loud? Ha!" I laugh and pretend to stretch. "Um, w-what did you have in mind?"

I have officially lost all control of my salivary glands in his presence. I hereby declare myself a depraved and shameless drool monster. How could I not be? Especially after licking chocolate off his fingers two nights ago.

Matthew looks at me with a lovely but painfully stoic expression, waiting for my flustered outbreak to calm. "I made plans for us," he says, hanging his towel on one of the closet door hooks.

"For us?"

"Yes, but only if you're up for a little surprise date today."

Has the sun catapulted through the ceiling of the closet and gone straight into my chest? Surely it must have. I'm glowing.

"A *date*?"

He coughs. "Well, we can call it a rendezvous if you prefer."

I don't care what we name it, a date or a rendezvous. I'm elated. Fire thrums through me. I rock back and forth on my feet again.

"And what are we doing for this rendezvous? That's *not* a date." I raise one brow at him.

I'll need to change. *Goodness.* I'm going on a date, which is not a date, but is so a date, with Matthew.

"It's a secret," he whispers conspiratorially.

"I've never had a secret surprise date before." I haven't been on a proper date since college. I search the closet, trying to find the perfect spot of color for the occasion. "What should I wear?"

He ignores my question. "What do you mean no surprise dates?"

"The only surprises I ever get are when my mother shows up at eight o'clock on a Saturday morning with a last-minute invitation to one of her many social events." I laugh to lighten the mood.

"What about birthdays?" A smidge of concern hangs on his question.

"Usually planned months in advance." I don't want to think about Socialite Molly. "Okay, no more chitchat. I have to get ready for a rendezvous!"

"So do I." He cracks a smile and grabs a clean shirt from his side of the closet.

Twenty minutes later, I enter the living room. A pink floral-print Rodarte midi dress with cream-colored flowers hangs off my shoulders. Since I don't know what we're doing, I threw on a pair of boy shorts underneath just in case. Matthew sits on the couch, engrossed in today's crossword.

I admire the crease running across his forehead. It would be nice to see him like this on a random weekday. Maybe his hair is shaggy after a long day at work. A book rests beside him as a fire crackles.

The fantasy is achingly beautiful and bittersweet.

Is there a reality in which Matthew and I could like each other?

And we could be real?

And I could see him curled up on his couch, petting Bear, and sharing longing glances with me?

Matthew drops his pen into his lap and stands quickly, tossing his newspaper onto the chair. "Molly. *Wow.*"

My skin is probably flaring so much that it's blending into the fabric of my dress. "Is this okay?"

"Flawless." His gaze lingers for a long time, on my body, on my hair, on me. "As always."

The compliment feels genuine, even if it's grandiose. *Am I seriously attracting him right now?*

I must be.

I may not be the most experienced lady, but I'm pretty sure his eyes are doing that darkening thing again.

"You look really handsome too."

"Shall we head out on our rendezvous, milady?" Matthew says in an indiscernible accent. He grins and stretches one of his arms out in an overly dramatic gesture.

I love this.

I pinch the edges of my dress and bend, feigning a curtsy. "That would be most delightful."

As he approaches, my breath catches in my throat. He's nothing like the fops I grew up with. Matthew's rugged and manly. His cologne engulfs me, making my knees weak.

As if it's second nature, I entwine my hand with his outstretched one, and we head out.

We've done countless activities over the last two weeks, but this one feels special. Maybe it is.

The same thought keeps bursting through the seams of my mind. *Would it be selfish to have something more than the life I'm destined for?*

A real love. A future that won't resemble my parents'.

Tonight, I just want to enjoy a rendezvous with my fake boyfriend. Like a normal girl.

The most normal girl in the world.

We pass the yoga studio, the pickleball court, and the lobby.

Where could he possibly be taking me?

As if reading my mind, Matthew glances over to me and asks, "How are you feeling?"

"Nervous."

He gives my hand a squeeze. "Good nervous or bad nervous?"

"Good—very good, I think." I manage the words through a high-pitched laugh.

"We're almost there."

The path through the resort is dotted with cacti and desert flora, making the air smell sweet. The quiet hum of insects buzzes in my ears. We turn around a bend, and the horse stables come into view.

My heart skips over itself. "Are we going to see the horses again?"

"We had so much fun visiting Honey and Maple, I thought we could take them out on the trail."

I glance down at my Christian Louboutin Mamadrague flats. "Wait; I can't ride in these."

"Don't worry, I already took care of it." Matthew shoots me an earth-shaking wink.

As we enter the stables, the musky scent of the oil for the saddles, the bales of hay, and the alfalfa transports me into memories of riding as a kid. It's like a warm hug.

A tickle shoots up my nose, and I sneeze. Over and over again.

Okay, this is the least nostalgic part of my time in dressage.

"Bless you," Matthew chuckles. "Are you alright over there?"

"Yes, just allergies. I should be okay once we get out of the stables." Last time we came to visit the horses, they were already on the pasture outside. The hay was far, far away from me.

"I had no idea; you didn't mention anything in your fact sheet. What are you allergic to?" He turns to me, leaning close.

"Hay." I play off the second sneezing fit as best as I can. "I didn't mention it because I started getting allergy shots this year and haven't had any issues since."

"Seems like pertinent information for a boyfriend to know," he voices calmly. I can't place whether his concern is for me or for our arrangement.

"Well, my own fiancé didn't—uh, ex-fiancé," I clarify quickly when Matthew's lower lip tugs downward ever so slightly.

"Hmm." Matthew doesn't say anything else, and we make our way deeper into the stables.

The stables have fifteen well-maintained horse stalls. On the walls, brushes and horseshoes hang in an assortment. Midnight, a shiny mustang, nickers as he sticks his head out over his stall door.

"Sweet boy," I coo, stroking his muzzle. "He used to always click his teeth together when he wanted something to munch on."

As if on cue, Midnight bites at the air, angling his head toward us. I grab an apple from the nearby basket and hold it out to him. His muzzle gently brushes against my palm, causing me to giggle.

Matthew watches me intently.

"What?" I tease playfully, although I'm a little embarrassed to be gushing over a horse.

"You're every definition of the word *joy* when you're being yourself," he states. My movements still, but my toes curl in my flats. None of my masks have made an appearance in front of him in days, and that fact doesn't spark the perpetual feeling to vanish. *Does he mean it?* "Stay here. I need to make sure we don't ruin your nice shoes."

I'm dizzy, almost faint. *A gift?* That's definitely not something a fake boyfriend does for his fake girlfriend.

"O-okay."

He walks to the front of the barn and returns with a large cardboard box. "Open it."

I'm more thrilled than I was when I got my Metallic Chèvre Birkin 25 shipped over from a silent auction in Austria last year.

I pull apart the twine and lift the lid. Inside, a pair of freshly oiled riding boots lie on a tuft of paper. There's a leather pull loop at the heel collar, and a set of long, lacy socks rests beside them.

They're beautiful.

More than that; they're perfect.

"*Matthew*. Riding boots?"

"I worked with Lolita to have them crafted for you after we visited the stables last week," he explains, a gleam shining in his eyes. "Pull the zipper down a bit and check the inside lining."

I do as he says and catch a scalloped leather label. Etched in a beautiful gold is an inscription: *Property of Molly Greene.*

My stomach somersaults. "This is—"

"I figured the boots can be an early celebration gift for your parents approving our marriage on Saturday. Why don't you try them on while I saddle up the horses."

I force my hands steady and glance up into his eyes. Beams of sunlight pour into the stables, casting shadows across his strong shoulders and spectacular face. My heart sings again.

He's real. This is real.

And if both of those things are true, then perhaps *we* could be real too.

Chapter 16
Matthew

"I'm having such a lovely time." Molly blushes beneath the permanent smile etched onto her face. "To be honest, I've never gone this far off the trail. It's beautiful here."

The breathtaking scenery of the canyons surrounds us. We sit in a shaded oasis nestled between two rock formations. Honey and Maple are tied up beside us, grazing on wheatgrass along the trail.

I look over at her. "Very beautiful."

From the picnic basket Lolita prepared for us, I pull out a pail of strawberries and oranges and hand Molly one of the red berries. As she takes a bite, she wraps her lips around the succulent skin. My eyes trace a path over her cheeks and neck before they settle on the delicate hollow of her collarbones.

Dammit. Why does the sight of her send me into a frenzy? *It's just a clavicle, man. Relax.*

A throb pulses through my body. I shift my knees on top of the blanket, attempting to ignore the persistent ache in my cock.

Watching Molly ride for the past hour was difficult enough. Her curves bobbing on horseback, her curls dancing in the wind.

Absolute torment.

"You're a wonderful riding partner." Molly places the strawberry stem in the pail and sets her palms behind her. "I haven't been on horseback with someone in a really long time."

"Why'd you stop dressage?" I take an orange in my hands and dig my fingers into its tough flesh. Molly watches my movements intently.

"I had a very close call with Sunburst Symphony. I didn't fall, but I did lose control of my reins. *Once*. By accident." She sighs. "I was always a nervous rider, but my safety stirrups weren't set up properly and I lost some footing. My mom got worried and asked me to pack up my breeches and spurs."

Maybe her parents do have pure intentions of keeping her safe. But life always has risks, and if it didn't, I'm not sure it would be worth living.

"Did you want to keep doing it?" I ask, handing her an orange slice.

"Yeah, of course. It crushed me, to say the least. I was even taking something for my anxiety at the time, but Vivian's word is final. I still don't really know why she felt the need to worry so much." Molly frowns, biting into the citrus.

She shares the personal story with ease. A small piece of her gets passed to me for safekeeping.

"I've seen you take something. I didn't want to pry about it, but my brother, Myles…he also struggles with anxiety."

She replaces the downturned corners of her lips with a heartfelt smile. "Really?" I nod. "It's more common than people think. I've never been ashamed about it or anything. It's kind of always been a part of my life. My anxiety and my meds, going in and out of therapy. Some days are harder than others, but I've been working to keep the majority of my symptoms at bay."

Myles always described his anxiety as if it were drowning him, cutting off all his fresh air. It wasn't long before he started taking medication that helped him find some oxygen. At least, that's how he described it. "Medical science is a real gem for that."

"So are therapists," she laughs.

I continue to pull apart our orange. "Thank you for sharing that with me. I know it's a very private thing." Her courage makes me want to reveal a part of myself too. "A few years ago, I—I was also in therapy. I know the impact it can have on your life. It helped me understand that vulnerability is power."

"No wonder you're so levelheaded." Molly gives me a soft nudge with her knee.

"That's just my nature." We sit together on the checkered picnic blanket. Peace and serenity. That's what I feel with this magnificent woman. "So, I guess we'll have to include a stable in your business plan." I hand her another orange slice.

Molly takes it, watching a stream of clouds pass above us. "I think you're right. I can't believe we'll be back in the city in only a few days. It'll be great to start scouting some locations on, um…Z…Zillow.com?"

I nod, failing to hide my smile.

On Saturday, we'll be back in New York. Back to our normal lives. Back to waking up without her sleepy amber eyes or messy curls right beside me. The haze of the last two weeks either making or breaking us.

"Just in time for leaf season," I say.

"The best time of year." Molly shimmies her shoulders again.

Fucking adorable. As always.

"Maybe we can dress up as Serienna and Damien in the Battle of Loria for Halloween, since it's only a few weeks away?" I joke, hoping the suggestion doesn't sound as awkward as it did coming out of my mouth.

I'm a grown man and a tad too excited to cosplay as characters from her favorite book. But *The Stone Court* has made it onto my top reads of the year. Plus, the image of Molly as an elf… The mere thought has my pulse humming in my veins.

"What?" Her mouth drops open.

Yeah. Definitely awkward. I rise from my forearms, sitting up. "I believe they're characters from your favorite book series."

"I know who they are." Molly feigns rolling her eyes above the playful smile on her face. "I just didn't know you've been reading. The Battle of Loria is book two."

Caught again.

I nervously stroke the back of my neck. "I bought the e-book after we finished the first one. That cliff-hanger wasn't letting me sleep." She studies me, lost for words. *Did I cross a line?* "I just got to the part where Serienna is on the back of her great griffin," I say, flashing her a wink that immediately snaps the tension from her face. "And she rides into battle, landing the shot that saves Damien. I thought he was a goner, but then she used her elven mind control and, well, I couldn't put it down."

What I can't quite explain is that there was no way I could lie in the same bed as her after she licked chocolate off of my fingers. Picking up the book seemed like the best distraction to keep my thoughts from morphing into memories of Molly's lips on me.

"Romantasy is a drug," she giggles, taking another straw-berry from the pail. "It can cause a full-blown addiction."

I'm starting to feel the same way about that little laugh of yours.

Molly brushes a heap of corkscrew curls over her shoulders, revealing the frills of lace along the neckline of her pink sundress. She's so painfully lovely. The smooth lines of her cleavage peek into view anytime she bends forward. My throat dries.

She takes a bite, her full lips curving over the red berry again.

Is that how her mouth would look wrapped around me?

Another ache surges into my cock. I've been at half-mast since we arrived.

"Matthew?"

I pull my eyes to her watchful gaze. "Hmm?"

"Remember Halloween, two years ago, when everyone went to the bar Lily was working at?" She smiles, reminiscing. "You, Ollie, and Robert went as the Ninja Turtles."

"And you went as that sexy pirate."

Her eyes widen. "Oh? A *sexy* pirate?"

"You heard me." There's no use in trying to hide what I said. Molly's leather corset and flowy dress are not something a living, breathing man can forget.

"Are women in costumes the equivalent of men in uniform?" She curves a brow at me.

"A thousand percent," I laugh. "What service attire gets you all worked up?"

Molly glances up at the sky, pretending to ponder the question. "I've always had a thing for park rangers."

"I'll have to see if the parks department will give me an honorary uniform when I launch EcoDrones."

She stretches her legs across the picnic blanket. The hem of her dress hangs mid-thigh. My gaze meanders over the pale skin of her leg.

"And, if your offer still stands, maybe the Damien costume…" She trails off, looking shy.

"As long as I can source a pair of riding leathers." I wink at her.

Her breath hitches, and her eyes dance back and forth along my face. "I'm sad Lily's bar closed last year. We had a lot of fun there, lots of trivia nights," she says.

There used to be some bonding activities at ORO, but once Molly got engaged she stopped showing up to all of them, and so did I. But I've missed those extra moments after work, where we always used to find a way to sit next to each other and laugh.

"There was one trivia night where we danced. It's still one of my favorite memories. Do you remember? When I first started?"

"Yeah…of course I remember." Molly looks at me for a long moment. Her gears are spinning, and I ache to know what she's thinking. "I always wondered what would have happened if we'd kept dancing."

"I'm happy it led us to where we are now."

Her eyes shy away briefly, then return to me. "I actually wanted to kiss you that night."

"Just that night? " I tease, trying to deflect from the tightening in my chest.

"Well…" She bites her bottom lip.

"Because if I wasn't lying to myself, I would tell you that I've thought about kissing you almost every single day since I started at ORO." I denied my crush on her for so long, and there's no use in holding back the truth any longer.

"Oh." The smile on her face widens. Her fingers walk to mine across the checkered fabric. I mirror the motion until our knuckles brush. "Actually, I want to reconsider my earlier decision," she whispers.

My pulse quickens. "About what?"

She bites her lower lip. "Kissing."

"Oh yeah?" My restraint collapses.

"I think so."

Desire returns to my veins. I pull myself closer and settle above her. I place my right hand on her hip and guide her down onto the blanket.

Molly blinks up at me. Her amber gaze is syrupy, the lush curves of her body only inches from my skin. I swallow, trying to calm myself, but it's no use. Gently, I shuffle a hand beneath her head.

The sight of her beneath me rushes over me like a hurricane. The past few years, I've lived my life parched. Ignored the fact that I was barely getting by without quenching this visceral need.

"Are you comfortable?" I whisper against her jaw. My free hand brushes over her neck and down her arm.

"Mhm," Molly moans through a sweet smile.

I want to drown in the sound.

"You look so pretty, darling." I begin the slow journey of kisses down her throat, allowing myself to suffocate in the scent of those damn red ruby apples. My adrenaline spikes. "Constantly, so fucking pretty."

"Matthew." She gulps, breathless.

Is she trying to kill me?

"I'm so lucky."

"Lucky?" Her chest rises and falls beneath me. My nose brushes against hers.

Molly's eyes shine like beacons, guiding me toward her and the promise of something I haven't searched for in a long time.

"To be here with you."

I never want to forget today. Our lips meet again, softly at first, mouths finding each other with a lazy slowness.

Kissing her feels like coming home after a long day, opening the door, and taking in the familiar. It's a safe resignation, a peace that fills every inch of my body. My mind spins with pleasure.

"You're a really good kisser." I smile against her lips. Molly grinds her hips over my thigh. Her tongue lazily brushes over my mouth. I haven't been this hard in years. Possibly ever.

"Am I?"

"Abso-fucking-lutely," I groan.

Maybe I'm not as numb to this devouring desire as I thought.

My palm glides down the curve of her waist, and I hike her closer. Heat dances between us. Her hands rake through my hair. She presses my mouth near hers.

When was the last time I just kissed someone because it felt natural—innate?

Maybe this is what Molly meant when she said she wanted to feel like flying.

She glides her tongue over mine. The sweet taste of her mixes with the citrus in my mouth. Her lips feel pliant under mine, and I savor them, take my time with every taste she gives me.

"Fuck," I breathe. This kiss is nothing like the frenzy in the library or the pounding adrenaline in the pottery studio.

No bumped teeth, no tentative touches.

It's easy. *No*—it's right.

I'm greedy for more. More Molly. My fingers itch to stain every inch of her.

Go slow, man. Take your time. Savor this.

A woman like Molly deserves every second. Every moment that someone didn't give her is mine for safekeeping.

The only thing I can taste, see, or feel is Molly.

A sharp gust of wind strikes at our skin, sending a tremble through her body.

I reluctantly pull away to see her rosy cheeks, swollen lips, and the open neck of her sundress beneath a blue haze. The buttons of my shirt have been undone. Her hair is frizzy from my fingers trailing through the strands. I let my touch linger there. The sight of the silky curls between my calloused fingers sends another spike of need through me.

The world continued spinning without us.

I have no desire to rejoin reality at all.

She giggles, swiping her thumb across my forehead. "You have a little dirt, just right here."

I plant my lips on hers again, savoring the warmth of her mouth. Then I will myself to sit up. "We should get going before it gets too dark."

The sky is a riot of dull blues and purples, with the last few rays of sunlight casting long shadows across the canyon floor.

"Thank you for such a lovely rendezvous." Molly bats her lashes at me, and I help her up, lifting her to my chest.

"My pleasure."

———

As we arrive back at the stables, the sky is peppered with glistening stars.

These last two weeks have been the first time in a long time I felt alive. *Truly alive.*

"I'm gonna give Honey a little snack, and then we can head back to our suite," she says nervously, walking the mare to her stall. "I really need to take a shower; I feel like I'm drowning in dust." Molly shakes out her hair, and red sprinkles collapse from the tresses.

I want to invite myself in the shower with her, but I smother the idea. "I'll meet you up front."

I carefully place my saddle next to the one I already took off her horse.

My thoughts refuse to cool. I'm already counting down the minutes until I can touch her again. Cover her body with slow, agonizing strokes. Listen to her hypnotic laughter and moans because of something I'm doing.

Molly's like a damn battery, charging me up.

Sure, our time at On Cloud Nine is ending, but we'll still have to be around each other when we're married. Hopefully?

Take it easy, man.

As much as I want to feel her mouth again—or, let's be honest, make her come with my fingers, my tongue, and my cock —Molly's calling the shots here.

She wasn't even given the gift of picking out her own wedding dress. I'm not going to trample over this situation. Until

Molly tells me she wants more than just kissing, that she wants to cry out my name until her voice goes hoarse, I'll practice every ounce of restraint I can muster.

"*Ahh!*" Molly's scream pierces through the barn.

Something in my chest collapses. I sprint toward her.

"What's wrong? Are you hurt?" I shout. She's sitting on a smattering of hay on the barn floor. "Molly?"

"Ow!" She winces as she grasps her right hand with her left. A thick tear slides down her face.

She's injured.

"What happened?" I drop to my knees beside her and carefully reach for her hands.

"It's nothing. I'm fine." Molly tries to put on a strong face. I despise the wall she still tries to shield herself with, especially after today. "I slammed my hand in the stall door. It was an accident."

"Can you show me?" She nods and gives me her palm. She bites her lip as I inspect the damage, but she doesn't flinch. Her knuckles are scraped raw and red. "It doesn't seem to be broken or fractured. I bet the impact was painful. Let's head back to our suite and get you some ice."

Instead of responding, she sneezes once, then again. Her eyes begin to water. Of course; she's sitting on the hay.

I need to get her out of the stables. Full-on evacuation mode.

My lips leave a soft kiss on her forehead. Without another word, I lift her up into my arms. Her body is small against my chest. I hold her tightly.

"What are you doing?" Molly gives me a hesitant look but relaxes in my embrace.

"Just let me take care of you, okay?"

"Okay." She hides her face in the crook of my neck.

"Damien would never let Serienna walk back to camp after being injured."

Her eyes find mine again. "Well, in that case, thank you for my rescue."

"You got it, little warrior."

Molly slowly runs her bruised hand across my chest, trailing through the hair there. A smile breaks through her teary face.

There she is.

Chapter 17
Molly

My hair isn't even that dirty.

I shiver and sneeze again. Who am I kidding. There's probably a pound of dust, hay, and maybe even tiny bugs making a home between my curls.

Okay, no, I can't skip a shower, but my hand is about as useful as a piece of overcooked spaghetti.

There's no way I'll be able to unzip my dress and wash my hair…alone. I eye the bathroom door, peeking beneath the crack at the bottom.

Matthew's footsteps pace outside.

I got to kiss him again! A giggle slips out of me, and my good hand flies to my mouth to stifle it. As much as my knuckles still ache, I'm thankful for being klutzy for the first time in my life. It's as if all those years of needless bumps and bruises finally amounted to something useful.

Matthew carried me, actually carried me, and he got all *who hurt you*. The reaction almost made me want to slam my other hand in the horse stall door and walk around with blown-up pasta fingers for the rest of our trip.

I'm still giddy. Over-the-moon giddy. No, better—I'm flying-on-the-back-of-a-griffin giddy.

When we got back to our suite, Matthew gave me a glass of water, an anti-inflammatory, and an antihistamine before I locked myself in our bathroom, insisting I was fine. But, really, I've never been cared for with such affection.

I want more of it.

More.

Matthew could've stripped me out of my sundress and ravaged me right beside the horses, hay allergy and all. Or, better yet, in the canyons.

I've never wanted to endure the embarrassment of indecent exposure until today. Is that what falling in love means? Risking it all just to run your hands through a man's chest hair?

Wait, *love*?

No, it must be lust. A feeling I'm not acquainted with. But being kissed for that long was my deepest fantasy come to life.

I can't help but recall his promise to take his time with me—well, with someone—when we participated in the Yearning Yoga activity.

Could Matthew take me to that place I've never been with anyone else?

Oh boy.

I turn on the faucet, filling up the spacious soaking tub, which is big enough for two people. I eye the showerhead, then the door again.

"Are you sure I can't help you?" Matthew asks. It's as if he has x-ray vision, or he can read my mind from the other room.

I hesitate for a moment, unsure whether to take his offer or struggle through the task on my own.

Maybe I can cut open my dress?

But I don't want to ruin one of my favorite Rodarte pieces. Especially when all I want to do with this thing is put it behind glass and frame it in my closet so I can remember today forever.

I groan loudly.

"Molly?" Matthew's voice is filled with concern.

Despite my reservations, I want to go farther with him. It'll probably make everything between us so messy. But my life's always been complicated.

What's one more thing to add to the list?

I inhale, channeling every ounce of bravery.

"Actually, I've changed my mind." I swing open the door.

"What can I do?"

"I need to get my dress off," I say confidently.

"Your dress?" He hovers in the doorway. I walk closer to the tub, turn off the water, and add in a dollop of bubble bath.

"Well, I…I don't think I can bathe with it on," I whisper.

"Of course not." His gaze is enveloped in darkness, the way it has been each time we've kissed. "Turn around for me, please."

Doing as he says, I face the bathroom mirror. He stands behind me with a hesitant gentleness. I can practically taste the blood beating in my heart.

A part of me wishes he'd snap.

Could I even make a man like him lose control?

In the reflection of the mirror, I watch as his fingers brush across the nape of my neck, gathering all my hair and moving it to the side. The sensation is electric. My core thrums with need, warm and seething.

"Is this alright?"

"Mhm." I nod.

My breath hitches when he tugs down the zipper of my dress. My vertebrae tremble.

His movements are slow and deliberate, as if he's savoring it. He slides the sleeves off my shoulders, and I suck in a breath.

The cotton is flimsy beneath his strong hands; the dress barely holds on to me. With the small movement of my inhale, it collapses to the tile floor.

Matthew lets out a heavy sigh and politely averts his gaze from the mirror. But I have no interest in him being a gentleman tonight.

No. Whatever has suddenly possessed me, I want him to do what he promised.

Because if I were in their shoes, I'd work tirelessly to show you colors you'd only see while you're with me.

I want to see the kaleidoscope of hues only he can show me.

"Matthew?" I say with a trembling voice. His eyes catch mine in the mirror. He looks primal. Predatory, almost. Then his focus slips onto the red, lacy lingerie still hugging my curves. Maybe it wasn't so bad that all my favorite pieces ended up in my suitcase.

"Yes, darling?" His tone is low and strained.

"I…I think I'm also going to need some help washing my hair."

I'm someone else, someone fearless—a woman who takes what she wants.

"Then we should remove this." He runs the pad of his thumb across the right strap of my bra.

My throat dries. "Please."

I tense, feeling myself grow wetter by the minute. I almost roll my hips back into him, curious to see if he's getting as turned on as I am.

He unclasps my bra, and the straps slip off my shoulders, leaving me in nothing but the shorts I wore under my dress. His eyes hungrily take in every inch of my exposed breasts.

I feel beautiful, vulnerable, and desirable.

I've never felt sexy before. But now, with him drinking me in, I'm every definition of the word. I'm sure of it.

He leans in close, pressing his body into me as his lips hover over my ear. "It's actually unfair how fucking perfect you are."

I swallow hard. His arousal presses against the dip of my lower back.

I am his, completely and utterly. I know he feels it.

Matthew's fingers hook into the waistband of the boy shorts I had on under my dress. I hold my breath as he pulls them down, revealing my panties.

"Thank you," I say. He helps me step out of them.

"No, Molly; thank *you*." His fingers trail up the backs of my thighs, over my hips, and up to my chest.

Oh my god.

He cups my breasts, softly kneading them. He pulls me closer, connecting my spine with his chest. He takes my nipples between his index and middle fingers, pinching them until they're stiff and aching.

My cheeks heat.

I'm on the edge with just a touch. *No way.*

Matthew's free hand slithers down the slope of my stomach until it reaches the waistband of my panties.

"How's your other hand feeling?"

"It's perfectly fine."

"Are you able to use it to take these off for me?" Matthew says in a voice I don't recognize. Thick and commanding, loaded with a charge I want to be on the receiving end of. "I want to watch."

I use my good hand to trace the lines on his skin. The ones with a decade more of experience than I have. Sure, ten years isn't much, but our age difference has never felt as apparent to me as it does now. I like it. He makes me feel cared for and safe.

Even if nothing happens, even if I can't quite get to *that* place with him, I ache for him to run the callouses on his knuckles over my skin. It'll be enough.

I slowly glide my panties down beneath his watchful, virile gaze. The act is making me all sorts of shy. I need to get into the tub as soon as possible before my whole body turns red from holding my breath.

"Fuck, Molly." He wraps his arm tighter around my waist,

pulling my naked body against his jeans. The rough, dust covered fabric feels like a livewire against my thighs. "You're gonna have to get in that bath before I lose my mind."

I smile. Guess he *can* read my thoughts.

As I sink into the tub, foamy water coats my skin, hitting the tops of my breasts. Matthew white-knuckles the countertop, his head tilted toward the floor. He looks as if he's as close to shattering every sense of control as I am.

He slowly turns and strolls over to me, grabbing the showerhead. I want to see more of him.

"Um," I begin.

"Yes?"

I play around with the words in my mind. "You might want to remove your shirt. So it doesn't get wet."

"We wouldn't want that, now would we?" His smile curls mischievously, and I light up again.

"No." I shake my head. My pulse violently slams against my throat. I can't believe I'm saying every thought I'm having out loud.

Matthew stands, his white linen shirt clinging to his skin, tufts of chest hair poking out. He gives me a sultry grin and slowly flicks open the buttons, exposing more and more of his tanned torso. I'm in awe.

He tugs his shirt off, sending it to the ground while revealing his lean, muscular build.

"How's that?"

"Better," I croak.

"I'll start slow." He kneels beside me, grabbing the showerhead again. "Just let me know if I'm doing this right. Can you do that for me?"

I almost yell, *You could do anything, absolutely anything you want to me!* But I focus my eyes back onto the bubbly surface of the water. "I will."

He turns on the water again, waiting for it to warm. Then he gently places the metal of the showerhead along my scalp. The stream cascades down my hair and over my shoulders. Matthew's fingers glide through my strands, gently massaging my scalp with every stroke.

The sensation is pure ecstasy. The stress and tension of the past couple of weeks wash away under his capable hands.

"You like that, baby?"

Baby. Oh god. My breathing is going to give out. "A lot."

"Good." I close my eyes and let out a moan, lost beneath the feel of his fingers. "Should I use this moisturizing shampoo, or the co-wash?"

Yeah. That about does it. A gorgeous man, rough and rugged, shirtless beside me, is asking about my curl care.

"The shampoo is fine, followed by the deep conditioner. *Please*."

"Perfect." The shampoo bottle squirts, and then his fingers return. He takes his time, working his way through every strand. "You know, I don't think I ever told you, but your hair was one of the first things I noticed about you. All these beautiful curls, like wildflowers tied together with lace."

I swallow. Hard.

My heart melts in my chest. Actually melts, I'm certain of it. Instinctively, I reach for my hair, feeling a little bashful again, but he gently guides my hand back into the water.

"They have a mind of their own," I say with a soft laugh.

"They're rather lovely, Molly."

Matthew rinses out the shampoo and then kisses me on the forehead. He holsters the showerhead and rummages around with another bottle before returning to my scalp.

Getting my hair washed by him is now my favorite thing in the world.

"Still feel good?" he asks, massaging my neck.

"Very." I inhale, sinking deeper into the tub. "Very nice."

"Can I make you feel any better?"

Yes. One hundred percent. I beg of you.

But the words don't come easily. Instead, I press my face against his muscular bicep. "Kiss me?"

He rinses his hands, tilts my jaw, and connects our lips. Even though it's only been a few hours since we last kissed, this one is just as passionate. He breaches the surface of my lips with his tongue, feasting on me.

My core pulses.

"I want you to touch me," I breathe against his lips.

He pulls away from our kiss. "How?" His voice is low and husky

"I—" I try, but my mind is melting.

"Tell me what you want, darling, and I'll give you everything."

"I want you to…" My feet slither down the base of the tub, and I part my knees. "Run your hands over my breasts again, like before."

He smirks. "Did it turn you on when I played with your nipples after I undressed you?"

A flare of embarrassment comes again. Those words. So blunt and tantalizing. "Yes," I manage.

He reaches for my breasts, somehow fitting them both into one of his strong hands. The weight of his possessive grip makes me want more. My stiff peaks ache beneath his touch as he kneads the soft flesh. The whisper of release echoes through my body.

Oh my, is he going to be able to make me come?

"Feels good, doesn't it, beautiful?" he murmurs, and I nod.

Matthew lets go of me, picks up the showerhead, and turns on the stream. The water cools the back of my neck, spilling over my chest. I nod some more because I'm unable to form words.

He returns to my breasts, his fingers teasing each nipple with slow, deliberate circles. The bath water sloshes as I lean back into his embrace, completely consumed with the pleasure spinning through me.

"I love making you feel like this." He moves in closer, his lips just inches from my jaw. "You're so magnificent, Molly, so responsive to me. I can feel you getting turned on just from my touch."

I moan. My body is on fire. His technique on my nipples becomes more deliberate, intense. I'm about to explode with pleasure.

Orgasming from a touch to your breasts? Can't be possible.

And then, just when it's all too much, Matthew stops, pulling away from me.

"Have you used this showerhead to make yourself come before?"

I can't even comprehend what he's asking. I need him to touch me again. "I—maybe. I…no, I have."

"What did you think about when you did?"

You. My heart races, and my toes curl.

"Th-the way it would feel to kiss you," I stutter.

"I love kissing you." Matthew breathes on the side of my neck. "What else?"

"Your touch," I moan. "I thought about what it would feel like to be touched by you."

"Where?"

My mind is vibrating in my skull. I'm having an entire out-of-body experience.

"Down my body." I force the words out. Matthew moves the showerhead over my chest. The stream is another overwhelming sensation over the heat pooling in my breasts.

"How low?"

I gulp. My thoughts are beginning to fade in and out of consciousness. *What is happening?* It's like I've collapsed into another dimension of all-consuming pleasure.

"All the way."

He submerges his hand with the showerhead. The stream runs over my stomach until it hits my navel.

"I want to see what you look like when you fall apart, Molly. Does that sound like something you'd like to show me?"

I nod eagerly.

"Words, my darling girl. You're going to need to keep using them with me."

"Yes, I want to show you."

He smiles, moving his hand lower and lower. My legs easily part for him. The stream of water hits my clit, and I gasp, my eyes still locked onto his.

"That's it, baby," he whispers, his other hand working my nipples. "Let me make your pretty pussy feel good."

I would let him do whatever he wants with me. That reality is startling.

The position we're in makes it easy for my head to fall against one of his arms. He's so large compared to me, and I'm happy to drown in his embrace.

Matthew keeps teasing me until I'm panting and gasping for air again. His touch, the showerhead. The water is warm, and the sensation is so intense. I'm losing all of my control. Every nerve buzzes with pleasure as he guides me to the edge. The edge I haven't walked with anyone before.

Well, I suppose right now, I'm running.

"Matthew," I moan through a heavy breath.

"You love it when I do this, don't you?"

My back arches. There's no way I'm going to climax. My body tenses up as my mind spins. The hum in my core skips a step. I'm not ready. *Am I? Is this too soon?* Nerves tickle up my chest, and I feel that reluctance start to flee.

"Eyes over here, baby," he urges, as if sensing my wandering thoughts. "Come back to me." I blink, finding my way to his gaze. "Good girl, Molly."

The hand on my breasts leaves and travels down my body until it kneads my inner thighs.

"I want to taste how wet your pussy is; I bet it's as sweet as your lips." His fingers inch closer to my aching clit. "Making you feel this good gets me so turned on."

"Please, I want more, more of you," I gasp. Matthew returns the stream to the spot right between my thighs, and then he places two fingers over my clit.

I buck my hips. *Oh wow. That's a lot. Too much.*

"Mmm," I sigh.

With slow, deliberate circles, he teases the swollen ache, awakening me once more. I've wanted this for weeks. Needed him so badly it hurt. My moans escape more quickly now. His fingers and the beating water are ecstasy.

He gradually picks up the pace. "You're so fucking sexy, Molly. Dammit," he growls. His hot breath heats my damp skin. "I love the way you react to my touch."

"D-don't stop." It feels like we've been here for hours, and I'm selfishly taking up every moment of time he seems eager to give me.

"This is mine now, right?" His fingers break their pace on my clit and press at my entrance.

"It is." I brush my face against his stubble. "I—I am." I barely notice the words coming out of me.

Matthew pushes a finger into me and holds the steady stream above my clit. My body was on fire before, but now it's a full-on inferno.

He inserts another finger. I feel so full, so fast.

"So tight. Fuck, baby. Your pussy feels so good around my fingers." My hips grind against his hand. I'm desperately craving more. He moves in and out of me with a steady rhythm. "I fit so well, don't I?" His voice drips with desire. "I've thought about this before, so many years ago, darling. But feeling your needy cunt is so much better than I imagined."

He plunges deeper, curling his fingers inside of me. They brush over my most sensitive spot.

Over and over.

He's thought about this before. *Years ago*. He's wanted this as much as I have. The pleasure is so intense, my mind goes blank again. It's just his touch and my heartbeat occupying every realm of my being.

I teeter on the edge for too long, but Matthew works me without a break, keeping his promise. My mouth is dropped open, my eyes on him. The fullness of him inside of me refuses to slow. The showerhead rushes against my swollen clit.

A drop of sweat falls off his forehead and onto my face.

It's so fucking erotic.

Abruptly, my orgasm rushes me off the edge. I'm barely able to understand what is happening as a storm deepens inside of me. My body explodes with pleasure as my walls pulsate around him.

"Matthew!" I scream, my toes curling, my fingers sinking into the arm wrapped around me. The pain in my hand vanishes, and the only thing I can feel are stars bursting inside of my skin.

"There you are, beautiful. I've got you baby. I've got you." His rich chuckle snakes over me. My hips buck, grinding over his thick digits. It seems to last forever.

The climax is so strong, I fear I'm moments away from cardiac arrest.

As I come down from my high, Matthew turns off the water. He doesn't remove the arm I'm clinging to, but he straightens his legs, and I lean back to rest on his chest. My vision is still blurry from the orgasm.

I peel open my lids to find him sitting in the tub with me, his jeans soaking up the suds.

Oh no.

"Your—" I begin, but he gives me a small shake of his head.

"Relax," he says in a quiet voice. "I just want to feel you

close." He turns me on my side, and I rest my cheek on his chest. The hummingbird rhythm of my heartbeat slows, and I nuzzle closer, melting beneath the possessive weight of his arms.

This doesn't compare to anything I've ever felt.

It's like being wrapped in a warm blanket on a cold night, or like feeling the sun on my face after a long, dark winter. Complete, like I belong. I'm exactly where I'm meant to be.

No matter what the future holds for us, our fake relationship or our pretend marriage, I'll always treasure the first time I felt like myself, wholly and truly.

Chapter 18
Matthew

MY MIND IS OCCUPIED with Molly. Everything she does, each subtle smile and glance over her shoulder has left me entirely shattered. I'm certain that watching her fall apart in my arms yesterday hasn't helped. There's also the fact that I about lost it this morning when we played a romantic version of Scrabble instead of our regularly scheduled activity, and Molly pulled out the word *concupiscence*.

Seriously. What starved man doesn't want to pin a gorgeous woman with a good vocabulary against their bed?

Not me. I'm the starved man.

But we made it. It's our last day at On Cloud Nine. Our last activity before we meet with Molly's parents.

At this time next month, she may be my wife.

A grin stretches across my face.

Lolita had us clear our afternoon to trial another new activity at the resort. Molly's panting a few stairs ahead of me, and the metal spiral staircase clanks with each step. We're in a greenhouse a mile from the main property. Dozens of variations of pothos, snake plants, and flowering birds-of-paradise litter the tables below us.

"What exactly are we doing today?" Molly's wearing a short dress, and every step exposes more of the dimpled flesh on her upper thighs. I want to sink my teeth into her, nibble at the notches in her skin until she's covered in my bite marks.

Christ.

"Painting." Lolita parrots the vague response she gave us in the golf cart over here.

Molly shoots me a confused look. Her nose wrinkles adorably.

We step onto the second floor and pass through a door that leads to an expansive art studio. Canvases of all shapes and sizes clutter the walls and floors. The shelves bend underneath the overflow of brushes, paint, and books.

 On the southern side, large windows start from the floor and extend to the skylight. The view outside is wondrous. The oranges and reds of the canyons blend into the colors of the sky.

Molly's hair is like a flame in the light. Amber eyes turning golden. She's breathtaking. While she's captivated by the view, I pull out my phone and snap a few photos of her. I want to remember today.

"Lolita, what is all of this? I'm pretty sure this isn't part of the program."

"Consider this painting activity a small gift before your departure. Therapeutic arts are my specialty, and I know you enjoy playing with colors." Ms. Deveaux gives me a knowing wink. "You'll find several tubs of nontoxic, body safe paint, as well as brushes, easels, and anything you may need for a very *enjoyable* afternoon."

Molly scans the supplies laid out on a large, paint-splattered, wooden table. Two chairs sit at opposite ends. Near the door, there are pillows and candles next to a jug of water, fresh fruit, and mini sandwiches.

The vats of paint are massive. There are so many colors. Molly's gaze is lush with excitement as she takes a seat.

This looks like it's going to be a lot of fun.

"What do we have to paint?"

"Anything you want, dear." Lolita spins on her feet. "Just have fun. Let your inhibitions loose, and sink into the sensations of your surroundings. I'll leave the golf cart so you can get back to the resort. Enjoy your last night at On Cloud Nine, lovebirds."

When she's gone, I sit at the main table, joining Molly.

Her eyes are glued to the sky. *What is she thinking?*

I've struggled to decipher the roller coaster of mixed signals from her. One moment, we're laughing, our lips almost touching. The next, it's as if she's willing herself to pull away.

Our horseback riding date was perfect. Watching her fall apart in my hands yesterday evening was one of the best experiences I've ever had. It's a damn shame no one's taken the time to watch her flourish. She's a wet dream and so incredibly unaware of how fucking sexy she is.

I'm certain that her parents' ruling in a couple of hours is weighing heavily on her. I want to distract her. To give her a break from her mind.

Molly shatters the silence. "Maybe we can do one of those splatter paintings."

"Splatter paintings? Like Mia did in *The Princess Diaries*?"

"Did *The Princess Diaries* make it onto your list of romance classics?" Molly props her feet on the chair, hugging her knees into her chest. Her dress cascades around her thighs, revealing a sliver of her lace panties.

My cock twitches against my trousers.

"'You saw me when I was invisible.'" I quote Mia Thermopolis.

"I love that part." She lights up. "Do you think Lolita will be upset if we get paint everywhere?"

Colors flake off the wood, the floors. There are even specks on the windows. "Art studios are supposed to be stained. Gives them more character. We'll be adding a piece of ourselves here."

"We can set up a canvas over there." Molly points and gives me a smile. There's an area toward the back of the room that's covered in plastic.

All I want to do is give her the freedom to let loose, a space to take control like she did in the bath.

Her parted lips, her reddened cheeks, her wide eyes locked on mine as I made her scream. *Damn*. I'm fucking hard again. Jerking off in the shower is nothing compared to the way it felt when my fingers were inside of her.

I'm starting to become some kind of obsessed servant. Wanting to care for her, give to her, and hold her in a way that makes our relationship feel real.

I need Molly.

"Great spot; I'll set it up." I do as promised, hanging up the canvas as her watchful gaze remains on me.

"I'm reconsidering the whole splatter idea," she laughs. "What if it looks like blobs of nothing?"

"Come on, you can blame any parts you don't like on me." I'd happily take the burden of being perfect off of her.

"Okay."

"What color should we start with?" I follow her to the tubs of paint. "Since you're the expert."

"Are you sure you don't want to take the lead?"

Fucking hell.

If I were taking the lead, she'd be in my lap, her delicious ass bouncing against my thighs. Then she'd be on the table, letting me taste her.

I clear my throat, trying to adjust myself in my trousers. "No, please, go ahead."

She grabs a brush from a glass jar, tracing her fingers over the bristles. With a sharp, metallic pop, she lifts the lid from a paint can, revealing the gooey paint within. "What do you think of this one?"

"Red?"

"It's crimson," she clarifies.

"It's great." I run my hand along the cool metal tubs. "Whatever you want is great."

Molly gets quiet, staring down at the paints. Then she rolls her shoulders back and flashes me a smile.

"You know what?" she says, and her entire demeanor shifts. "You're right. It's our last night here. I want to make a mess."

"Me too."

Molly gathers the colors like they're speaking to her.

A carnal hunger fills my veins. She's a work of art, every curve and contour perfectly sculpted. She bends over slowly, and her dress lifts. I should look away, but I can't help myself. Her lace panties stretch tight across her skin, outlining the lush curve of her ass.

The need to lay her on this table and hear her moan my name again is overwhelming. Or scream it. Growl it. Anything.

I'm a wild animal, imagining all the ways I want to touch and taste her.

Take her. Possess her.

"I'd like these." Molly opens her arms over the tubs of paint she's arranged, showing off a rainbow of saturated pinks, purples, reds, oranges, and yellows. "They'll look like the sky here, and I'd love to remember it."

"Great idea." I grab two cans and make my way to the canvas I set up. Molly follows me, a tub of paint in one arm as she drags a chair with the other. "Hey, hey." I rush to seize the chair and paint cans from her. "Don't you worry about a single thing. Let me take care of this."

"Thank you." She runs her hand across her forehead. We settle the tubs on the ground and open them. Molly passes me a brush. "What now?"

"Let's jump off the deep end together." I dip a brush into the vat of purple. "Here." We share the brush, our fingers locked around the handle. Globs of color drop onto the floor. My free palm rests on the curve of her lower back.

As her brows lift, she gives me a sweet, innocent look that's hard to resist. "We're doing this? Just going for it?"

"Count us down, darling."

She nods. "One, two, three." We lift our arms and flick our wrists, sending a spray of color across the canvas. "Okay, so fun."

An orchestra of giggles, breaths, and snorts pours out of her. My chest warms.

Over the years, I've become an expert in making her laugh, even during casual office conversations that seemed insignificant. It's a gift I haven't fully appreciated until this moment.

She hands me a brush drenched in red paint.

"Ready?" Her pupils widen.

For the next hour, our movements synchronize as we toss paint onto the canvas, watching colors blend and mix, creating new shades and patterns. Paint stains our skin, Molly's dress, and my pants.

It's beautiful, the picture we're creating together. I'll have to ask Lolita to ship it to me when it's dry. I want to hang it in my house, above the mantel of my fireplace. Or maybe I can give it to Molly as a parting gift after we split her trust. The thought dims my mood slightly.

Suddenly, Molly grabs one of the half-empty vats, cradling it in her arms.

"What's your plan for that?" I ask, setting my brush down.

"The big finale." Mischief swims in her eyes. "It's your turn to count me off, Mr. Hudson," she says in a playful tone. Her posture is that of an Olympic diver.

"One, two…" She drags the tub over her head and, in one fell swoop, tosses it to the canvas. "Three."

Bright crimson paint splashes everywhere, seeping into the canvas, staining the plastic, and drenching my shirt.

Molly turns to me, and her eyes widen. Her laughter ceases. "Oh no. I'm so, so, so, sorry!" She speeds over to me, swiping at the paint on my chest.

"Hey, it's okay." I guide her hands into mine. The paint is tacky between our fingers. "We're making a mess, remember?" I tap her nose, leaving behind a splotch of color. "Now we match."

"Well, in that case." She pushes up onto her tiptoes and trails her paint-covered touch along my brow. Then she bolts for a brush.

"You're not getting off so easily." I sprint after her, but she's quicker, darting around the room.

"I'm not sure if you can keep up with me," she teases. Blue paint from the brush she's holding drips down her legs.

I dip my finger into a vat of yellow and flick it at her. Molly shrieks, swatting her own brush in retaliation. Blue paint hits my arm. My button-down clings to me.

"Alright, that's how we're gonna do this?" I yank off my shirt. Molly halts, her eyes glued to my chest.

She notices me watching her and then whisks her brush again. Sticky paint coats my torso.

I snatch my brush and run toward her.

"No, no, no!" Molly yelps and rushes behind the table, leaving paint in her wake.

"Playing dirty, huh?" I dip the brush into the pink. When I dart left, she speeds right. "Really, darling, you're going to make me chase you?"

We move like pieces on a chessboard, soaking each other in colors.

"Only if you can keep up." She laughs. "Are you having fun?"

"Molly." I land a shot on her exposed shoulder. "I never want this day to end."

"Me either." She stills behind the table and pops her hip, holding the brush out nonchalantly. "But maybe we should call a truce?"

"I didn't realize you were ready to give up so easily."

I stroll around the table. Molly doesn't try to run.

"I'm beginning to feel bad for you," she says, nodding toward my chest. My torso looks like a Pollock painting.

"You've got quite an arm."

"It's all the yoga we've been doing." She flashes her paint-splattered biceps.

In a breath, I'm beside her.

Her skin is a canvas of colors, from shades of pink to bright bursts of orange. And her lips—*damn*, her lips. Plush and aching to be kissed, tasted, loved. I tower over her, wanting nothing more than to lean down and claim her.

"Our masterpiece is missing one small thing." We're so close. A brief movement of my fingers, and I could be beneath the hem of her dress.

"What's that?"

She grips my hand. My heart thuds. With a few swift flicks, she paints *M.G.* onto my palm. "A painting is not complete without a monogram."

"May I?"

"It's only right."

I lift her hand and mimic the motion. Her eyes trace over my initials, *M.H.*, on her hand.

Our palms face upward, and a bond to her fills my chest. My pulse pounds erratically.

M.H. M.G.

Molly left her mark on me, in more ways than just this paint. She reminds me of everything I've ever loved, of home. I shouldn't feel like this. We said we didn't want our relationship to turn complicated.

But it already has. There's no way I can go back to

pretending that what's unfolding between us means nothing.

I don't want to be like everyone else in her life, trying to take from her and control her. I want to build our connection based on mutual trust and respect. Molly deserves someone who gives her space to shine and blossom. Who makes her feel safe. I want to try to be that man for her.

Can I be?

Surely, she's meant to have that with someone she can start a family with. I can't take up only a piece of her heart, nor do I want to give her the broken fragments of myself.

But perhaps it wouldn't hurt to keep pretending for one last night.

"You don't even mean to torment me, do you?" I whisper.

"I torment you?"

"Molly, you've infiltrated my thoughts." I place a soft kiss on her knuckles.

"I think about you too, so much." Her voice trembles.

"Tell me, baby." My hands wrap around her petite waist, and I lift her onto the table. "I want to know everything in that pretty head of yours. Every thought, every feeling, and every fantasy. I want it."

"Take it, Matthew." Molly slings her arms around my neck, spreading her knees and pulling me toward her. "You can have everything."

Her thighs hook around my hips. "When you say things like that, beautiful, I'm not sure you know what you're asking for." I breathe into the crook of her neck, my hands sliding into her hair, across her skin.

"Then show me. Teach it to me."

Those words are like solving the last crossword clue. *Relief.*

I lean and kiss her. Her breath is sweet, her mouth hot.

Molly arches her back, pressing her breasts against my chest.

"I need you," I admit, covering her paint-splattered jaw with my lips. My left hand cups her breast, kneading the tender flesh beneath the fabric of her dress.

"Then, p-please," she moans, pushing her hips into me and fumbling for the clasp of my belt.

"Be patient." I kiss her neck. "I've thought about this for so long. I'm going to savor every second of you."

Molly's gaze is drunk with desire, and I know exactly what to do to make her melt beneath me.

I just want her. Not to think about tonight, or tomorrow, or any fucking day I have to spend without her.

Molly gasps as I pull her closer and settle her perfect ass on the edge of the table.

"I'm going to savor this pussy until I get my fill. Is that okay, darling?"

"Mhm." She nods, sending both of her palms back onto the table.

My right hand slides down her thigh, hovering at the edge of her dress. There's no going back.

Molly. Molly. Molly.

I kneel, and my pulse increases as I slowly push my hands up her dress.

"Have you thought about what it would be like for me to have a taste?"

"Yes." She moans, biting her lip. I tug at the waistband of her panties, remove them, and drop them to the floor. Her amber irises flare. "But wait." Her cheeks flush. "I've never—"

My cock surges against my pants. "Am I the first man to devour you, Molly?" She nods, sending her face onto her shoulder with a bashful squirm. "Don't be timid, baby." It's adorable, but it won't do. "Don't hide how fucking divine you are."

"I—I won't, I promise." She spreads her legs. There's no way I'm going to last long once I get inside of her. Hell, I want to come right now with her splayed out like this for me.

I lift the hem of her dress over her thighs. Waiting for me is her wet, gorgeous cunt. I spot a towel on the table and grab it, wiping my fingers clean.

"Fuuuck," I groan into her thigh. "Perfect, so damn perfect." Molly's chin connects with her shoulders as she shies away again. "Keep your attention here, okay?" I rub my clean thumb gently across her leg. "I'm going to take you, baby. Fuck you with my tongue and fingers until you drown me."

"O-okay."

I brush my tongue along her, tasting the salty slickness already waiting there. "And I will not be polite about it, beautiful."

She nods. "Mhm."

"But if there's anything else you'd like me to do to you, all you have to do is ask. Can we agree to that?"

Another teasing kiss from me. Another shallow moan.

"Yes." Her voice quavers. She white-knuckles the edge of the table.

I start with slow, teasing licks across her swollen clit. Molly's body vibrates. I rub her hardened nipples through her dress.

She tastes like she was made for me. I drag my tongue across her entrance, and Molly shakes, her fingers raking through my hair. Her body tenses.

"Ride my face, darling; don't be shy," I say, and she does, gripping my head harder and grinding herself over my lips.

All I see is red. The color of her hair, the tone of her lips, her blush, her cheeks. All I smell, taste, and feel is Molly.

I want to fill every fucking inch of her tight, delicious pussy until her mind's lost somewhere between climax and heaven.

Her body convulses, and the amber of her eyes vanishes behind her lids.

"I—uh—I," she attempts through gasps. "I'm—need more. Please."

I can't resist. I slip one of my fingers inside of her. She

writhes beneath me as I keep a steady pace.

"Yes. Yes, more," she begs, and I oblige.

My tongue traces circles across her swollen clit, and I push another finger into her. The fullness causes her body to tremble harder. Her gasps grow heavier, more erratic. Her walls pulse around me.

I latch onto her as if my life depends on it. The edges of my vision blur.

My cock throbs painfully in my trousers, but I don't hold back. Not a single break.

I keep my movements deliberate, mimicking the motions in the bath that kept her present. With my free hand, I pull off her sandals and prop her feet onto my shoulders, deepening the motions of my fingers inside of her.

I could spend the rest of my life on my knees in front of her.

"Oh." Molly groans, easing her forceful grip. "I—I lost it." Her face scrunches.

"Hey, that's okay." I stand.

"This is what I was talking about. Sometimes it—" She frowns and shrinks.

"Molly, darling." I bracket her jaw. "We're in no rush. You lost it? I'll find it. What would feel good?"

She furrows her brow, deep in thought, then blurts out, "Kiss me."

"I'd love to." I smile. I go to wipe the wetness of her pussy off my chin, but Molly catches my hand.

"No, don't," she whispers, eyes dark beneath her lashes. "I want, um, everything."

Oh fuck. This woman will be the death of me.

"Anything, baby. Anything you want."

Our lips lock again. The kiss is slower, deeper than the last one. My tongue breaks the seam of her mouth. I drown in the taste of her tongue and pussy on my lips.

Marvelous. There's no better word to describe her.

Molly is a marvel.

"You, now," Molly says against my lips. She pulls at my belt. The clink of metal rattles as the buckle comes undone, followed by the soft sound of the button and zipper being released.

There's no way this is happening.

"Are you sure?" I pull back, holding her face with both of my hands. "I don't have a condom."

"Yes, so sure." She nods. "I—I'm on the pill and, um, tested clear."

My entire body goes rigid. My balls ache.

I can't remember the last time I finished inside of a woman. I want to explain everything to her. How it wouldn't matter if she wasn't on the pill. But Molly's fingers push past my boxers.

Later. I'll tell her soon.

"I'm clear too." I connect my forehead to hers. "I'm one lucky bastard, Molly. I don't deserve this."

"You do. You deserve me. I deserve you."

And I foolishly believe her. Maybe I am worthy of a woman like her.

My pants and boxers drop to my ankles. My cock springs out between us.

Molly's eyes widen. "Oh, wow." Her voice is a soft giggle. "You're, uh, very thick…um, and big."

I break.

"C'mon, darling, let's see how much of it you can handle." I give her a wicked smirk.

Molly's gaze is full of lust as she falls back, her forearms meeting the table, her knees curling up. Her glistening cunt exposed to me.

Yeah. Lucky, *lucky* bastard. Whatever I've done in my past lives, I must've paid penance repeatedly.

"Open up, baby girl." I center the swollen tip of my cock at her entrance. Fuck. Even a small touch feels so right. "I'm going to show you how a man takes his time."

Chapter 19
Molly

I'VE BEEN SOARING for hours, balancing between the point of shattering and passing out, because there's no way oxygen is actually circulating inside of me anymore. I melt beneath Matthew's touch on my skin.

He devoured me. I didn't think it was possible. He absolutely, positively, in every definition of the word, *devoured* me. My insides are still scorched from the way he fucked me with his fingers. Then there's the taste of myself on my own lips, mixing with him.

I'd never had anything like it. Never let myself indulge in an experience that felt so…filthy and yet so right.

"I'm ready." I inhale as his tip presses at my entrance. My body hums with anticipation, to be taken by him, to give myself over. I want him so much.

His blue eyes are drenched in darkness.

He's all man. The paint across his chest, the purple above his brow. Matthew's hair is slicked back with sweat as the tight rods of his muscles envelop me.

He pushes himself into me with such agonizing slowness, I may die from how overwhelmingly large he feels.

"I—" My words catch in my throat. My heart thumps out of my own chest. "You're—too—thi—"

"We'll make sure it fits," he promises and notches in another inch. My heart feels like it might burst. "That's right, baby." Matthew brushes his palm over my damp forehead. "You're going to take this dick like a good girl, aren't you?"

I am. I do want it. I force the heavy weight of my head into a nod. He's stretching me beyond my own limits. There's no way, absolutely no way, I can handle him filling every bit of space inside of me.

But apparently, I'm barely aware of my own limits. Matthew slouches forward, his hands dropping onto the table beside my hips as he thrusts deeper. His gaze is like light across my skin, searing it to life.

"The things you do to me, Molly. *Fuck*," he groans against my shoulder, almost in a growl. Hearing him curse may be my most favorite thing in the world.

Apart from his mouth.

And his eyes.

All of him is my favorite.

Matthew takes me. Each stroke is deeper, slower, as if he knows exactly what I need. I drop my eyes to where he and I meet. Softness and hardness. Him and me. It's everything and more.

I'm wound up past the point of sanity.

There was no guilt, no disappointing huffs when I couldn't come. It's like he could spend all the time in the world making me feel good. And I want him to.

"Play with your pretty pussy." Matthew rests his forehead on mine. His sweat gliding against my skin sets my body into a blaze. "I want to watch you come all over my cock. Can you do that?"

"Yes." I slide off my forearms. Paint sticks to my skin, but I don't care. I may be washing the colors off for the next two weeks.

I'm free. Entirely myself again, and only with him.

I keep myself propped on my left arm as my right hand travels below the skirt of my dress. I brush my fingers over my clit, making my bones tremble in my skin.

"Just like that," Matthew groans. His own hands wrap around my waist as he continues rocking in and out of me. "I know that feels right, doesn't it?"

I rub myself softly, circulating the pads of my fingers against my clit until my core tenses. As his thrusts pick up pace, so does my rubbing.

"You look so lovely when I fuck you." His grip on me is rough, manly. I'm on top of the world watching the way he's claiming me.

I press onto my clit more frantically now. A drop of weight falls to the base of my spine. I'm close.

"I love it when you do that," I say, not even recognizing my own voice but loving every second of it.

"Good, baby." The table rocks beneath me, and Matthew starts to fuck, hard, actually *fuck* me. "Because this is the only dick you'll be taking from now on." His hands rush down my body, gripping at me so tightly, sending him deeper into my core.

He fucks the spot buried in me with precision, not once changing his tempo or tiring out. It's blissful, maddening. Mind-melting.

I've never had sex like this before, and I never want to have any other kind of sex ever again. That's final.

"Matthew," I warn, the crescent of my climax building inside of me.

"You're so fucking wet, Molly. So tight around me," he grits through his teeth. My walls clench even tighter, flooding the veiny thickness of his cock with slick wetness.

"I—ah." The words don't appear, because I know what's

coming, and I'm certain that, this time, it's going to come. "Can —are?"

"I'm right here with you." His lips cover mine. "Right here with you."

I shatter at his words. Matthew follows, the hot shot of his cum filling the deepest parts of me.

Beautiful stars sprinkle my vision. My heart is exploding in colors. We're a mess of limbs, sweat, and lips.

This was so much more than sex. We made love.

Every one of my senses is alight.

Matthew pulls my limp body into his chest, holding me carefully and not breaking the connection between us. His lips brush against my temple, bringing me back down to earth. There's paint everywhere, but I like it.

"I've never felt this way before." My voice is husky as my lips press into the stubble on his jaw.

"Me either." Matthew smiles warmly.

We linger in the silence for a few moments, and I let myself enjoy it. Allow myself the opportunity to listen to his breath, the sound of the wind outside. It's peaceful, not numbing.

He pulls out of me slowly. "Molly, I actually have to tell you —" he begins, but a crackle sounds through the room. I swing my head toward the door, yanking myself out of his arms in a hurry. "What was that?"

"I'm not sure," I say.

"Hello, lovebirds!" Lolita's voice sounds through an intercom box by the entrance. "Hope you've had a splendid afternoon. Sorry to cut your time short, but dinner has been moved up to six thirty. Your parents are expecting you at the restaurant."

My heart speeds up into a full-blown frenzy.

"We need to get back." I slide off the table and run around the room looking for my underwear. My right sandal must've fallen off during…oh no. I indulged in being Just Molly too much, and now I'm going to pay for it. "Where on earth is my sandal?"

Matthew says something I don't register as I rush through the stained studio, getting paint splotches everywhere. Our large canvas is soaked with color, and I can't spare a moment to admire the fun we had. Can't even find a way to breathe.

I hurry over to the intercom and press the speaker button. "We'll be right down."

My parents are here. They're going to decide.

It's all so, so soon.

"Molly." Matthew appears in front of me. His pants are on, his shirt half buttoned. He holds out my Cult Gaia sandal, and I take it from him and slide it on. "It's going to be okay. We got this."

There's paint all over my skin. How am I going to scrub this off?

Matthew's initials on my palm, my own on his. My heart sinks even further into my stomach. I don't want to wash them away yet. Not yet.

"Look." He lifts one of his fingers and rubs at the paint, like he knows what I'm thinking. "It comes right off, okay? I'm going to help you get ready, and no matter what happens, I'll be with you every step of the way."

The nagging in my chest warns me not to trust him, not to get too close. Because deep down, I'm afraid that, however pure this feels to me, it's still pretend. He's said he doesn't want a relationship, that he can't give someone what they want, and that reality hasn't quite left my thoughts.

But right now, I don't listen. I have Matthew.

A man who's made me feel like I belong, like I'm enough as the person I am. Not the person I can be for others.

I love Matthew Hudson, and I'm going to marry him.

Chapter 20
Molly

I'M sure I've been trapped in a montage sequence from one of my books. Except the genre I'm being written into is unclear. The past couple of days have been surreal.

My time with Matthew in the art studio was a sweet shock to my system. I've discovered how it feels to want to sin—to collapse into the freedom that only he can make me feel. Even after the two showers I took in our suite, paint hides in the crevices of my knuckles. My skin tingles with the memory of his touch.

The true reason why Oliver and Clara named their resorts On Cloud Nine is a lot clearer now. Falling in love is euphoric, terrifying, and so damn real.

Perhaps once Matthew and I tie the knot we can see if there's an opportunity to make the feelings between us work before we go through with a divorce.

Whatever happens, I'm safe with him here.

Oh gosh. This is the first time I'm introducing someone I genuinely care for to my parents. My nerves fret.

It's fine. Everything will work out for the best.

I know it.

Matthew wraps his fingers in mine as we step into the restaurant.

Vivian and Ray Greene's presence is obvious, ritzy, and commanding, as if an empire is resting on their shoulders. I suppose it is. And only a few weeks ago, it was my responsibility to ensure that it keeps expanding.

My father's gaze sears his phone screen. My mother is to his left, flipping through a leather portfolio. Are those the plans for my wedding to Matthew?

The waitstaff watch them with hawkish attention, ready to pounce at any indication of dissatisfaction.

Matthew is fixated on my father. I can't blame him. Dad's face is like a painting, every line and wrinkle from years of hard work and time he's committed to the resorts. I straighten my spine, raise my chin, and focus on putting one foot in front of the other.

"Hi, Mom; hi, Dad," I say brightly. "It's nice to be here together again. The last time must've been when I was, I don't know, ten?"

My father sets down his phone. The leather portfolio slams shut. My mother looks displeased that I brought up a memory from *before*.

"Vivian." Matthew gives her a polite smile. "Mr. Greene." He extends his hand to my dad. "It's a pleasure to make your acquaintance."

"Ray is fine." My father works through his autopilot pleasantries, standing up, fixing his jacket, shaking Matthew's hand before retaking his seat. To him, this is just a meeting with a fleeting stranger.

My chest deflates. Sure, I didn't expect him to throw Matthew into a big bear hug and smack his lips against my boyfriend's—uh, fake boyfriend's—face, but he could've at least given him a pat on the back.

I take the seat beside Mom. Matthew sits on my right.

"Molly, what's wrong with your hands?" My mother frowns, catching the paint in my cuticles. I toss my palms onto my thighs, rubbing my fingers across the napkin settled there.

"Sorry, I—"

"We had a painting class earlier today," Matthew interjects. "You'll have to forgive me. I'm not much of an artist, and Molly had to help me clean up my mess."

His mess.

"Hmm." Mom turns the tip of her nose toward the ceiling.

"Did you have a pleasant flight over here?" I offer, keeping the conversation on neutral topics. As though that'll do me any good.

"Doll, we're going to cut straight to the chase." Dad faces Matthew, looking at him with an unsettling frankness. "You passed your wedding course with flying colors, like we agreed. But there's still the matter of signing off on your match, and we're hesitant to give our seal of approval, given how *new* this relationship is to us."

Trusting them was a mistake.

"If we're to consider Matthew as a part of this family, as a father to future Greenes, we need to ensure that this connection you have is real," Mom says.

I was naive to think they would keep their promise to me. They must've never planned on letting me have autonomy.

And why are they bringing up the topic of children? Mortification spreads through my bones.

My heart thunders in my chest. Does Matthew want kids? Do I?

Tension strains me, freezing me in place. The lump in my throat makes it difficult to swallow.

I nod my head in agreement. I can't even look at Matthew. I'm a coward.

"Don't look so solemn," my mother remarks. "There are people here."

"I'm fine. You don't have to pretend to worry about me," I bite. Her eyebrows shoot up.

Oh no. I've never snapped at my mother, but the words just shot out of me.

The world spins out of control like a malfunctioning carnival ride, leaving me powerless in the seat of anger and disappointment.

"Vivian, Ray, if I may interject here." Matthew's voice is steady. "I'd love to better understand your reasoning. If it's a matter of pedigree—"

My mom raises a hand. "Nonsense. I hope Molly hasn't led you to believe such lowly thoughts of us."

"Of course not," I say, but she doesn't pay me any attention.

"In fact, I was as much of an outsider as you before I married into the family. The adjustment to this life was exigent, but it's necessary." Mom's neck lengthens in annoyance. I'm shocked. My mother never speaks of her life before she became Vivian *Greene.* "Oh, no need to be surprised. I grew up in a small town outside of Syracuse, and if it wasn't for Ray's mother sitting on the board of Cornell University and listening to the commencement speech I gave, I doubt I'd even be here today. She didn't hesitate to arrange our marriage as quickly as possible."

Dad winces, but he masks his expression. Work and societal expectations took a toll on my parents' happiness, causing it to slip away into the past.

"I appreciate you sharing that with me." Matthew nods. "I'm only trying to understand your decision regarding our relationship."

"Molly's first match would be a better fit for her future," Mom explains.

I don't bother holding back my eye roll. The Bradbury investment must have fallen through. Or maybe my mother's so intent on Lance because she likes to control every aspect of my life.

I need my trust now more than ever, or I'll be stuck under their suffocating grip, letting them snuff out any hope of a life of my own.

"Is this about the resort expansion?" I probe, growing impatient.

"Doll, we care about you," Dad chimes in. The nickname forces my molars to grind together. "This is about the family. The deal with the Bradburys is being sorted. Just let the grown-ups handle it."

Annoyance drills through my entire body. "I'm not as sheltered and clueless as you think I am."

"Molly, don't start," Mom snaps.

I rub the tops of my thighs to displace the energy coursing through me. My napkin falls to the floor.

This is all too much. Matthew's face stays neutral, though there's a small tick in his jaw as he studies both my parents. I'm certain their lack of decorum and belittling is making him uncomfortable.

He jumped through hoops, sacrificed his time. Now, that may all be for nothing. I'll have to find another way to get him the money for EcoDrones.

Ugh. What is he feeling? Probably abased, uncomfortable. Because of *them*.

The seams of my heart break apart in my chest. I reach down to retrieve my napkin, but Matthew beats me to it, flashing me a knowing look. "I have a plan to get that money. Trust me," he says quietly, so my parents can't hear.

My pulse races. *Trust?*

Matthew's words carry no hidden meaning, no games. Over the past two weeks, he's shown me that he has no need for my perfectly-acted performances. He sees me, listens to me, and—dare I say—even cares for me.

Although I don't have a clue how he truly feels about me, and I don't know what can actually come of our fake relationship. But Matthew has given me an introduction to my voice, however shallow it may be.

If he believes there's a way out of this, I trust him.

"What can we do to change your mind?" Matthew chimes in.

Confidence oozes out of him. He's not questioning *if* there's anything we can do, but he's insisting that there must be a way to win them over.

"In our life, love isn't an indicator that a relationship will work. Even after your father and I passed our course, there were still expectations we had to uphold as Greenes," Mom insists.

Be brave.

I don't want to live in a state of fear and anxiety.

I don't want to be the perfect daughter, the perfect friend, the heiress to a legacy.

"Matthew is important to me, and if you take some time to see that, then you'll understand that there is no difference between his world and ours," I explain.

"To Molly's point, I'd love to know the expectations you have of my role in her life, and in yours. I'm sure they're aligned."

"I don't think so—"

"Let's hear him out," Dad interrupts. My mom's face pales.

"I know you're looking into a business expansion. I worked at a VC firm and started my own business. If there's one thing I know how to do, it's convince people to invest money."

"Hmm." Dad's eyebrows yank down in thought. "What if they help plan the Winter Ball this year, Vivian? All of our investors, employees, and business connections will be there, along with new prospects. I suppose if there are leads, it wouldn't hurt to exhaust another opportunity to help fund the Gold Coast expansion."

"That event is nearly planned," Mom snaps.

"On the jet over here, you mentioned that your list of tasks was miles long, Vivian." My father glances at her over his wiry frames. "Why not enjoy a rest? Give these two something to do that can showcase Matthew's commitment to our family. The kids can get reacquainted with our society, and then we can get the full picture." Dad looks over at Matthew. "If you truly love my daughter, then this shouldn't be an issue."

"It's not, sir."

Something about Matthew's enthusiasm sags a greater weight on my shoulders. Why does he actually want to keep trying and not cut his losses? Assisting with the Winter Ball would be exhausting and time consuming. Matthew already had to rearrange his life to come here. Does he have ulterior motives?

Maybe the past couple of days meant nothing to him.

The sex? The moment in the tub? All of our spontaneous dates?

It felt real. Like actual, real love.

But maybe it *was* all an act, and Matthew is the greatest showman of all. I mean, he just said he wants to get the money. Twenty-five million dollars for EcoDrones.

My mother gasps. "Ray, you know the mess our daughter had me smoothing out for two weeks. Molly can't possibly show up in society with a new man when she was just engaged to someone else."

"I think you meant to say that Lance caused the mess when he was making out with the caterer at our wedding shower," I deadpan.

The table simmers with silence.

My stomach flips inside out. Nausea burns my throat. Anger is pulsing in my blood like a runaway steam train.

"Doll, our approval isn't off the table," my father assures me. But I don't believe him, and I hate that nickname. *Doll.* That's all I am, aren't I? A sweet puppet for them to play with. "Vivian, if Molly's going to get married, the pair will have to show their face around town sooner rather than later. Our lot has seen worse things."

"But we have a surefire investment from the Bradburys at our fingertips," Mom insists, her voice unusually pleading. "You know what that could mean for us."

"Yes, Vivian, I do." My father swirls his drink, the ice clanging against the side of the glass. "But we also only have one daughter. Let's see if they can manage this. Sure, people will talk; let them get it out of their system. It's not like any of them are going to stop booking our resorts for their family vacations."

"Fine. The Winter Ball is the first of December, at The Plaza." My mother's glare bores into Matthew and me. "There will be over a thousand people there."

"That's not quite two months away," Matthew confirms, looking uneasy.

"Do you think you can handle something of that caliber?" Her eyes target us. She never acknowledges that I've put together galas and events of double that size for ORO.

"Molly and I are a great team." He squeezes my hand beneath the table, but I barely feel it. "I'm sure we can complete whatever tasks you need us to do." Matthew throws on his most confident business cadence.

"We lost our caterer after the wedding shower incident…" She glances at me. "And the cocktail-hour entertainment went under, so we need something to keep the guests busy for an hour before dinner."

Bookings like this need to be planned months in advance. Especially with the fall socials lining up, there are fundraisers and galas left and right. If we have only a month and a half left before December, there's no chance that two in-demand companies will be available.

"I have a task to add to that list. Get my brother, Davis, to come to the event," Dad says.

"Why isn't Uncle Davis coming?" I frown. *What is happening back home?*

"I'm sure he'll give you an earful when you see him." Dad's jaw clenches. He and his brother are always fighting about something.

"I have three brothers; I definitely understand." Matthew attempts a smile, but it looks as phony as the one I should be wearing. He's become good at putting on *the act*. "We'll do it."

"Fine," I regale, trying to squash the growing discomfort in my body. It feels terrible—too potent, too loud, too big. But it's there now, and I'm concerned it may not go away any time soon.

"And if you don't succeed, you'll have two months to patch things over with Lance before your twenty-seventh birthday." Mom smiles.

Two choices sit in front of me. Either plan the impossible, or be the only one in my family who didn't fulfill the stipulations in the Greene trust. Both will surely make my life even more difficult than it has been. Reality sets in. I may lose everything I hold dear: my parents, my independence, and the man who has captured my heart.

Chapter 21
Molly

MY SUITCASES RATTLE against the hardwood floors as my driver drags them into the foyer of my townhouse. "Would you like me to take these upstairs?"

"No, thank you, Dylan. I'll deal with them later." I rub my eyes. Fatigue burns my lids.

Nobody slept on the five-hour flight back to New York. I was hoping my parents would doze off so I could get a word in with Matthew, but they stayed wide awake, choosing to pore over their binders and computers in an agonizing silence.

After we landed at the Westchester airport, we all shuffled into our respective cars. One for me. One for Mom and Dad. One for Matthew, to take him home to Greenwich.

Perhaps Dylan could drive me there now and give me the opportunity to talk everything through with him. Guilt gnaws at my chest.

I've kept him away from his house, his cat, and his routine for two weeks. Now, my parents are forcing us to take on the impossible. The last thing Matthew wants to see is a Greene.

"Nice having you back, Molly." My driver grins. I will my cheeks up, echoing his kind gesture.

"It's great to be here," I lie, hating the way the falsehood feels in my mouth. Maybe I could share a small truth, especially with Dylan. "But I do wish I got to stay in Sedona a little while longer."

"Even the best journeys always bring us back home. Enjoy the rest of your weekend, and have a good night."

When the front door clicks shut, an anchor of loneliness drops into my stomach. The dark, muted townhouse is colder and emptier than it was before I left.

Five years ago, when I moved in here, I got a taste of my own life. Now, I realize that the place I thought was my home is just another hold my parents have over me. They made it so easy to get stuck in their clutches. I let them.

I slip out of my horse-bit-detail loafers and leave my Métier tote at the foot of the spiral staircase. Even turning on a light is an impossible task. Instead, I roam into the sitting room off the entryway and slump into the window seat, closing my eyes.

The swing of highs and lows from the past twenty-four hours has me hungover.

I want to run away or pick up a book to escape. Flee to a world where all those vanishing powers I dream about having actually exist.

But the wrench in my plans isn't going away. I have to confront what's happening. My parents lied to me. I can't run away from that any longer.

They probably never planned on approving the marriage after we completed the course. I'm sure they thought Matthew and I would fail, or I would give in to the weight of our legacy.

I inhale a sharp breath. I should get to bed. It's the middle of the night, and I only have one more day before I face work on Monday. Although, I doubt I'll be able to sleep.

A smattering of cobalt blue hides under my nails. The ache in my rib cage deepens.

What's going to happen now? Did I imagine what was unfolding between Matthew and me?

I'm so gullible.

The twenty-five million dollars are the only thing keeping him tied to another month and a half of pretending. His commitment is unwavering for his project—not for me.

I've been kidding myself.

He never pursued me in the three years we've known each other. Why would two weeks change that?

I truly have no idea how to read him. Sedona, and everything I felt there, must've been a long dream. My stomach sours at the plethora of memories replaying behind my lids.

Yesterday, in that paint studio, Matthew made me feel complete. I'm pretty sure he felt it too. Felt how perfectly we fit together.

Didn't he?

Ugh. I need to cry. My palms drag over my cheeks. No, wait —I'm already crying. *Great.* I almost feel sorry for myself. The pain in my chest is becoming unbearable, causing each of my muscles to strain.

Being brave and fighting for my parents' approval is my best chance at freedom, but I barely have it in me to keep trying.

I roll off the windowsill and push my legs through the downstairs.

How am I going to keep it together at work? Matthew and I are going to see each other daily, except I'll come home every night and be alone again.

I miss him terribly.

Did I remember to pack his pajamas?

Three suitcase explosions later, I find Matthew's clothes.

To a stranger, these would be nothing special. A white Calvin Klein tee and a pair of gray shorts.

But they're my most prized possession.

I hurry to my bedroom, ready to wash off the stress of the

past couple of weeks and throw on Matthew's things before hiding in bed.

The moment I get upstairs, I smell it. Pungent, sweet, and musky.

I push open my door. The vases of orchid bouquets shake my senses. The white and dainty petals sit in droves on my desk, my nightstand, and my vanity.

Are these from Matthew?

No way. Not after everything that's happened. Besides, he would never get me white flowers. He knows me better than that.

The arrangements are replicas of the flowers at my many wedding events.

I pluck open a small envelope attached to one of the vases.

Since you're back in the city, come see me.
- Lance

The text is printed on thick cardstock with a small flower medallion stamped onto the back. A logo I've seen many times in my life. My mother's favorite florist in the city.

My chest caves in, and my spine curves forward. The weight of the world is too heavy to bear. A grief-choked wail escapes my lips, echoing through the empty house.

I want to burn it down.

This is my mother's doing. She must have told him I was coming back.

Lance never purchased me gifts. He didn't even make this much of an effort when we were engaged.

All these hideous white flowers belong in the trash. I swipe a vase off my desk, sending it into the bin. My heart aches for the flowers—it's not their fault.

Another card reads the same words as the first.

I snap.

Anger, boiling and flashing, seeps into my bones. I've never felt this viscerally broken.

How dare Lance or my mother encroach on the only place in this house that's all mine?

The cool fall air beats against my skin as I rip open the window. I grab a vase and chuck it off the balcony and into my backyard.

A loud crash ricochets. My back patio glistens with shattered glass, mimicking how I feel. Messy. Fractured. A delicate flower waiting to be destroyed.

I laugh or cry; I'm not sure at this point. My vision burns red as I grab another victim, tossing the bouquet out of my window. Again and again. One after the other, I drop the vases into my backyard.

For all the times my parents refused to listen to me.

For every part of myself that I sacrificed for them.

For each unwanted advance from Lance that I let slide.

For letting my voice turn into a whisper in my own mind.

No more.

Tears stream down my face.

A message chimes on my phone.

Is it Matthew?

I reach for my phone and unlock it.

LANCE

Made reservations at Carbone at 7 on Monday

I scroll through the graveyard of ignored messages from the last two weeks.

It's just like Lance to not give me a choice. When we'd be forced to go to dinner, on the rare occasions we needed to be seen in public, he would always order for me, comment on the waitresses, or ignore me completely.

I can't deal with this.

With the next vase, I let go of my phone, sending it to the ground below.

The broken glass glimmers like diamonds in the moonlight. The white flowers lie strewn among the debris, their petals bruised and torn. They still look too perfect, too fake, probably just like my existence always has.

I'm going to need to clean this up. My house manager, Olivia, shouldn't have to fuss over another one of my disasters.

It can't be that hard, right?

An hour later, the backyard is as clean as I could manage. The stewing anger in my veins is dragging me down with fatigue. My palms sting; bandages cover the small cuts from the vases.

My parents will continue to move the goalposts until I'm backed into a corner and forced to put our family business before myself. That's not an option. I'd rather forfeit my trust and become the outcast of the family than marry someone I do not want.

The realization feels sobering, but with it comes a trickle of guilt.

Matthew's rightfully owed the money I promised him. I can get through the next month and a half, like we agreed in Sedona. Then we'll just get back to being strictly business.

There's no need for my silly, fleeting feelings to ruin that.

For the time being, I need to secure a backup plan.

I pull my laptop off my desk, lie back in my bed, and use my sore, cut-up fingers to type *Zillow.com* into the search bar.

One way or another, I'll take my life back. Even if I have to go at it alone.

Chapter 22
Matthew

MOLLY'S PHONE goes straight to voicemail again. I toss my cell onto my lap. The sound of passing cars rushes by me in my Rivian's driver seat. My temples pound, and my neck strains under the weight of a headache. I should've rested before driving into the city to see her, but we need to talk.

Immediately.

All the lights inside of her townhouse are off. She's probably already asleep, and I'm peering into the windows of her home at three o'clock in the morning like some kind of madman.

What has gotten into me?

Molly.

I beat my palms against my steering wheel, attempting to cool the worry in my veins.

There's no point in denying it. That damn dinner with her parents has left me feeling unworthy and inadequate. *For fuck's sake.* I haven't felt quite this small since I told Laura about my azoospermia. Those memories sting despite how much I want to say I've moved past them.

But the moment Vivian brought up heirs and carrying on the Greene family name, I felt myself shatter.

Do Molly's parents know about my infertility? Could they be looking out for her best interest?

They only have one daughter. Some part of her must want to carry on the esteemed line—a gift I wouldn't be able to give her.

Lance, on the other hand, can provide the Greenes with money for their expansion *and* a grandchild. Vivian's words burn in my mind.

A much more suitable match.

My teeth clench. That boy has no respect for Molly. She'd be better off with anyone else. Dammit. This would be easier if I didn't care so much.

In the painting studio, something shifted between Molly and me. There's no point in denying it. Sure, it's only been two weeks, but I felt it. I'm certain I did.

My confusing feelings are distorting reality.

We can't have a future—not one in which she has everything she deserves. With me, there's only a partial life. Half a man who could only provide her with a small family of two.

I'm not even ready to tell her about my infertility. Seeing Molly look at me with pity and reject me will plummet me back to the time when Laura left. It will break me all over again.

Focus on the promise you made to her.

The trust.

I will do anything to get Molly her money. I made her a promise. After witnessing her parents' behavior at dinner, I realized that, now more than ever, she deserves a chance at a life that resembles the ones she reads about in books.

Sure, I could push my reforestation project off a few more years. But there's no point in denying that the twenty-five million would be helpful now. This week alone, one of the deadliest fires in over a hundred years occurred. EcoDrones can help repair the ecosystems and homes that are being destroyed worldwide.

We need each other. There's no way around that.

A light sparks up in one of the upstairs windows. She's awake. I rush out of my car, wrapping my wool coat around my body. The crisp October air stings my cheeks.

I rap my knuckles against her door.

In a moment, Molly appears on the other side.

The sleeping shirt I gave her in Sedona hangs over her small frame.

She's wearing my clothes.

My throat dries. My palm shoots up to the cold skin on the back of my neck.

The soft creases around her eyes, the slight dip of her chin. I see it.

I see Molly.

She's hurting, like I am.

I hate this.

"You're here," she whispers.

"You're wearing my shirt."

She looks down at it sheepishly and swipes her hands across the fabric. *Why are her fingers wrapped in bandages?* A pain mines itself into my jaw.

"What happened?" I reach for her. She pulls away.

"Nothing," Molly replies, devoid of any emotion. "What are you doing here?"

Ouch. This is what I feared. She's not opening up to me. She's back behind her walls, hiding herself again.

The reality hurts.

I want my Molly.

"You weren't answering your phone." I try to keep my voice steady, but the tickle of worry in my throat makes it almost impossible.

"I had an accident, and it broke. You don't have to worry about it." She shrugs. "I already left a note for Olivia to replace it."

How on earth did her phone break? I saw her on the tarmac only a few hours ago.

"Are you okay?"

"Does it look like I'm okay? Uh—please don't answer that." She frowns, swiping at her hair. Betrayal is scribbled in cursive all over her face. "My parents, my whole life is…infuriating. They lied to me and to you."

The pain in my body intensifies, dealing a final blow that shatters my heart into pieces.

"We can figure it out," I attempt.

"What's the point? Nothing I do will ever be right for my family." Molly spins on her heels and walks into the foyer. I follow her inside, shut the door behind me, and lean against it. The grandiose space feels cold and colorless. "That dinner showed me what their priorities are, and now they're just playing their little games until I call my own bluff and end things with you. I'm not sure how much longer I can tolerate the way they treat me." She paces in front of me, arms crossed over her chest.

I've never seen her this angry before. Anxious, worried, sad —yes. Molly's entire body is vibrating with vexation. How do I help her?

"If we plan this holiday party, are they going to give you the trust?"

She halts and aims her pursed lips and sour expression right at me. The fire behind her eyes is something I've only witnessed when we made love. But now that same intense gaze burns through me. "The trust." She lets out a sardonic laugh. "Right, of course. That's why you're here."

My own annoyance flares at the hidden meaning in her words. "Yes, Molly. Your trust. Your ticket to stopping the suffocating grip your parents have over your life."

She rolls her eyes again. "Back to business, I guess."

"I drove here in the middle of the night to check on you." My voice drops an octave. I don't mean for it to, but the tension in my body is becoming unbearable. "After Sedona, you can't possibly believe I'm here for any other reason."

"No, Matthew. I genuinely have no idea why you're at my house at three o'clock in the morning. Apart from funding your project, I can't see why you'd come all the way to the city." Her lip quivers slightly.

Molly looks at me with raw hurt. The air feels more frigid in the townhouse than it did outside. The ground beneath my feet feels unsteady. She's got me all wrong.

I force a deep breath into my lungs. "What are you saying?"

"There aren't any cameras here. No one to monitor all of our pretending." She waves her hands around. Her bandages send a pike into my gut.

"Molly," I try.

"What? Isn't that the truth?" Pain races in her eyes, except she doesn't run away this time. Molly is here, experiencing this with me despite how much she's hurting. The trust we have built is a testament to how close we've become.

It's exactly why I'm here.

"I haven't been able to relax since sitting at that dinner table with you. The way everything unfolded made me feel like I'll never be enough for you or anyone else."

A tear spills across her cheek. "You are—"

"Please, let me finish. I feel pressure to succeed in this for you. And, Molly, you have every right to be angry. At your parents, at the way they treat you, but, baby, don't be angry at me," I say calmly.

"Why not? I'm so tired of being given permission to feel, to exist. I'm sick of apologizing for acting however feels most natural to me." Molly sobs. I want to hold her so badly. "I barely know what's right anymore because anything I do is wrong."

I take a step toward her, and she doesn't retreat. "I hear you, but I'm here. I'm putting you first."

"I don't need to be saved, and I don't need your permission to be upset."

"No, you don't." I shake my head and take another step closer.

"At dinner, you told me that you wanted to get my money," she cries. Her bandaged hands swipe at her cheeks. "Is that it? Is that really all you want?"

My rib cage tightens. "My motivations are you. I want to get your trust for *you*."

"What about your project? I know that pretending to be in love with me has been exhausting, but you didn't hesitate to come to the rescue again."

There is so much I can't say right now and so much I want to. My hands flex, and I roll my neck. "Molly, the entire night, I only had you in mind," I explain. "After what happened at the paint studio, I—I don't know how you could presume anything else."

She looks up at me. The faint streetlights outside cast shadows across her face. It's killing me not knowing what happened to her hands, or, at the very least, what she's thinking. I can always read her, but not now.

The pads of my fingers tingle with the need to touch her.

Molly shatters the quiet between us. "Did the past two weeks mean something to you?"

The years I spent numbing myself to these feelings were obviously a mistake, because my mind refuses to approach this logically. Not one ounce of rational thought swims in my head. I should let her push me away, except I can't.

It's selfish, helpless, foolish, even, but what I've started to feel for her isn't going to disappear.

These last two weeks have made me understand that I want to be cherished and desired again. I want to cherish and desire someone else.

Molly.

I want to shine in her light. I want to feel like I'm flying. I want to wake up and count the freckles kissing her mouth. Make her laugh. Make her fall apart and then help put her back together, like she's been doing to me without even realizing it.

She bites her swollen bottom lip and stares up at me, expecting an answer.

"They meant everything to me." I reach for her, and she doesn't stop me. "For fuck's sake, darling. I'm certain that I can still taste you, practically feel you wrapped around me. I didn't drive here for your money. I'm here for you."

Her mouth slopes down. Worry wrinkles her forehead. "But what about—"

"What do you want?" I ask, towering over her.

"I—I don't know," she whispers.

"Molly, what do you want?"

"*You.*"

"Finally." I exhale with so much relief.

In a blink, my hands cup her face. Her lips are on mine again. Right where they belong.

We have so much to talk about. So much to fix. However, we both need a moment to escape and get lost in each other.

Our tongues clash together, and we scatter to the base of the staircase.

I want to consume her. To savor the sweet taste of her lips and the smell of her hair.

A fucking dream.

That's what this must be—a dream, and although I've never been much of a religious man, I pray I never wake up.

"I want you," I rasp against her swollen lips. I take the bottom one between my teeth. My length grows in my trousers, aching to be inside of her again. I need her close.

"Please," she gasps. Her wet mouth finds its way to my jaw as she pulls the coat off my shoulders.

Is this all happening too fast?

I pull away to check on her. Molly stares back at me with swirls of amber in her eyes and a puffy face.

This woman.

A complex, loving, heart-too-big-for-her-own-good woman.

"I fucking hated that dinner. Hated how quickly it pulled me away from you." I kiss the slope of her jaw. "Mine." My lips connect with her nose. "Mine." Her still-damp cheek. "*Mine.*"

I claim her mouth again. Molly wraps her arms around my neck and drags me closer.

"Yours," she mewls against my lips.

My balls cinch at the mere promise from her.

"Best fucking thing I've ever heard." I drag her body along the handrail, her back pressing into the banister. "God, my girl. You've taken over my entire mind." Involuntarily, my hips thrust against her. I won't last even a minute longer without feeling her wrapped around my cock. "Did you wear this shirt because you missed me, baby?"

"Yes," she moans, pulling at the collar of my sweatshirt before she strips it off me. "Missed you. Need you."

I must oblige and give her everything, anything she asks.

My thoughts race fast. I almost forget where we are. I can take her up against these steps, even this wall, but I should find her bed.

"I'm gonna get my girl upstairs and give her everything she needs," I promise.

"No." She presses her palms into my chest. I pull her to me by her waist. "Now, please. Here," Molly pleads.

"Are you sure?"

Molly looks up at me with a stern expression. "I'm a grown woman, Matthew, and I'm telling you I want you. *Now.*"

Fuck. I won't deny her a minute longer.

We spill out onto the staircase. Her shoulders rest on the marble steps. Molly locks her hands together and hangs on to my neck. She parts her legs for me and winds them around my torso.

I fumble for my belt buckle, sending my pants and boxers down my legs. One of my knees leans on a stair for support. Molly's heavy breathing knocks against my chest.

"Are you ready to take all of me, baby?" I rest a hand beside her head while the other pulls her panties aside. I center myself against her heat, wet and slick against my swollen tip.

Don't rush through this.

Do not waste the moment with her.

Get it together, man.

Get it the fuck together.

"Yes." Molly nods, and her eyes land on the place where she ends and I begin. "I want you always. All the time."

My willpower fades.

I brace my hand on a step and notch the first inches of my cock into her scorching core. I lost my mind somewhere back in the car. Or, most likely, at On Cloud Nine.

All I want to do is please and worship her, but not tonight.

Tonight, I'm claiming her.

My Molly.

I thrust my hips upward, sending my full length into her at once. She chokes on a scream, arching her back. Her thighs squeeze around my waist, and my grip on the marble hardens. My other hand wraps beneath her waist, lifting her hips to me.

"Good, be loud," I slur. My mind falls victim to the feel of her around me. I drop my mouth to her lips. "Let the world know who's looking after you."

Molly obeys, as if she's been waiting for permission. With each pump of my cock, her voice grows louder and louder.

"You," she pants. "It's y—*oh*—you. Ah—*woah*—you."

She's weightless in my arms. Her teeth find my jaw and leave their mark beneath her gasps.

Nails scrape into my neck. My heart races fast.

"Fuck, Molly, I'm obsessed with you, your body, your thoughts." I drill into her, her moans guiding me with every feverish stroke. Her beautiful mouth parts wide. "You've made me think of things I never imagined. I feel mad when I'm around you, entirely out of control." Her lips curve up, her eyes drunkenly rolling back into her head. "You like that, huh?" I groan with a labored chuckle. "Love knowing how out of my mind I've been because of you?"

I angle deeper, lifting her closer to me so that I can hit the spot that makes her lips tremble. The moment I do, Molly's eyes widen with pleasure, but I don't break my pace.

"T-tell me, how." She smiles at me. *I could fall apart right now.*

"You want to know the power you have over me?" My smirk turns wicked. I pump my cock deeper. "Fuck, Molly, it's sickening what I want to do with you. Move you into my house. Pamper you, feed you by hand, and watch you try on every pretty dress you own. And then I'll buy you hundreds more, just so you can do it all over again."

My mind is lost. I don't know what I'm saying. I don't know what I'm thinking. But everything I've ever felt for her comes pouring out of me.

Her walls tighten around me. She takes every inch without hesitation. The heat in my body escalates. My own climax is teetering on the precipice. I can't hold back for much longer. The muscles in my arms strain.

"Wash your hair, fill your belly with laughter, and bring you books, so you can read them out loud to me, and I can listen to the sound of your voice for hours on end. Fuck, baby."

"Matthew," she moans. My cock swells with need again, and Molly begins to heave.

I slam into her with one determined thrust, filling her to the brim as she regains her breath. I stay here as she adjusts to the fullness of me. The grip of her sweet cunt around me is nirvana.

I balance on my knee and pull up the shirt still hugging her body, revealing her full breasts, reddened nipples already hard.

"Most of all," I say, my voice low and husky against her mouth. I run my hand over each breast, tugging and pulling at the stiff peaks. "I want to drink you in. Taste you, touch you, feel you all around me. Lose myself in you, drown in you, until I am drunk out of my fucking mind."

Molly squeezes around my cock. My entire body freezes over as the heavy weight of need almost shatters at the base of my spine. *No. Too soon. Too fast.* My balls ache for release.

A drop of sweat makes its way down my face and collapses from my chin to her chest.

Damn.

She looks at me, her eyes mimicking what I can only assume is the awe in mine. Raw and intense.

"You do that one more time, and I'll really take this pussy. Take it all for myself." I release her breasts and drop both of my hands around each side of her face. "You hang on now, okay?" She nods, and her thighs tightly hug my waist. She steadies herself on her forearms. I resume my strokes, slow and steady. "I should be scared that you've terrorized every spare second of my thoughts. But I'm so fucking alive with you." I attach my mouth to her ear, teeth grazing her lobe as I force the words through my lips. "I want more of you every damn day."

My legs almost give out, thighs burning as sweat drips down the backs of my knees, but I refuse to stop.

"You're making me—Matthew—" Molly's tone is panicked, and then her walls tighten around me with another heavenly grip.

There's no going back to how things were before this. I'd fight however many fights she needs me to. I'd commit to breaking down my own walls for her. Anything for this precious girl who fills my life with color.

"I know. Give it to me." I escalate my steady pace and drill into her, dragging my forehead to hers. Molly's breasts bounce with every rough thrust. "Let me feel how good I treat our pussy."

"I'm—I—gonna—" she whimpers, her face blurring the lines between disbelief and astonishment. "I'm gonna come."

"Every. Single. Time."

Her cunt convulses around me, and it's enough to turn a starved man like me into an addict. That's what I was before her, a man with a hunger I'd grown used to.

Molly's eyes are glazed over as she refuses to break our stare. My hips batter into her, skin slapping against skin. She grows wetter around my cock.

She tugs my hair. "N-now," she begs. "Please, together." Her request sends me over the edge.

"I'm here, my girl. I'm going to fill this tight pussy with my cum, and you're going to take all of it, aren't you, baby?" Our swollen lips crash together, teeth against skin. I pull away, needing to see her beautiful face. "So beautiful with me dripping out of you."

"Y-yes, I—I," she screams, guttural and loud as she lets herself crash into bliss.

"I know, that's it. Let go for me." I keep my pace a while longer, letting her ride every ripple of pleasure as her body writhes beneath me. "I gotcha; I'm gonna be right here for you," I groan. The flood of her heat around me becomes too unbearable. My breaking point snaps, and I cannonball right through it. My release rushes into her.

Fuck.

My joints tremble, bones somehow breaking and rebuilding in my skin as the low, rushing simmer of my orgasm liberates.

I collapse my weight against her.

Molly begins a soft laugh, the sound bubbling up inside of her like the rise in a symphony. "That was the best thing I've ever felt in my entire life."

A smile breaks across her face like the dawn of a new day. I can't remember the last time I felt as whole, as much of a man, as worthy as I do right now.

"Me too, darling. For me too." I join in her laughter before carefully pulling myself out of her. I caress her limp body with a trail of kisses. One on her lips, her neck, her chest, each of her knees. I find my sweatshirt and use it to clean up the release on her thighs.

"I'm pretty sure I still feel you in me," Molly whispers, watching me.

The words unlock something primal in me, hardening my cock, and I almost pounce on her again.

"I love hearing you say that." I collapse beside her, pulling her onto my chest and leaning my head against one of the marble stairs. The stone digs into my side, and another presses against the strain in my thigh, yet I'm in a state of bliss. "We should talk…about earlier."

"We will. But maybe we can get some sleep first?"

Smart girl. Both of us must be spent from not having a moment of rest in over twenty-four hours. I have no idea how I would've lain in bed without her at my side. Molly's eyes close. I plant my lips on her temple, tasting the salty sweat on her skin.

"Let's get you to bed."

"I HAVE TO BE HONEST," Molly says, slowly wiggling out from beneath my arm and sitting up against her headboard. I prop a pillow behind my neck, grab my glasses from her nightstand, and put them on. "I haven't had a lot of physical relationships."

"Okay." I nod, beckoning her to go on. The sky outside is hazy again. We must've slept through the entire Sunday.

The walls in her room are draped in green wallpaper. Books brim the shelves. Her walk-in closet is massive, overflowing with clothes in the corner of the room.

"I just—I mentioned it's always taken me a while to *get there*, and, well, I haven't been with many people, and I never even slept with Lance because, well…" I cringe at the mere mention of his name, let alone the image of him going anywhere near Molly. "But last night, and the night before, it was just, wow…*woooowie*. You did everything right. Maybe too right, *ha*! So, what I'm trying to say is, expanding the, um, the scope of our relationship may make things confusing."

"If I'm understanding this correctly, you had several enjoyable orgasms—thanks for the compliment, by the way." I tip my head at her and land a soft wink. "But you don't want to have any more of those orgasms because it would make all the stuff between us difficult to manage?"

"Exactly," she agrees. "And we have to get back to real life tomorrow, and work. I just don't know how to handle a casual thing."

"Honestly, I've never had a *casual* anything." Nor would I ever define the feelings between us as casual. I adjust the pillows behind me. "We've known each other for years, but these past two weeks have made me realize that I don't want what's starting between us to end." I offer the information so calmly, it surprises even me.

Molly's eyes widen. "Well, me either."

"There's no reason we can't try to secure your trust while exploring this new part of our relationship."

She looks flustered. I shouldn't be enjoying the pink tinge on her cheeks, yet I am. "Even if it becomes messy?"

"I think it already is, darling."

Molly hesitates. Her eyes scatter over my face. "But if at any point you wanted to see other people, then our arrangement shouldn't stop you from—"

I wrap my palm on top of hers. "No, Molly. I only want to see you."

"Okay."

"*Okay.*" I smile, and her worried expression finally breaks. "If we're going to give this a go, and if it's alright with you, I'll be sleeping in this bed now, baby, and leaving my things here."

She nods before falling against my chest and snuggling up into my neck. "That works for me."

"Good," I say. I'm the luckiest man alive.

"You should bring Bear here," she whispers. "There's no reason for him to be left alone."

Christ. This goddamn perfect woman is worried about my cat. What on earth am I going to do with her?

"He'll love that."

Molly's breathing matches mine for a few moments as her cheek warms my skin.

"Matthew?" She pulls herself up again, looking at me with hesitation in her eyes.

"Hmm?"

"Are we really going to try to get my trust?"

"We've come this far, right?" I brush away a stray curl dangling in front of her eye. "No point in breaking up our team now that we're so close."

"I'm sorry for earlier."

I tilt her face up to mine. "You have nothing to apologize for, Molly."

"You're the only person who's ever seen me blow up like that, and I'm feeling guilty for getting mad at you—"

"Hey, no, none of that." I trace the worried lines on her face with my thumb, and she relaxes. "You had every right to be upset at me when you thought my priority wasn't you."

"Did you mean what you said during…" She trails off.

Fresh memories of us falling apart on her staircase flash across my mind. My body is still sore from taking her so fearlessly.

"I did," I assure her. "I want to take care of you, Molly. Starting off by prioritizing how important The Griffin is to you."

"The forests are important to you too," she says in a small voice.

I hate how much she's doubting me, but can I blame her?

I've barely wrapped my head around the reality that I'm… I'm falling for her. I still have so much to share with her. Yet the fear of everything between us crumbling when I do looms over me. "They are, but it's you, baby. I'm here for you."

"For us." Molly gives my chest a pat. "Oh. What are we going to do about ORO? I mean, we'll be at the office together now, and, well, how should we act?" Her mind must be working on overdrive.

"Let's keep things how they always were. There's no need to add more to our plates right now." At this, Molly frowns, and I realize how cold my words sounded. "Hey, I just mean that I don't want to put pressure on either of us to act differently. Whatever feels right is what we do. For now, let's try to focus on taking care of ourselves before we have to rejoin the real world."

"Ugh," she sighs, and then a small grin tugs up her lips. "I hate the *real* world. But speaking of, I should probably tell you that Lily and Avery know about what's going on with us and the trust."

I let out a throaty chuckle. I'm glad she had someone to talk to besides me. "I told Ollie and Robert too."

"How'd they react?"

"Haven't given them too many details, but I'm sure I'll be bombarded with questions tomorrow." My friends don't believe that we were ever pretending, and I guess, starting today, we're not.

I'll never hear the end of Ollie being right about this.

She blushes, looking shy again. "Don't you need to get home to get some fresh clothes for the office?"

"Trying to get rid of me already?"

"No, Mr. Hudson." She smiles, a toothy one this time.

Finally, things are getting back on track. "I think I'm going to keep you around for a little while longer."

My chest fills with warmth. "Good. And don't worry, I have a gym bag with some clean stuff at my desk." Though I should pick up Bear tomorrow and pack up my essentials to bring here.

"Okay." She slumps back down onto the mattress and tangles herself into my arms.

I pull her bandaged fingers up to my lips and plant kisses on the small cuts on her fingers. "Want to tell me what happened?"

"I broke a vase. Well, several vases, and then my phone," Molly says, not looking up to see the concern on my face.

"Did those vases do something to you?"

"Lance sent me a bunch of orchids. I guess he got news that I was coming home and thought they would impress me."

Him again. My pulse hammers, and from the way her face presses into my skin, I'm certain she can hear its feverish pace. "Lance? I didn't realize you were in touch." I try to sound calm.

"We're not." She shakes her head. "He's tried to reach out a couple of times, but I've barely read his messages. The flowers were out of nowhere."

"Gotcha," I say. My teeth grit together again.

"Are you jealous of him? Because there's absolutely nothing—"

"No." The response comes so fast, it's barely convincing.

Am I jealous of the prick? No.

Do I hate the fact that he has access to Molly? Yes.

Does her family's favor of him make me feel less than? More than I care to admit.

"Just let me know if he causes any more trouble. There's no reason you should be getting scratched up because of him…ever."

"Thank you." Molly's breath shallows. The scent of my favorite red ruby apples washes over me, calming the tension in my body. Her softness rests against my roughness. It's natural, right? Heaven help me, I'm a goner.

"I'm here for you," I promise.

"I'm here too," she whispers.

I've always been the kind of man who follows logic and reason, trusting my gut above all else. It's time to give my heart a chance to take the lead.

Chapter 23
Molly

THE HASTINGS' Athletic Charity Luncheon is at the Mandarin, overlooking Central Park. My dad gave me a tip that Uncle Davis would be a keynote speaker. It presented the perfect opportunity to try to win him over for the gala.

Tables scatter around the intimate space, each adorned with a flickering candle and an arrangement of fresh flowers. Soft strains of jazz music echo in the background as some of Manhattan's elite mingle and chat.

I did not miss this life. I've been here for a half hour, but the reality still shocks me.

Since coming back to the city, I spent the past week flying through pages and pages of Zillow.com. Who knew browsing properties would be more fun than shopping for clothes?

The thrill of real estate barely compares to the way my heart hasn't stopped doubling since Matthew and Bear moved in.

I can't really believe that we're exclusive. I'm on top of the world. Matthew and I are *together*. An item. All those years spent sketching his name beside mine were worth it. Maybe I do have magic?

Alright, that's a bit juvenile. But my three-year crush is now living in my townhouse, waking up beside me every day. What living, breathing, human woman wouldn't kick and giggle about it every chance she got?

Olivia and I bought every toy and accessory a cat might need. However, Bear seems to prefer the gift boxes to the actual gifts. I'm warming up to having a pet. Bear's constant love and attention have me gushing over more than one man in my life.

"…we are addressing the devastation caused by wildfires," Matthew says from beside me. My schedule at ORO this week was hectic, but he's had plenty of time to focus on EcoDrones. "My drone technology will reseed damaged lands with vegetation that's local to its operating region. Pine and aspen forests in Alberta; koa and ironwood trees in Maui."

He's in his element. Eyes blazing with enthusiasm. A charming smile. The handsome lines in his face are creased with an achingly magnetic focus.

Ugh. Simply irresistible.

Sam Kaitlin, a flashy private equity executive, leans in, handing over their business card. Their buzz-cut hair and prim, well-tailored suit shine beneath the radiant lights above us. "You had me at vegetation, Hudson."

They share one final laugh before I watch Sam disappear into the crowd.

"That was impressive." I give Matthew's shoulder a nudge, delight swelling in my chest. "I now understand the hype around having arm candy."

"Is that all I am to you?" he teases. "I'm more than just a pretty face, you know."

"Oh, I'm sure of it." I snake my hand up his arm. "All this brilliance and brawn, just for me."

"Don't flatter me too much." He playfully raises a brow at me. "Besides, you've seen me work before."

"I know, but nothing like this."

I reach over to fix the knot of his tie. Matthew shyly looks down at me. My heart sings. "Glad I'm not too rusty. I haven't pitched in three years. But I wouldn't be able to do it without you being here. Honestly, it's all you. You really make people come to life."

"I only let them see what they want to see." I wink.

"Well, I've never been more thankful that I get to see all of you."

My cheeks heat a degree. I glance around the thirty-fifth floor of the Mandarin, feeling mischievous all of a sudden. "You know—"

"Molly?" A familiar voice pulls my attention away from Matthew's intrigued eyes.

I turn to find my uncle standing right behind us. "Hi, Uncle," I say and flash him a little wave. We're not huggers in our family. We can't risk wrinkling each other's wardrobes for the sake of affection.

"Haven't spoken to you in ages." Davis loops around us. He's a carbon copy of my father—same wiry glasses, same stone expression. But my uncle always had a bit of softness to him. Maybe being the oldest sibling gives you a certain *je ne sais quoi* that makes you tenderhearted. "Have you talked to Dave and Larson yet?"

I didn't realize my cousins were here. "No, where are they?"

"Who knows?" Davis shrugs. "I can barely keep track of my wife, let alone those two."

We laugh, but not too loud. This man is my family. Yet I don't feel any closer to him than I did to the private equity manager.

"This is Matthew Hudson." I present my man with a swell of pride. My feet rise and fall in my Maysale suede buckle mules.

"Ah, I've heard your name through the grapevine." Davis shakes his hand, looks toward me, and lowers his voice. "Your mother's not a fan of this one."

"Mom's not really a fan of anyone," I say plainly, making him laugh.

"It would be polite of me to disagree, but, given the whole situation, I'm on your side. Your father didn't tell me that the Gold Coast expansion was riding on your marriage. I was under the impression the Bradbury's wanted to invest without there being a wedding involved."

The statement hits me like an unexpected blow. Why would my parents initiate the expansion without telling Davis about my arranged marriage?

Davis is my father's brother and his business partner. Shouldn't you be able to rely on and trust the people you work with every day? "I—uh, I had no idea." I stumble through my response.

"Well, that's just how it goes sometimes. Perhaps he was too excited by the opportunity of what this deal could mean for both of us. Still, that didn't give him the right to start the expansion project without me," Davis explains. Why is this expansion so important to my parents that they would trample over Davis and me? I would never hurt someone to get what I want. "We're scrambling to secure funding." He shakes his head with disappointment. "There's no reason you should've been caught in the cross fire, but I'm not helping Ray get out of this one."

"One of my brothers is exactly like that, quick on the draw." Matthew joins the conversation. He straightens his back and flashes me a knowing glance. *He's got this.*

Davis nods. "See, this one knows what I'm talking about."

"It's always hard with family," Matthew says. "Yet, if I'm being honest, it's even harder for me to remind myself that if it hadn't been for Mac's go-getting, I probably wouldn't have had the courage to launch my own company."

Davis's stiff posture eases slightly, and he tilts his head toward Matthew. "That's right, Plastech? A buddy of mine, Carl

Williams…do you know him? He's at Lemon Venture Capital. They were looking at your tech before the ORO acquisition."

"Of course. We met with them shortly before the Ellington grant."

Alright, it looks like my man has this one covered. Time for me to make the rounds. Someone in this crowd must have a caterer or entertainment connection I can tap for the Winter Ball.

That was our plan: attack and conquer.

I give Matthew's bicep a quick squeeze. "I'll be back." He shoots me a wink. "It was lovely to see you, Uncle Davis." I bid him a quick goodbye and prepare to enter the lion's den.

THE NEXT HOUR FLEW BY, and my leads for the Winter Ball remain at zero.

I forgot how tiring it is to mingle and laugh at jokes that aren't all that funny. My mules pinch my feet.

My shapeshifting used to be so much easier. Figuring out someone's soft points and playing into them was effortless.

If someone had children, I'd ask about their extracurriculars.

Recently married? *Oh, where was your honeymoon? Antigua! That's fabulous.*

Started a new job? *You know, my father must know their executive team. Let me see if I can pass on a good word or two.*

Okay, but that dress is so fabulous! *A custom piece? You have to tell me your contact at Versace.*

Now, however, *the act* feels trying. As if I've thrown on one of my masks, except it no longer fits right.

A shiver whisks down my skin. I take a sip of my seltzer water to calm my nerves. From the far corner of the room, I spot Matthew still speaking with my uncle. They're both red in the face from laughing, and I'm pretty sure Davis has tears in his eyes. Tears of joy.

What on earth could they be talking about?

"There you are," someone says. I spin on my heels, and my eyes shoot up to find Lance. "You've been ignoring me." He puffs out his chest like a bulldog, posturing for lord knows what reason.

"Yes. I have been." I turn away from him. The last thing I want is to be seen with Lance under the watchful eyes of Manhattan's socialites.

"Molly, I've already said sorry for the slipup at the wedding shower." I can't recall any form of apology from him. "We agreed that we could hook up with other people. Sure, that probably wasn't the best time, but please, doll; I need you to hear me out."

The nickname sours the bubbles still dancing on my tongue. "Please don't call me that."

"Let's walk through all of the perks that'll come from us getting married," Lance attempts again. "Our wedding was meant to be two months from now; we can still turn this around."

"Sure, if you can tell me what benefits there are for me, I'll humor you," I sigh.

He looks flummoxed. "The resort expansion, obviously."

Of course. I frown and glance into his brown eyes. "No, Lance. I asked about *me*. Not my family, not the On Cloud Nine resorts. What's in this marriage for me?"

He hesitates, his mouth hanging open. Lance has no idea what I want or who I am. This is all an ego play to him, and I'm collateral.

"We could be great together. New royalty. A beautiful family," he continues as I emotionally withdraw from the conversation. "It's clear that we'd have handsome kids together."

The suggestion makes me nauseous. "No, thank you."

I'm not even sure if I want to have children of my own. I barely have a handle on my own life. How responsible would it be to bring someone into this world when it feels like I'm just learning how to walk?

Lance ignores me. "Once my family's investment goes through, I'd give you the life you're used to. Better—what have you always wanted that you couldn't have?"

I'm almost tempted to remind him that my family are billionaires. But my heart gives me another answer. *My inn.* That's what I really want, but I won't marry Lance to get it.

"Happiness, Lance." I share the truth without hesitation. "There are some things that money can't buy."

"In our world, everything has a price. I doubt that guy you've brought here can afford you." He looks at me with great displeasure, blond brows collapsing, straight nose almost folding in half. "Molly, this is the biggest account of my life. Come on. There's no way you're going to be content as some ordinary, suburban trophy wife."

"Greenwich is hardly ordinary." There's no point in reasoning with my ex-fiancé, but I have to try. How do I make him understand and get him to leave me alone? "All your efforts and arguments aren't going to work on me, Lance. I'm in love with Matthew Hudson," I explain. However, unlike the previous times I've said those exact words, I might actually mean them now. They feel right. It's like the truth just clambered out of my mouth like gumballs in a machine.

He rolls his eyes. It's terribly unbecoming. "He'll never make you happy, doll."

Frustration boils beneath my skin, hot and potent. Enough. I'm sick of Lance and his antics. "I'm not a doll, and I don't care about you or your money. Please, just leave me alone."

"Everything okay here?" Matthew's deep voice rumbles over Lance's shoulder. His tone is severe and unrelenting. I glance up to find him skyscraping over my ex-fiancé.

Oh no. I didn't want Matthew to get wrapped up in all of this. I had it handled. Everything was under control.

Heat flames my face.

"I'm having a discussion with Molly," Lance hisses, spinning on his Ferragamo loafers to face Matthew.

The pair are night and day. Matthew is all man. A heavy crease in his forehead, a strain in his jaw as he looks—no, glares down at Lance, who resembles a scared little boy with his hands in his pockets.

My skin pebbles.

Matthew looks over at me and asks, "Do you want to continue your conversation?"

"She—"

I cut Lance off. "No, I don't." Matthew extends his hand out to me. I wrap my palm in his, worming my way out of Lance's vicinity.

"Great, let's get out of here." Matthew nods, and we take a step forward.

Our spot in the corner in the room has been helpful in keeping attention away from the kerfuffle Lance is causing. *Thank goodness.*

"She needs to be with someone who—" Lance seethes, but there's an unmistakable crack in his voice. He's desperate.

"Listen here, boy." Matthew turns and straightens his shoulders, somehow growing taller. He lowers his voice into a whisper. It's barely audible, even to me, and I'm right at his side. "You don't deserve her. Hell, you don't even deserve to look at her. Now, we're in public, and I care about Molly too much to cause a scene. We can either take this outside, like two gentlemen, or you can choose to come near her one more time and see what happens then."

Lance winces, his brown eyes darting around. As if in a final plea, he looks at me over one of Matthew's large shoulders. "You're going to choose this caveman over me? He probably doesn't even have a spot at Augusta National."

"Neither do you," I snap. Another perk Lance would have received from *my* family.

"Well, fine, but I'm wor—"

Matthew steps forward and leans down into Lance's ear. "What did I say about looking at her?"

Lance frowns. There's no way he's equipped to handle whatever comes after Matthew's words. Goodness, I'm barely able to understand what's going on between my wild pulse and the thrumming fire in my veins.

"You know what? Fine, whatever." Lance forces another sneer and stalks off.

I'm left entirely glued to the floor. It takes a few moments and some shallow breaths for Matthew to stretch out his neck and turn to face me. "You good?" I nod, because it's the only thing I can do when the reality of seeing Matthew go all man and protective of me actually kicks in. "Let's go home."

"Matthew." I halt, scanning his face. "That wasn't—he didn't say or do anything that meant something to me."

A calmness returns to his face. "Darling, I get to be with you every night. I couldn't care less about that boy."

My lips roll together, and I turn to a puddle where I stand. "Every night, huh?" I say playfully.

"Damn straight." He nods. "Plus, I have more important news. Your Uncle Davis agreed to come to the Winter Ball."

The first task is crossed off our list of impossibles, and only five more weeks to go. "I guess we have lots to celebrate."

Chapter 24
Molly

We stumble into my townhouse, laughter bouncing off the walls and ringing through the chandeliers. "Best Halloween ever," I giggle, pulling off the equestrian boots Matthew got me back in Arizona. They were the perfect match for Serienna's costume. Bear runs to the front door and loops between our legs. "Hey, Beary!" I give him a pat on the head.

"I have to be honest." Matthew kicks off his own boots, giving his cat a scratch behind the ears. "I could get used to carrying this sword around."

His Damien costume has had my heart galloping all night. "Oh yeah? All that steel does look good on you." I wink. "You were the perfect warrior. It must be because you're a natural at pretending."

He brushes his hand into my straightened curls and says, "The only pretend I want to do with you is role-play."

"Well, we could start that right now." I brush one of my fingers over the leather waist of his pants.

"Oh yeah, you into that?"

"There's a lot you don't know about me, Hudson." I laugh

when he pulls my hand to his lips and leaves kisses along my knuckles.

"Becoming fluent in everything about you has been my greatest honor, milady." He throws on his indescribable accent, lowering his voice. The words are part of our little game, but I can tell he means them. For real. "Though next year we're going as Lysa and Jordy."

Next year. We haven't spoken about our future much since returning to New York. We've been trying to take it day by day and focus on wrapping up the tasks for the Winter Ball. The mention of a time so far from now makes my knees weak.

"Of course you'd like that," I tease. "An elf and a human. Will they overcome their differences, defy fate, and be immortal mates?" It's my turn to take on a dramatic voice, one that makes Matthew smile.

"What is it they say? True love prevails." I'm not sure we're talking about my book anymore. "Lysa reminds me of you so much."

"Well, I'm definitely no elf." I push the hair out of my face, swiping against my golden ear cuffs. "I mean, except for right now."

"Lysa's strong, resilient. Even when she loses her magic, she does everything to keep her friends safe. Sure, Serienna begins the story, but it's Lysa who's the real lead. I always picture her with curls as red as yours, the same beautiful amber eyes."

My body comes to life beneath his touch. The half a glass of wine at Lily and Nico's Halloween bash is causing my cheeks to flush.

"Well, don't get too attached," I joke. He doesn't need to know Lysa's life is at the mercy of a cliff-hanger in book five.

"Jordy did, and I believe he's doing just fine." The space between us shrinks. Bear gives us a look and runs off. The things this poor cat has witnessed in under two weeks—he already knows when we need privacy. Matthew reaches for my cheek, and his fingers wander lazily into my hair.

More.

"I hate to break it to you, but I'm pretty attached to you in these leather pants." My laugh turns into a snort.

Matthew was the perfect Damien all evening. The shirt beneath his suede vest is loose around his collar. His chest hair peeks out, tempting me to grab it. And don't even get me started on the trousers.

Can someone become addicted to muscular thighs?

"Oh yeah? Is the whole battered warrior look getting you going?" He cocks a brow at me, his hand falling to my nape.

So much more, please.

"Definitely." I rise onto my toes and bring my lips to his. It's electric. Perfect. The way it always is.

I shuck open the knots that hold his vest together while Matthew undoes the string around my neck. My cape drops to the floor.

I want to kiss him, his neck, his chest, down the trail of hair leading to his…

An idea pops into my head, likely all too scandalous and ridiculous. But when else will a gorgeous man be dressed up as one of my favorite book boyfriends?

"I want to do something for you," I whisper against his lips. No chickening out now. "Meet me upstairs in ten minutes?"

He tilts his head. "What do you have planned?"

"As they said at the Battle of Loria: *tonight, we ride,*" I announce in a voice that mimics a war cry and run upstairs. His deep chuckle rumbles through the foyer.

Please let me keep this spell of confidence through the night.

In a blink, I'm in my room, and my costume is on the floor. My emerald La Perla slip is heavenly soft. I zip the leather warrior's corset around my waist, cinching the lingerie. My heart drums against my chest.

Am I doing this? No. Yes!

A gorgeous man in leather pants is waiting for me downstairs, carrying a sword. I'm doing this.

My reflection stares back at me, except it's not just me. It's Molly Greene: elven princess. I'm on top of the world.

Maybe all of this chameleoning for other people could've been put to better use—cosplaying.

A knock comes from the door.

"Come in," I call out. My nerves thump beneath my skin.

"Molly?" Matthew enters. His jaw clenches, straining his neck. "A-are you…real?"

I haven't been good at knowing when a man wants me. Except right now, I'm certain of it. Matthew is speechless because of me.

"If you want me to be." I stroll over to him with power and control.

"Fuck." His voice strains, and his spine goes rigid. "I must've died out there, because this can't actually be happening." He lets out a gruff laugh.

My insides tense as I lower to my knees.

"Well, *my* Matthew told me he's always had a thing for elves." I smile, locking my eyes on his. "I have to be honest, I've never done this before." The nerves coursing through me aren't enough to stop me. I'm really looking forward to making him feel good.

"I promise you can't do anything wrong."

"Does this feel nice?" I run my hand over him.

He attempts to speak. "I—so good, baby."

The corners of my lips curl even deeper. The leather-clad bulge near my face is a pretty good gauge that he likes what he sees.

My hands land on the thick belt around his waist, and his hands envelop mine.

"I want you," I say, taking the lead.

"This is a fucking wet dream, Molly." He cups my face, and I turn, dragging his touch to my lips. Goosebumps spread across my chest. He gently presses on the slit of my mouth, and I part for him, running my tongue over his fingers. "Look at me."

I do as he says, straining my neck. I'm too vulnerable under his gaze. It's terrifying.

But Elven Princess Molly, girlfriend of Elven Prince Matthew, is not shy. She takes her lover and shows him that he's hers.

All hers.

My Matthew.

"You're mine," I say, sucking on his fingers until I gag.

The heat between my thighs escalates, and I lean into that fire—into the power of having Matthew entirely under my own control.

Is this what it feels like to be alive?

To take?

To be given?

My tongue swirls around his calloused fingers. He's man, all man, with strong hands. They're nothing like the clammy ones I've touched in the past. Every one of his movements is confident.

"You love this, don't you?" he heaves. "Let me hear how much."

There's no use in pretending I don't. I'm loving every second of this. I wiggle around on my feet and moan, bracing my hands against his thighs.

Matthew's gaze burns into mine. From down here, he's achingly beautiful. Every wild dream I've had from the pages of my books flips through my mind. Except now it's real.

I'm the main character of my own story. Even if this one doesn't involve any griffins or dragons.

He pulls his fingers from my mouth, a trail of spit connecting from my lips to the pad of his pointer. The ache in my core multiplies. It's filthy, maybe the filthiest thing I've ever seen, and I adore it so freaking much.

"These lips," Matthew says, tracing the damp skin along my jaw. "These gorgeous eyes, your smile." I blush, stifling a small giggle. "That fucking laugh. Fuck, baby, your laugh makes me so hard."

I'm restless and need to taste him. My fingers pull apart his belt buckle, stripping it off his waist. I yank his leather trousers down his legs, Matthew's erection tents under his boxers.

"Molly." He sounds desperate. "Do you have any fucking idea what you do to me?"

I nod. At that, he flexes in his boxers, and I set him free. Then, I'm face-to-face with Matthew's cock. His handsome, thick length. *Sheesh.*

"You put these ears on for me?" He brushes the hair out of my face, fisting the strands at my nape. "Got all dressed up just for me? Molly, you're better than any fantasy I've ever had."

The praise strokes a tempestuous side of me. I part my mouth and present my tongue to him. It's bold, maybe a little wicked. His gaze fully darkens.

"You want me to take it?" Matthew yanks my hair. The pinch sends a blissful shiver up my spine. "Fill your pretty mouth with this cock?"

I like him rough.

I nod, and he pulls me closer, bringing me only an inch away from all of him.

"Please," I say through a breathless moan.

"Begging, baby?" Matthew laughs. His length hangs heavy in front of me. "Are you going to show me how much you deserve this?"

I nod again, feverishly this time.

"I want you," I moan. "To have me."

He sucks air through his teeth. In one fell swoop, he pulls his tunic off and then reconnects his grip on my strands.

"Suck this cock, my girl. Get it nice and soaked. You're doing so good."

I do as he says, wrapping my lips around him for the first time. I lick the precum already waiting there. The salty taste tingles along my tongue. It doesn't feel scary. If anything, I'm powerful with him in my mouth.

"Oh, fuck," he growls again, actually growls. Desire pierces me. I want to make him feel as good as he makes me feel.

I start with soft strokes of my tongue along his shaft, working my way up and down his length.

"That's it, baby." Matthew's voice is strained. His palm flexes in my hair. "You know just what I want."

I suction my lips around his erection.

"Dammit. I'm going to fuck your pretty face, take you shamelessly, fill up every inch of your throat. You just open your mouth wider, okay, darling?"

"Mhm."

His dick hits the back of my throat. My core flushes. My panties are entirely ruined from how wet I'm getting just sitting here, letting him do exactly as he said.

The man I'm in love with is fucking my face while he's dressed as one of my fictional crushes.

What is my life?

I glide my hands over his taut stomach, tracing the lines of his abdomen.

In some twisted way, I give in to being used, to being had this way, because it's like a liberation. Submitting to him entirely of my own volition. It's a choice I've never made before, but now it's heavenly.

"Touch yourself." He drags my head along his length at a pace he likes. Feverish and fast. "Get that pussy ready for me."

I do as he says, zoning out to the sound of his cock in my mouth. No thoughts, no decisions. Just here. I get to be just here, drowning in the trust and intimacy of giving up control to my man.

My mind is euphoric when I push away the lacy fabric of my slip and glide over the wetness waiting underneath. I follow the rhythm of Matthew's thrusts, growing almost too drunk with lust.

"Such a sweet, dirty girl," he groans. "You choke on this cock. See how good you're making me feel? This is all you, baby. In your pretty outfit, my elven princess, all fucking mine."

My eyes widen. My hands cup his balls, squeezing and pulling with abandon.

There's nothing to second-guess. I push him deeper into my mouth. His cock jerks. My eyes sting, but it's bliss, pure and utter bliss, making my man feel this good.

"Slow down, my girl." His mouth lifts in a half smirk. "It's been a while since I—since I felt this good, and I don't want to waste this."

I shake my head. *No.*

It's a challenge. I'm going to make him come, and I want to do it right now.

My eyes scan over his chest, the rough, virile hair, the strong lines in his pecs. It's godly and intimidating, even from all the way down here.

I yank him closer, stretching my neck to try to take more.

He's at my mercy now. All mine.

"Molly," he breathes, and the sound of my name on his lips is ecstasy. "I'm going to…"

He tries to pull back, but I don't break my pace, sealing my lips around him even harder. Both of his hands grip my head, and the fucking turns slow, the thrusts longer and deeper into me. I don't second-guess anything I'm doing.

My own body hums.

Matthew's mouth parts, his eyes narrowing. *"Molly."*

And suddenly, he's falling apart. Giving in. The hot shot of his release explodes on my tongue as his eyes refuse to break away from me.

"Fuck." He strokes my hair, and I draw away, looking down at the mess that's escaped the tight seal of my lips. "Oh, fuck, baby, you're covered in me."

"W-was that good?"

Matthew drops to the ground next to me. His mouth crashes against mine. Clearly, he has no care in the world for the mess.

"You're the best I ever had," he breathes against my lips, and I laugh. He pulls us both up off the ground and drapes me in a hug. "I'm going to have to show you how thankful I am for making my dreams come true."

"Well," I say playfully, "how do you top the best?"

I'm on top of the world.

"Lie on your back." He looks over to the bed. "Let's see how many times I can make you come before you feel like I've sufficiently shown my gratitude."

Matthew makes me feel safe enough to indulge in my wildest fantasies. For the first time, I'm free enough to be *just* me.

Chapter 25
Matthew

Outside the glass walls of the office headquarters, the city skyline is a blur of grays and blues. "It's feasible for me to develop a prototype and complete a beta software by the end of the year," Robert says without looking away from the strings of code on his screen. Large headphones cover his ears as he types vigorously.

It reminds me of when we first started Plastech together. The late nights, the bubbling nerves of not knowing what the next day would look like, and getting to work with my best friends. I'm glad Ollie and Robert are joining EcoDrones.

"That's perfect." I clap my hands together and sit back in my office chair. "I'm scheduling meetings with a few ecologists in forest hotspots; I'll send you a summary of my notes, and you can take their feedback into consideration."

"Thanks for including me in this endeavor, Matthew. Ocean Tidy's self-sustainability has led to a noticeable deceleration in activities within ORO," he says in the same tone of voice I've heard since we were at MIT together. Robert has always been the brainiac of our group.

"There's a chance that if our prototype and seed money come together quickly, we may be able to quit ORO by the end of the year."

Robert nods. "That would be beneficial for me. It's been a great three years, but it's time to say goodbye."

Our new venture has already received a lot of interest. Of course, with Molly's introductions, we'll have a much easier time securing capital than we did for my first company. Even if we don't get the trust, I should be able to fund the majority of EcoDrones's operations with the new leads I've been making around town.

"Mornin', mates." Ollie bulldozes into our shared office. Robert gives him a quick glance while I shoot him a tight-lipped smile. He halts in the doorway, his six-foot-five frame taking up the cramped space as he peers straight at me. "Why are you looking so grim?"

"I barely got any sleep last night." I rub my tired eyes. It's impossible to hide anything from Ollie.

"Ooo la la," he sings before tossing his backpack onto his desk and collapsing into his chair.

Although I did have the pleasure of knocking role-playing off my bucket list, that's not why I haven't caught any shut-eye in the ten days since it happened.

"No, it's not that, you scoundrel." I shoot him a glare. "There are only three weeks left before this Winter Ball thing. Molly and I have been racking our brains to find entertainment for the cock-tail party. We've tried every acrobat, fire-juggler, and stilt-walker in a hundred-mile radius. There's nothing available. Apparently, all of New York City is having their holiday party that week."

An ache settles in my temple. Molly's been on the phone for hours each day, tapping every connection she has. We've been met with a brick wall at every turn.

Ollie rolls his chair closer to mine. "Why can't those fancy folks just drink? It's called a cocktail party for a reason."

"Trust me, we've tried all the wineries and breweries in the tristate area. *Nothing*."

"I may have a way to help ya." He considers me for a moment, stroking the auburn beard on his chin. "But it's gonna cost you one of the biggest favors of all time."

"Ol, I'm desperate," I say, dropping my forearms to my knees and leaning forward.

"Ma called me last week. Business ain't looking good in Scotland, and, well, if you wanted, I could maybe make some magic happen."

"Are you serious?" The first year I met Ollie, he had a box of whisky shipped from the Andersons' distillery in the Highlands. He rarely talks of home or his family business.

"Need I remind you of the favor you'd owe me." Ollie cocks a brow at me. "But yes, they could probably ship a few crates, and I can help you host an artisanal tasting for these stuffy folks. Can't let you go making a mockery of real whisky."

"Make it happen." My heart thuds in my chest.

Two tasks completed, one to go.

"When was the last time you hosted a tasting?" Robert asks in a hushed tone. "Hasn't it been almost two decades since you've been back home?"

"Pipe down, Robbie." Ollie's friendly demeanor slips.

"I'm sensing some discomfort from you," Robert notes.

"It'll be fine, like riding a bike. I was giving tours when I was a boy," Ollie grumbles. My friend hates any mention of his time away from Scotland. "Anyway, Mattie, how are things going with Mols? You've been living together for some time now. She sick of you yet?"

I inhale and peek outside the glass walls of our office, making sure the door is firmly closed.

I've been trying to ignore this unsettling feeling. No matter how much I try, it keeps coming back to torment me.

No time like the present.

"I actually need some advice."

"Should I be charging by the hour?" Ollie laughs and leans back in his chair. It bucks beneath his weight.

"Well, I really like Molly and—"

"*Like? Like?*" Ollie wiggles his eyebrows up and down. "I knew ya wouldn't be pretending for much longer. Robbie, you owe me lunch."

"I thought your relationship was meant to help with the initial funding for EcoDrones." Robert doesn't look away from his screen.

"It was, but…" I suck air through my teeth. "There's something else now."

"You've always liked her," Ollie says.

"That's beside the point. I'm feeling uneasy because I haven't told her about my infertility."

"Oh." Robert's keyboard stops clattering, and a silence falls over the room.

Nerves pinch my chest. "Kids haven't come up in our conversations. We've only truly been getting to know each other, on an intimate level, for a little over a month."

Ollie frowns, tapping his knuckles on his desk. "Aye. She's not going to judge you. Molly's not like that."

"I know. That's not what I'm concerned about." My voice trembles as I run my fingers through my hair. "We have a lot going on with the party planning and both of our businesses. I'm worried that if I bring this up and she wants kids…what would that mean for us? Can I make her my real girlfriend or even go through with this marriage if I don't tell her?" I pause, trying to steady my breathing.

"Are you afraid of discussing the personal topic with your betrothed because you haven't fully healed the wounds from your history with…" Robert pauses. "Lau—Miss Eye of Sauron, and you're using that as an excuse to avoid sharing the details of your biological insufficiency with the woman you're living with and denying your feelings of true love for?"

Christ. I'm slack-jawed. Never put it past Robert to read you better than you could ever read yourself.

"Well, Bobbie's got you pinned." Ollie chortles. "Has Molly given you any reason to believe that your happily ever after is gonna be filled with tots?"

"No, but her parents have." Isn't that why we're doing all these tasks—to prove to the Greenes that I'm suitable enough to produce heirs with Molly? "I don't really know how she feels about that. She's only twenty-six, and she loves her family."

"Understandable," Ollie says, his voice soft and reassuring. "But you gotta trust that she'll tell ya what she wants. That's all you can hope for out of people, that they're telling you the truth."

"Or you can assume they're all lying," Robert suggests before returning to his typing. "Obi-Wan has yet to move past Anakin's betrayal. Lack of trust has been proven to be an effective method of self-preservation."

"Aye, you're on fire today, ain't you?" Ollie tosses a pencil at Robert, who dodges it and seems entirely unfazed.

I ignore my friends' chattering.

I need to know how Molly feels, even if the truth ends up breaking us apart. My pulse erupts in my veins. As much as I wanted to believe it, years of therapy haven't quite fixed my feelings of inadequacy. Not when I'm faced with falling in love again. I'll likely have to work on this for years to come.

But I want to be enough for Molly. Desperately.

"After the Winter Ball, I'll tell her everything," I say, more to myself than to my friends.

"What happens if it's a deal-breaker?" Ollie notices my distraught expression.

Would she shuck me out of her life as easily as Laura did?

Maybe there's a way for Molly and I to work through this, except I can't get my hopes up. "Then we get married, split her trust, and get divorced." The words feel hollow, meaningless. "The original plan."

Ollie frowns. "Messy stuff."

"It is." The strain of my worries presses down on me. "I'll wait for her parents' approval first."

I don't have it in me to face two rejections.

"What if they say no to your marriage?" Ollie asks, his voice hesitant. "Would you consider being with Molly without their permission?"

The question catches me off guard, and I pause to consider it. "I don't know if that's up to me."

What would happen if we were to just run away together?

I'd take care of Molly. Maybe not to the standard she's accustomed to, but I'd provide for her, always. Give her anything she'd like, even if it meant stuffing my house with tulle dresses and silk pillowcases.

I want to be with her.

"Aye." Ollie nods. "The things we do for love."

Love. That's what this is becoming, isn't it?

It's been so long that I can barely remember what it feels like. But Molly's been reminding me of all the different ways love can take over your life. "We haven't exactly said that we—"

"You don't have to say it. It's written all over your face."

"What do you know about love, Ollie?" I slump deeper into my chair. "Didn't you leave a girl back in Scotland and never look back?"

"He did," Robert confirms.

Ollie's face blanches. "No."

"Right, it's normal to carry around pictures of your first love in your wallet," I deadpan.

That seems to annoy him even more. "It's for safekeeping. Case she goes missing."

"You haven't seen her since you were, what, a teenager? Doubt she looks anything like that battered photo." I chuckle.

"Some best friend you are." He feigns annoyance, but there's a grin spread across his face.

Chapter 26
Molly

"I'll be home late," Matthew says softly over the phone. On the line, children's laughter booms before a door opens then closes.

"Boo, I guess I'll just have to play this game of strip Catan by myself," I joke, tapping my pen on the kitchen island.

After our role-play, the fun we have had together has exceeded my untamed imaginations.

Matthew has been the most patient, giving, and caring lover. There are nights when he just kisses me for hours. On other occasions, we play silly games or re-create more scenes from my favorite books.

The Catan game arrived earlier this morning, and we were saving it for a special occasion. The first player to ten victory points gets to pick out our next costumes for another salacious act in the bedroom.

"Don't worry, darling; I'll give you all my wood when I get home." He laughs, and the sound feels as good as one of his hugs. "Though Aaron's game doesn't end until nine. Who decided to close out a hockey match for six-year-olds that late?"

"People say go big or go home, but honestly, I don't know

why the latter is a bad thing. I'd love to spend all night in the house with you." Bear brushes up against my ankles, purring loudly. I've never spent so much time alone with him. Nerves drum in my veins. He's my responsibility tonight. *It can't be that hard, right?* "Okay, well, Bear and I will be waiting for you."

"Thanks again for watching him; I hope he doesn't give you too much trouble," he says. "How's property hunting going? Seen anything new?"

A sprawl of business plan drafts lie before me. They're in disarray beside the platters of food I've been taste-testing for the Winter Ball. All the catering options haven't been up to par.

"The buildings that are big enough need a ton of repairs, and the others are out of my price range." I tap my pen more harshly against the island. "So, I guess I'm still looking."

I've never had to think before swiping my credit card, but now I'm counting every dollar. Without my trust, it may be hard to start The Griffin. I'll have to sacrifice clothes, books, shoes, and my aesthetician. I gulp.

"New listings go up every day; don't be discouraged," Matthew assures me.

"Yeah. Scrolling has been a helpful distraction from the fact that we still don't have a caterer," I sigh, looking at the assortment of desserts staring at me. They're pretty and sweet. However, knowing my mother, if they aren't pavlova, mille crepe cakes, or something equally decadent, she'll consider the task a failure.

"We'll just have to serve hundreds of bacon, egg, and cheese breakfast sandwiches." Matthew chuckles over the phone. "Hope you've been practicing."

I love that he tries to lighten the mood anytime a situation gets overwhelming for me.

"Could you imagine everyone in their bespoke Michael Andrews suits and Elie Saab gowns eating my greasy food?" My laughter turns into snorts. "I'm going to leave the cooking to the professionals."

"We'll figure it out together."

Silence fills the line. Would a normal couple typically say *I love you* before hanging up? Is it too soon?

"I'll let you go," I whisper.

"Okay, see you soon." Matthew hangs up the call.

"Beary." I look down at the vibrating bundle of brown fur at my feet. "How do you feel about pizza?" If I eat one more bite of cake, I may actually throw up.

He blinks at me, then lets out a penetrating meow, which I'm pretty sure means, *Yes please.* But even though I've been around him for almost a month, I'm not quite fluent in cat yet.

"Okay, buddy. I'm going to throw on some slippers, then I'll put in a delivery order for an extra cheesy pie, and we can watch a movie in bed. How does that sound?"

Wow, I must be tired if I'm actually speaking to a cat.

A few minutes later, I return to the kitchen, wrapped in my Agnona cashmere sweater and my shearling slingbacks.

Oh no.

To my horror, Bear is on the kitchen island, his little furry face in a jar of caviar. Frosting is caught in his paws. The remnants of a crab puff are stuck to the tip of his tail.

No, no, no. My blood sloshes in my veins, my heart pounding louder and louder.

"Bear!" I scream, running toward the counter. He doesn't look up. *Is he okay?* Animals can't eat people food. That's like rule number one of pet care. "Bear, no; please get out of there."

Carefully, I help dislodge his head from the jar. Caviar sticks to his whiskers. He purrs the moment his body is safely tucked into my arms.

"No, kitty. How did you even get up here?" I riffle through The Griffin's business plans spread out on the island until I find my phone.

I chew my bottom lip.

Quickly, my fingers type *Can cats eat caviar?* into the search bar. Then I delete the search and try again. *Can cats eat caviar, cake, and crab puffs?*

I skim the results, and they all declare the same thing—only in moderation. Is a whole jar of caviar and a couple large bites of vanilla sponge cake considered moderate?

Bear yowls and claws his way out of my arms, collapsing onto the floor. He scurries away as I skim the copious articles. Then a retching sound comes from the other side of the kitchen.

"Bear!" I cry, finding him again.

He peers up at me with the saddest eyes as he retches.

Panic ripples in my cells. *Matthew shouldn't have trusted me with his cat.*

Should I call him? Or a vet?

No. I can do this. I can try to fix this.

"You're okay, little guy." I kneel beside Bear, scratching the top of his head. "I've been there. Trust me. When cronuts were all the rage, I must've eaten four boxes of them all at once."

He stills, seemingly done with his fit of nausea. In a blink, his entire body goes rigid, and he sits up, spine rippling as he vomits on the shearling fabric of my slipper.

"Oh god." I gag. How do people do this with their children? *Hold it together, Molly. This is Matthew's cat. He might be your cat in the future.*

You need to take care of him.

I abandon my slippers and rummage through the pantry and cabinets for cleaning supplies. Where does Olivia keep the puke soap? Is there even such a thing?

My nerves dance around in my body. I finally stumble upon some kind of all-purpose spray. This feels like an all-purpose situation.

I grab a roll of paper towels and return to the scene of the crime. Holding my nose shut with one hand, I use the other to wipe Bear down.

"I'm so sorry; I shouldn't have left you alone with all of those tasting platters," I say in a nasally tone, and he purrs loudly. "I had no idea you could climb that high up. Or can you fly?"

He sits watching me clean up his vomit. My slippers likely won't survive this disaster.

When Bear is all clean, I pull off my sweater and wrap him in it. The smell in the room is horrendous. I scoop Bear up, grab my phone, and rush him over to the living room. "You're going to be okay now. I got you, Bear." Tears roll down my face. "Please be okay, buddy."

Bear purrs, closing his eyes. He seems fine, but guilt weighs heavily on my chest.

What if this is the calm before the vomit-induced storm?

We fall back onto the couch. My vision is a blur as I scroll my phone, searching for an emergency vet nearby.

A call flashes on the screen. *My mother.*

I decline. I don't have time for this. But the buzzing returns, this time in the form of a text.

What's that saying, when it rains, it pours?

I open it.

MOM

> Worried about the Winter Ball. Do you have a caterer yet?

Ugh. The world obviously only revolves around her desires.

MOLLY

> Little busy, will give you a call back.

MOM

> This is urgent.

> The event is only a few weeks away.

MOLLY

I have someone.

Lying used to be my forte, but right now it's making me feel rotten. I'm not in the mood for her shenanigans. Nothing is as urgent as making sure Bear is okay.

MOM

Who?

MOLLY

You wouldn't know them. I'll arrange a tasting menu for you this week. I have everything under control.

Maybe Matthew was onto something. I'll cook for the entire party if it will prove to her that I can handle this.

MOM

You never stop by the estate anymore.

MOLLY

There are a lot of things to do for the Winter Ball.

MOM

Are you sure that man isn't keeping you away from us?

The only person preventing me from seeing my mother is my mother. I've been trapped in her abstract world. If it wasn't for my life filling up with the love and happiness I feel for Matthew, I wouldn't be able to open my eyes to the fact that I spent years letting myself be belittled, mistreated, and shut down.

My trust will help me put more distance between my mother and me, and it might be best for us both.

MOLLY

I've been busy.

MOM

> I would've appreciated an earlier update about the food. I was moments away from having to call around town and ask for favors.

On a Saturday night? I doubt it.

I glance down at Bear. He purrs quietly as he sleeps in my lap. *Poor guy.*

He's more important than a trivial party.

My mother's overbearingness is the last thing I need right now. I'm almost tempted to call it quits. No fifty million dollars. No more fake relationships. No more Greenes.

But there's Matthew and his project. The Griffin and my future.

I need to figure out a way to protect my peace, but first I need to keep Bear safe.

Chapter 27
Matthew

IN ALL THIRTY-SIX of my years, I've never lost my head this much over a woman.

Projects? Sure.

Deadlines? Definitely.

The way I mixed up the words *kick* and *kink* in a presentation during Plastech's early funding days? One hundred percent.

But a woman? No.

No one's infiltrated each and every one of my thoughts the way Molly has. I hadn't realized how much she occupies my mind until I spent a few hours back in my normal life. *Normal.* I don't really know if that word means the same thing it used to.

Every time I watched Aaron's team, The Wee Warriors, out on the ice, I saw her.

Their red jerseys reminded me of her fiery red hair. The cheering and laughter in the stands sounded like her. The puck was her wide amber eyes.

Molly.

I even worked up the courage to tell Maya that I'm bringing a woman home for Christmas. My arm is probably bruised from where my sister punched me for waiting so long to tell her.

Looking back, I should've delivered the news over text.

Would've been easier to dodge the full-on interrogation that broke out. But Maya will have to wait to meet my girl like everyone else.

The locks on the townhouse click into place, and I push the heavy weight of the door open.

"I'm in here," Molly yells from the kitchen.

When I enter, she's sitting on a barstool. Her curls are tied up into a messy knot above her head, and a pen sticks out from behind her ear.

"Hey." I smile at her. She frowns, and her forehead creases. "What are you still doing up?"

Did Lance come over while I was gone? Has he convinced her to marry him instead?

Christ. The jealousy in my veins is impossible to ignore.

"I messed up, Matthew, so, so badly." She slides her laptop aside. "I was trying to make sense of the budget template and get through all of the platters those caterers sent, but I just…I went to get my slippers, and I was going to order pizza and—" Molly sucks in a deep inhale.

"Slow down, darling." I drop my coat on the kitchen island and place both palms on the stone top, waiting for her to go on.

"Bear ate a jar of caviar, and maybe some cake and crab puffs. He threw up," she says, her lip trembling. "I called the emergency vet, and they said he's probably fine but I should keep an eye on him for any signs of distress. He's been sleeping for the past two hours, and, Matthew, I hurt your cat—"

My laughter bursts out of me, interrupting her. She looks at me in bewilderment. "Baby, relax. Bear's got a stomach of steel. Seriously, this cat once ate a tub of strawberry ice cream, chewing the compostable lid for dessert."

"But…" Molly hesitates. "He got sick, because of me."

Her pout is making my heart burst at the seams.

"He got sick because he hasn't got a clue about self-control.

Cats get sick sometimes," I assure her. "Thank you for being worried about him. I love—" I hesitate, worry needling the back of my mind. "How much you care."

"You're not upset?" Molly bats her lashes up at me, then she lets out a lion-sized yawn.

My dick springs to life. Dammit. This woman can't do one sweet thing without me turning into a neanderthal.

"Of course not." I loop around the island, settle myself between her legs as she sits on a stool, and pull her into a hug. Molly leans her head against my chest. The smell of her hair sends a deep comfort through me.

She spent the night fussing over my grumpy beast as if he were her own.

Fuck. I'm head over heels for this girl.

"I'm not cut out for motherhood," Molly chuckles into my knit sweater.

The hollow feeling in my stomach returns. Is she just saying that because of the stress she felt tonight, or does she mean it? It doesn't matter. I have to stop assuming what she's thinking. After the Winter Ball, Molly will have a clearer picture of her future. Then we'll sit down and discuss what our life together could look like.

"You've been a great cat mom." I plant my lips on the top of her head. She pulls away and looks up at me.

"Do you think Bear hates me?"

"With a belly full of caviar? I doubt it." I spot him lying on top of one of her fancy sweaters. He's definitely living the high life here.

"There's one more thing," Molly says, keeping her arms wrapped around my waist. "While I was trying to find a vet for Bear, my mother reached out, and I was so overwhelmed with the situation that I kind of lied to her and told her we already found a caterer."

Her eyes are swimming with worry. Not being able to take

the pressure off her shoulders is hurting me. Even if we do everything right, I don't know if her parents will think it's enough.

I manage a deep breath. "I can't imagine the stress she's putting on you."

"She thinks we're going to fail, and I just want to prove her wrong." Molly's beautiful bravery and determination shine right through her.

"We will," I promise. "Our little team already succeeded at two of the impossible tasks. We can finish strong." Out of the corner of my eye, I notice the Excel sheet I helped create on her laptop screen. "How's the budgeting for The Griffin? Any new listings in the last few hours?"

Molly spins in her chair, dragging her laptop over to us. "Miserable. How on earth is real estate so expensive?"

"Ah, innocent Jedi, you will soon learn that everything costs more money than you budget for." I give her thigh a playful pinch.

"Do…or do not. There is no try." Molly echoes Yoda's famous proverb. Blood rushes to my cock, which hardens against my jeans. My hands flex as I resist the urge to pick her up against this counter and show her how irresistible she is to me.

"Since when are you a Star Wars fan?" I pry.

"You, Ollie, and Robert always make references I don't get, so I just watched everything from *Episode I* to *The Mandalorian*." My smirk is impossible to hide. Is this how she felt when I read her favorite book series? "After this year's Halloween activities, maybe we'll skip the Lysa and Jordan costume next year, and I can get you to throw on that bounty hunter mask." Molly giggles.

"There are humanoids called Sephi in the universe; you'll be able to reuse those elf ears."

"Have you given this a thought before?"

"Once or twice." I join her laughter until we're both red in the face. "Now, come on; show me what you've got so far." I nod at her laptop.

"Okay, well, I did actually find a place." She bounces her knee in her stool. "It's a castle—I know, *extreme,* but hear me out." Her eyes rapidly blink up at me. Delight oozes out of her. It makes me weak in the knees. Yeah. I've been giddy over this woman on so many occasions, you'd think I was under some kind of spell.

"Go on," I say, keeping my cool.

"It's in Tarrytown, and it overlooks the river." On her screen, a spectacular property is displayed in dozens of images. There are gothic windows and a brick exterior. "Twenty-two rooms."

"And only twenty-five miles from the city," I note. "A perfect hotspot destination for anyone seeking a weekend escape." I put on my best travel-agent voice.

"That's what I was thinking too. And the grounds are stunning." She beams, scrolling through the images of the gardens. "There's a barn on the property, so I could actually have a stable. However, the structure probably needs a lot of work."

As Molly clicks through each picture, she looks up to gauge my reaction. Pure joy is etched onto her face.

She's radiant.

There's nothing like finding a passion to ground you and set you free at the same time. That spark is evident in Molly.

The property is everything she's described and more.

A castle suited for a queen.

I glance at the hefty price tag. "Nineteen million dollars?"

"I know." Molly slumps in her stool. "That's almost all of my assets without the trust. Well, unless I start selling off my bags."

"No, you won't be selling off anything," I promise. Not on my watch. Molly's going to have her inn and get to keep all the frilly and sparkly things she likes. "This is actually pretty reasonable. Sure, it needs an inspection, but it's been on the market for four years; there's a chance the owner would bump down the cost. And, yeah, you're going to have staffing and renovation expenses." I peruse the listing, picturing her there so vividly. "Even without the trust, we might be able to swing this. There are plenty of grants and opportunities for early investors out there."

"We?" Her amber eyes shoot up to me.

"Yes, we," I confirm and reach for her laptop. "We've met plenty of people who would place a bet on you, Molly. Me included. I may not have had enough capital of my own to launch EcoDrones, what with all of its research and technology costs, but I invest in start-up businesses all the time. I believe in you, and in this vision."

She smiles. My favorite, genuine one. "Thank you."

"Of course. Now let's see which of your costs we can realistically cut. How much is the rent on your townhouse?"

"My parents own this place, so I don't pay rent. But I've actually been thinking about moving out. That probably means my personal expense category is going to go up." Worry coats her voice. She clicks around the spreadsheet a few times. The cells turn a blaring red.

"If you move in with me, you won't have to pay rent." The words slip out, but I can't imagine going back home and spending any of my days without her. "I mean, if you buy this castle, it's only a half-hour drive from my house."

"I can't ask that of you."

There are so many reasons we shouldn't be agreeing to this, so many parts of our future that sit unknown. But I want to figure them out with her.

Molly has taken over my life for the better, and I refuse to let that go.

"You're not asking me; I'm inviting you." I trail my hand down her leg. "I'm sure I can spare a bedroom for your books and shoes."

She sets an elbow on the island, her chin into her hand, and looks up at me. "Oh, but where would I sleep?"

"I've got a spot for you in my bed," I say, leaning down and planting my lips on her cheek. "It's perfectly sized for my girlfriend."

"Girlfriend?" I wish I could memorialize the way her amber eyes are lit up.

I know the timing may not be perfect, but Molly's sleeping in the same bed as me and taking care of my cat. I need her to be fully mine.

"No more pretending, darling. I'd love to make this real." I brush my thumb along her cheek. My commitment to her is rooted still. Whatever happens with her parents' decision, I'll be by her side. "Would you like to be my girlfriend?"

"Yes. Yes. Yes." Molly shimmies her shoulders, jumps out of her seat, and wraps her hands around me. "I'd love to be your girlfriend, Matthew Hudson. And move in with you." She kisses me before briefly pulling away. "Again."

My heart soars so far that it hits the clouds of guilt hanging over my head. I'm weak and selfish, for not sharing everything with her, but there are only two more weeks until the Winter Ball. *It can wait until then.*

Chapter 28
Molly

"I was nervous about wearing this today." My Huishan Zhang Madalena gown is a flurry of pretty pink sparkles and feathers. I smile up at Matthew. "But I feel so freaking cute. Honestly, all this time, I let myself believe that if I wore even a splotch of color out into the world, my parents would disown me. I know, super dramatic, but—"

"Not dramatic at all." He rubs my lower back, looking oh so handsome in his tuxedo.

"I am who I am, and everyone will have to deal with that."

It's hard to slowly chip away at the grip my parents hold over my life. They've dictated so many of my decisions that it's hard to let myself be comfortable in my own choices. Even if it's just a dress; I'm prioritizing Just Molly.

Sparkles, color, and all.

"Damn right." Matthew nods as we step into Gotham Hall.

The Climate Convergence Gala is in full swing. About a thousand people chatter and chortle in their best attire. We make the rounds, saying hello to those who have shown interest in EcoDrones over the past couple of weeks.

In an hour, my stomach is bursting from all the food I've eaten. Everything has been delicious.

"It's the hors d'oeuvres apocalypse over here." Matthew kisses me and grabs a glazed fig with a tempeh chili reduction from my plate on the high-table. My Judith Leiber Couture ruby heart-shaped minaudière sits beside the array of food.

"I'm certain this is the chef we need." I chew through the final bite of my crème fraîche tartlet.

"Do you think they'd be available?" Matthew regards the overflowing ballroom.

"Probably not, but we're running out of time." My nerves are frayed, all my contacts exhausted. We only have a week before the Winter Ball, and the backup caterer I have on call is miles away from the incredible flavors here. I want to blow my mother away, not scratch the surface of her expectations. I take another bite of the pancetta, pear, and pecan puff. My mouth waters. "*Ugh*, Matthew. Yum. We *need* this."

"If you keep moaning and groaning like that, I may have to throw you over my shoulder and carry my girlfriend all the way uptown." A hint of mischief flashes in his blue eyes.

My heart races with each reminder that I have a boyfriend. Matthew's my first, in so many ways. First *real* relationship, first love. I wouldn't have it any other way.

My pulse sings through my veins. I want to touch him so badly. "Now that sounds like—"

"Hudson," someone calls out from beside us. Sam Kaitlin, the private equity executive we met at the Hastings' Charity Luncheon, strolls toward us. Another shimmering suit hangs off of their lanky frame.

"It's great to see you." Matthew nods, extending his hand.

"Likewise," Sam says, giving him a firm shake. "Molly, you're looking lovely."

The compliment squashes any lingering doubt I had about my outfit being too much. "Thank you."

"So." Sam lowers their voice. "I've spoken with my partner, and we want in on EcoDrones."

"Excellent." Matthew nods. "The prototype is coming along very nicely."

"Of course, we'd need to do some due diligence once you have the initial iteration. But, given your business plan, we foresee a hefty investment from the ReClaim Fund."

It's amazing—no, motivational watching Matthew at work. He's a real-life Superman. Saving the world one tree and cocktail party at a time.

With this amount of interest, he definitely won't need the trust. But the money can't hurt if my parents approve our marriage, and if they don't…well, all those nagging daydreams about separating from my family may become more than just daydreams.

"You won't be disappointed." Matthew smirks.

Sam tips their drink to us. "Can I introduce you to a few people here? I'm sure they'd be as eager as we are."

Matthew gives me a glance to confirm I'll be okay by myself. I nod. It's nice that we can speak with just a look.

I swallow the remainder of my puff pastry, holding back the audible moan. A burst of spice and sweetness explodes on my tongue. This is nothing like I've ever tasted before.

That's it. I need to find out who this chef is immediately.

A force bursts in my chest. *Okay, girl. You got this.*

I ruffle the pink feathers of my gown and follow the waitstaff through the crowd of people. Once I locate the swinging kitchen doors and push through them, pure chaos envelops me.

I hear sizzling pans, chopping knives, and orders being read out. The air is hot and stuffy with the smell of garlic and seared meat. Pots clang as chefs in stark-white coats bustle around the large kitchen.

Amid the commotion, I see the head chef standing tall and composed, clad in a crisp white chef's coat and black pants.

Under her chef's hat, her deep purple hair is swept into a low bun. She surveys her domain with purpose and confidence.

That's who I need.

Before I can back out, I march my Valentino Garavani platform pumps over to the woman in charge. The seven-inch heels make me roughly the same height as the chef.

"Hi," I pipe up, coming to her side.

"Behind," someone shouts. "Behind!"

"Move, sweetheart." The head chef notices me, and I do as she says, quickly stepping back, wobbling in my heels. A cook carrying a tray of large bones misses me by an inch. *My goodness*.

"Oh, so sorry." I press myself into a metal table next to a sink overflowing with dishes. "I've never been in a real chef's kitchen before."

"Obviously," she groans, swiping a pastry off a passing tray.

Okay, we're not off to a great start.

"I love your food." The chef doesn't look up at me as she inspects the sweet treat before nodding and waving the waiter away. "Are you new to the scene?" I ask.

Her eyes narrow on me like a predator. "New? I'm Analise Roche, and I do not have a spare moment of time to give to tipsy partygoers who want another truffle caprese bite."

"This is nothing like that. I barely even drink! I simply want to hire you," I explain.

Analise speeds away, and I follow her.

There's no way I'm losing out on the opportunity to have her work the Winter Ball. I dodge the shouting chefs and cooks scattered around the kitchen. Knives flash through the air, and flames lick the pots and pans on the stovetops. I'm sweating through my dress as I try to keep the long, feathered sleeves tucked firmly at my side.

"*No*," Analise snaps at me before pulling a spoon out of her coat pocket and tasting a sauce on one of the burners. "What have I told you, Druk? Unless you're cooking for a herd of deer, ease up on the salt."

"Yes, chef." Druk wipes the sweat off his brow and starts pulling ingredients from a shelf.

I refuse to give up. "No? Is there anything I can do to change your mind?"

"Do you not see that I'm slammed here? My schedule for the next two months is packed. Holiday parties here, Christmas this, New Year's that. Then there are the birthdays and private events." Analise turns to face me, her hands firmly on her hips.

I gulp. She's terrifying.

"Dead plate!" Analise yells over me. A chef groans, pulling the plate off of the counter. "You grumble like that one more time, Petey, and I'm sending you back to the Le Cordon Bleu."

Okay, maybe this was a bad idea. I still have the other caterer booked. But their food doesn't compare to Analise's. Not by a long shot. My mother made that clear when I put together a tasting menu for her, as promised.

"Where are the clean dishes?" She eyes the sink, which looks fuller than it did when I arrived.

A waiter rushes up to Analise. "This came back."

"Flash it and get it back out there. Come on, people, we've already lost Van and Carmine tonight. Where are those replacements, Tessa?" Analise looks at the person manning the ship.

"They're not coming," Tessa yells.

I'm growing dizzy from the thick smoke and steam.

"What do you mean not coming? We don't have dishwashers, and our industrial machine isn't cleaning the plates fast enough."

"I'm trying to solve this, Ana, but we don't have someone right now." Tessa shakes her head and goes back to reading out orders to the frantic kitchen.

This might be my chance.

"I can help," I pipe up. *Pfft*. I've washed dishes before.

Okay…I've helped Matthew with a few plates after the dinners he's made. But it can't be that hard. Sponge, soap, scrub, and rinse.

"What?" Analise faces me. Her thick brows stitch together.

"I can do it."

"That shoe can probably barely make a fried egg," Petey pipes up from behind me.

Shoe? "These are Valentino Garavani pumps, and you're right, but I'm not offering to cook." I shoot him a glare. "Dishes, however, I can do."

Analise studies me as another batch of dishes gets tossed into the sink. If those don't get cleaned soon, her night will be impossible. "Fine. Get her some rubber and wrap her up," she shouts and stalks off.

Tessa throws me a pair of yellow rubber gloves from beneath her call podium. I catch them and put them on as I run over to the sink.

"You're really doing this, princess?" Tessa raises a brow at me.

"Watch me."

I turn on the tap, the sound of rushing water filling my ears, and toss back the sleeves of my dress. Am I in over my head? Not even a little bit.

Stop doubting yourself, Molly.

An employee empties the industrial dishwasher at my side. The hot steam coats my skin. My hair is surely bubbling into a frizzy frenzy.

Inhaling a calming breath, I grab the soap and sponge and start scrubbing. The dishes slip out of my hands a few times, but the staff pay me no mind as they run around like headless chickens. In a few minutes, I fall into rhythm, scrubbing, rinsing, and repeating.

I'm unstoppable.

Chapter 29
Matthew

Where is Molly?

For the past fifteen minutes, I've looped around Gotham Hall about a dozen times, but I haven't been able to find my woman. I've scanned the entire hall, and there's no sign of her pink dress. The investors Sam introduced me to were so interested in EcoDrones that I let time slip by me.

Christ. My pulse pounds.

I've already asked the waitstaff to check the ladies' room. I can't even call her, because she left her heart-shaped purse on the high table. Thankfully, no one decided to take it home with them. It looks very expensive.

After a few more rounds, a flicker of bright pink flashes through the swinging kitchen doors.

Molly? *No way.*

Maybe she's still chatting with the caterer. I follow a waiter and enter the hectic kitchen. It's filled with a flurry of white coats and frenzied cooks.

Molly leans over the sink in her seven-thousand-dollar dress, very tall heels, and yellow rubber gloves. Her feathered sleeves are damp with soapy water. Sweat coats her neck and back.

What in the world? *Is she washing dishes?*

Yeah. This is another bucket list item I'm going to have to check off.

My darling Molly Greene in yellow rubber gloves. *Check.*

An urge sparks up in my body. *Can we bring those home with us?*

"So, you going to cater my event?" Molly shouts at the chef.

"I told you, I'm booked."

"And I just saved you tonight, Analise."

"That you did." Analise joins Molly's side, drying off the clean dishes on the rack.

"I'll double whatever they're paying you."

The chef cocks her head. "Tempting offer, but I'm not sure."

"Trust me, you're not going to want to doubt me." *Atta girl.*

"I like this one; she's fiery." The woman at the head of the kitchen laughs before catching sight of me. "Sir, you're blocking the door. Are you lost?"

"Uh—no, I'm looking for my girlfriend…" I scamper out of the way. Molly doesn't seem to notice I'm here.

"December first. The Plaza Hotel. A thousand people. I need you there," Molly says firmly, not giving the chef the opportunity to decline. A shiver zooms up my spine at her assertive tone. *She's so attractive.*

Two people push past me, throwing on aprons and running to the sink.

"Fine," Analise sighs reluctantly. "You can stop scrubbing those dishes now. Our backup is here."

"I'll email you the details." Molly nods and abandons her sponge.

Then she spots me. The entire front of her gown is soaked. Her cheeks are red, her brow is damp, and there's a wide smile across her face. She shucks off the rubber gloves.

"Matthew?" Molly says, looking surprised.

"I've been looking for you for ages." I rush over to her.

"I got us a caterer." A glimmer lights up her eyes. She's perfect.

I wrap her in my arms and spin her around. "You did it."

"No, we did. We finished the list." She laughs before connecting her lips with mine. Euphoria washes over me, and my heart rate speeds up.

I don't think I've ever been more sure that I'm in love with her. I mean, how could I not be? This precious, tender woman whose skin is as tough as a suit of armor. No masks in sight. Just Molly being entirely herself.

We break from our kiss, and I fall to pieces at the look in her amber eyes.

"Hey, get the hell out of my kitchen before I change my mind!" Analise yells.

Molly laughs, wiggling out of my grasp. "Let's go home, Hudson."

Gladly.

* * *

WE BARELY KEPT our hands off each other on the drive back to the townhouse. Molly's chauffer definitely needs to invest in a privacy screen.

My Molly.

"I feel like I've barely been able to calm down since we left the gala," Molly says, turning off the shower.

I lean against the doorway, hand her a towel, and she wraps it around herself. "You were marvelous, darling."

"Did you see? I was literally a dishwashing warrior," she giggles.

I inhale the steam from the shower. Red ruby apples flood my senses. *Home.* "You know, I don't think I've ever been more attracted to you in my life."

"Oh yeah? You're attracted to me, are you?" She playfully arches her brow at me.

A little more than that. She swipes at the condensation on the mirror. The cotton towel rides up her thighs, revealing her soft, pale legs. A little more forward, and her perfect ass covered with dimples would be peeking out of her towel.

I swallow.

"So much."

Molly faces me. Mischief coats her face. "Be honest; did the rubber gloves get you going?"

"You get me going. Everything about you." I approach her, brushing one of my fingers along the slope of her shoulders.

"Really?" She inhales deeply, watching my reflection in the mirror before she spins around in my arms.

My heart leaps from my chest. My palm brackets her jaw, and I pull her in for a kiss.

She is pliant and receptive, effortlessly opening her mouth to me and welcoming my tongue.

"Have I told you that you're perfect?" I whisper against her lips.

"Only once or twice." She smiles, turning back toward the sink and straightening against my chest.

I pull her damp curls off her shoulder and plant a kiss on the crook of her neck. "Only once or twice? That won't do." I let out a sardonic laugh and gently sink my teeth into her nape. "I don't think *perfect* is a good enough word to describe you."

Molly croons beneath my lips, rising onto her tiptoes and pressing herself into me. My cock throbs in my tuxedo pants, grinding against her back. At On Cloud Nine when I undressed her in front of a mirror, she was nervous. Now, her confidence is obvious. I love when she takes control.

"No?"

I trace my palm up her waist. "No, it's too plain. Maybe

venust." She whimpers beneath my touch. "Or, better yet, *elysian.*"

"I'm not familiar with that one." Her lustrous gaze connects with mine through the reflection in the mirror.

"Heavenly, almost like paradise." My fingers push past the fold in her towel, the pads swiping against her damp skin.

"Oh." She shivers. "Good one."

"Still not quite the right word for my girlfriend." Her skin pebbles beneath my touch. "*Resplendent.*" My hand glides against her stomach until it reaches the dip between her waist and thigh. "That's the one."

"You think so?"

"Richly colorful, a pleasure to enjoy, glowing." Another kiss along her neck, and then I pull her towel off, sending it to the ground.

"I think that's fitting." Molly's cheeks turn red in the mirror.

Fuck. She's *everything*. "Christ, baby, you look too good like this."

She catches my gaze in the reflection. "How else can I look good for you?"

Surprising me, she bends over the countertop, her perfect ass on display.

My pulse races. "You drive me wild all of the time, darling."

Her body trembles, and she props both of her palms in front of her, arching her spine. "Speaking of wild, I've always had a bit of a fantasy..." She bashfully tucks her lips between her teeth.

"Now's not the time to be shy." I trace my hand over the curve of her back. "Tell me what happens in it; tell me how I can make you feel good."

Her nipples harden. Her amber eyes are alight with fire as she puts on a timid voice and says, "Well, I've been a little bad. I made you look for me all night, and now I think I need some setting straight."

This woman must've been forged in heaven just for me. She's taunting me, and I happily slip into the role she wants me to play. "I was so worried while searching for you." I throw on a disappointed voice. "What am I going to do with you?"

"That was so naughty of me. I could probably use a bit of… punishment." She wiggles her behind against me.

"You want me to mark this delicious ass, Molly?"

"Yes."

I pull my hand away from her back and down the plump curve of her behind. "What else happens in this fantasy of yours?"

"I do anything you command." Her grin is laced with wickedness. "I like it when you take me and make me beg. You always know exactly what I need."

I grab a fistful of her breast, the other hand kneading into her ass. "You're so good when you let me care for you, when you give yourself over to me, aren't you?"

She nods. "Mhm."

"I'll do whatever you ask of me and make all of your fantasies come true, but I need you to agree with me here, okay? Say *red* if you want me to stop anything I'm doing. Anything at all. Otherwise, I'll enjoy making you beg."

"Red if I want you to stop," she whispers.

"You're safe and in control here, remember?"

"Yes, I'm in control." Molly thrusts her hips against my crotch.

"Good girl. Now, are you eager for this cock already?" I let out a gruff chuckle, descending onto my knees behind her, and instead of waiting for a reply, I trace the tip of my tongue over her already wet pussy. "Open wider; let me show you how lucky I am to give you everything."

"And what if I don't?" she coaxes.

"Then I'll make you." I run my finger along her cunt.

"Mhm." Her legs spread open wider, pushing her ass closer

to my face. Her knees tremble when I push inside of her. "Matthew," she cries, and I just let myself get hypnotized by the sight of her soaked pussy taking one of my fingers, slowly and tortuously.

"I adore this," I say, planting my lips across the line where her ass meets her upper thigh, then sinking my teeth into her skin. "Hearing your whimpers, your moans, and knowing that I'm the only one who can do this to you."

"You are."

"I bet you look beautiful, eyes wide, as you wait for me to take this pussy for myself." I pull out slowly and connect my mouth with her clit. "Tell me how good you look."

My cock throbs, begging me to end this little game she's created while simultaneously wanting to stretch it out for as long as possible.

"Uh—" She hesitates. *No, that won't do.* I open my palm and land a smack on the pale flesh of her ass. Gentle but firm.

Molly growls, her body colliding with the countertop.

"Be good and describe how lovely you look, darling," I repeat, sending my breath against the swell of her clit.

"I—I…now?" I cut her off with another smack, harder this time, my handprint clear against the reddening skin of her ass.

Molly yips, but her legs don't shut together. She keeps herself perched steadily against the sink, pussy still sopping wet.

"Try again."

"I look beautiful," she mewls, and I catch her eyeing her own reflection, her cheeks reddening.

"Good girl." I gently palm the skin of her ass and push two of my fingers into her wet pussy. "Tell me how much you deserve this cock," I groan against her cunt, lapping at the slickness that's starting to drip against her thighs.

"I—" Another spank, the other cheek this time. Molly heeds the warning. "I deserve your big cock," she says, her voice growing more confident than before.

It's bliss watching her fight the embarrassed part of herself that wants to resist. I want to shatter that part. Make her feel safe.

"Red yet?"

"Not a chance," she groans.

"Stubborn girl. I bet I know why."

"Why?"

"It's because you know who makes you come, don't you?" Her gasps rattle in her throat, and my erection scrapes against my suit pants. "Who worships this pussy?"

"You do." Her stomach grinds against the countertop.

A smile stretches across my face. I work my fingers with languid strokes. Molly looks over at me—another smack.

"Eyes on yourself, gorgeous," I command. Her ass is a bright red. My favorite color. "I bet you're desperate for a release, aren't you? Fuck, I love the sight of your body marked by me, love watching your legs tremble with every pump of my fingers."

Molly's lips split into a silly grin. "I love it."

"Me too, baby; look here." I keep my eyes glued to hers and retract my fingers from her swollen cunt. Then I lift them to my lips. "You're my sustenance," I say before running my tongue over the slick feel of her. She watches with awe. "Now you're going to have a taste."

She nods.

I tower over her, bringing my fingers to her lips. She puts them in her mouth and sucks hard. The pinch in my balls is agonizing. *Fuck.*

"How do you taste?" I ask.

"Like I'm yours."

Yep. That does it.

I use my other hand to undo the buckle of my belt, stripping off my pants and boxers until my aching cock is only an inch away from her.

"Listen up." I lean into the thicket of her hair, searing my teeth into her earlobe as she vibrates beneath me. "Keep sucking your taste off my fingers as I stretch out this pussy with my cock, you got that?"

"Y-yes," she grumbles through the pressure of my pointer and middle finger between her teeth.

"That's right, and if you're good, if you take every inch, I'm going to fill you up to the brim. I know you like that, baby," I groan. "Love it when my cum is dripping out of your pussy, my sweet dirty girl."

In a blink, I slam against her. Molly chokes on a scream, but she keeps sucking the pads of my fingers. My punishing strokes increase rapidly, and from this angle, I'm hitting the sweet spot buried within her with such precise agony that all Molly can do is suck, gasp, and roll her eyes back with every push.

My orgasm feels too fast, too soon, but the teasing did as much to me as it did to her.

"It feels too good having you wrapped around me like this," I confess. Her walls clench around me. "You know exactly what you're doing to me, don't you?"

Another tight grip of her pussy, and I feel the point of no return right on the horizon.

"Tell me, Molly." I slam into her, pulling my fingers out of her mouth to pinch each of her hardened nipples. "Tell me how much you want this."

"I want you, Matthew," she says desperately. "I want your big cock to fill me up, to claim me, to take me."

"Good girl; you get rewarded for saying things like that." I land a firm smack against her ass again, drilling deeper into her. Molly's face is almost pressed up against the mirror.

My blood rushes in my veins, my breath leaving my lungs as I will myself to keep going, to let her reach the edge before me.

It's adrenaline and passion and fucking explosions all at once.

"You own this cock. You own me." I grind deeper into her, and Molly almost screams again. "But you're aware of that, aren't you?"

I bury deeper, and she tightens again, another wash of heat pooling at the base of my spine. I've never been this hard in my life.

"M-Matthew." Molly's voice vibrates. She's resisting her release again, her mind way too consumed to simply let go.

"Stop fighting it and come," I demand. "I know you need to. I can feel it."

As if it's the encouragement she needed, her walls clench around my dick in a few thrusts. A wail pushes out of her throat, and I let go with her, my cock jerking inside her tight pussy. I push as far as she can take me and empty myself inside of her. My body collapses over hers, my weight draping her against the countertop.

My hands cup her skin, and I turn her, dragging her right into my chest. Molly's damp forehead collides with my pecs. Her eyes are red, her cheeks splotched with color.

"Oh, I'm sorry," she laughs, swiping at the tears in her eyes. "That was...*so* much. I don't know why I'm crying."

"Never apologize, darling. You have nothing to be embarrassed about."

"I've truly never felt anything like that. It was so overwhelming." She's a hot mess in my embrace, her body pliant, a dazed look in her eyes. I pull her closer.

"Was it how you imagined it? Did you feel safe?"

"I felt so in control, so free. Everything was up to me." She smiles, and I plant a kiss on her temple.

"That's how it'll always be, you hear me?" Her head nods against me as her breathing slows. "With us, you're in control, and I'm just your humble servant."

"What does that make me?"

"My woman." I reluctantly unglue from her, walk over to the bath, and turn on the faucet. "Now let's get you cleaned up."

It's instinctive, helping her let loose, and I want to do it endlessly.

Chapter 30
Molly

The Grand Ballroom at The Plaza Hotel is breathtaking, with gilded designs adorning the walls and a chandelier sparkling above. Fresh calla lilies, orchids, and ranunculus arrangements tower over guests at each table. Crisp white linens line the high-top tables and shimmer beneath the hues of blue lights.

We did it.

All three tasks are complete, and the Winter Ball is running smoothly. A tray of Analise's specialty glazed figs speeds past me. I grab one and plop it in my mouth.

Success sure does taste delicious.

Matthew whispers in my ear, "You know, girlfriend, we make the best team."

"You better not get used to that title. After tonight, you'll be my fiancé," I say with confidence.

"I look forward to it." His fingers trail down the fabric of my Oscar de la Renta ruffled Georgette dress. I can't wait for him to take it off me tonight. He's so tall, and handsome with his jet-black hair slicked back. His round frames on the bridge of his perfectly crooked nose. "Have you seen your parents?"

"Not yet. They're probably holding out for dramatic effect,

or they're making sure this first hour goes smoothly." I scan the crowd again, looking for them.

Tonight, they'll make their decision about my relationship with Matthew, and I just want to get it over with. Anxiety hums in my belly. I don't want to cut my parents out of my life, but if they fail to put my needs first, I'll have no other choice.

Matthew has funding for EcoDrones. I can do my best to swing an offer on the Tarrytown property without the trust. Or I'll find another location for my inn. Nothing and no one will stop me.

I'm certain we'll both be fine without the trust money. At least, I hope so.

However much I want my family's approval, my future is more important.

"Your Uncle Davis has been in line for Ollie's whisky tasting twice. So I would say we did a pretty good job." Matthew tugs at the cerise tie around his neck. It's a perfect match to my gown.

"Agreed." I nod. "Did you try the figs?"

"Already had two of them," he laughs, but I barely notice as I continue searching the room for Mom and Dad. Matthew's hand settles a possessive weight on my back. "Hey, don't worry. We got this."

My heart soars. It's nice to know that, whatever happens tonight, we have each other.

"I know, I'm just nervous." The butterflies in my stomach refuse to stop multiplying.

Fake dating my work crush, falling for him, making it real, and then marrying him for money isn't the most traditional love story, but we've made something beautiful together.

The past couple of weeks, we've skirted around our true feelings with the anticipation of what happens today. Tonight, I'll tell him I don't want a divorce.

We must feel the same for each other. I doubt he'd make me

his girlfriend and ask me to move in if he didn't share my feelings.

I need to be brave, because I want this.

Cocktail parties, philanthropic pursuits, cosplay on the weekends, volunteering, Bear snuggling with us on the couch, and book club. Staying up late working on my inn while he launches EcoDrones.

Matthew Hudson is the love I deserve.

In the crowd, I spot Dave, Larson, and their wives chattering beneath the haze of the lights. There are whisky tumblers in their hands and a wooden flight board on their high-top table. They wave me over. "I'm going to say hello to my cousins. Want to come?" I ask Matthew.

"I would; however, Ollie is giving me a pleading look. I'll make sure everything's okay and join you in a moment." He places a kiss on my forehead.

"You better." I meander toward their table, passing a few of the guests and making sure everyone looks happy.

Tonight, for the first time in my life, I don't feel like a complete fraud amid all of these people. My boyfriend, my clothes, and my words are all my own. Second-guessing my every single move isn't suffocating me anymore.

It's freeing.

Sure, I've caught myself mirroring a smile or laughing at something that isn't particularly funny, habits I've been trapped in my whole life. Except now I'm aware of them.

I reach my cousins, and Dave pulls me into a hug. I laugh at the unusual gesture. "Molly!"

"Someone's happy," Larson slurs, the stench of whisky heavy on his breath.

"Enjoying the drinks?" I eye their almost empty tumblers.

"We're going to need to stock this at every On Cloud Nine resort," Dave says approvingly, showing off his glass of the burnt umber liquid. I should ask Ollie for a case for The Griffin.

"Has your father told you about the new line of resorts we're opening along the Gold Coast?" Larson asks casually.

Did the Bradburys agree to invest without Lance and I getting married? Or did my dad find a new investor? I've been so distant from my family lately that I cannot answer his question.

"He mentioned it. I thought he was waiting for the funding to come in before finalizing the build plans." I try to gauge how much they know.

"Ray just told us about a new investor this morning. Some Aussie." Dave shrugs.

Someone new? I must be off the hook from marrying Lance for good.

Elation pours over me. If what they're saying is true, my parents may actually approve my marriage. It would've been nice for anyone to tell me the news and not string Matthew and me along all night. But it doesn't matter.

I'm going to get everything I want without sacrifice.

"We'll be flying out there next year." Larson raises his glass to Dave, and they cheers. "Maybe you can join us."

"I'll try, but I'm likely going to be busy working on my own project."

The Griffin, here I come.

A new surge of confidence soars through me. My mother may have kept me out of the resort business, but I'll make my family see that I was always supposed to be in hospitality. Just like them.

Perhaps after everything goes well today, I can show my father the ideas I've been working on for the Tarrytown property. We could even find a way for my business to become a subsidiary of the On Cloud Nine resorts.

Is something like that even possible?

"Tell us more," the wives coo. I barely know my cousins' spouses, yet they all seem happy in their arranged marriages. Matthew and I will be able to make the best of this situation.

"You'll have to wait to find out. Now, I need to talk to my parents, but I'm so happy for both of you."

"We'll see you from the stage at the announcement later tonight."

I nod my head and stalk off. Let's get this over with. I circle around the crowd, looking for my mother's copper hair. Nowhere to be found.

Maybe they're in one of the suites, or even the downstairs foyer? I turn down a hall, and my breath hitches.

Lance strolls toward me. His dirty-blond hair is combed over, and a navy bow tie sits at his neck. His cologne is pungent, even from several steps away.

Can I run in the other direction? No. I don't hide anymore. He's the one who needs to leave.

"Molly," he calls out.

"What are you doing here?"

He stops in front of me, clicking his teeth. "Your mother invited me." He says the words like they're a well-known fact.

Panic sloshes in my veins. I shake in my Mach & Mach embellished bow pumps. "What? Why?"

"Vivian said you've reconsidered my proposal."

He can't be serious. My cousins just told me that they secured other funding. Why would my mother still invite Lance? Why would she tell him I want to marry him when they're going to approve my marriage to Matthew?

Right.

How could I be so naive? Again?

Hoping for the best in them all the time is completely useless. I'm so done with this family.

"I have no idea what my mother has told you, but it's a lie. I'm never going to marry you, not now, not ever," I snap, sending a target of gazes our way. No trace of embarrassment flares in my body. I don't care.

"Calm down. Th—"

"Do not tell me to calm down." My fingernails carve crescent moons into my palms. "You shouldn't be here."

"Molly, are you really going to give this all up?" Lance throws his arms out around him, gesturing to the inside of the Grand Ballroom.

"You need to leave." I'm not wasting another breath on this man.

"I canceled my Vegas plans to be here tonight. If you're not interested in marrying me, then why'd Vivian invite me?"

"Not my problem." I push past him and clatter down the hall. My anger returns. Heat burns my throat, my chest, and fills my veins. My mother must be in the Terrace Room. It's the only place I haven't checked.

I wasn't foolish for spending the last six weeks preparing for the worst. Deep down, despite how much I wished I'd be able to please them, I knew they would pull something like this. They probably expect me to roll over, cry, and give in.

But the old Molly is dead.

I doubt my mother spent a second of her precious time considering how this would make me feel, how small and overlooked.

They just want me to be miserable. Pliant. I'll never be enough for them, no matter what I do or don't do.

My last ounce of patience oozes out of me. I'm over it.

I have Matthew. I have my business. I can figure the rest out.

My life will be an endless loop of unhappiness if I don't set boundaries, and with boundaries come consequences.

It's about time they start listening to me—the real me.

MY MOTHER IS ENGROSSED in a conversation with an event coordinator in the Terrace Room. Only a handful of guests admire the harpists playing a peaceful song as I storm into the gilded hall.

"There you are," I snap. Months ago, I wouldn't be able to recognize the bite in my own voice, but now I hear myself. I'm finally breaking through.

A look of disbelief stuns Mom's face. "What on earth is going on with you?"

My vision blurs at the edges, my heart screaming in my chest. "You brought Lance!" I don't bother tempering the rise in my tone.

Her eyes bulge as she darts her head around then looks back at me. Lowering her voice, she says, "This is not the time or place, Molly."

Of course she cares more about what others will think than her own daughter.

I, on the other hand, don't care that I'm yelling at my own mother at the biggest social event of the year. I'm not the one who should be concerned about how I look right now.

"Why did you invite Lance Bradbury?" My palms burn as my nails sink deeper into the skin. My stomach flips, and I tremble in the ruffled silhouette of my dress.

Two months ago, she blamed me for my ex-fiancé cheating on me at my own wedding shower. Going on and on about the scene *I* made. Well, now she'll get to be the star of the show.

Mom looks away, dragging the coordinator back to us with a simple glare. "Get everyone out of the room, now." The woman pulls her clipboard close to her chest and shuffles the guests and harpists out of the Terrace Room. When the space is abandoned, Mom huffs. "Do you want to calm down before speaking to me?"

"No. Frankly, I would like to continue yelling at you until you find it in yourself to actually listen to me," I say plainly. A weight lifts from my chest at the confession. "Was this your plan all along? To put me and Matthew through hoops just to parade

Lance around? Can you honestly tell me this ridiculous Gold Coast expansion means more to you than I do? It's not even your company!"

"This is my family, Molly, and I have always done what I can to protect all of you," she bites. Deep lines etch into her forehead, and her lower lip quivers. Her once-impenetrable façade is crumbling, revealing the vulnerable woman beneath it all.

"You can't make decisions regarding my life without me anymore," I bark.

She takes an unsteady step back. "I'm looking out for what's best for you."

"What's best for me or for *you*? What's riding on this Australian resort? Seriously."

My mother pauses, bewilderment flooding her eyes. She looks at me as though she barely recognizes me. "It'll give your father the opportunity to retire."

Dad's never brought up wanting to retire before. Ray Greene has given his life to On Cloud Nine. He's been CEO for over fifteen years. There's absolutely no way he'd be interested in stepping away now. My cousins are barely in their thirties; taking over as co-CEOs would be too soon.

She's just playing another one of her games.

"And? What does that have to do with me? Dave and Larson just told me that funding for the expansion has been secured. You don't need to use me as your little pawn anymore."

She stares back at me in confusion. "What?" she whispers.

My father struts into the ballroom. His polished black dress shoes brush against the red carpet, and his tuxedo, tailored to perfection, makes him look like a general who's returned home from a victorious battle.

However, there's nothing to celebrate here.

"There you are, Ray." A nerve swells in the brow above my mother's right eye.

"What's going on?" he interjects.

I turn to him, my hands flying to my hips. "Did you find funding for the expansion in Australia?"

"Yes, just this morning. We had an investor come in on the condition that we continue to preserve the lands we purchased," he says, eyeing me behind his glasses. "How do you know about that?"

"You have?" My mother's voice cracks, and she reaches for her pearls, counting each one with her fingers.

"Yes, Vivian, I haven't had a chance to tell you—"

"Can I marry Matthew and get my trust?" I ask sternly. Their lack of communication is not my problem.

I'm over this charade.

"If you marry that man, you'll feel like an outsider for the rest of your life. You do not want that. Trust me," Mom croaks. "Everything we do is for you, and Matthew Hudson is not someone we would choose."

Ha! I almost laugh out loud. I get it now.

My mother lives in a world of grandeur, expecting everyone to play a supporting role in her existence. My heart thumps against my rib cage.

She's a narcissist. How have I not seen this before?

"You have the funds for the resorts. I have a love match. What more do you need from me?"

"For you to have the life we've always planned. To never have you feel on the outskirts of society. That's where you'll be if you choose someone from outside of our world." Her voice shakes. "You'll be a constant outcast with that man. He's a nobody. No name, no legacy, no way to support you."

It hits me like the spike of cold on the first snowfall. The filth coating her words and how they pierce through me one by one.

Matthew is the love of my life. He's everything to me, and I will not stand for her disgusting accusations.

"I don't want any of those things." The truth feel bigger in my mouth. "I'm so done…with you both." I look at my father.

He's the only person I ever had a chance at reasoning with, and even he hasn't been there for me. "I spent my whole life looking up to you; I wanted to follow in your footsteps. I even put together a business plan for my own inn, but I'm over being a part of this family," I say.

He looks stunned. "An inn?"

"Yes, Dad, in Tarrytown."

"No. We won't approve your trust," Mom cries.

My father turns to her. "*Vivian*, I don't think that's necessary."

"Let me handle this, Ray." Her piercing glare shoots at me. It's heartbreaking to look into eyes that so closely resemble mine and see them abandoned of an ounce of love. "That's right. No trust. No money. What will you do now?"

"Had you actually paid attention to me, you'd know that I can figure it out," I state, holding my ground.

The fear of losing my parents' financial support is terrifying, but it's also liberating.

I will set myself free.

My mother mumbles under her breath.

"Molly, Vivian, why don't we all try to discuss this after the party?"

As I open my mouth to speak, another set of footsteps echoes through the ballroom.

Matthew rushes toward me, and relief seeps through me.

"Oh, look, the knight in shining armor has arrived to take our daughter away," Mom sneers.

Matthew ignores her, coming to my side. "Molly, are you alright?" One of his hands brushes against my cheek, swiping away the damp line of tears I hadn't realized were there. I nod, hoping that the pain in my eyes is enough of an explanation for what's happening.

"This doesn't concern you," Mom snaps. "Molly is *our* daughter."

I whip around, baring my teeth at her. Matthew clears his throat. "If you're talking to my woman, it concerns me."

"Your *woman*?"

"Matthew and I truly care for each other, and I'm as much his as he is mine," I sigh, reaching a point of done I haven't felt before.

"Absolutely not." Her cheeks turn beet purple.

"Doll, let's reconsider this." Dad looks small beside her. "I'm sure we can all come to some kind of—"

"Don't call me that anymore," I interrupt.

"We won't support this relationship. It's final." She gives us a once-over. "The family legacy must carry on, and it needs to happen with someone who fits into our—"

"Don't even think about finishing that sentence," I snarl. The rage and indignation coursing through my veins threaten to consume me entirely, leaving nothing but a shell of myself.

But I won't let that happen, and I refuse to let her disrespect me or Matthew any longer.

The man who has held me together through all of this, the one who has been my rock and my source of comfort.

The man who has helped me realize that I've lived my life in fragments, barely able to make sense of the pieces. The kind, consistent, reliable man I am lucky to call my partner.

It's not about me anymore. It's about him too. He doesn't deserve to be treated this way, not by my parents or anyone else.

I won't stand for it.

"Neither of you have ever acted like you cared about me, and until you start taking responsibility for all the things you did wrong as parents, you won't get to have me in your life anymore."

"Molly," Dad pleads. He's as complicit in this as she is.

"We're done." I straighten, my chin lifted as I pull my dress up off the ground. "Enjoy the whisky and hors d'oeuvres." I grab Matthew's hand and turn toward the exit.

He pauses for a second, looking back at the stunned expressions on my parents' faces.

"Your daughter is one of the most incredible people I've ever met. It's a shame you've never taken the time to get to know her."

With that, we leave the ballroom.

My mother shouts after us, demanding to know where we're going, but I'm not listening.

All I can focus on is the fact that I need to get away from this, away from the suffocating expectations and demands of my family.

As Matthew and I step out into the cool night air, my pulse continues ringing in my ears. A new sense of freedom washes over me. I'm taking control of my own destiny. It won't be easy, but I'm stronger than they've led me to believe.

Chapter 31
Molly

"I KNOW this was quicker than expected, so thank you for letting me stay here," I say, watching Matthew's muscular arms lug forty pounds of books up the flight of steps in his house.

"Stay? You think I'm installing shelves and a new closet for you so you can pack up and leave? I don't think so," he chuckles.

"I'll help," I chime in. He looks at me over his shoulder, cocking a brow. "Hey, don't look so surprised. If I'm going to be running The Griffin, I have to learn how to be handy."

My favorite boyish grin dimples his left cheek. "Being handy isn't an issue for you."

"Tsk, tsk, Matthew, your mind is filthy," I tease. Our laughter fills the house. I tug up the sleeve of my Stella McCartney Smile wool sweater as I continue to drag my suitcase up the stairs.

"You're one to talk. Sweetest and filthiest person I know."

My cheeks heat. "Only sometimes."

Matthew sets the boxes down in his office, which already has a desk set up for me right beside his. Even with assistance from the moving company Matthew called last night, we've had to unpack the majority of my stuff ourselves. He wipes the shimmer of sweat off his brow with the back of his hand.

After what happened at the Winter Ball, I can't stand having anything tie me to my parents. That meant moving out of my townhouse and cutting up my Centurion card. The years I spent in that place were lonely. I was constantly surrounded by things that weren't my own.

Are those days finally behind me?

"Thank you." I avert my gaze from Matthew, feeling shy. "Not only for helping me pack up my things, but for being here for me. For having my back against my parents."

"Of course, darling." He walks toward my spot in the doorway and pulls me into a hug. Like he knows exactly what I need—to be held by him.

I inhale his vetiver scent and lean into his damp shirt.

Could this really be home now?

Am I even capable of sharing a life with someone when I've yet to pick up the pieces of who I am?

Matthew's warmth encases me, and I squeeze my arms around him harder. I'm not sure how long we stay glued together.

A minute, ten?

My body trembles as memories of the past twenty-four hours flash behind my closed lids. My eyes sting from last night's crying. He gently rubs circles on my back and kisses my fore-head. "It's okay, baby. I'm right here."

Power courses through me from taking a stand against my parents. No matter how many times I've sat with the idea of cutting them off over the past couple of weeks, I couldn't have predicted how painful it would actually be.

I don't regret my decision, but they're still my mom and dad. Apart from one missed call from my father, they haven't reached out.

"Are we going to be okay?"

Matthew's embrace falters as he releases me, lifting my chin to his face. "Yeah, we are," he says.

I believe him.

"Last time I was in your house, I told you that this whole thing wasn't going to be easy, but I never expected everything to play out this way," I whisper, my voice a little hoarse. "I have to ask, are you upset you didn't get half of my trust?"

"Are you serious?" Matthew frowns.

"Hey, my trust issues are flaring." I hide away in his chest again. "Ugh, the irony!" Matthew cups my cheeks with his warm palms and pulls my gaze to his.

He laughs softly. "Baby, I got you. I'm not concerned about the money. I managed to secure enough funding to get started with EcoDrones. Robert is finalizing our first prototype. I'm only worried about my girlfriend."

"Don't worry about me; I'm fine..." I plaster on a smile. Matthew gives me a look of disbelief. "Okay, maybe not right now, but I'm *going to be* fine. This morning, I made an appointment to start seeing my therapist again. And, hey, I realized that my mother's a narcissist. It's kinda like the badge of honor for every rich kid. Right?"

He's not amused by my joke, and he pulls me into another firm hug. I never shied away from getting support in the past, and now is no different. I'm going to surround myself with as many people who love me for me as I can.

"I'm proud of you," Matthew says.

I need to start accepting my parents for who they truly are. No more rose-colored glasses or excuses.

The doubt they created in my mind. The confidence they slowly drained from me. It was all real. The distance I've put between us will hopefully benefit everyone in the long term.

I told them what I needed, and when they're ready to take

ownership of the way they've treated me, then we can start figuring out a way for us to have a relationship—on my own terms.

"My parents may never change, but it's not my problem to solve. The only thing I can do is work on forgiving them at my own pace. Now, however, I want to focus on being kind to myself and living my own life. Finally."

"That's a plan I can get behind." He beams. "And look, I don't want you to feel pressured to come to Christmas."

I pull away from him and slap on my game face. "Hey, Hudson, I've been practicing my egg-frying since you moved in with me in the city. We're gonna crush the Olympics this year."

"And if at any point you feel like you don't want to help me destroy my siblings, that's fine too."

I love that he gives me a choice and an out, but I need to blow off some steam. My visit to and potential offer on the Tarrytown property is on hold until the owner gets back from their holidays, and all the unpacking won't keep me busy for long.

"Honestly, it's the distraction I need."

My stomach grumbles. *When was the last time I ate?*

"Well, until then, maybe I can distract you with a homemade meal?"

I sigh, trying to gauge if he has any mind reading abilities again. *Nope.* My radar is either down or it never activated correctly. "You always know just what I need."

"That's kind of my specialty."

"Oh yeah?"

"Yeah, I'm fluent in Molly Greene." He gives me a wink that makes my knees weak.

A moment later, we're in the kitchen. Matthew throws a towel over his shoulder and riffles through the pantry. I sit on one of the stools, glancing around my new home.

Our home.

At Matthew's suggestion, the movers brought over two of my favorite burgundy Eames lounge chairs to replace one of his couches, a colorful Persian rug, and golden Antonangeli Mamamia table lamps. They fit so nicely among his things.

I scan the boxes we still need to carry upstairs, and something catches my attention. One of my mother's Toteme scarves hangs over the cardboard. She bought that for me when I set off for freshman year at Cornell.

Ugh. A weight slumps across my shoulders. This is going to be a long road to healing, isn't it?

My gaze slips to something else. The vase Matthew and I sculpted at On Cloud Nine. It's filled with winterberry. Above it hangs the painting we created on our last day. Splatters of color, messy and beautiful.

"My mind has been so busy that I didn't even realize you kept these." I stroll to the mantel and run my finger over the vase. The clay is bent, the structure all wonky. It's perfect.

Ours.

"I had Lolita ship them out," Matthew says from the kitchen.

I turn back to look at him. "When?"

"Right before we left On Cloud Nine."

My mind turns mushy. "What would you have done with them if we didn't work out?"

"I would've kept them anyway." He gives me a soft nod, as though it's the most obvious answer. "I love being surrounded by things that remind me of you."

Happy tears brim my eyes, and I let go of the vase. I am going to get through this next chapter in my life. My own business, a cat, and my man. I glance over at him again.

Yeah, that's my man.

"They're perfect," I say, and I make my way back to the stool beneath the kitchen island. There are no words to describe my appreciation for how welcome he's made me feel, so I settle with, "Thank you for thinking of getting them here."

"Anytime, darling. Now, what are you craving?"

You, I almost answer, but then I realize he's talking about dinner. "Pasta. A big bowl of pasta."

Matthew lands a peck on the top of my head and retreats to the fridge.

"*Quattro formaggi?*"

"Extra on the *formaggi*." I laugh and watch him get to work. My body heats as my eyes track his movements around *our* kitchen.

"I wish the herbs in the garden weren't frozen, but I'm sure I have some thyme around here."

"*Mhm*." Now I'm all sorts of antsy for spring to come just to watch him work in the garden out back.

Matthew's biceps flex as he pulls a block of Parmigiano Reggiano from the fridge. At what point in my biology was it coded that I would become a horny hooligan at the sight of Matthew Hudson grating cheese?

First he made me an extra cheesy pizza in Sedona. Then we shared countless dinners in the city. Now he's working that slab of cheese so well that I wish I was the block trapped in his fist.

Oh goodness.

The rooster-print kitchen towel draped over his shoulder, his rolled-up sleeves, and his focused gaze are making the cave-woman part of my brain take control of my facilities.

"Do you want to give me a hand or watch from afar with that bit of drool on your lip?" He raises his eyebrows at me.

My nerves shoot up, and I swipe at my mouth, feeling a trail of spit on the back of my palm. *Wow*. I'm depraved.

"Uh—I'll help." I slip off the stool and join him.

"Good girl." Matthew winks and walks over to the tower of copper pans stacked neatly by the window. The ones we agreed to bring from my townhouse.

My heart sings in my chest, my mood brightening almost instantly.

AN HOUR LATER, my belly is full, and the cloud that was hovering over my head earlier is now a blaring ray of sunlight.

I'm not sure how true the old saying is about a way into a man's heart being through his stomach, but a way into a woman's heart is definitely a giant plate of extra cheesy spaghetti.

I yawn.

"Let me finish up here, and I can get the fire going for us in the living room. It's been a long day."

"Why do you insist on doing those dishes now? I can take care of them later," I say over the kitchen island with another big yawn.

"I like taking care of us." Matthew places the last plate in the dishwasher and wipes his hands on a towel. "Cooking for you, then cleaning up after you. Few things make me feel manlier than that."

The words turn the building tension in the base of my spine into a full-on puddle.

For a moment, I dream up all sorts of things I can do to make him feel all man. But Bear croaks at my feet.

I give in to the comfort of knowing my man and my new cat are here, making me feel all woman.

Home sweet home.

"I still can't believe you're mine," I say.

"Get used to it, because I love you."

My breath stops. My knees go weak.

Did he just say that?

"What?"

"Oh man, that's been sitting on the tip of my tongue for

weeks." He shuts off the faucet and faces me. *Weeks?* "Dammit, this isn't how I meant to tell you."

"I love you too," I say, pushing out my stool and rushing toward him.

Matthew takes my hands in his. "Molly, I don't want you to feel any pressure to say it back. I know with everything going—"

"No, I do, Matthew," I interrupt him, squeezing his fingers tighter. "I love you. I've…I've loved you for such a long time."

"You make me feel complete, darling, and I haven't felt that way in years. It's like, before you, I let myself give up on the part of me that could have *this*. On the part that wants to love fearlessly and loudly." He plants his lips on my forehead, nose, then lips. "It's everything about you. I get nervous around you," Matthew chuckles under his breath. "Christ, I'm nervous out of my mind right now, baby, but you're…you light up my life, Molly."

I glow beneath each of his words. As if my chest is a holiday display, bright enough to be spotted from space.

Over the course of my life, I've experienced things I wish I hadn't. Despite my mind and heart being covered in scars, Matthew has always seen past them. He's witnessed who I am and the woman I'm becoming. He makes me feel safe.

I can barely find the words to explain that to him. "I love you."

He pulls me closer, wrapping me in his arms, and I breathe in the mouthwatering vetiver of his cologne. "I'm sorry," he whispers, and I find his blue eyes. "I was waiting to tell you after the holidays. After what happened with your parents, I wanted to give you space."

"No, don't." I shake my head. "The stuff going on with my family is awful, but it was inevitable, and I'll get through it. I know I will. I'm strong."

"You're the strongest person I've ever met."

"I promise, I love you and have loved you, and I think, if it's okay with you, I'd like to keep loving you."

"I'd like to keep loving you too."

I rise onto my toes, connecting my lips to his. Every one of my cells is singing, humming a melody that only he and I can know. Bear comes bolting at us, meowing loudly at our feet.

My own little family.

Chapter 32
Molly

THE ICY WIND whips across my eyelashes through the cracked window of Matthew's Rivian. Heat pours in through the vents, keeping my body warm. For three hours, my nerves have been pounding in my throat.

I've met all kinds of people, from celebrities to humanitarians to politicians and businesspeople. And I've gotten pretty good at charming crowds, shapeshifting my way through society with ease.

Right now, however, as we drive through the town that Matthew grew up in, all of that schmoozing and socializing feels entirely useless.

His family's approval means the world to me. Not in the same way I needed my parents to sign off on my decisions, but in a different way. He loves his parents and siblings. I just want to fit into his life, wholly.

I inhale deeply, watching the rows of snowcapped trees slip past us.

"Robert sent me an almost complete EcoDrones prototype earlier this week." Matthew breaks through the Christmas carol radio that's filling the air.

"How are you feeling about that?" I turn to face the stark lines of his profile.

"Honestly, really good. I thought I would've been more nervous about handing in my notice at ORO, but it feels right."

"Yeah, same." I nod. "I figured Luca would be upset about losing me at the beginning of the year, but I think the replacement résumés I sent put him at ease."

I'll only be at ORO for another week after the holidays. Handing in our resignation letters was scary. I loved my job, but it represented another tie to the life my parents chose for me. It was time for me to cut myself loose.

"You were very considerate to do that for him," Matthew says, keeping one hand on the steering wheel and reaching over with the other to squeeze my leg. "Are you excited for The Griffin?"

"I really am." I wiggle in my seat. "Look at us go, two entrepreneurs chasing their dreams."

"*Achieving* them," he reminds me. Matthew makes another turn down a narrow, snow-lined road. Colonial houses and twinkling Christmas lights make it feel like we're driving through the set of a Hallmark movie.

Am I about to have an Amanda Woods winter like Cameron Diaz did in *The Holiday*?

I put my hand on top of Matthew's and give him a warm smile. Come to think of it, he kind of looks like a way sexier version of Jude Law.

You're supposed to be the leading lady of your own life, for god's sake!

I am now. Even if I have to remind myself of that fact repeatedly.

"I have to be honest; I'm really nervous." I squeeze his hand, which is still on my thigh. "I just want your family to like me."

"Be yourself, and everyone will love you as much as I love you. I promise."

Matthew loving me makes me feel invincible.

Be myself. I can do that.

If his family is anything like him, they will all be warm and welcoming.

"Do you mind if we go through everyone's names again?" I ask. "I've been practicing, but I'm pretty sure my head just emptied itself on I-90."

"Of course, darling. So you already know Aaron, whose mom is Maya." Matthew flexes his hand on the steering wheel, keeping his focus on the road.

"Maya is married to James, and they just had a baby named Sophia," I recite from memory.

"Good girl. Maya is the oldest sister too."

I got this.

Nerves be gone.

"Okay, then there's Myles. He's a veterinarian, right?" Matthew nods. "Myles is married to Helene, and they have three kids, Taylor, Willow—who's the reason we have Bear—and baby Riley."

"Perfect." He pats my thigh.

"Then there's Mitchell and his husband, Theo. They have two kiddos, named, um…" I pause, racking my brain. "Wren aaand…Finn?"

Matthew chuckles. "Are you sure you haven't met my family before?"

"You're sweet. Okay, then your baby brother Mac and his wife, Korina. They have a little boy named Isaac. Finally, your youngest sister, Madison?"

"You've got a better memory than my own parents."

"Years of memorizing people for ORO and family events have paid off," I laugh, but my chest aches.

Even though my parents and I don't usually spend Christmas together, it's still going to hurt not sending them a present or giving them a call this year.

I'm glad I booked an extra session with my therapist when we get back next week. The holidays and being around a happy family may be harder than I anticipated.

My parents have made their choice. *I have nothing to feel guilty for*, I remind myself.

I've fallen so in love with the freedom to be who I am without criticism and overanalysis. I'm not giving that up ever again.

We pull up to the Hudsons' two-story brick house. It's gorgeous against the snowy landscape. The red and green Christmas lights on the roof, windows, and banisters make it look like one of those homes trapped in a snow globe.

How in the world did Matthew's parents raise six children here? The house I grew up in is four or five times this size, and it always felt like I took up too much space inside of it despite there being only three of us.

We park and get out of the car. Matthew grabs our suitcases, which are stuffed to the brim for our weeklong stay. He gives me a quick kiss. His lips are warm against my temple before he laces his free hand with mine and leads us up the salted path to the front door.

"Hello, it's us," he says, entering the house.

Us.

A simple word that makes me feel like I'm flying.

Aaron tumbles toward us before I even have my Moncler snow boots unlaced. He wraps his small arms around Matthew's jeans. "Uncle Mattie," he squeals, following his excitement with a jumble of gibberish. "I have to show you the f-fort thing outside. You come? Please, come, please."

"Of course, buddy." Matthew shucks off his beanie. His hair is adorably messy, and he hasn't shaved in a few days, so his jaw is peppered in a thick scruff. "Let us get settled in, and I'll make sure that the fort is fortified."

"F-fortified?" Aaron cocks his head curiously.

"Protected. Safe," Matthew explains.

"Aaron?" A woman's voice echoes through the hall, and when she comes into view, I recognize her from the photos. Maya, with a baby on her hip. "Oh, there you all are. Everyone's in the den except Madison and Mitchell. They got stuck in traffic." She lets out a sigh, tossing her cropped brown hair over her shoulders. "And you must be Molly, the woman who's taken over my brother's life," she laughs. "I'm Maya, and this little gal is Sophia."

"It's nice to meet you." My nerves spark like fireworks in my chest. Maya reaches her free arm toward me and loops it around my shoulders in a halfway hug.

"Wait, do you do hugs?" She cranes her neck back, pulling away slightly.

Um. I've never been asked, but I'd like to be the kind of person who does hugs from now on.

"Yes, I do." I nod, and she pulls me back into a full embrace. I lean into her arms. Baby Sophia giggles between us.

Oh goodness. Am I actually about to cry? I blink a few times, willing the tears not to fall.

It's quite lovely to be greeted this way.

"We're so happy to have you here." Her cheeks dimple before her eyes light up. "Now…"

Matthew cuts her off with a hug, then places a hand on my lower back. "Come on, can we at least get Molly in front of the fire with a glass of Mom's cider before you start bombarding her with questions?"

"I didn't even start." Maya passes him Sophia.

"The next words out of your mouth were going to be something along the lines of, *So, how do you handle him?*" Matthew says in a tone that's similar to Maya's frank cadence.

"Fair." She sucks on her teeth. "Take off your coats and come in."

We do as she says, and Maya lugs one of our suitcases

through the house. Matthew shoots me a quick nod and follows her down the hall.

Aaron grabs my hand. "Come on. Mima said you have a present under the tree, and I could ask you, n-nicely, if I can maybe help open it."

"Aaron, you have your own presents to open," Maya calls out from down the hall. His tongue shoots out at his mom, then he smiles up at me.

A rush of warmth swoops over me as the tot leads me into the house.

There are trophies, ribbons, and framed diplomas. An abundance of photographs, stockings with initials hanging off a mantel, and handprints in clay with various dates that adorn the walls.

The den is filled with people. They're lounging on a large couch and scattered on the floor, all gathered around the beautifully decorated fireplace. The tree is bursting with colorful lights, handmade ornaments, and garlands of popcorn and cranberries.

This is what a home is supposed to feel like.

"Everyone, this is my girlfriend, Molly," Matthew announces, his face stuck in a permanent grin. A wave of heads turns toward me. My pulse rushes like I'm on stage at a school play.

Almost all the siblings share a likeness to Matthew. The same dark brows and a smattering of light eyes.

"She's a hugger," Maya announces, and within moments, I'm swarmed with welcomes. I'm a cozy mush beneath the sea of limbs looping around me and the smiles beaming off of everyone's faces.

"We'll quiz you on all of our names at the end of the night," Mac says, giving me a toothy grin. His choppy, bright green hair makes his pale face glow.

"No, we won't." Matthew playfully rolls his eyes and gives each member of his family a giant hug.

"Hi, you're pretty." A young girl with bouncy chestnut curls that mimic my own and a tinge of pink under her deep-brown cheeks peeks up at me. "Are you *Brave*?"

She thinks I'm a Disney princess? I must get my ego boosted by little girls more often.

But the word is also a reminder that I am, in fact, brave.

I crouch. "Only sometimes, but don't tell anyone. Today, I'm Molly. What's your name?"

"Taylor," she says, pulling her sibling to her side. "This is Willow."

"It's nice to meet you both."

The girls giggle and rush back to their spot by a beanbag.

As I stand, trying to take everything in, an elderly woman appears from a door at the opposite side of the room. Her eyes are a replica of Matthew's, shades of deep blue peeking through the smiling crease on her face.

At her side, a man with familiar jet-black hair, peppered gray, wears a matching apron. Both of them are covered in flour, specks of it clinging to their arms as they make their way toward me.

"It's swell to meet you, Molly." She pulls me into the biggest embrace, smelling of sugar and freshly baked cookies. "Oh dear, sorry; we've got a mess all over us, and I've just smattered your pretty cardigan." Matthew's mom wrangles herself away from me and gives me a once-over. "Well, aren't you just so adorable."

I blush at her assessment, then at the wink she shoots Matthew. "Thank you for having me, Mrs. Hud—"

Her hand shoots up immediately. "None of that. You'll call us Mary and Jack, that's that."

"Okay." I nod. "Mary and Jack, your home is so beautiful."

She cocks her hip, sending her palm to her waist. "Lots of

memories in this house, and we're so delighted to make some new ones with you."

If my heart could combust, I think it would. Frankly, it still might.

This feels so right.

Jack pulls his wife closer to his side. "We wanted to pop in and say hello, but if we don't get those cookies out of the oven, we'll burn them...*again*."

"Oh, hush, we're not burning them. He's always such a worrywart." Mary looks at me as if I'm being let in on an inside joke. "The cider's on the stove. Matthew, be a dear and get settled in upstairs, then come back down and help Dad sort out his new computer."

"It's working perfectly fine," Jack sighs.

"What did you do this time?" Matthew appears at his father's side, giving him a pat on the back. It's like I'm on the set of a movie, watching a closely-knit family interact. The urge to throw on a mask appears. I want so desperately to fit in, to be accepted by everyone here. But I hold off.

I'm good enough as myself.

Jack goes to speak, but Aaron pushes past their legs, looking up at Mary with puppy-dog eyes that I'm sure could melt even the coldest ice caps. "Mima, please, you said Molly opens it?" He holds up a box wrapped in bright red paper.

"Ah, of course." Mary takes the gift out of his hands and passes it to me. "It's just a little something that everyone gets when they come to their first Hudson Christmas."

"Oh, th-thank you, you shouldn't have," I stammer. Mary waves her hand dismissively.

Aaron turns to face me, all wide-eyed and grinning. "Can I help you open it?"

"Sure." I smile, holding out the box.

"We want to help too," Taylor and Willow sing in unison. Then the rest of the kids rush over, forming a circle around me.

"I don't see why we can't all open it together." I lower myself, coming eye level with all the giggling faces. "Why doesn't this side pull apart the bow, and the other side can rip apart the paper?"

A frenzy ensues, like a piranha tank during feeding time. As the kids disperse, seemingly satisfied with their unwrapping task, a white garment box is left on the floor.

Inside sits a bright red sweater in a thick cable knit. On the front, the letter M is stitched in beautiful gold thread. I run my hands over the soft fabric.

A prickle of tears pinches my lids.

"Just like all of my kids." Mary grins. "Matthew said you like it bright, so I dug up my most brilliant yarn. You look like you're into fashion, wearing names I'm sure I can't pronounce, but I hope you like it."

I look around and notice that most of the family is wearing their initials on knits of every color of the rainbow. I strip off my Alaïa cardigan and pull the sweater over my head. I grip the sleeves in my palms. The fabric is soft, the perfect amount of cozy.

"I—it's the best gift I've ever received," I say, not bothering to hold back the tears welling in my eyes.

It's official. I've been overwhelmed with love.

"Oh, she's a charmer, isn't she?" Jack laughs. "Alright, get comfy. We'll discuss the rules for this year when Madison and Mitchell arrive."

"Thank you," I whisper as they shuffle away and the rest of the room resumes their conversations. Matthew's hand wraps around mine, guiding me out of the den.

Every Christmas for the rest of my life will be compared to this one, and I've only just arrived.

Chapter 33
Matthew

THE FIRST FULL day of the trip couldn't have gone any better.

For breakfast, Madison and Molly threw together an epic fashion show for all eight of my nieces and nephews. Even the little ones who can't walk yet were part of it—they were strapped onto their dads' chests, if somewhat reluctantly, to partake in the catwalk.

It was hilarious and adorable all at once.

Madison and her girlfriend, Gabby, showed off the jerseys they designed for this year's games. They are giant hockey jerseys with *Hudson* embellished in big white letters, and *Family Olympics* written underneath. Instead of a team logo, they had a picture of our family trophy.

I'm pretty sure I won't be able to forget the image of Molly throwing on her green jersey over her ski jacket. The moment she was wearing my last name, I wanted to make her mine all over again.

Will she take my name when we're married?

Who am I kidding, though? It hardly even matters. I'd take *Greene* if she wanted me to.

There are so many other things to talk about before that, but I can't help but picture our future together.

One day, really soon, I'll have the honor of making her my wife.

The opening challenge in the Hudson Olympics was a somewhat tame version of Monopoly. We placed second, coming behind my mom and dad. Frankly, no qualified mathematical genius like my mother should be allowed to play a game developed on economic theories.

"Hey, wait up," Maya calls after me on the snowy hill.

"I'm going to go scope out the challenge," Molly says. She looks back, checking if that's alright. I nod for her to go ahead. I've barely had a chance to talk to my sister.

"Hey, sis. You ready to get your ass handed to you today?"

"Don't get cocky, okay? I still can't believe you brought *the* Molly to Christmas."

"*The* Molly?" I hike up my brow at her.

"Yes, *the* Molly you said you had a crush on three years ago. That would have been very useful information to mention when you told me you were bringing home a mystery girl." Maya raises her voice, and I glance around. Thankfully, everyone's already at the base of the hill.

Curse her good memory.

"I didn't even think about telling you," I joke, knowing my sister would have definitely made this into a big deal.

"Oh, please. You've been ever so casually mentioning Molly since you started at ORO." Maybe this whole being-close-with-your-siblings thing is one big scam. "Alright, I'll lay off. I'm just elated. This is the first woman since Lau—" She catches the name in her mouth, her eyes springing wide.

Maya's always been protective. The fact that she's *my* baby sister hasn't seemed to matter to her. After what happened with Laura, she's been skeptical of the rare occasions I've mentioned a fleeting interest in someone.

I don't blame her. Maya has a grudge she hasn't quite been able to shake. My sister was the one who had to deliver the news to me when I participated in a one-off oncology study for her research thesis at the time.

I was only twenty-eight, but I'm sure she feels like she ended my life then and there.

"You can say her name," I sigh and stop in the snow. "Laura's not Beetlejuice."

Maya gasps. "Do not say that name! What if Aaron heard you? I'm just looking out for you, big bro. After what happened with the—" She pauses and shakes her head, likely choosing not to dive into my sperm's lack of existence in the middle of the Hudson Family Olympics. "Look, never mind that. I'm only talking about it because I may have heard something through the grapevine…"

My mother was never good at keeping secrets from us. "Well, you heard right."

"You're gonna do it?"

I nod. "I got the ring."

Last night, when Molly was showering, I had a talk with my parents. Our family ring was always meant to go to me. With Laura, it never felt right to pass on a family heirloom—which should've been my warning sign.

With Molly, there's no hesitation.

I want to ask her to marry me. I don't just want to date her and *see what happens*. Calling her my girlfriend barely sums up the array of feelings I have for her. I'm thirty-six, and I'm ready to start living my life with the woman I love.

"Can I just ask, have you told her about—"

"Not yet." I cut Maya off. "But I will. *Today*. Right after whatever they have planned for us."

Since the Winter Ball three weeks ago, it was easy to convince myself not to tell her about my infertility.

Molly was already under enough stress from separating from

her parents, having to move out of her home, and give up a large part of her life. Her world was falling apart, and there was never an appropriate time to add more things for her already overwhelmed mind to process.

Even when we confessed that we loved each other and she promised that the split from her family wasn't affecting her, I still let myself believe that it was.

I'm a coward. Terrified that Molly's reaction would be similar to Laura's.

I feared that Molly would think I am no longer worthy of her love, that I am not the man she wants to spend her life with.

I've let myself be convinced by the fact that Molly has a history of hiding her true feelings. It's a pathetic excuse, considering how much she has worked on opening up to me. But she had just run away from her family. I didn't want her to run away from me and the future we're building together.

I didn't want her to see that I was just another broken person in her life, weighing her down.

I can't continue to let my fear hold me back.

It's time.

"Good." Maya nods, and I try to shake off the tension in my chest. "I won't let you make that same mistake again."

"Molly would never be a mistake." I just hope she understands why I waited so long to tell her.

"I know." My sister gives me a nudge. "But I care about you."

We join the rest of the group at the base of a hill. There are six deflated tubes at our feet.

The children are running around the backyard, while all the adults stand in a straight line. The snow has let up, and the sun shines down on us. *What on earth is this challenge?*

I wrap my arm around Molly, who's buzzing with excitement. God willing, our talk later today doesn't ruin the rest of the trip.

"Did we need to go all *Survivor* this year? I mean, come on," Madison exclaims, and I realize I zoned out the entire time Dad was explaining the rules of the second challenge.

"It's way worse than *Survivor*, because we're stuck trudging through two feet of snow in thirty-degree weather and not frolicking on a sandy beach," Mac says.

Myles drops both of his arms around my younger siblings. "Y'all are just mad because this challenge is physical."

We all roll our eyes. Myles definitely bench-presses three hundred pounds before he has his morning coffee.

"Okay, meathead, we'll see how well you do." Madison gives him a solid push, but Myles barely sways.

"*Kids.*" Mom's voice is heavy with warning. "Everyone will have a chance to showcase their skills. Now line up."

At this point, we're all talking over each other like we always do. Molly watches, smiling. Her nose is red, and she hikes up her fuzzy scarf over her face.

"Okay, settle down," Dad shouts. "We've only got a couple of hours before the storm rolls in again. Let's go through the rules one more time. Who remembers what we're doing?"

Molly chimes in, "We race to our tubes, blow them up, run back up the hill, and whichever couple is the first to slide down over the finish line wins."

I'm so grateful that I have my girl at my side—my *hopefully* forever teammate.

Her eyes are clad with focus. Yeah, we've got what it takes to crush my siblings.

"Atta girl." I pat her on the butt, and the red in Molly's cheeks deepens. "We're going to destroy you guys."

"Strong claims, brother," Maya says from beside me. James's fair face is painted with stripes, and he's towering beside my sister.

"We better watch out; there's a new kid on the block," Myles laughs. He throws up his hand to high-five Molly, and she slams her gloved hand right into his. "Damn." He pulls back, shaking out his palm. "Let's keep that level of destruction for the field."

"Sorry. I'm just excited."

"Come on, let's give them something to be afraid of," I whisper in her ear.

We all make our way to the starting point, about a dozen feet from the deflated tubes.

"Ready," Mom yells, "set, go!"

The whistle zooms through the air. My heart pounds, and we sprint. I struggle to keep up with Molly. She's surprisingly fast for someone so small.

We reach the tube marked for us at the bottom of the hill. She picks up the black inflation valve and wraps her lips around it as I frantically search for the inflator.

Of course, we don't have one.

I glance around at my siblings, who all seem to register the fact that my parents have decided to test our lung strength today. Mitchell and Theo appear to be in the lead. Madison and Gabby are bickering. Myles and Helene are taking turns inflating the tube. Mac and Korina are giggling as Maya and James blow up theirs.

With a few breaths, Molly's tube is more than halfway blown up. She hands it over to me to finish.

"How'd you get so good at this?" I ask between critical gasps for air.

"ORO birthday parties," Molly pants. Her eyes are almost bloodshot as she ushers me to go on. "Sometimes the balloon pump is broken."

"You're brilliant." In two more passes, our tube is fully inflated.

We take off like bats outta hell, leaving my siblings in the powder. The hill's elevation may only be three hundred feet, but after blowing up that damn tube it feels like climbing Mount Everest.

I'm gasping for air, trying not to collapse onto the icy snow. The pressure to win builds as we fight tooth and nail to maintain our lead. There's no way we're letting those suckers catch up to us.

Molly is a few steps ahead of me. I hold on to our tube for dear life. Our boots sink into the snow with each step.

Maya shouts from behind us, "We're gonna win!"

"In your dreams," Molly yells back. She's trying to sound competitive, but the edge in her voice turns into a bout of giggles. "C'mon, Hudson; keep pace." Her eyes glimmer as she glances at me over her shoulder.

"There's no way I'm letting my sister beat us."

"James, no! Get up!" We turn to check on the chaos. Maya has her hands up as James tumbles backward on his tube, taking out Myles and Theo like a bowling ball.

"Go, go, go!" We laugh at the havoc unfolding around us. "We have a chance."

"We're coming for you," Myles taunts, but I don't even spare him a glance.

My attention is fully focused on Molly, wearing my last name on her back, scaling this hill like her life depends on it.

Holy shit. I've got to marry this girl, or I'll regret it for the rest of my life.

At the top of the hill, I turn to Molly, breathless. "You ready for this, baby?" I ask, swinging the tube off my shoulder and plopping it onto the ground.

Her eyes widen as she settles into it. "Let's do it!"

I jump onto the back of the tube and push us off.

We're going to win.

Molly's screams echo off the trees and snow as we spin in circles down the hill, the wind whistling through our hair. We hit a bump in the snow, and she slams into me, sending her cushioned ass right into my crotch.

Ouch.

Other tubes whoosh behind us. Mac and Korina, Myles and Helene close in on us.

Faster and faster, our tube propels down the hill.

We're the first to slide over the finish line.

Molly leaps off the tube, jumping in excitement. "We did it! We won!" Her voice is drowning in glee, and she reaches over and kisses me.

The world slows down around us as I pull her tighter, our cold lips interlocked. She collapses onto me. Her nose feels frozen as it hits my cheek. I lean in, coaxing the warmth out of her.

"*Eww!*" The children's laughter and teasing fill my ears, but I don't care.

I'm too focused on the woman of my dreams kicking ass on the slopes with me.

My first Hudson Olympics win in a long time, all thanks to my girl.

"Come on, let's go rub your siblings' noses in our win." She tries to untangle from me, but I realize the blood has left my head and traveled down to my cock. I'm so hard that I doubt my thick snow pants will even be able to conceal my length.

"I'm going to need a second, baby." I give her a shy grin.

Molly lights up. "Here? Now?"

"That fire in your eyes really turns me on," I whisper. *And your hair, your button nose, your red cheeks, and corkscrew curls.*

"My determination got you all worked up?"

"Something like that."

Fuck, I'm so in love with this woman. It's dizzying.

Chapter 34
Molly

UPSTAIRS, a shrill scream echoes through the house. The kids insisted that Matthew read them a story after dinner. From their laughter, it's obvious that he's doing a phenomenal job at mimicking a funny voice for the dragon in their bedtime story.

My legs are sore from today's tubing challenge. I still can't believe we won. Matthew kissing me after we crossed the finish line was a feeling I could never get sick of.

I settle into the large downstairs sofa, draping a cozy blanket over myself.

Maya enters the room. We're both wearing blue pajamas with small polar bears on them. Willow got to pick the matching family jammies this year, and Mary promised that I'd get to do the honors next year.

I couldn't be more thrilled. I literally started browsing the Eberjey website in the shower.

Matthew's sister stretches out onto the couch and gives me a sleepy smile. She reminds me of a mixture of all my favorite people. She has Matthew's humor, Lily's directness, and Avery's work ethic.

"How did you get so good…at, well, everything?" Maya picks up her hot chocolate and pats my leg.

"Rich parents who didn't want to spend time with me," I laugh. A little weight lifts off my shoulders from admitting my life hasn't been perfect.

She scoots further back into her seat and snorts. "I would've preferred that to my mother's helicoptering."

"Grass is always greener, isn't it?"

Her blue eyes stay on me for a while. The fire crackles in the comfortable silence. "Does your family not celebrate Christmas?"

"Oh, um." I want to lie, but if I'm to be a real part of this family, I won't start our relationship off by concealing parts of myself. "We're actually not on speaking terms at the moment."

"Oh, I'm sorry." Maya frowns.

"That's okay." I shrug, pulling my legs into the couch. "I recently realized that I wasn't living life for myself. Everything I ever did was to live up to my parents' expectations, and frankly I wanted to change that. It's not a way to spend your days."

She nods as though she deeply understands, and I appreciate her lack of judgment. "I don't know if this was your experience, but I had a boyfriend in college…he was a bit of a narcissist." Maya takes a small sip of her cocoa before continuing. "Honestly, that jerk made it seem like each one of his needs came before my own. He was so obsessed with what people thought that it got to a point where I felt uncomfortable going to our shared lectures because I was afraid I'd somehow make a bad impression on him."

The familiar description is so vivid.

My mother's concern about how I was perceived made me think that other people's opinions were the most important things in life.

She turned love into a transaction, rewarding me with gifts

when I did what she wanted and criticizing me when I didn't. I did everything to please her—putting on a mask that mimicked whoever she needed me to be that day. I grew fearful of making mistakes and disappointing others, and, most importantly, I lost touch with myself.

Since I got back from On Cloud Nine, I'm able to see that it's not my responsibility to conform to my mother's standards.

"Ah, are you sure you didn't just date my mother?" I let out a sardonic laugh.

Maya rubs one of her feet against my own in a comforting gesture. "It took me a long time to figure out how to love again and how to trust my instincts. But, when the time came, it made loving James all the more rewarding."

I can't wait to curl up in the safety of Matthew's arms. I force a calming breath into my chest. My happiness is my own. My future is my own.

"Yeah. Even finally calling my mother a narcissist helped me release the guilt and blame I used to put on myself for everything going wrong with their world. Our legacy."

"Right. The *Greenes*." Maya says my last name with a heavy emphasis. I quirk a brow at her. "I looked you guys up online." She gives me a playful wink.

"I don't blame you. Matthew mentioned that he hasn't brought someone around in a long time. I would've tried to dig up all the dirt I could."

We giggle. It's lovely being snuggled up on the couch, talking like sisters. If Matthew and I ever do get married—and I really hope we do—I'll have so many more siblings than I ever imagined.

"That's one of the many reasons I like you. You seem prepared."

"I try to be," I admit.

The fire crackles, and I stare at the wisps of flames.

"Has Matthew talked to you about Laura yet?" Maya asks.

"Yeah, he's told me a bit." I nod. Maybe this ex has had a bigger impact on Matthew than he has led me to believe. But it doesn't matter. The past is the past.

"Good." She nods. "You know, I never imagined my brother with someone like you, but I'm so glad it happened this way."

"What do you mean?"

"It's hard to articulate." She pauses, her eyes creasing with a smile as she sets down her mug. "I guess, someone so full of life."

I mirror her relaxed expression. "He brings it out of me."

"Well, thank you for bringing it out of him," she says. "I know I may sound like I'm exaggerating, but I truly haven't seen Matthew this happy since before I broke the news to him about his infertility."

I stop breathing, straightening my neck. My brows knot in confusion. "W-what?"

"His infertility."

I stare at her blankly. My heart splinters.

"Oh, crap. What did you think I was talking about with Laura —oh, never mind." Maya scampers over to me and grabs my hands. Her eyes are as wide as mine, worry and panic both flooding her face. "You said Matthew told you about Laura. What has he said?"

I shake my head, not able to find words. "Just that she was his only long-term relationship."

"Fuck." She panics. "Molly, I—I just assumed. Matthew said he was going to tell you today and I—" Maya searches my face for something, and I don't even have the energy to throw on a mask for her, to help calm her down. "He's gonna kill me."

I try to process what I'm hearing. It's as if her words are Scrabble letters being thrown at me, forcing me to piece together words I can't quite spell.

Matthew can't have children.

He didn't tell me.

My mind spins from confusion to anger to frustration, until it lands on disappointment.

Maya continues her scattered whispers. I don't even hear her.

Why would he hide this from me?

Did he think I would judge him for it?

Or, worse, that I couldn't handle him telling me the truth?

We've worked to fill in the gaps in our communication, building trust and honesty. Heck, we said we love each other a few weeks ago. My heart sinks further in my chest, free-falling into my rib cage.

All this time, Matthew had a secret.

I need to talk to him.

Pulling myself up out of my seat, I catch the look of pure fear in Maya's eyes.

"Molly, I'm really sorry."

I shake my head, hoping I look even remotely reassuring. "It's not your fault; I just need to find Matthew."

As I stand, she tugs on my wrist, yanking my attention to her once more. "Please don't be mad at him. She said some of the most heinous things to him before ending their relationship. This is the first time I've seen him be himself again, and I'm sure whatever reason—"

"I'm not mad," I say truthfully.

Matthew's only long-term partner hurt him. This Laura who he once loved broke his heart. Probably to the point where this made him feel ashamed?

I know exactly what it feels like to want to conceal pieces of yourself.

Is that why he put off telling me? Because he thought I'd do whatever she did?

My strong, sincere, and passionate man who had to wear this chip on his shoulder for years.

I hate it. Anger pulses in my veins. I hate that anyone ever inflicted wounds that deep over something beyond his control.

But the man I love needs to tell me the truth, the whole truth.

Chapter 35
Matthew

THE KIDS finally fell asleep after I read to them for an hour. Exhaustion seeps into my bones from today's running around. When I enter the bedroom, Molly is sitting on the edge of the bed.

"Hi, darling." I give her a soft smile, but she looks sullen. My favorite amber eyes are bloodshot and heavy. "Are you alright?" Worry strums in my veins. Molly doesn't reply. I sit on the bed. She drapes her arms around my neck and pulls me into a suffocating hug. "Baby." I fail to conceal the panic in my voice. "What's wrong?"

Everything's been fine. I mean, more than fine. I look over at the dresser, where I hid the ring I want to give her. It's closed. Did she find it and think this is all happening too fast? What could've possibly gone on in the few hours since our first win in the Hudson Olympics?

Did something happen with her parents?

"I'm sorry," she whispers against my chest.

"You don't have anything to be sorry for, Molly." I pull away from her, searching her face.

Her full lip quivers, and I'm concerned that on her next

breath she'll simply fall apart in my hands. "Maya, she didn't mean to, but she told me about…"

She knows.

Christ. I should have told her before dinner. I was waiting until…well, now, when we were alone.

"Let me explain," I interject. Every cell in my body ignites with terror.

"I know why you didn't tell me." Molly frowns, wincing.

Acid burns my throat. "Please, give me the chance to explain everything."

"No, Matthew, I—" Her voice trembles. I slide off the bed and collapse onto my knees in front of her, lodging myself between her legs.

"I know it doesn't make it any better, but I was going to share this with you tonight, if you can just let me try," I beg, stumbling through every word.

Molly stares at me blankly. The tightness in my chest strangles me.

Have I already lost her?

I knew I was being ridiculous for not telling her the truth sooner, before this weekend.

I may have made the biggest mistake of my life.

"Okay." Molly nods. Her eyes are glassy because of me. The seams of my heart begin to strain.

"I'm infertile. I found out when I was twenty-eight," I begin. "Maya was in medical school at the time, focusing on her oncology research. She was running this big data-gathering project. It was extensive, and it required a lot of, uh—contribution samples. When her testing pool was short on donors, she asked all of the brothers to pitch in. We didn't even hesitate.

"I was working up in Boston, at my old venture capital firm. The whole experience took an hour of my time." My chest feels as if it's being constricted by a boa. "Three weeks later, I took Maya's call in between meetings, thinking she's ringing me to vent about her asshole boyfriend or the research that's been bothering her for weeks. Instead, she told me that I needed to make an appointment with my doctor. When I pried for more information, she explained that my sample didn't carry any sperm in it whatsoever, and that I should get tested again soon."

"Maya found out first?" Molly frowns, and the sight makes me want to break. "Is that why she brought it up to me?"

"Yeah. Trust me, I can't quite explain how strange it was having my baby sister break the news that I couldn't father any children." I swipe at the hair falling onto my forehead.

"At all?" she chokes out.

"At all. I'm in the rare one percent of men who have azoospermia, which basically means I have absolutely zero sperm." I drop my head, averting my gaze at the discomfort that speaking the words out loud still brings. "Anyway, it took only another week to confirm the findings with my doctor."

"What did you do?" Her lip quivers.

"Panic, worry. I felt like a failure, like I had somehow caused this insufficiency myself. Sometimes I still wonder what could've gone differently in my past to prevent it from happening." I pause. Molly's eyes remain blank. I hate that I can't read her at this moment. "I already told you a little bit about Laura, but what I didn't mention was that we had discussed being one of those dual income, no kids families. However, after she found out...." I inhale a sharp breath. "Laura wasn't a bad person. I guess. If you ask my family, they'd tell you that they knew she was awful the whole time but we had been together long enough that I assumed we'd get married, like everyone else does.

"When I broke the news to her, she got angry. Fuming angry. She called off the relationship and told me I wasted four years of her life. She acted like I kept a secret from her the entire time we were together. I never assumed my infertility would be an issue. Christ, we even talked about me getting a vasectomy when I turned thirty." The hurt rushes back in full force. I remember that night so well, her telling me all the ways I'd deceived her as I sat on that ugly brown couch Laura insisted we needed.

A tear rolls down Molly's cheek, and I swipe it away with my thumb. Her face blooms with pity. "That's terrible. You had no idea."

I didn't want my girl to look at me like this. But it was inevitable. This is on me.

Guilt drowns my lungs. "Yeah, but the positive thing that came out of our breakup was that it led me to quit my old job, move to New York, and start Plastech." If anything, I'm thankful for the pain that somehow managed to help me find my way to Molly. My breath hitches for the next part of the story. "A year after we broke it off…I was scrolling through Facebook and saw that she had her own child. A little boy. I don't know. It made me hesitant to tell a partner about my infertility because I believed that maybe everyone wanted kids, and that's not something I would be able to provide."

"Did—did you love her?"

"I cared about her," I say honestly. "We met at work, and it was one of those things that seemed easy. We meshed into each other's lives because of circumstance, and we moved in together because rent in Boston is horrid. But whatever I had with her could never compare to what I feel toward you."

Molly's lip is still trembling.

"It's not something that haunts me anymore. The infertility, I mean." Though the way I handled this situation with Molly is proving otherwise. If we can get through this, we're definitely going to have to talk about the topic for the rest of our lives, maybe even see a counselor. "I've gone to therapy, I've done support groups. There are podcasts and a plethora of information on how something like this can be handled. There are always alternatives, adoption or fostering. I never wanted to put someone in a position to make that decision and, honestly, I never thought I'd find someone who would want to face those hardships with me."

"I'm not like her," Molly says, slumping. Her hands glide on top of my palms resting on her thighs. Outside my frosty windows, the wind howls like a pack of wolves.

"Every cell in my body knows that's true. You have every right to be mad at me for not telling you; I owed you my trust like you've given me yours. But, darling, I was so fucking terrified. The love I have for you is unlike any feeling I've ever had."

"I love you too, but—" Her forehead creases. "Why didn't you tell me sooner?"

The one question I knew would be the hardest to answer. I look down, staring at my hands in hers.

"I didn't want to make you decide something so important about your life. Hell, you're only in your twenties, and anything you may want now could change later. I was afraid there'd be a part of you that would always feel like you gave something up for me, for us. You've spent your whole life sacrificing parts of yourself for others, and I couldn't ask you to consider a future without a family of your own. Your mom brought up carrying on the Greene name, which made me feel ashamed because it's something I couldn't give you.

"I was going to tell you after your parents' decision, except then the Winter Ball happened, and I wanted to give you time to process everything with your family without adding another thing to your plate."

Molly sits on the bed, looking down at me. The floor beneath my knees feels like it's splintering.

"You're my best friend, you're marvelous, and you deserve to have a life I wasn't sure I could provide. It's not fair to you that I assumed you were going to respond negatively. I was a coward. I was falling for you, and I selfishly wanted a moment where, regardless of your decision, we could be in love." When I glance back up, there are tears in Molly's eyes. "Where we could be real."

"Matthew." Her voice cracks open like a rusty music box. "I'm so sorry that Laura said those things to you. You didn't deserve that at all, and thank you. Thank you for sharing this part of yourself with me, but I need you to believe what I have to say." She pauses, and I'm dizzy awaiting her next words. "I—I don't think I even want kids."

I pull back, studying her face. She's made comments in the past about not wanting to be a mother, but many young people do. "Molly, you're twen—"

"No," she says flatly. "Don't do that."

The edges of my lips curl down. "What?"

"You don't get to treat me like a child. You've taught me to stick up for myself. That my voice and my wants are important." She shakes out of my grip, pulling her feet up beneath her. "I love you, Matthew Hudson. I know how I want my future to play out."

I'm awestruck. My heart races as I watch the very determined stare in Molly's eyes. "You're right, I don't get to do that."

"No, you don't." She knots her brows together, narrowing her eyes at me. "I'm angry."

"You have every right to be."

"Not at you." She softens. "No one's ever asked me if I want kids. My mother would bring up the importance of expanding the Greene name. You, rightfully, thought that I couldn't make that decision for myself. That may have been true a few months ago, but, Matthew, you're the only person who's seen me for me, let me feel safe and…" Molly pauses. "I'm just learning how to take care of myself." Her amber eyes well with tears again, and I want to pull her close to me so badly.

"I know." I drop my forehead to her knee.

"I'm not ashamed about it—maybe I'm still a little embarrassed, but I'm a work in progress. I can't possibly even begin to consider a child before I've given myself my own life back. I'm angry because I've spent a lot of time worrying about what everyone else wants and never listened to myself."

The truth slaps me right in the face.

Molly has her own reasons, her own desires, and I was too afraid to consider that she may not see children as a part of her future. "I understand. Please know you're allowed to change your mind about wanting a family at any time. We can check in with each other constantly and make sure that the plans we have for our future are always aligned. We can see a couples therapist about it as well."

"I'd like that a lot."

"If you want to try fostering or adoption, I'm more than open. They are arduous processes. I watched my brother and Theo go through it twice, and both times they were in a cycle of high hopes and devastation before finally matching with their babies. I—I would never wish that on you."

"Thank you for giving us the choice. Thank you for wanting to go through that with me if the time ever comes." She runs her palms over my face. "I love you, Matthew, all of you. Every single hair, every perfect blemish, your brain, your patience, and your undeniable loyalty. You're my family, my team. Whatever our future holds, I trust that we can figure it out together. You, me, and Bear."

My heart bursts open. The ache in my throat deepens. I heave a heavy sigh, not sure if I'm about to cry or break in half.

You're my family.

"I love you too."

"I want you, kids or no kids. I would be proud to live my life with you, and I'd feel fulfilled every single day just knowing that I have you by my side." Molly's lips draw to mine, pressing softly into the flesh. "Just us."

"Just us, darling." I kiss her, tasting my future on her lips.

My eyes feel heavy with sleep as the early dawn pokes through the window. I search around my bed, but Molly's nowhere to be found. We fell asleep holding each other, I was sure of it.

Did she leave after last night's conversation? I rise up onto my forearms, and then I see her.

Molly's wearing the thick-knit sweater my mom made for her, her silky pajamas hidden beneath it.

"Good morning," I say, my voice feeling hoarse. The house creaks with silence. I glance at the clock. Five in the morning. "You're up early."

Nerves awaken in my chest. I hope that everything we talked about last night still stands.

"Good morning." Molly smiles at me from the bookcase by the window. Her red curls sprawl across her shoulders. "I didn't want to wake you."

"Are you feeling alright…after yesterday?"

She nods. "I am. Nothing's changed."

"Okay." The worry barely settles. "I have to be honest; it's my turn to feel my trust issues flaring."

She lets out a soft laugh and sits beside me on the bed. "Matthew, I fell in love with you for you, not because of your ability to make a child. I love you because you're a choice I want to make every day of my life. And I know that if having kids is something we want to do, we'd figure it out together. I'm certain that if we ever decide to, I would love any member of our family with the same fierceness I love you."

My body relaxes onto the bed. Yeah, I was a complete fool for allowing my past to shame me from telling her. "Thank you for saying that." I finger the soft curls resting on her chest.

"I mean it. I would much rather have you and no children than children and no you." She nods, running her warm hand over my torso.

I never wanted to admit what those words would mean to me, especially from someone I love as deeply as Molly. But hearing her say them causes some part of me to unlatch.

"What I said last night stands; we can always revisit the conversation and talk about our options."

"I know that, thank you. I'm certain we'll never stop talking about it and checking in with each other," she says, and I squeeze her hands. "It won't be an easy decision for us to make, and I'm not oblivious to the way this could affect our life in the future, but I'm committed to you. I trust us to get through this."

To be loved and accepted by her is the biggest gift I've ever let myself have.

Not sharing the truth about my infertility was silently crushing me. But it's the first morning in weeks, maybe even years, that I haven't felt some kind of chain wrapped around me.

It's my turn to feel safe in my own skin.

I pull her into a hug, and she rests her head on my chest for a while. "I feel lighter than I have in a really long time."

She looks up at me. "I value you so deeply. You're my man."

Her man. "I could spend my whole life making sure that I'm worthy of the title."

"You are, you're worthy of it. Yesterday, today, tomorrow." Molly gives me a sleepy smile and pulls away, returning to my bookcase. "Now, I have to ask, *Moby Dick*?" She pulls a book off of a dusty shelf.

I catch the mischievous grin on her lips. "It's the first book that made me fall in love with the ocean."

She peruses the artifacts in my childhood bedroom as I readjust my back on the silk pillowcases. I picked them up at Bergdorf's before we left because they would be better for her curls.

A little piece of her normal, nestled against my full-sized childhood bed.

"Just a man and his whale," she giggles quietly. She reshelves the book, continuing to examine my room as if she's attempting to absorb my past. "You played hockey?"

The trophy she's glancing at is tarnished and dusty. "Not very well," I chuckle, stretching my legs out on the navy sheets. "It's a rite of passage to at least attempt hockey when growing up in this neck of the woods." Molly returns to bed. I tug her to my side, and the old, springy mattress bucks under her weight. "How are you actually feeling, darling?"

"Close to you. Happy that I have you in my life," she whispers. I kiss the edge of her smile. "This is what I want." Molly taps her pointer finger onto my chest. "This feeling. Forever."

"I want that too."

The blood in my cock makes it tent my plaid pajamas, and I attempt to readjust beneath her weight. She turns, settling her forearms on my chest and laying her body flat on top of me.

Molly plants a little kiss on my lips and hovers her face over mine. "What do you think younger Matthew would make of our relationship right now?"

My chest expands beneath her weight. "I think he wouldn't believe that he ever managed to get a girl like you to fall for an ordinary boy like him."

"Ordinary? Since when?" She exaggerates a quiet gasp that makes me laugh.

"What about you? What would younger Molly think about us?"

She softens her amber eyes, smiling. "She'd be really surprised to know that she's found someone she can be herself around. That she doesn't have to hide the ugly or the silly parts just to feel loved. That being noticed could feel as good as it does when it means being noticed by you." *The way I don't have to conceal the ugly parts of me any longer.* "Oh," Molly giggles. "And, if we had been the same age as teenagers, she would've been drooling over your glasses and books."

"You think so?"

She nods, shifting her weight on top of me. Her hips tilt deeper into my thigh. "Yep. She would've abandoned all social decorum and found her way right up into this bedroom."

"If you would've come up here, I wouldn't have known what to do with you. I'd probably just stare at you, gobsmacked, as you looked at my shelves."

"You wouldn't have tried to kiss me?" She quirks her brows at me, a little hint of mischief nestling in her eyes.

"I'm sure I would've wanted to, so much." I tighten my hold around her waist, pulling her closer into the hardness beneath my pajamas.

Molly's fingers follow the path down my chest. "What about now?"

"Dying to," I breathe, pulling her face into mine and savoring the inevitable.

Molly's fingers fumble with my pajama bottoms. My heart races as she sends her soft hands down the trail of hair leading to all of me.

"Really, darling, right now?" I ask between the feel of tongue and lips.

"Yes. I want to be close to you."

My clothes find themselves in a heap at the foot of the bed, Molly's panties near my things. Just as she reaches for her sweater, I wrap my hand around hers. "Leave this on for me, will you?"

"Another fantasy come to life?" Molly smiles, all too elated.

"Something like that."

I kiss her neck and the crook in her shoulders, and then I lift up her woolly sweater and silk slip. I trace my lips along her breasts, and she arches her back.

Molly grinds her cunt over my cock and guides herself to my tip, her mouth agape and her eyes wide. In a blink, her warmth hugs around me, slick and wet.

I'll never get used to how good she feels. It's so early, but I can already feel the hint of my orgasm build at the base of my spine.

"I would never give this up," I whisper into her ear. Her body hangs over mine, her hips lazily grinding against my own as she settles into a pace above me, riding my length.

"Me too," she moans. "Just like this. Just like we have been."

My mouth hovers by hers. I close my eyes, listening to the gentle creak of the mattress, her shallow breaths, and the sound of her wet pussy gliding over me. I use my hands to guide her onto my length, picking up the pace.

"Ah!" Molly gasps when I hit the spot that makes her fall apart every time.

"Quiet, my girl." I gently palm her mouth. "Can't go waking up the whole house moaning like that," I chuckle. The gleam in her eyes, cresting over my hand, causes my heart to throb in my chest.

We move together, our bodies entwined.

This is what love feels like. *Molly*.

It's the kind of sex you can only have with someone who's seen every side of you, the good and the bad. A trust that only comes from giving without expectation. In such a short time, I've somehow managed to have this with her.

"Hush," I remind her. Molly doesn't listen, just grows louder and louder beneath the grip of my hand. Her eyes bulge with pleasure, her teeth sinking into my skin.

"Be quiet, or I'm going to flip you over and drill my cock so deep into you, you'll forget how to breathe," I say more roughly. I take control of the grinding thrusts, forcing her into my own rhythm. Molly's spit coats my palm. Her eyes burn with fire. She feverishly nods against my grip, desperately struggling to keep quiet.

It's so fucking hot.

"Baby," I warn, but Molly only works herself harder against me. Not breaking pace. In only a few moments, I feel my control fall apart. "I—I'm going to..." I heave a heavy sigh, steadying her above me and dropping my hand from her mouth. "Get over here."

She connects her lips with mine. Her hot breath and panting beat against me. My hand massages circles against her swollen clit. She grows wetter and hotter, and I pump my hips upward until, with her heavy groan, the moans cease.

When her pussy clenches around me again, I'm done.

Without a word, Molly knows it too.

Our teeth slam together, our hands finding themselves clasped around one another as we both push ourselves off the brink together.

Molly's body falls against mine, snuggling close as I'm still throbbing inside of her.

"I love you," she whispers, and I can hear the smile in her voice.

I push the sticky strands of hair from her forehead and plant my lips to the damp skin there.

"You can claim all I have, Molly."

Chapter 36
Molly

It's the last day of the Hudson Olympics. Myles and Helene are our only competition. We're tied by nine points each, with this last, unknown challenge being the deciding win. The duo stands a few feet away from us, huddled together, aggressively whispering out of earshot.

The other siblings aren't even trying to win first place. They're just avoiding doing the dishes on Christmas Day, a task that has been assigned to today's loser.

We only lost the baking challenge because our peanut butter chocolate chips were missing— well, only the chocolate chips were missing. Courtesy of me. I made up for it the next morning during the lake-skating challenge, surprising even myself when I landed a triple axel.

I firmly plant myself on the ground, freezing my butt off, with snow falling all around. The Hudsons stand on opposite sides of me, smiling and nodding with encouragement.

I don't have to be afraid of the future anymore. After Matthew shared a raw part of himself with me, I've never felt closer to him.

A part of me still aches about how afraid he was to tell me.

Seeing the fear and hurt in his eyes as he explained what happened with Laura is a memory I won't be able to easily shake.

I would never think of him as less than for something that's entirely out of his control.

Having children is the furthest thing from my mind, but it's nice to know that if I do ever feel the desire, Matthew is open to the conversation. However, at this point in my life, I just want my man all to myself.

Matthew stands beside me and gives me a wink. His game face is on.

Time to win this thing.

Even though I've fallen in love with every single person in Matthew's family, I don't want to play nice.

We will not be settling for second place. We both deserve this win today.

Jack speaks up. "Your last task is to make a snowman."

"Oh, come on, we did this one three years ago," Mitchell groans, holding the gilded Hudson family trophy in his hands.

"We know, and we've added a twist this year." Mary smiles, sporting a vibrant purple snowsuit. "You can use any items around the house to embellish your snowman. The most magnificent design wins!"

"Wha—" Maya starts, but Madison cuts her off.

"Is there a theme?"

"No more questions; you have an hour." Jack claps. "Ready, set, go."

Panic ensues as everyone sprints off into the house, grabbing whatever they can find. Matthew takes my hand and pulls me upstairs to the second floor. "They're trying to disorient us by giving us creative freedom."

Out of the window in the hallway, we spot Myles carrying a ladder. Helene adjusts the fuzzy beanie covering her long brown twists and tosses a shovel over her shoulder.

"Let's think outside the box," I say, feeling like the world is spinning.

"They're gonna go all out. Myles is building a yeti or something even more massive. We gotta keep it simple."

"Tiny snowmen?"

"Perfect." He nods, gazing down at the ground. "But how do we make it interesting?"

"All of us," I blurt out.

"What?"

"Your entire family is all kinds of interesting. Let's make a snowman to represent each one of you. Maya the rockstar oncologist, Korina the badass social worker, Myles the buff veterinarian, and Helene the talented barre instructor. Then there's your dad, a commanding principal, and your mom's a financial whiz. And then there's you…" I trail off, at a loss for words.

"You're amazing." Matthew brushes my cheek with his gloved hand. The tip of his nose is red, and I want to tiptoe to kiss it.

"Matthew, I want this—*us*—forever," I say confidently. "I mean it. For the rest of my life."

"Yeah?" His eyebrows quirk up, and a wide smile pulls across his face.

He wants this too.

"I do." He pulls me right into his arms in the middle of the cramped upstairs hallway. "I love hearing you murmur at the crosswords in the mornings. I love the way you give Bear and me a kiss on the forehead when you get home, and how nerdy you are and how nerdy I can be with you. I want to be your family."

"I want to spend my life with you too." He picks me up off the ground and kisses me.

My heart flutters with joy, almost rupturing at the seams.

This is seriously the kind of thing that only happens in books. I mean, the man I've had a crush on for years is kissing me in his childhood home, and we're agreeing to spend our lives together?

Madison rushes past us, shoving us out of the way. "See ya, losers," she chides, bringing us back to the present.

We'll talk about our plans, and maybe even our real engagement, after we beat his siblings to a pulp.

"We have a game to win." I spring into action. We need, um —" I count the members of his family in my head, adding myself. "Twenty-two medium-sized snowballs and twenty-two small ones. Go get started; I'll collect everything we need."

"On it." Matthew and I exchange another kiss, but it's not just any kiss. It's the kind of kiss that lingers long after it's over. He sighs, pulling back. "But only because I want to crush Myles."

"Me too."

I speed through the house, grabbing ribbons and twigs, searching frantically for supplies like my life depends on it. This isn't a snowman-building competition anymore—it's war.

By the time I return to Matthew, he's rolled most of the snowguys and snowgals, each one standing two feet tall.

We scramble to put together the final touches. Charcoal stains my gloves as I make each snow face out of the coal Mary handed me when I rushed out of the house.

The ribbons around Madison and Gabby's snow necks whip in the wind. A pair of my Chanel ballet slippers lies by Helene's snow feet. I drape a stethoscope over the snowlady meant to be Maya.

Maya and I had a chance to talk and clear the air. I know she would never intentionally try to cause a rift between her brother and me. She was so concerned that I'd hurt Matthew, I don't even blame her. In a way, I'm glad she told me first, because it gave me a bit of time to process the reality of what Matthew was going to share with me.

"Those are going to be my mom and dad." Matthew motions

to the larger snowmen in the back as he drapes a scarf over the one that resembles his father. I shuck off my bright green ski jacket, tossing it over the snowman that's meant to be Mary.

"Perfect." I smile, barely feeling the cold. Matthew stabs branches and sticks into the sides of the snowy bodies.

An idea springs into my mind, and I drop to my knees, shuffling over to the pair of snowmen resembling Matthew and me. He has a pair of glasses on his snow face, and mine is holding a small book and wearing bright pink lipstick. Quickly, I form a small shape on the ground beside us.

"Is that Bear?" Matthew asks behind me, noting the pointy ears I'm finishing up.

"Of course; he's family."

"You're something else." He picks me up, kissing me again as the airhorn sounds.

Game over.

"Time to wrap it up, folks! Let's boogie to the deck," Jack hollers in a voice that only a man who's been the principal of an elementary school for twenty years can manage.

In the distance, the other siblings' creations stand tall and proud. Myles and Helene's snowman is massive, probably ten feet high, with a Red Sox baseball cap perched on top like a cherry.

"Boooo!" Madison jeers. "Yankees all the way!"

"You don't even like baseball." Myles pulls his sister under his arm, scrubbing his knuckles over the top of her head.

"If I did, it would only be to root for your rival."

The bickering is so casual and familiar, it's like they're speaking their own language. This is how Matthew learned that fighting is okay as long as you have each other's backs. I suppose he taught me that too.

He squeezes my hand as we admire his siblings' creations.

Mary and Jack are *oohing* and *aahing* as we walk through the museum of snow creatures.

Mitchell and Theo made a pair of snow angels holding hands. Maya and James crafted a simple snowman in flannel gear holding up a tiny tree with an axe leaning at its side. Mac and Korina's snowman has a guitar and a tattoo, while Madison and Gabby used paint to give their snowman a retro, tie-dye vibe. It's adorable.

We end up in front of our array of snowmen.

Mary beams. "It's our family."

"How'd you get Mac's hair so green?" Korina kneels, inspecting the snow.

"A packet of Jell-O," I laugh.

Myles feigns a huff, his nose bright red. "I'm not that round in my midsection, am I?"

"Let it go, Myles." Helene gives him a hug, her own cheeks looking flushed beneath the deep brown of her skin. "You guys nailed it."

Mary and Jack share a knowing look, one only a couple who has been married for forty years could understand. A look that's sweet and tender. As Jack leans in to kiss Mary's cheek, her entire face lights ups like a thousand suns, radiating with joy and love.

I want that with Matthew for the rest of my life.

And I'm going to have it.

"Wonderful job." Mary reaches her hand to mine, giving it a squeeze. "We're ready to announce a winner."

"Please return last year's trophy," Jack says.

Theo and Mitchell reluctantly hand the trophy over to Jack. Mitchell winks at me. "Good luck."

"This year's competition was intense," Jack's voice booms. "The battle was bloody, the sweat was real, and the tears were… well, let's just say there were tears."

"For the last time, I wasn't crying! I got hit with a branch," Maya groans.

"Our two eldest had the closest race." Mary holds up the

trophy, and all of the siblings collectively hold their breath.

Myles places his arm around his wife, who's nervously biting her lip.

"Ladies and gentlemen, the moment you've all been waiting for. The winners of this year's Hudson Family Olympics are…" Jack pauses, letting the tension build. "Matthew and Molly!"

Everyone erupts into thunderous applause, cheering and whistling. I barely register the words as my feet lift off the ground.

"We did it!" Matthew says, spinning me around the deck. "I knew we had it in us."

I land back on the deck, smiling brightly. "I don't know, Matthew," I tease. "I think I carried us to victory."

The group bursts into laughter, and Matthew showers my face with kisses. I'm dizzy with happiness.

"Mattie has finally won." Myles slaps his brother on the back, dragging him into a bear hug. "Get over here, Miss Molly Greene. You were a fierce competitor."

Matthew pulls me to his side, and then suddenly everyone's arms are draping around us.

My heart is bursting with so much love. I never want this day to end.

Ever.

I don't want to vanish or escape from my life anymore. I want to experience every single day, with all the good and bad.

When we all unravel, Myles narrows his eyes on Matthew, who walks hand in hand beside me into the house. "Are you sure you didn't just hire Molly to help you win? I don't think I've ever seen someone think on their feet so quickly."

My bones stiffen in my skin.

Did Matthew tell them this started as pretend?

"You married a barre instructor." Matthew gives him a nudge. "That seems entirely unfair, especially when, two years ago, we had to do a full-on ab challenge."

Helene shakes her head and gives me a nudge, lowering her voice as she says, "They assume we're giving them an advantage, but the Hudson competitive gene runs deep."

Maya gasps. "Now that I think of it, Mitchell is married to a history teacher, and last year the trivia questions were strangely skewed toward the olden days."

"You guys are just upset that Theo is smarter than all of you," Mitchell calls from inside the house.

Mary and Jack watch their kids with smiles plastered on their faces. I'm going to look forward to this every year.

WHITE FLAKES FALL outside Matthew's bedroom window. My present for him is probably getting ruined by the snow. My efforts to wiggle out of his embrace are thwarted with every inch I move. He only pulls me closer, wrapping me up in his warmth.

"Stay in bed, darling," he grumbles.

I breathe in the vetiver and musk of his skin.

The way he holds me, as if I'm every definition of the word *precious*, makes me feel loved. Nothing could harm me as long as he's here. I believe that's true. In the deepest parts of myself, I know that I'll have the life I've always wanted with Matthew.

The world beyond the windows grows whiter, the wind whistling against the roof. I can't wait a moment longer.

"I'll be right back." I place a kiss on his lips, quickly unhinge from his grip, and throw on Matthew's oversized green sweater with a golden *M* on it. I sneak downstairs and retrieve the box Dylan, my old driver, dropped off this morning on his way to Montreal to see his family.

Thankfully, the fallout with my family hasn't caused everyone from my old life to pull away from me.

I return to Matthew's bedroom, finding it filled with the soft glow of the bedside lamp. He's sitting up, his glasses resting on his nose and the blanket draped around his waist. My heart flutters, and I fumble to conceal his present behind my back.

Matthew gives me a lopsided grin, his eyes narrowing with curiosity. "What are you hiding over there?"

"A surprise." I sit on the bed and hand him the messily wrapped gift.

"I'm a big fan of Molly surprises." He pushes my hair back, inspecting my ears. My face flushes with a smidge of bashfulness. "Just checking that one of the elves didn't escape this year."

I could strip off his beyond-erotic flannel pajamas right now. I mean, seriously, who designed these things?

Nerdy lumberjack chic is most definitely my type.

"We'll save that surprise for when we're home." I chuckle loudly, the sound ricocheting off the walls before I clap my hand over my mouth. Everyone is still asleep.

Matthew pulls my palm away and kisses my smile. "Merry Christmas, baby."

"Merry Christmas," I whisper. "Okay, are you ready for your actual gift?"

"You are my gift, darling."

"*Matthew.*" I feign a scolding tone, passing the present to him.

We sit cross-legged in his childhood bedroom, wearing matching pajamas, facing each other. With a tantalizing slowness, he pops off the tape one piece at a time, each sound sending shivers down my spine. The paper unravels, and his brows furrow in confusion. I may shoot up through the roof like a torpedo from how giddy I am.

"The newspaper?"

I smile. "Check the crossword."

He flips to the page I've watched him go to dozens of times. His curiosity melts into awe.

"H-how?" His voice cracks.

I wrap my fingers around his palm. "I have elves at *The New York Times*."

He reads the clues:

ACROSS:

1 Actor who played the witty Chandler Bing on the sitcom Friends

5 Aureate

7 Literary character written by James Joyce, known for her spirited personality

8 Crimson Red rocks, formed about 210-370 million years ago

10 Start-up company eliminating the pacific trash vortex

11 Camping treat

12 River home to the elusive Lake Tear of the Clouds

13 Round, or bulging

15 Classic New England dessert

DOWN:

2 Book where the Battle of Loria takes place

3 Mythical eagle-lion hybrid

4 Sephi Humanoids

6 Animal with ursine characteristics

9 Biggest oceanic conservation organization (Acronym)

14 Animal with ursine characteristics

Nervously, I watch him scan the newspaper and piece together the puzzle I had designed for him.

"When did you...? How did you make this happen?" He looks up at me, setting the paper down in the space between us.

"I took care of it a couple of weeks ago. The new puzzle-master is an acquaintance of mine." The *Times* hired an old Cornell peer earlier this year. In exchange for this particular favor, I gave her my Metallic Chèvre Birkin 25.

Writing the clues took the longest time. Avery and Lily helped me piece together a few of the hints, but I've been tinkering with the idea for a while.

The grin that splits his face is priceless. I melt beneath the way he takes my hand and kisses each of my knuckles with care.

"Nothing will top this gift," he says. "I have to be honest; when we first arrived at On Cloud Nine, I started putting together a bucket list of all the new things I got to experience because of you. You've made my life so full, Molly."

"Stick with me, Hudson. I have a whole world of experiences I want to share with you."

My words seem to have an effect on him. Matthew's blue gaze glides over every one of my features.

Today can't possibly get any better.

He shifts, reaching beneath the bed for a box wrapped in gold foil.

"I have something for you too." He hands it over. I trace my thumb over the small dragons printed on the paper.

"This is lovely."

I like that we're exchanging presents alone. It's special. Maybe it could be our own little Christmas tradition. I carefully unwrap my gift.

Inside the thick cardboard box is the first book in *The Stone Court*. It's an edition I recognize almost immediately because it was a limited run, and there are only fifty prints of the full set in the world. I own the series collection, but he must've searched tirelessly for this copy.

I run my hand over the foil cover. It ripples beneath my palm.

"Flip it open." He smiles, and I do as he says.

On the inside, written on cardstock, is a note.

To my brave warrior, Merry Christmas. Love, yours forever and always, Matthew.

Tears well in my eyes like heavy droplets of rain. When I flip to the first chapter, they fall.

Matthew's handwriting is in the margins, along with scribbles and highlights along the text.

"You annotated it?" I sob.

"There's more." He nudges his head toward the box. Inside sits a small, velvet pouch. I pick it up, undo the button, and peek inside.

My heart stops; the air drains out of the room. His blue eyes ogle me.

We didn't have time to discuss my impromptu plan to spend our life together yesterday at the snowman contest. Part of me thought that he may have been caught up in the moment when he said he wanted to spend the rest of his days with me.

But that's not the case.

I pour the ring out into my hand. It has a gold band, and small diamonds encircle a beautiful pear-shaped ruby in the middle.

"It's beautiful."

Matthew takes the piece and hovers it by my ring finger.

"Molly Greene, I know you beat me to the punch yesterday, but I want you to understand that I'm serious about what I said. When we first met, I was taken by you. And now my life has bloomed because you're in it. You've flooded me with happiness, and I want to spend the rest of my days doing the same thing for you. I want to read all your books and cosplay as all your favorite leads." I laugh through my happy tears. My skin tingles with warmth. "I want to make that pretty smile appear on your face every day. I want to watch you build The Griffin and grow my business alongside yours. Anything you want, darling, I'll give it to you. I love you, Molly. Would you do me the honor of being my wife?"

"Yes." I nod vigorously. "Of course I'll marry you."

The cool band slips over my finger. It doesn't feel heavy because it's not another noose. This is a symbol of love, the feeling I was so afraid I'd never have.

Now, my life will be filled to the brim with it.

The perfect engagement.

Just us.

On our own terms.

He holds my hand, staring down at the ring. Wrapping paper crinkles around us as he leans over and kisses me. A happy-teared, salty kiss with my oh so real fiancé.

When we break apart, our lips are swollen. I run my left hand over the stubble on his jaw, down his chest—these manly chest hairs are mine forever. I giggle at the thought.

"What are you thinking over there?" He smirks as if he's reading my mind; he probably is.

"Just that I'm so lucky to call you mine."

"And Bear, if you'll have him."

"My favorite boys," I say, and we fall back onto the silk pillows with me tucked safely between his arms. "Do you think Bear would like a sister?" I ask.

He turns his head to me, and we roll over onto our sides so we're facing each other. "You want to adopt a cat?"

My pulse claps. "I know it may be a lot to take on another pet right now, but I think our Greenwich house is big enough.

And there's a long winter ahead. Think about all those poor kittens waiting to be loved by us. Is that too much?"

A smile pulls across his face. "Not at all. Bear's going to be glad to have someone else to annoy."

Sure, kids aren't in our plans for now. I'm certain that I don't need a large family of my own to be fulfilled, but every crevice of my being brims with love, and I know Matthew feels the same. Another bundle of joy might be really nice to include in our life.

"I love you." I smile.

"I love you too."

"I have to ask, when did you get this ring?" I say, flipping over onto my back and holding my hand above me. This ring, unlike the Harry Winston diamond Lance gave me, represents a freedom the other didn't.

"It's a family heirloom. My mother wore this, her mother before her, and so on. They've all had very happy marriages, so I'm inclined to believe it carries a little luck."

"Luck is exactly what I need if I'm going to secure the Tarrytown property," I say.

I don't care that I'm not getting my trust, especially with all the ties it would bring to my parents. But I've been changing all my budgeting models, and hopefully I can find an investor for my inn like Matthew has for EcoDrones.

"I have a feeling luck will always be on your side, darling."

"A lot of things are changing next year. New home, quitting ORO, starting The Griffin, getting EcoDrones off the ground, a new cat, and now…a wedding." I smile at the future that awaits me.

"Are you excited?"

"More than I've ever been."

Matthew kisses me again, and all the pieces fall into place.

Chapter 37
Matthew

Our closest friends are here, celebrating New Year's with us.

There are wineglasses stained with lipstick and bottles of scotch on the bar cart. Candlelight glows through the crowded kitchen in our home. Laughter echoes, mixing with the aroma of apple pie.

"You know, if you'd like some help on the EcoDrones interface, I'm your guy," Nico says, tipping his drink to me. "Lilium is doing so well that I have some free weekends. Lily has been working on her new book 'round the clock, so she'd probably appreciate me getting out of her hair."

I never would have imagined that the creator of two of the most downloaded apps in the country, someone who has made it onto the Forbes 30 Under 30 list, would be interested in helping EcoDrones.

"Robert will appreciate that." I extend my hand, and he laughs, pulling me into a hug. "Especially since Ollie is ditching the project."

"It's the least I could do. You had to tolerate—I mean, work with my brother for three years. I gotta pay you back somehow." Nico grins at Luca.

"Seriously?" Luca scowls, bouncing Kaia on his hip.

Their relationship reminds me so much of me and my brothers.

"Alright, stop your frowning," Nico laughs. "Now give me my favorite niece." He holds out his hands. "You wanna play airplanes, Kaia?"

She giggles.

"Don't you even think about it," Luca says.

"I promise, once your second one comes, the whole experience becomes less doomsday. I practically put a helmet on Aaron as soon as he got home from the hospital." James laughs as he pats Luca on the shoulder.

"I'm just protective of her," Luca sighs.

Reluctantly, he hands Kaia over to Nico, who launches her high into the air. She squeals loudly. "Kaia here is a little daredevil."

My former boss doesn't relax at my brother-in-law's words. A vein on the side of Luca's neck seems to pop out as he picks up his drink.

"My turn, Daddy," Aaron chirps, pulling at James's sleeve.

"I got him." Nico nods and sets Kaia down, offering my nephew a toss in the air.

I never thought I'd feel so complete having my friends, family, and future wife all under the same roof.

"Nightcap, anyone?" I grab the bottle of red wine from the counter.

"Fill 'em up, birthday boy," Ollie calls out, nodding toward his empty glass. He wipes down one of the final dinner dishes and sets the towel beside the sink.

"Lay off. It's tomorrow." I give him a nudge.

I've never cared much for my birthday, especially since it

overlaps with the holidays. But Molly gave me a peek at the gift she got me, and, well, I'm going to be looking forward to the first of January for many years to come. An intricate Rey costume from *The Last Jedi* for her, with a set of Kylo Ren robes for me.

Yeah, best birthday ever.

I top Ollie off and make my way to the living room.

Molly sits in front of the roaring fire, a blanket draped over her legs and Bear snuggled in her lap. Maya's sprawled out on the couch, typing away on her laptop. Lily's lying across the colorful rug, and Avery's sitting cross-legged beside her.

My fiancée notices me coming and gives me a toothy, wine-stained smile.

"Last call," I announce, flashing the bottle at them.

Avery, Lily, and Maya hold up their glasses, and I refill each one.

"Thank you," they say in unison as I finish off the bottle.

When I turn to Molly, she shakes her head. "I'm good." I make a quick mental note to bring her some water when I go back into the kitchen.

"Did you decide on a venue yet?" I ask Molly. "I know we talked about the New York Public Library, or The Met Cloisters this morning."

"As much as I loved those options, what do you think about a wedding for thirty people in our backyard?" Molly strokes Bear's brown fur. He purrs so loudly, I can hear him vibrating over the crackle of wood in the fireplace. *What a spoiled boy.*

"The backyard?" I clarify. We agreed that our ceremony would be low-stakes, just how Molly described it to me a few months ago at On Cloud Nine.

The only thing missing would be her parents. But I know this is how she prefers it. Whatever makes her happy is fine by me.

"Under the patio deck, in the snow. We can have s'mores, and Analise said she'd put together a dinner for us." Our gazes connect, and she smiles brightly.

A jolt of electricity runs between us. My radiant woman in her burgundy dress and a swipe of gold across her lids.

Watching her masks fall away in the presence of those she's most comfortable with makes me grateful that I'm one of the lucky few who get to witness her for all she is. I'm glad she has been leaning on her friend group and me since the split from her parents. She never has to be alone when we're all here.

"Your girl sure knows what she wants," Maya says, tipping her wineglass toward me.

"That she does." I give Molly a quick wink. Another item to check off of my never-ending bucket list.

My soon-to-be wife, smiling widely in all of her glory. *Check*.

I itch to tell her about the surprise I planned for The Griffin next week, but I push down the desire.

She always makes things special for me; I want to do this one thing for her.

"Except for your bachelorette party, which I'd argue is far more important than the ceremony." Lily reaches over and tickles the bottom of Molly's foot. She jolts with laughter, and Bear scowls at Lily.

"Apparently, doing a repeat of tonight isn't good enough," Molly giggles.

"Fine. As long as Matthew doesn't get upset when I hang up sparkling dicks everywhere." Lily props up on her elbows, shooting me a curious look. "Would that bother you, Mr. Hudson?"

"Lily!" Avery backhands her friend's shoulder.

"Did you know they make phallic-shaped pasta?" Maya joins in on the raunchy fun.

"And that's my cue to leave."

My girl peers back at me with mischief in her eyes. "You're no fun."

I lean down and kiss Molly's hair, which is warm from the

fire. "I'll show you how much fun I am tonight," I whisper into her ear.

"*Ooooo laa laa*," the women sing.

Christ. I thought I was quiet enough. The Anderson scotch obviously went straight to my head.

"Guys, stop." Molly's cheeks turn bright red as she waves off their suggestive whistling.

Her friends cheer, whooping and clapping as I make my way back to the kitchen.

Ollie pats me on the back. "Why are you smilin' so big over there?"

"What are you on about?" I stitch my brows at him, tossing the empty wine bottle into the recycling bin. I pull out a glass for Molly and fill it with sparkling water.

"It's all her, isn't it?" He leans back on the counter, somehow managing to look too large in this chef-sized kitchen, the way he typically does. It's as if his life has always been just too small for a man of his size. "You're in love, and now you're getting married," Ollie sings. "Love, love, love."

"Oh, hush." I give his shin a soft kick.

"Let me tease ya! I can't joke with you like this when I'm in Scotland." Ollie uncaps another bottle of scotch and pours us another round.

"Still can't believe that the whisky tasting was so popular, your folks are making you move back home to run the business." I force a grin, trying not to think about my best friend leaving.

"I should've sabotaged that Winter Ball after findin' out you all left," he chides. "But it's my own fault. I was trying to help them out, and, well, I helped a bit too much."

"I'm going to miss you." We cheers with the small glasses and take a sip. Smoky whisky coats my throat.

"Don't get all sentimental yet, Mattie." He gives me a nudge that almost knocks me off my feet. "I'm just sorry I'm bailing on EcoDrones."

"If you don't think I'll call you every week with questions and updates, you've got another thing coming." I laugh.

"Good." He tips his auburn beard toward me and pulls me into a huge hug. "Now, where did Bobbie run off to?"

"Probably upstairs. Molly's got a special edition of *Lord of the Rings* he's never seen before." I smile, catching a glimpse of my bride-to-be. Her head is thrown back in laughter as her friends encircle her.

Only one more hour until we bring in the new year, and I can confidently say I've never known happiness quite like this.

"WHERE ARE WE?" Molly peeks outside, rolling down the window of my car to get a better view, but the snow comes down in thick flakes. Pieces melt against her skin, and I let the cool air fill my lungs.

After her final day at ORO yesterday, she seems in really high spirits. Hopefully, my surprise will inspire even more confidence in her future.

"So impatient," I tease. "We're almost there."

We've been on the road for less than a half hour, but Molly hasn't stopped questioning me the entire trip.

A huge iron gate comes into view. This must be the correct turn.

The Tarrytown property is even more stunning than the pictures we saw online. The building appears through the snow-covered trees. An actual high tower stretches up toward the hazy white sky. The architecture is grand, with all kinds of carvings and decorations covering the walls and pillars.

"Is that…? No. The Griffin?" Molly's mouth gapes open. "Matthew, what is this? Is the owner here? When I spoke to Shauna back in the city, she said she wasn't going to be back for weeks!"

"Well, let's just say I put forth a very good argument over the phone, and there may have been a winter storm that made Shauna come home early." I place my hand on her thigh.

It took about two weeks of pestering phone calls and constant emails to convince the woman who owns this property to meet with us. But every second was worth it for the look of shock on Molly's face.

"I don't even believe it. What if she doesn't knock down the price? Oh my goodness, I would've put on a blazer or something if I'd known we were going to meet her today." Molly glances down at her cashmere sweater as though it's some kind of Snuggie.

"If there's one thing I'll always bet on, it's your ability to negotiate." I give her leg a squeeze.

We roll into the driveway and park by the grand entrance. I get out first and loop around the Rivian to open the door for Molly.

She shudders and runs her hand over her long skirt. "But I don't hav—"

"Baby." I drop my hands onto her shoulders. "You prepped all of December for this moment. Your laptop is in the trunk, your business plan is up to date. You got this."

Molly sets her hands on her hips and puts on a very bossy tone. "Mr. Hudson, one might get the impression that you're trying to seduce me with all of this business talk."

"Well, Mrs. soon-to-be Hudson-Greene, what if I am?" I give her a wink and grab her purse out of the trunk.

"I'm just speechless, that's what I am." Her eyes take in the grandeur of the property. "This is perfect. Better, even—it's real. The pictures on Zillow.com didn't even begin to do this place justice. I mean, do you see that tower?"

"It's all for you, darling."

"Well, consider me seduced." She nods and threads one hand through her bag, the other into my arm.

The crisp air stings my cheeks as we make our way inside.

We walk through the stunning maze of stained glass windows, which cast a beautiful array of colors all over the floors. The main entrance is bare but in good condition.

"Electricity is a good sign." I tip my head up to the chandelier above us. Molly nods with glee.

"There you are," a voice booms from behind us. At the corner of the room, a woman with graying hair and a stout frame comes shuffling toward us. She's wrapped up in a pink snowsuit that I'm pretty sure is sparkling.

Oh, Molly is going to love her.

"You must be Shauna." I offer my hand. "I'm Matthew Hudson, and this is Molly Greene. Thank you so much for meeting us here."

"Well, you wouldn't stop pestering me." She gives us a playful smile.

We exchange a quick round of introductions. Shauna's family has owned this property for decades, but her sights are set on Europe now.

All the better for us.

Molly laughs, holding on to Shauna's hands. "I have to say, I absolutely adore your snowsuit. I bought a purple Modena from Cordova, and it's my favorite to this day."

"You've got a brilliant eye, dear." The woman shines. "Of course you do; you're holding a Claire Tabouret Lady Dior."

She blushes. "Don't tell anyone. The world thinks there are only two of these out there, but this is number three."

"A woman with resources." Shauna claps her hands together. The cheerful sound bounces off the walls. "I like you already. Let's discuss business, and then maybe we can see what I can offer you for the bag."

Molly shoots me a quick glance, excitement glimmering in the amber of her eyes. I give her a nod, beckoning her to go on.

"I've been interested in your property for months," she

admits, following Shauna through the archway and down a long hall. I tag along behind them. "I grew up in the luxury hospitality industry, and I'm looking to turn this beauty into an inn where people can experience all of the wonders I grew up with, minus the resort price tag."

Shauna eyes Molly up and down. My fiancée straightens her shoulders. Her expression is all business, and I have to be honest—Molly's looking positively scrumptious right now.

"An inn? Most of the buyers I've met want to turn it into another vacation home, but I don't want my property to sit empty. It needs repairs, maintenance, and care."

"Yep." She nods. "And that's exactly why I want to discuss my offer."

Molly pulls out her laptop and brings up the plans as we get a walk-through of the property.

Within the next three hours, Shauna's lawyers send over the purchase contract and ownership paperwork.

"We'll be in touch, dear." Shauna smiles beneath the grand entrance.

"Enjoy the bag." Molly hugs her new friend and hands the elderly woman her purse.

The moment we're back in the car, Molly's alight with joy. "Can you freaking believe it? I can't even feel my hands or my face," she laughs. Her shoulders shimmy as I pull out of the driveway. "Nine million dollars below the asking price. Is this real? Am I awake? Pinch me!"

"You killed it in there, baby. Offering Shauna a stake in The Griffin was a brilliant negotiation tactic." I smile, admiring the pink blush stuck to Molly's cheeks.

"Don't forget the bag." She winks. "Sure, the Lady Dior was priceless, but my inn matters so much more to me, and I have dozens of other limited-edition bags already."

"I doubt anyone would've given Shauna a better offer."

There wasn't a minute where I doubted my woman, but her savviness surprised even me today.

"Plus, did you see how happy Shauna was with the renovation plans and the concept?" Molly gasps. "And she even asked to be one of our first guests. I may actually cry from pure happiness."

My heart is almost bursting with as much elation as hers. The blood traveling below my belt is also very eager for her news. "You're so sexy when you go all Business Molly."

"It wasn't even a mask; it was all me." She claps.

"I know, darling. My cock's hard beyond belief right now from the way you took charge." I look over at her and grin.

She hikes up one of her brows at me. "Oh yeah? If that gets you going, maybe I can take charge right now?"

"Don't tempt me, or I'll have to pull over and take you in the snow." I howl like a wolf, exaggerating the sound, and my throaty chuckle fills the car.

"Now that's something I'd like to try." Molly reaches one of her hands for my thigh, stroking the denim fabric. "If all the paperwork goes smoothly, do you mind if we have our wedding there? It just feels right, don't you think? I know it needs renovations, but half the rooms are good enough to sleep in, and the grand room with the fireplace would be perfect for a private vow ceremony and then a small party afterward."

Anything you want, baby. "That's perfect."

Chapter 38
Molly

THE EARLY MORNING sun peeks through the stained glass windows, causing my dress to shine. My dream gown. A gorgeous, custom-made masterpiece, with a deep crimson bodice and delicate lace designs that trail down the front. The sleeves are long and sheer, with sparkling fabric that makes me look like a maiden in a love story.

Except today, I'm the main character.

There's been a tinge of sadness permeating my thoughts as I got ready, casting a shadow over the morning. Even though I haven't spoken to my parents, I still wish they were here. But I know that I want my wedding to be mine. I'm certain that, despite how much my heart aches for them to be here, I get to have this day all to myself.

Just like I wanted.

My life begins again, with the person I trust most in the world.

There are no whispers from unknown guests. No judgmental glares. No contracts or business deals. I can't believe at one point I almost settled for being just *fine*.

Our friends and Matthew's family are arriving in a few hours to celebrate with us, but I knew I wanted our vows to be just for us.

It's my moment. My time.

Today, I'm choosing me…and Matthew.

My real love match.

Sure, I don't have my trust, but money's never mattered less than it does now.

As nerves swarm through my belly, I run my hand over the stone walls, grounding myself in the present.

The morning, last night, and every hour leading up to now have been drenched in memories I've shared with him.

How we rode horses together, stargazed, and made art in Sedona. How his musk and vetiver scent stuck to the bedsheets until it became my familiar source of comfort.

The years Matthew and I spent laughing among the glass walls of ORO's offices. The way my breath stills every time I find myself beneath his blue-eyed gaze.

There are the renovations we've been undergoing at The Griffin over the last three weeks, and Matthew's handiness has been saving us left and right—from the leak in the chef's kitchen to the four-poster bed we managed to break.

Bear's purring, the trips to the animal shelter to find us a new cat, the meals we've shared, and the dishes I've cleaned when we're done.

The smallest things. From the bend in his nose to the freckles above my lips that he kisses every morning.

I'm fluent in our life now, not just in him.

As I near the grand room, a strum of piano keys plays Taylor Swift's song, "Today Was A Fairytale."

Matthew's choice, and all too perfect for today.

When I turn into the doorway, my husband is waiting for me.

The nerves I thought I'd tempered sneak up on me again. My lungs seem to have stopped working.

Matthew's dressed in a three-piece tuxedo. The crisp black suit jacket hugs his muscular arms. I swallow a steadying inhale. His eyes find me, and the effort to remain calm shatters.

His hand shoots over his mouth when he sees me. He tosses his head back. The whites of his eyes quickly turn red.

Tears sting my eyes. Thank goodness I wore waterproof mascara.

A boutonniere of winterberries is notched into his satin lapel, matching my red dress.

"Molly." Matthew steps toward me, outstretching his hand. Tears stream freely down his face, and mine start gliding over my cheeks. This is the happiest I've ever felt in my life. "You are —" His words get caught in his throat.

My knees shake as I approach his spot under the arch made of winter wildflowers.

Lolita stands beside him. The relationship expert not only agreed to marry us, but she became the second investor in The Griffin and will be leading classes here once we open.

She was eager to get out of the Arizona heat, and her excitement about officiating our wedding makes me think that she missed having us around.

"Hey, you can't cry, or else I'll keep crying," I laugh through my sobs.

Matthew pulls my fingers into his hand, holding me with a firm grip, as though I might float away. But I'm not going anywhere.

The air feels thick as I make one final step up to our altar. Bear and Brave—an orange barn cat we adopted five days ago— are snuggled up on a large blanket next to the fire.

He reaches for my cheek, gliding his warm hand against the damp skin. "My darling girl, you are the most beautiful thing I've ever laid my eyes on." My heart glows, surely visible through the tight lace of my corset. "I—god," he chokes out. "I can't believe I get to spend my whole life with you."

"You better believe it, Hudson." I pull his fingers to my lips, staining his knuckles red.

"My favorite lovebirds," Lolita fawns. "Should we begin?"

Taylor Swift's voice sings in the background.

Today was a fairytale

I'm getting my happy ending. Though I suppose it's more like a happy start.

THE SNOW outside is draped with shadows of blue and gray. Our upstairs bedroom in The Griffin is warm.

I barely remember Matthew lighting the fire last night. The moment I reached our bed, I was asleep.

Who could possibly have the energy to make love after a full day of wedding activities?

Our wedding was small, but we danced for hours. Matthew's family, the kids, and our closest friends. Our bellies were stuffed with Analise's amazing dinner and loads of bubbly. I even broke out some old salsa moves I hadn't done in years.

At about four in the morning, my husband carried me up the stairs. I'm giddy as the word glides through my thoughts.

Husband.

Today is my first official day as Mrs. Hudson-Greene.

I feel so freaking complete.

I'm turning twenty-seven in only a few weeks, and my birthday always felt like a dreary day. Specifically when it was tied to my trust.

Now it feels like my life is just beginning. I wish I'd known that while I was growing up, that it can start whenever.

"Good morning," Matthew says in a sleepy voice.

From my place by the window, I glance over my shoulder, admiring the rugged look of *my husband* in bed.

Yeah, I'm never going to get tired of that.

"Good morrow." I smile and tip my head toward the snow outside. "What do you think about going out there?"

Matthew stretches his large, muscular biceps over his head.

"Now?" He quirks a brow at me, a very tempting look in his blue eyes.

"Yes, now. We need to consummate our marriage," I tease, walking toward him. "I have to be honest with you, I read something in a book once, and today feels like the perfect day to give it a go."

At the foot of our four-poster bed, I slowly bend and pick up a pair of my woolly thigh highs from the floor.

My lips curl, and I flash Matthew a challenging look. I hike my leg up onto the edge of the mattress and begin sliding one of the socks up my leg. My thick cashmere sweater barely covers my behind.

"I'm starting to think you only married me so that I can help some of your fantasies come to life." He sits up, watching me intently. Matthew swipes his hand over the five-o'clock shadow coating his face.

"Maybe." I blink my lashes at him innocently. "Are you going to come outside with me and see if you can live up to the task?"

"You sure you don't want me to keep you warm right here?" He pulls back the covers, inviting me.

"Tempting offer, Mr. Hudson-Greene." Yeah. I'll never get over him taking my last name. I lower my voice and say, "But I'm a married woman now, and my consummation deserves some *pizazz*."

"Who says we can't get started now?"

"Me," I snap playfully. "I think that if you want your wife, you're going to have to come and fetch her."

"Already thinking about running away from me?" Matthew smirks, fire lighting up his eyes.

I make a slow effort with the second sock, savoring the way his gaze devours me. "Only for a little while."

His breath shallows, and he palms the hardness that's forming beneath the sheets.

"Fuck, baby, you're driving me out of my mind with those." His voice is deep and seductive. My body trembles in anticipation.

"Well then, you better come catch me. Fare thee well; I must away!" With my socks firmly in place, I take off sprinting through the door.

My light footsteps tread through the stone corridors and down the twirling stairs. I grab my Max Mara shearling coat off a nearby chair and throw it over my long sweater. As I'm lacing up my boots, I catch Matthew's tall frame shuffling down the steps.

I bite into the smile cresting my lips.

"Did you think you can escape me, princess?" Matthew asks in a voice that sounds like it belongs to a commander of some kind of knight's watch. *Ugh.* I love how much he enjoys playing with me.

My heart beats wildly against my rib cage.

This is going to be so much freaking fun.

"I know I can," I squeal, pulling open the front door and setting off into the early morning light and toward the small forest surrounding our property.

Snow crunches beneath my feet. Laughter spills out of me.

I'm free, so free.

The cold breeze barely registers as I dash through the white meadow. Thank goodness winter mornings in the Northeast tend to be warmer, because the cool air doesn't even bother me.

When I reach the forest's edge, I turn around.

Matthew isn't running. He's taking his sweet time treading over my tracks. A thick leather jacket drapes his shoulders, revealing the plaid flannel of his pajama shirt and a pair of jeans hugging his muscular thighs.

"You're not even trying to keep up, husband," I yell out to him. The fresh smell of pine fills my lungs.

He doesn't smile or break his targeted stare on me. His piercing blue gaze licks over me. Warmth and adrenaline course through my veins.

Okay, I'm in trouble.

I burst into the forest, darting toward a tree and hiding behind it. The thick bark is cool to the touch, rippling beneath my fingertips. Snow crunches as Matthew comes into view.

"I knew marrying you would keep me young." He lets out a sardonic laugh that shakes the snow-covered branches overhead. Powdery mist falls from the sky.

"Tired already?" I call out, giving up my hiding place. I run, not looking back. But this time, I hear the heavy drag of his boots as he chases after me.

I'm weightless and light-headed.

I want him to catch me.

I want to find out what he'll do when he gets a hold of me.

When I reach a small clearing, I steal a glance over my shoulder.

Matthew's only a few feet away. His jet-black hair is peppered with snowflakes. His features are sharp. Intimidating.

"You turn me into an animal; you know that, don't you?" He hikes up the collar of his leather coat. My lungs struggle to fully expand as I inhale the icy air.

"Do I?" The bow in my hair is flimsy as I pluck it from my curls and throw it in the snow toward him. When he moves forward, I step back. He grabs the ribbon and rubs the silk against his fingertips.

"All the time."

My skin pebbles at the darkness in his voice.

"Then come get what's yours. I'm here for the taking, aren't I?" I throw my hands out, putting myself on display.

"I'm in no rush. You're going to tire yourself out soon enough." His teeth tug at his bottom lip like he's planning on eating me alive.

"Aren't you eager to take your wife?" I coax. The bashful girl I was in our bedroom minutes ago fully melts away. Now that he's my husband, I get to share all the parts of myself with someone who cherishes me.

"I think you like the chase, don't you?"

"Most definitely." I let out a loud, thrilling laugh. I absolutely love the game we're playing.

"When I get my hands on you, you might grow to regret that, wife."

Yeah, it's official. Never, ever getting tired of that.

"What are you going to do?" I narrow my eyes on him.

"Take you."

My spine trembles, my core tightening.

"Here?" I feign innocence.

"Yes, darling, right here, in the fucking snow."

"Good luck completing your mission, knight," I squeal and sprint off, surging through the snow with a wild, reckless fervor. The wind whips through my hair as I push myself forward.

I'm invincible.

At least, until a root under the snow snags my foot, tearing me down to the ground.

Ugh. Now I understand why heroines are always falling when they're being chased.

Honestly, Mother Nature must know Matthew is an ally. As if the universe is shouting, *You're reforesting me, sir? Here, take your prize.*

A wild laugh escapes me. My head whips side to side, scanning for my captor, but he's nowhere to be found.

I'm alone in the snowy forest.

The trees loom overhead, casting shadows that shift with the wind. Snow continues to fall heavily, sticking to my coat and curls.

I press my hands to my chest, trying to warm my fingers. I should have grabbed gloves. A shiver runs through me. My panties are already soaked, but as I try to steady the adrenaline coursing through me, I realize they're growing wetter from the snow below me.

Panic sets in. I don't have my phone.

Where is he?

How far have I run?

"On your knees." A deep voice comes from behind one of the trees. Thrill replaces fear in an instant. I search for him. "Now," Matthew says, seemingly closer this time.

Electricity zooms up my spine. I follow his command, pressing my knees and palms onto the cold, unforgiving ground.

A low, guttural growl emerges from the tree line. *My wolf.*

"Eyes forward," he commands in a husky tone. His boots crunch behind me.

The cold breaks through my woolly socks. A shadow looms in front of me. My core floods.

The ribbon that was in my hair falls like a leaf in front of where I kneel. The scarlet fabric is stark against the blanket of white snow. Without a word, he shucks my coat to one side. My lower back, behind, and thighs are exposed to the frigid breeze. The icy chill only intensifies the heat rising within me.

My thighs cinch together.

"Tell me the color of your ribbon," he says.

"Red." My pulse sloshes in my ears.

"You remember what that means?" It means everything we do is in my control. On my terms. One small word, and all our games can shatter.

"Yes." I nod. But I won't be using it.

"Did you think you could outrun me?"

"You're getting slow at your age," I tease.

"I guess I'll just have to teach you how wrong you are." From behind, he lands a sharp smack against my ass. My eyes flutter shut, enjoying the delightful burning sensation dancing against my skin. "I'm more alive than I've ever been."

"Prove it." I want to push him, see how far he'll let himself go, how far he can take me.

In a second, his icy fingers glide down my spine and over my waist. He hooks into the fabric of my panties and, with a sudden tug, rips them off of me.

I yip loudly.

He runs his fingers against my wetness, igniting a fire within me.

"Is this pussy mine, wife?"

I shake my head.

His fingers push into me all too fast, rough, and deep. Not an ounce of tenderness because he knows what I need right now.

To be consumed.

"Fuck," I shout at the unexpected fullness. Cold and heat mix together. My breath becomes ragged as I lean forward and steady myself on my palms on the icy ground.

"I'll ask you again." He leans over me, and his minty breath caresses my earlobe. "Is this wet cunt all for me?"

I mewl under his calculated strokes, until his movements still and he retreats from me.

"Use your words."

"Yes. Every inch of me is yours."

This time, he presses on my clit and creates slow circles with two of his fingers. His free hand gathers my hair and gently tugs, pulling my head back. "How much do you want my cock, Molly?"

"So much." I let out a beastly groan.

He counters with a menacing laugh, his fingers not breaking

pace on my clit. I struggle to keep myself steady on my hands and knees. I rock back against him and gasp for air.

My socks are completely drenched.

The cold earth penetrates my senses.

Fear mixes with excitement. Snowflakes blur together as I lose myself in the dark pleasure of his touch.

"That's too bad," Matthew says, letting go of my hair and landing a searing palm against my ass. The sting hurts so good. "You ran away from me, and only good girls get to be filled to the brim."

"Please," I plead.

I'm delirious, caught in a dream.

"Keep begging, beautiful."

"Matthew, please." My wetness overtakes the sound of my heavy breaths and Matthew's heaving. "Please."

"Louder." Matthew leans over me again. His hand makes a path from my ass to my stomach until he's clutching my breasts under my sweater. A mix of pain and pleasure shoots through me every time he pinches my nipples.

The motions on my clit stop, and his fingers slip back into me. He pumps them exactly how I like it.

"P-please." The trees shake beneath my amorous screams.

"I can't fucking hear you, darling." Matthew abandons the tender skin of my breasts. His hands are in my hair again. He yanks at the strands, forcing me off of my palms. I do my best to balance on my knees as he keeps fingering me.

"Give me all of you," I yell with everything I have. I'm possessed. Euphoric and wild as the orgasm starts to crest my spine. Everything is out of my control, and I love it. "Please, please, please."

"Good girl." He nips at my ear, and I groan.

"Matthew, don't stop," I cry.

What am I begging for? Release? Conquering? Wanting him to shatter me?

"My sweet wife, all dirty in the snow. What am I going to do with you?" he growls.

"Matthew!" I choke on another scream. The inevitable fall of my climax begins to blur my vision. My husband connects his lips with the back of my neck, his teeth dragging along the sensitive skin.

"You're so pretty when you beg for the release only I can give you."

"Yes." My knees spread wider into the ground as I rock against his fingers. "Yes. Only. You."

My scalp burns from his firm grip around my hair. I moan on the brink of oblivion.

"There she is." His teeth sink into the nook of my neck. He bites hard, and I yell. Spots attack my vision. This must be nirvana. When my orgasm stops, his lips caress the bite mark he left on me. "Christ, Molly, you're fucking dripping for me."

"I need you."

"I'm right here." He lets go of my hair and rests his hand on my back, guiding me to topple forward onto all fours again.

The thick head of his cock pushes at my entrance.

I swallow deeply.

"This is mine, isn't it?" Matthew demands. "Because I'm going to claim it."

"All yours."

In one thrust, he drives himself into me, stretching me past my limit. My walls are sore from his unforgiving fingering. He can get so deep at this angle. I spread my knees into the ground, arching my back and pushing my butt back toward him.

"Fuck, baby, you feel so good." He pauses.

Without leaving me, he strips off his coat and drops it in front of me in the snow. I quickly pull it beneath me and lean my forearms onto the warm shearling fabric inside.

The moment I steady my balance, Matthew drags me off the

ground by my hair again. My back presses against his chest as I balance on my knees.

The grip on my strands sends my face to the sky, and Matthew moves my jaw to one side for a kiss.

We devour each other. Tongues. Teeth.

The fullness of him is unbearable, and he refuses to move. Each time I try to rock myself along his length, he forces me steady. It's torture to feel him occupy every inch of me without a single stroke.

I doubt in my wildest and darkest fantasies I could have ever wanted someone this much. But Matthew now owns every part of those. Every part of me.

My neck strains. My legs tremble. I barely manage my balance. As my tongue hungrily explores his mouth, my teeth sink into his bottom lip, and I taste copper.

"Fuck," Matthew growls against my lips. He drops his hold on my hair, and I fall forward onto my palms. He's not gentle as he reaches over and grabs each of my wrists, gathering them at the base of my spine. My face meets the shearling. "You bit me, princess."

"Just tasting my prey," I laugh.

I turn onto my cheek, making out his towering frame from the corner of my vision. The blue of his eyes is entirely replaced by a burning darkness. Blood spreads across his mouth like a wild beast. Matthew wipes his lip and pulls out of me.

"You, my sweet girl, are my catch," he says, low and heavy. "You brought me all the way out into the woods. You're going to make it worthwhile."

He spits on my swollen pussy. A gasp rips out of me. The act is filthy and possessive.

My core vibrates, and I spread my knees wider for him, putting myself on display.

Vulnerable and exposed.

Matthew doesn't wait. He pushes himself inside of me in one

go again, stretching me. My teeth grit against his coat. My body convulses, shaking around him as he fills me to my end without mercy.

His bucking halts.

Why'd he stop again?

I need him. More of him.

"Please." I flash my eyes at him, trying to coax him to move again.

"Get to work," Matthew commands. His hands tighten around my wrists. I oblige immediately, digging my knees into the snowy ground and rocking my hips against his length. He feels so good. "Harder, Molly. Like you mean it."

My lids sew shut as I fuck his cock. Matthew's hold around my wrists pinches my skin. My cold fingers turn numb.

"You're going to be good and come all over my cock. Aren't you?"

"I am," I heave. Matthew's cock grows bigger and bigger with every stroke.

He unlatches from my wrists, and I take my arms back into my possession. My muscles are sore, but I hike up onto my forearms, staring ahead.

Matthew grips my ass, digging his nails into my skin as he takes over my ragged rocking. He angles his cock deeper into me and, with punishing strokes, tempts another orgasm from me.

"My."

Thrust.

"Precious."

Thrust.

"Wife."

I howl, loud and animalistic. I let him ravage me.

"Are you going to take every drop of cum that's about to fill you up?" His hips slam against me viciously.

"I want it." My moans grow louder.

Involuntarily, my walls tighten around him. My own demise,

so close. He feels incredible. My eyes burn. My spit drips down my chin.

"I'd spend my whole life chasing you."

My husband.

My safety.

My Matthew.

"I'm right here," I say to him and myself.

The words shatter us both. My climax rocks me to my core, sending my soul into fragments. My muscles go slack, and I fully collapse onto his coat as Matthew's hot release empties inside of me.

He pulls out of me, drapes my coat over me, and cuddles me in his arms, planting a string of kisses across my damp face.

"I love you." He cups the side of my neck. "Was that how it played out in your book, darling?"

"My book barely compares to how amazing that was. I've never been happier."

"Let's get you home, and I can spend the rest of the day taking care of you and keeping you warm."

Matthew gently tends to our clothes, wiping any trace of himself from my thighs before helping us both dress. Then, with a tender embrace, he lifts me into his arms and carries me back to The Griffin.

The brilliant sun casts a warm glow across him, shimmering against his blue eyes and the snowcapped trees above.

Scratches and red marks line his lips and jaw. *I did that. I marked my own husband.*

The reality undoes me.

Matthew wants me, my whole heart and soul. He wants to watch me break apart and be there to care for me after.

I'm so blissfully in love.

"Where have you two been?" a voice calls out from the inn's entrance.

Maya and Lily tip their steaming mugs toward us. They're

both bundled up in coats and sweaters, watching the smattering of snow fall from the sky.

"Just enjoying the snow," I call back, kicking my feet with glee in Matthew's arms.

"*Oh*," Lily says in an exaggerated tone. "Nico and I also enjoyed the snow this morning."

I laugh into Matthew's chest. He strolls toward them. "You know, James and I had a lot of fun in the snow last night," Maya chimes in.

"Alright," Matthew scolds. "That's more than I needed to know."

"I see my *Toasty Inside* novella gave you all the best ideas. Naming your inn after the grumpy recluse and then having a little fun in the snow?" Lily teases.

"Oh my goodness." I burst out laughing. "I totally forgot about that. Guess it's time for a reread."

"How could you forget about Griffin and his hairy wiener, Comet?"

Matthew quirks an eyebrow at me in curiosity. "It's the main character's dachshund," I explain.

"Do I need to check out this book?"

"There are some things that happen in a hot spring you would enjoy." I wink. My cheeks hurt from smiling so much. "We'll be down in a bit," I yell to my friends. "We've got frost-bite to take care of."

The pair laugh as Matthew carries me over the threshold of The Griffin.

Chapter 39
Matthew

Molly and I are spending half of our nights at The Griffin since the winter storms have been getting worse as we renovate. The other nights we share at home, snuggled up in our bed.

My wife twirls under the giant chandelier in the grand foyer. She has Brave hugged over her shoulder, and Bear paws at her feet, waiting for a turn.

Guess I'm not the only jealous man in the house now.

Life since we've been married hasn't felt real.

I'd never imagined myself as a man of hospitality, but since EcoDrones will take at least a year of research and development —all of which I've outsourced to my team of MIT mentees from Enviroworks, who were eager for new jobs postgraduation—I have free time on my hands.

I also never saw myself as someone who would fall in love again or own a cat.

I suppose that's the strange thing about getting older: your life blossoms around you, and you just need to sit back and enjoy the blooms while plucking all the weeds that come your way.

"Maybe we can hold our opening day reception in this room." Molly sets Bear down and strolls over to me. She pulls a pencil and a small notepad out of her back pocket, tapping the eraser on the side of her mouth. Her journal is already halfway full of ideas. "We could build a stage in the corner to host a live band. I'm sure the kids would love to dance around, and with these windows, we won't even need lighting."

"In June, the rose garden should be full of blooms. We can fill the rooms with their own bouquets." I wrap my arms around her thick wool sweater and pull her close.

"Maybe we should ask guests if they're allergic or what color they want on the intake form," she says, her eyes bright.

"My wife has the best ideas." I give her a small kiss, but Molly has other ideas. She pulls on the collar of my shirt, pressing me close.

So achingly sweet.

There are times when her melancholy has her wrapped up in blankets at home, nose in her book, a flash of smile over the bound spine. Then there are times like this, when her delight strums up her life.

She's been back in therapy for almost two months, working through the ups and downs of the adjustment with her family. Maybe even the grief of losing the person she was always pretending to be.

I know from experience that it's easy to dive headfirst into a project without taking the time to process everything that's happened. Plastech would not have been the same without the impact Laura had on my past—it might simply not exist. No grand vision of helping future generations, no technological advancements.

Though I believe that having something of our own is a good thing, a permanence.

"So, out of the twenty-two rooms here, there are five left to design," Molly chimes, pulling away from me and putting her serious face back on. I have worked with plenty of founders and entrepreneurs, and I must say that Molly's mind is one of a kind.

"I was thinking the one farthest from the stairs could be the Honeymoon Suite. Or maybe we should name it the Fairytale Frolic."

"Or the Lovers' Lair."

Her laughs turn into my favorite snorts. "I love that. We may be able to open up for the summer season. Can you see it? Birds chirping, horses, hikes?"

I close my eyes. "I really can. You in a bright pink dress, welcoming all the guests. Me trying to rally the cats together." The agendas have already been drafted, and Molly's been working overtime processing her ideas with Lolita. "I'm most excited for the painting class in the southern part of our property." I give her a playful grin, watching her cheeks turn the color of her hair.

"Our property," she sings. "What have you done to me, dear husband?"

We loop around the grand hall and into the back room leading out to what will be the outdoor patio and garden.

Every time I look out into the woods, I remember Molly sprawled out in the snow. My heart races at the mere memory.

"Now, Lily and Avery will be here tomorrow. They're bringing the guys, and the three of you can move the grand piano into the room right over there." Molly nudges her head to the small nook by the stairs. Her laser focus, the pencil tucked behind her ear, and her firm nodding are causing my body to warm. "Oh, Lily also asked if she and Nico could book a room for an entire month, for research on a Renaissance romance she's writing."

"Did anyone ever tell you that you're absolutely irresistible when you're bossy?"

"You might need to remind me," she laughs.

"Shall we go now?"

"Tsk, tsk, Matthew. We're at work."

I playfully lift my brows at her. "Don't worry; I won't tell the boss."

Molly's focused stare scatters around the room. "I think we should look at some linens this week. There's a whole world of fabrics out there, and we need to pick just the right ones." She scrunches her nose in amusement. "Are you taking notes too?"

"I'm a bit distracted." I kiss my wife.

"Maybe you can take me upstairs once we finish up down here?" She smiles, a mischievous look folding into her eyes.

"Must we wait?" I exaggerate a sigh that makes her laugh.

"Hmm." Molly pretends to consider me for a long moment, deliberating the question with great care. "Maybe we mustn't."

I bend, scooping her off the ground, one arm beneath her thighs, the other at the groove of her back. "As milady commands." I rush out of the room, causing her giggles to escalate to the point of tears on her face.

Molly's phone vibrates in her pocket. She removes it and looks down to see her father's name on the screen. Ray has called four times this week, but she tucks her phone under the journal in her lap.

"Not yet?"

"Soon, very soon." She shakes her head back and forth. "They're trying to arrange a meeting."

"What do you think?"

Molly drops her temple into the bend of my neck. "I'm going to reach out next week and invite them over to our house for a talk. I want to speak with them before my birthday next month."

"Sounds like a plan." I squeeze her close.

"Do you think I'm weak for waiting this long?" Her voice feels small.

"Hey." I pull back, getting a better look at her face. "Of course you're not. Besides, watch what you call my wife. She's the strongest woman I know."

Chapter 40
Molly

"Hɪ," I say, standing in the doorway of my house.

"Hi, Molly." Dad adjusts the wiry frames on his nose and puts his hand on my mother's back, nudging her forward.

I hesitate, inhaling a deep breath and pulling open the front door. "Come in."

Two days ago, I called my father and invited them here. The conversation was brief. It didn't feel right to discuss what's unfolded over the past two months over the phone.

Our relationship may never be perfect, but Vivian and Ray Greene are still my family, and as much as I'm enjoying my life, I want them to have the opportunity to be a part of it. Slowly.

Both of them apprehensively shuffle into our house, leaving their shoes in the entryway.

Unlike my dad's torn-up expression, my mother hasn't changed since I last saw her at the Winter Ball. I didn't exactly expect her to grow a second head or shed a new skin, but I thought something would be different.

My own life has changed so much.

Do I look different to her?

Her gaze trails down my Johanna Ortiz sweater dress,

splotched with print and color. Then her eyes slide over to the living room. Our shelves, the mantel, and our kitchen are brimming with red crocus flowers and heart decorations that Matthew put up to celebrate our first Valentine's Day yesterday.

"We've missed you." My father pulls me into a warm hug, somewhat awkward and unsteady.

"Ray, Vivian, it's nice to see you both." Matthew shakes my father's hand and takes both of their coats.

"This is a lovely home." Dad spots the photo from our wedding day at the entryway. A small frown tugs at his lips. "Thank you for having us."

"Our pleasure." Matthew nods. "Would you like a tour?"

Dad pauses for a moment, looking over at my mother, who, uncharacteristically, has barely said a word. Then he turns back to Matthew. "I would love that."

"Right this way." My husband leads my father up the stairs and into our shared office space, which mimics a war room right now.

Both of our businesses are taking off, and we've been back and forth between here and The Griffin for weeks.

I'm left alone with my mother, who looks small without the lift of her Toteme booties and Moncler puffer. I spent all of yesterday's therapy session rehearsing what I'd say to her, the different approaches I could take. But, looking at her now, I know I need to speak from the heart.

"I have tea," I offer, and she takes a seat on the plush couch, crossing her ankles one over the other and lacing her fingers together. "Lemon verbena?"

"Thank you." I fetch us two mugs, ushering them to the coffee table and joining her on the couch. "If I may start?" She rolls her finely lined bottom lip into her teeth. Her eyes nervously shoot from the floor up to mine. I nod, letting her continue. "Molly, I'm sorry."

She's never apologized for anything. Sure, this is the best-case scenario, the one I've waited an eternity for, but I'm stunned. Genuinely flabbergasted.

"Sorry?" I repeat, clarifying. I need to hear the words again.

Mom looks away. "Yes. I want to apologize for how I acted at the Winter Ball and…" She inhales, wincing. "And how I've acted toward you all of this time. Your entire life, I mean."

My heart aches, and even though she apologized, I'm not satisfied yet.

Is she being genuine?

After discussing the situation with my therapist, I realized that my mother's behavior may have been driven by her own fears and insecurities, causing her to overreact to situations she deemed dangerous or risky. Though it hasn't quite helped me move past the scars her words have inflicted, it has helped me let go of some of the anger and resentment I had been holding on to for so long.

"Thank you." I nervously trace the lines in my palm. "I've spent the past few months trying to understand your motivations, why you insisted I get married to Lance. Why you'd hurt the man I love. Why you'd hurt me. But guessing the reasoning behind your behavior was pointless." My voice cracks, and instead of brushing away my tears or hiding the fact that I'm hurting, I let myself cry. "I just want to know one thing: why was I never good enough for you?"

She doesn't look at me for a long while, and then her amber eyes brim with something that's causing them to turn red.

Is she allergic to cats? Or, wait. Is she…crying?

Impossible.

"You've always been good enough for me, Molly. For me and for your father."

"You never made that known."

She frowns, her hands trembling on her thighs. "There's no excuse. I wanted to protect you; we both did. Though I won't speak for your father now. I want you to hear my side—not so it changes anything, but so maybe you could understand some of my…" She pauses again. "*Shortcomings* as your mother."

"Okay."

"Your father and I got married when I was twenty-one," she reminds me. "He was older than me, somewhat similar to your situation with Matthew. Except our relationship wasn't quite the road to love that you've had." I want to quirk an eyebrow at her, but it seems like she's having a difficult time. "Ray's mother approached me at my Cornell graduation and offered me a ticket to this life. I was set to work at *The New Yorker* that fall—"

My mouth juts open. I had no idea. "What?"

"At one point, things looked different." My mom sighs, picking up her tea. Surprisingly, it's easy to picture Vivian running around with a pen and paper, trying to get the latest scoop. "I told my parents about the Greene trust, about how I'd marry into this dynasty and have a shot at something bigger than what was awaiting me after college, and I took it. I chose riches over my dreams, over real love. Little did I know, despite all the money, I agreed to spend my entire life as an outsider."

It's heartbreaking that my mother had to give up parts of herself to fit into a life she didn't truly belong in. A reminder that sometimes the people closest to us are dealing with their own struggles and challenges, and we may not even be aware.

Like how no one knew I was suffocating for years.

"Fitting into society was arduous. Everyone made sure to remind me that I didn't belong, that I wasn't quite the right fit. But, with time, your father and I learned to love each other. We became friends, and it made things easier." She takes a long sip of her tea and sets it back on the coffee table. "When we had you, our love shifted into something more, and I found that feeling I'd been searching for…like I belonged. My own family. You probably don't remember this, but I submitted a few pieces to *The New Yorker* before you were five. A part of my identity was coming back."

My heart quakes in my chest, caught between the betrayal of never knowing this side of her and the fact that, despite her feeling like an outsider, my mother made me think I didn't belong either.

Her shoulders slump as she continues, "Then Ray had to step in and take over the business, and the small life we started, the life that felt like home, crumbled. Suddenly, I was responsible for planning galas and benefits, as all the other Mrs. Greenes did before me. There was no room for me in my own life, and I didn't want that for you."

"But why Lance, Mom? Why did you risk pushing me away? Was the expansion really all you cared about? I don't understand."

"Your father promised that the Gold Coast would be his final impact on the business. He was going to retire, come home to me —to us—and we would be a family again."

"Why didn't you just tell me that?"

"Because it seemed simple in my head. I wanted to take care of it."

"Lance cheated on me the entire time we were together. You were glad to leave me in a loveless marriage. You'd rather give *me* up so that *you* could be happy with Dad?" I say, anger in my voice.

"I know. I was wrong. I was so focused on what I thought was right. I got stuck playing the game, moving around the chess pieces, and I was willing to… You're right, Molly. I was willing to sacrifice you for an opportunity to get the old days back."

It hurts more than I expected.

I reach for her, pulling one of her hands into mine and holding on to it tightly. "I'm sorry that you felt like you made a mistake, Mom, but you've tried to do the same thing to me. Except, unlike you, I wasn't given a choice. I've spent years being afraid to be myself around you." I laugh at the ridiculousness of it all.

A few months ago, when my world shifted and I saw an opportunity for freedom, I knew I had to take it. Everything I left behind, including the many years I spent crafting parts of myself to please others, no longer mattered. While I may never get that portion of my life back, I did learn, the hard way, that being true to myself is the best choice I could have made in this one life.

"Molly." My mom's low voice cracks, and a tear rolls down the pale skin of her cheek.

"There have been so many times when I felt that I was sacrificing myself for you, hiding pieces of me so that you'd love me." My own tears return. "I can't do that anymore. If you're going to be in my life, I need you to accept me for everything that I am, for every choice that I make. And I need you to hear me, loud and clear: you will never make a single decision for me again. I can stand on my own two feet, and I don't want to grant you the privilege of knowing me just so you can chip away at me again."

I don't know what I expect. Maybe an objection, a wince. Except my mother reaches over to me shakily and wraps her slender arms around my shoulders. "I'm sorry."

I sink into her embrace. A warmth spreads between us, one I haven't felt in so many years. It's bittersweet and long overdue. Vivian will have to do a lot of showing me that she's sorry. We could probably talk about boundaries for hours, but right now, I simply let myself be held by my mother.

A faint sense of safety rolls over me. I'm in control.

When we break apart, I give her a tissue from a nearby box. "Do we have an understanding?"

"Of course." She stifles a cough.

"I also want you to know that this doesn't mean that I don't appreciate aspects of my childhood. You've given me a confidence that I doubt I'd have picked up anywhere else. And Dad, for all of his years away at work, taught me perseverance. Both of you gave me pieces of yourselves that I love, and right now, I'm trying to exist with both the good and the bad."

My mother gives me a lopsided smile, mascara coating the bottom of her lids. "We got lucky with you, Molly. You have such a good head on your shoulders." She pulls in a steadying breath. "You're right. I was refusing to see that I forced you to have the life I had. In my own fear and protectiveness, I thought I did the right thing, but in reality, I was only passing down the pressure that made me the person I am today. The mother who hurt you."

Maybe there's a chance for us to be happy together.

"Thank you for listening to me," I say. "It would probably be best if you started getting help with your narcissistic tendencies. It's also important to me that you fix things with my husband."

The term causes her brows to crease, a pain pushing into her eyes. "I will. I have a lot to work through on my own. I crossed a line—many lines, and I want to make it right." She looks down at my left hand, her gaze tracing over the diamonds and ruby on my ring finger. "It fits you perfectly."

In her pale Burberry cardigan, my mother is starkly out of place in my house, with its bursting flower arrangements, loose ribbons, books, and trinkets.

Now, she and my space can coexist. Hopefully.

"Thank you." I give her a shy smile. "This life fits me quite well too."

"It was wrong of me to cut you off and not give you your trust. But you're married now, and even if you weren't, that money is yours. All yours, Molly, no strings, or expectations attached. Happy early birthday."

My chest tightens. I hug her, squeezing so strongly. Although my husband and I have enough investors for both of our businesses, the extra fifty-million will be nice.

We remain hugging until Matthew and my father find themselves in the kitchen, talking like two old friends.

"Matthew." My mother unhooks me and clumsily makes her way to him. My husband shoots me a questioning glance, gauging whether or not I'm alright. I give him a nod. "I'm sorry to have made you feel less than. It was hypocritical of me to ever judge your background, especially when I came from…" She looks around. "Nothing like this. You're as worthy of our daughter as anyone else."

"No hard feelings, Vivian." Matthew tilts his head to one side. "I know what it feels like to want the best for Molly."

I shuffle over to the kitchen island and take a seat.

"I also have an announcement." Dad clears his throat. "I'm going to be retiring, for good."

"Really?" Mom's eyes light up.

"Yes, Vivian. I know I abandoned you for many years, and I want us to try to be a family again." Ray turns to me and places his hand on my shoulder. "I'm sorry, Molly. We're sorry. Losing you was the biggest mistake we'd ever made. Your mother and I have been doing a lot of work on our own, and together, to try to make sure that the remainder of our lives aren't spent without the most important thing to us. *You.*"

"Thank you, Dad. Maybe you both would like to see The Griffin?" I straighten my back, feeling myself return to my skin.

My mother smiles. "Truthfully, we drove by a couple weeks ago. It looks stunning."

"Would you come to my opening?"

"We wouldn't miss it for the world."

"So, are you staying for dinner?" Matthew yanks an apron off the hook by the fridge and ties it around his waist. Bear and Brave waddle into the kitchen at the mention of food.

My mother looks concerned, but Dad puts his arm around her, pulling her close into his side. "What do you say, Viv? Think we can show these kids how we used to do it back in the day?"

"Cooking? Um, what are you making?" She swipes at the dampness on her cheeks and readjusts her cardigan.

I laugh. "We're making pizza."

"Extra cheesy?"

"Yes."

She looks surprised. "I don't think I've had a slice since you were a kid."

"It's still my favorite." I stroll over to the pantry, pull open the door, and take out a jar of tomato sauce. "Think you can open this for me?"

Mom nods, taking it and then pulling me into another hug.

It's everything I've ever wanted. A life on my own terms.

The beginning
(Well, for Molly, that is.)

Epilogue
Molly

MY HANDS ARE WRAPPED around Matthew's neck as we sway to the live music. All around the ballroom, our friends cling to each other. Lights cascade in the room like they're bouncing off a disco ball.

The Griffin's grand opening is going absolutely perfect.

The last six months have flown by unexpectedly quickly. With the money from the trust, we were able to build a cute cottage on the property that we stay in most nights. Our daily commute was treacherous, and we wanted to be around for the first couple of years in business.

Matthew has a research site set up down the road where they're testing the various EcoDrone prototypes. The park rangers gave him an outfit to wear out in the forests—I love taking it off of him when he comes home.

It's like an elven fantasy come to life. Bear and Brave frolic through the gardens, chasing each other's tails. Next month, there may be a puppy on the horizon. Motherhood—well, pet motherhood—is bliss.

"Can you believe we did it?" I whisper.

"Of course I can." He smiles at me. "All of your hard work has paid off, darling."

After our announcement, which my father helped publicize, our inn booked up almost immediately. The Griffin is like an adult summer camp that helps you connect with your inner child.

We are working on growing most of our own food, and we offer courses similar to the On Cloud Nine resorts, except we don't have a massive upcharge on nightly rates. Yoga, cooking classes hosted by Analise, and a neat spa for all. Matthew even designed an entrepreneurship course to help newlyweds turn their passions into viable businesses.

My husband has been a man of many surprises. He built me our very own horse stables. We brought over Sunburst Symphony and rescued four beautiful, retired dressage horses—Sir Gallopsalot, Jar Jar, and, because I couldn't resist, Lysa and Jordy.

The Griffin has been a place of joy and play, a place to call my own—*our* own.

"We're definitely having the games here this winter." Myles spins Helene around. She just found out that she's pregnant with their fourth child. "Mom already invited your parents, Molly."

"I cannot wait to see your dad rushing around on the slopes."

"Are you kidding me?" I giggle. "You know my mom is going to try and swing the ability to judge the competitions."

The idea of blended family Christmases at my own inn makes my heart sing.

"She would actually be pretty good at that," Matthew says.

We sway toward my mom and dad, who are entwined together. Retirement, and copious amounts of counseling and family therapy, look good on them. "You know, sweetheart, you've really made Oliver and Clara proud," Dad says.

"Have I?"

"Absolutely. This is what On Cloud Nine was always meant to be. A place that felt like home. But you never told us how you came up with the name…The Griffin?"

I look at my husband, blushing and beaming. "It's from one of my favorite books."

"Maybe you can let me read it sometime," my mother says. She's wearing jeans today. Actual denim ones. Sure, there are Chanel ballet flats on her feet, but if this is Vivian Greene letting loose, I'm happy for her.

Matthew shoots me a very suggestive wink.

"I think you'd love it."

My family is still a work in progress, but they've been respecting my boundaries, and we're learning how to be around each other again.

Matthew and I stop dancing when the melody ends, and we go out onto the patio, where there's a bonfire. The nights are still cool in the summer heat. Guests gather around the firepit with kits for s'mores. Lolita has organized a stargazing session that will begin soon.

Suddenly, Bear zooms through my legs, followed by Brave. The nieces and nephews chase both of the kitties, giggling and screaming after them.

"Oh, there you guys are," Avery says from a chair by the fire. She's rocking Kaia in her arms. "Ollie's on the phone; come say hi."

"Mattie, Molly." Our friend's grin takes up the entire phone screen.

"Ollie, we miss you so much." I give him a small wave.

"I'm so mad I couldn't make this," he sighs.

"How's the distillery going?" Matthew asks.

It's so sweet that Ollie moved back to Scotland to help run his family's business while his parents are on the honeymoon they never got.

"Oh, you know hospitality. Loads of tourists this year, so I can barely get away."

"And how's the girl?" Matthew smiles.

"How many times do I have to tell ya? If you want to know about my love life, ya gotta come visit," he laughs. "Speaking of which, I gotta go. Happy opening."

"Love you," we say in unison.

I hand Avery her phone. "Where's the rest of the crew?"

"Nico and Lily are hosting a puppet show in the barn for all the kids. Luca is chaperoning the content." She flips her cropped blonde hair over her shoulder.

I laugh. "I can only imagine what those two are teaching our nieces, nephews, and the guests' kids."

"I should probably go check on him." Avery squeezes my shoulder, beaming at me. "Thank you for having us. I like that Kaia is getting a taste of the beach, the city, and now the forest."

"Well, you guys always have a room here."

"We'll take you up on that." Avery shucks off her heels and walks barefoot across the grass.

I was worried that moving outside of New York City and quitting ORO would make it hard to maintain friendships with Avery and Lily, but they've been here monthly, helping out and catching up.

We even went away on a spa weekend in the Hamptons.

"How are you feeling, my darling wife?" Matthew caresses the side of my cheek. I look around at our parents dancing beneath the chandelier, my new siblings exploring, my friends laughing, my pets running around, and my husband supporting me and loving me with every step.

"This is the happy beginning I always imagined but never thought I deserved."

He kisses me. "You deserve everything."

"What about you? Are you happy?"

"My life is resplendent." He lights up, then his blue gaze

burns a little brighter. "Though I always pictured my happily ever after with you in those elf ears."

I move my hair to the side, revealing a little golden ear cuff with a slight point on it. "You mean these?"

"There she is. My warrior." He picks me up. "Do you think people will notice if we leave?" His head swivels around.

"Who cares? Let's get out of here."

Acknowledgments

With each book we publish, we grow more thankful for the astonishing team of people we've surrounded ourselves with.

To Caroline A., you are such a joy to work with, and we truly appreciate how invested you are in our books. You have understood our voice and vision from the start, and with each book we learn invaluable lessons from you. We respect your commentary, feedback, reactions, fun tidbits, advice, and anecdotes above all else. Thank you for helping us do Molly and Matthew justice.

To Caroline K. and Isabella, thank you for your attention to detail, and for your exemplary support along the way. To our beta readers, Sophia Welch, Isabella F., and Nicole McCrane, we loved how much you related to Molly and Matthew's stories. Your input was extremely helpful in bringing this book to life. You all deserve a night in with Matthew, Bear, and maybe some elf ears…

To our cover designer, Chloe, thank you for another beautiful cover. To our showstopping character artist, Kristen, you are such a talented creative, and the way you've brought each of our characters to life makes writing such a treat.

To the amazing book communities online—BookTok, Bookstagram, BookTube, Book Twitter, book blogs, book podcasts, and book clubs, thank you for taking the time to share your love for our stories. We are so grateful for each message, post, video, and review. Thank you.

To you, our reader, if you related to Molly or Matthew while you were reading their story, just know that we see you and we think you are worthy. It's okay to set boundaries and put yourself first. It's time to shine bright for you.

To the companies who are actively working toward mitigating the effects of climate change, thank you. Without you, EcoDrones and ORO would be mere ideas.

Lastly, to our partners, thank you for always being interested in hearing about our stories. It's easy to write about men like Matthew (and Luca and Nico), who love their partner so deeply because you guys show us what love is daily. Does this dedication count toward your guys' words of affirmation quota? Love you both.

K: Denise, what a whirlwind few months. Thank you for making me feel like I'm finally on a team project with someone I can fully trust and rely on. This last year has been a rollercoaster, and for two girlies who get motion sickness, it's to be said the journey hasn't always been easy. But I wouldn't want to spend all the highs, lows, loopity loops, and sudden heart-wrenching drops with anyone else.

D: Kels, thank you for sharing another masterpiece with me, for wanting to grow and learn together, for being every definition of the word partner. I do and will endlessly enjoy your brain, ideas, humor, and heart. Now *Thor voice*: ANOTHER! I'd also like to dedicate this book to my anxiety, but my therapist would probably advise against it. So, I'll dedicate it to my Bee, who has shown me a no-strings-attached kind of love. Molly's journey with her family and mental health was so personal and dear to me. It is with the sweetest hope that if she speaks to you as much as she spoke to us, you will be inspired to become the main character in your own life by putting the side character script to rest.

Playlist

"I Write Sins Not Tragedies" by Panic! At The Disco
"mirrorball" by Taylor Swift
"Run Away With Me" by Carly Rae Jepsen
"ballad of a homeschooled girl" by Olivia Rodrigo
"Love Affair" by UMI
"Please Notice" by Christian Leave
"Shapeshifter" by Kathryn Gallagher
"Happy Girl" by Jensen McRae
"Cloud 9" by Beach Bunny
"Kiss Me" by Sixpence None The Richer
"Sweet" by Cigarettes After Sex
"Hunger" by Florence + The Machine
"NFWMB" by Hozier
"I Guess I'm in Love" by Clinton Kane
"Glory Box" by Portishead
"This Must Be the Place" by Talking Heads
"Adore You" by Harry Styles
"Look What You Made Me Do" by Taylor Swift
"Flowers" by Miley Cyrus
"Vertigo" by Nick Hakim
"Today Was a Fairytale (Taylor's Version)" by Taylor Swift
"Easy on Me" by Adele

About The Authors

Kels & Denise are authors, best friends, and the definition of the found family trope. The pair bonded over their love for romance and turned all their late-night chats into writing together. Their love for storytelling morphed into writing strong heroines and rugged, swoon-worthy love interests with lots of dirty talk. While Kels travels the world with her high-school-sweetheart husband, Denise is making her way through every restaurant with her boyfriend.

Stay in touch!
@authorkelsdenisestone
kelsdenisestone.com

Join our newsletter *The Sticky Note*
kelsdenisestone.com/the-sticky-note
Join our Patreon for exclusive content

Also by Kels & Denise Stone

<u>**Perks & Benefits Series:**</u>

Water Under the Bridge

Workplace Romance, Avery and Luca's Story

Our Scorching Summer

Friends to Lovers Romance, Lily and Nico's Story

On Cloud Nine

Fake Dating Romance, Molly and Matthew's Story

Falling for Meadow

Small Town Romance, Ollie & Meadow's Story

<u>**The Hastings Series:**</u>

Close Knit

Sports Romance